PRECIOUS BABY

"My baby, my precious," Rose whispered. She sat on the floor, facing the window and the moonlight. Holding the doll to her breast, she rocked back and forth, humming softly under her breath.

The real Angela lay in a dark hole in the ground, out at the edge of the forest. But for now Rose could pretend she had her baby again.

She was very tired. Exhausted. A strange, deep weakness reached into her bones.

Soon she was drifting between sleeping and waking, between dreams and reality.

Suddenly she couldn't breathe. She was suffocating.

It was the doll. *The doll was taking her breath.*

She tried with her hands to push the doll away, but it clung to her. She turned her head back and forth.

She tried to rise, but all strength had been pulled from her.

Help me. She had to get up and find her mother, tell her what was happening. Tell her about the doll. Before it hurt someone else.

But she was too weak to get up . . .

RUBY JEAN JENSEN
BABY DOLLY

ZEBRA BOOKS
KENSINGTON PUBLISHING CORP.

Prologue

In the stillness of the cold, dark night Sybil could hear sleet pecking against the window. It sounded like small fingers scratching to get in, searching for a weakness in the panes, for cracks around the edges. Small fingers like the fingers of the new Christmas doll that lay facing her like a real newborn baby on the pillow and beneath the covers in her bed.

A dim light from a lamp turned low on the dresser between her bed and Rose Marie's in the opposite corner outlined the pinched and ugly features of the doll. A bonnet covered its painted hair. Couldn't she at least have a tiny, grown-up doll with real hair, like Rose Marie's new Christmas Eve doll? A lady doll, a dancing doll perhaps, with dainty slippers and real stockings. This doll that was just like an ugly newborn baby was not what she had wanted.

Couldn't Papa have bought her a brooch like the one he bought Mother? It was beautiful coral in filigreed gold. Or even the gold necklace such as he had given Rose Marie, with the little heart that opened. A locket, to hold her secrets.

Why had Papa thought she would want a baby doll? She was twelve years old, only one year younger than Rose Marie, and almost as grown-up. She didn't want an ugly baby doll. She didn't like babies very well anyway.

Her papa had seemed proud of it. He had gotten both dolls in South America, he said, on his last business trip. They were under the tree, wrapped in colorful Christmas pa-

5

per and tied with real ribbons. The ribbon, at least, she would use in her hair.

Sybil whispered to it, "I hate you. You're ugly."

It stared up at her. She had never seen such dark glassy eyes. She began to feel uncomfortable. She stared back at it intensely, her frown deepening. It was like looking into the eyes of another creature, a living thing different from herself, yet very clever and knowing in its own way.

"You can't have been listening to me," she whispered. And then in shocked realization, *It knows every word I said!*

The pungent odor of the candles that had lighted the Christmas tree had found its way up the long stairway and into the bedroom. Or was there something in the clothing or body of the doll that stank?

Sybil bared her teeth at it and whispered, "You're so ugly. Tomorrow I'll put you away, and I'll never touch you again. And I will never forgive Papa for bringing you to me."

Tonight she'd had to accept the doll in her bed because her papa had come to tuck her and Rose Marie in, and he had placed this hideous doll in bed with her just as he had tucked Rose Marie's doll in with her. Rose Marie slept peacefully, like the angel Papa had called her. But he had called Sybil his big girl, not his angel.

"Don't you know you have to be beautiful to be loved?" she hissed to the staring eyes of the doll. "Like Rose Marie. Or maybe you don't know what love is. Our old cook, the one that died, said I don't know. But I do. It's having people be nice to you." She shoved it away and turned over.

Sybil's eyes closed, and she drifted toward sleep, feeling the hammock-like swing of drowsiness as she slipped away from this disappointing Christmas Eve. What would her stocking hold tomorrow morning? Maybe Santa Claus would be more understanding than her parents had been, and bring her a necklace.

The sleet sounded like thousands of pecking fingers, like strange creatures running on tiny hooves, like miniature voices chortling in evil glee.

She began to smother in the strange world of the elves outside her window. They were transporting her to an alien world where she was helpless, where she could no longer breathe.

She struggled to open her eyes, and the features of the room drew her away from the evil world of the elves. But there was something pressed against her face, smothering her.

Sybil pushed weakly at it, and felt the soft, stuffed body of the doll. Its face had moved against hers and its mouth sucked leech-like at hers, and she had a horror-filled vision of it filling with blood, like a real leech, but it was not sucking her blood, it was sucking away her breath.

She grabbed it and threw it, and it fell on the floor at the foot of her bed. She lay still, gasping desperately, feeling the way she had the day she'd fallen out of the big swing onto her back, all the breath knocked out of her.

When she was able to breathe again she slowly sat up, staring toward the doll on the floor. The low, flickering light from the lamp cast shadows on its face. There was a frightening look in the dark, swollen slits of eyes, and its mouth was open a bit now, as if pursed for nursing, for gathering nourishment. When she had gone to sleep the lips were in a small, round, closed pout.

It had tried to take her breath . . . her life.

Slowly she crawled out from beneath the down-filled warmth of the comforter and into the chilled air of the room. The sleet at the window rattled the pane.

She stared down at the face of the doll, then she picked it up by its long white gown and carried it to the bed across the room.

Rose Marie slept on her side, her back to the tiny, beautiful lady doll on her other pillow. It was dressed in scarlet and black lace, and its small, stiff arms pointed upward toward the ceiling.

Sybil carefully placed the baby doll on the pillow beside Rose Marie's head, turning its face toward hers.

Rose Marie's rich and glossy black hair made a bed for the doll.

Sybil slipped back into her own bed, snuggling beneath the warm comforter. She covered her head and her ears, shutting out the night and the memory of the disappointing Christmas Eve.

She awoke to silence. A dim dawn had filtered into the room, and a bit of warmth from somewhere below.

Papa was up and had stoked the furnace. The beginnings of Christmas dinner would be started. She could imagine her mother in the kitchen with the cook and maid, doing part of the cooking herself as she liked to do at special times.

But Rose Marie was quiet.

Sybil sat up and looked toward her older sister's bed. There was the rounded form beneath the comforter, lying still, so still.

Sybil slipped out of bed and stood with her flannel gown touching the tops of her feet as they grew cold on the woven rug between the beds.

Rose Marie lay in the same position as she had at midnight, and beside her on the pillow lay the baby doll, with its long white gown and its lace trimmed bonnet. Its face looked more rounded, its cheeks rosier. Its puffy eyes had closed and it was sleeping.

Sybil stepped closer to stare at Rose Marie.

The pinched and narrow look that had been the doll's seemed now to have been given to Rose Marie instead. She looked a lot older than thirteen. She looked thirty, or even forty, or more.

Sybil carefully removed the doll from the bed and went out into the hall. She stood still, listening. But the kitchen was too far away. She could only feel a bit of the warmth from it, and hear none of the bustle.

She carried the doll to the end of the hall, where she paused to open the door of the enclosed stairway to the third floor. She climbed the steep stairs and went down the cold, dim, third floor hallway.

The doll felt heavier than it had last night. Its long, white gown reached far past its feet and swayed whisperingly against Sybil's legs as she walked; the round, stuffed body hidden beneath the gown. The doll's cheeks had a rounded,

8

full look, and the eyes remained closed, even when Sybil tilted it upright.

Sybil stopped in front of the old cabinet that held odds and ends of things she had collected since she was small. She placed the doll back in a corner on a lower shelf where it wouldn't easily be seen, and closed the glass door.

Then she went downstairs to tell her mama and papa that Rose Marie was dead.

Book One

Fatherless Child

Chapter 1

1910

Outside the open window the summer insects and frogs filled the night with sound. Fragrances of honeysuckle, of wild grape from the woods, from flowers in the garden below drifted upward into the window. Touches of perfume in the air. Rose sat in a rocking chair near the window, looking down at the infant in her arms. Against Rose's breast and stomach her daughter curved outside her body in yielding warmth as three months ago she had curved within. Rose listened to the night sounds, to the suckling of her child, feeling suddenly as if she were one with the complexities and mysteries of nature. A sudden sense of rapture, like the wafting fragrances of flowers, lifted her in a brief happiness beyond anything she had ever known. The grief of the past year seemed suddenly worth her moment now, filled with the completeness motherhood had given her and her sense of oneness even with the katydids, the jarflies, the frogs.

Rose smiled, and the baby unexpectedly returned the smile around the nipple in her mouth. Rose laughed, and the baby kicked, her eyes bright and wide, as if bedtime was hours away.

"Haven't you learned there are rules in this house?" Rose whispered. "Lights out at ten o'clock, no exceptions. Except, perhaps, the night you were born. Go to sleep. Be very quiet. Don't disturb Grandma and Grandpa."

The three month old girl released her mother's nipple with

a comical insouciance. Her lovely little face was as beautiful as a dream. Rose held her tighter, cuddling her close to her breast as she rocked gently in the old chair her mother had allowed her to bring into her bedroom. A milk drop, as creamy white as a pearl, clung to the baby's lower lip before it slid down and disappeared into the soft flannel of her gown. Rose slipped her breast out of sight beneath her shirtwaist.

Grandpa. Grandma. Rose's feelings of happiness fled, as swiftly and silently as blackwinged birds through the night.

"Angela," she whispered, and the baby's gaze became serious and more intense as if she already recognized her own name. She seemed to sense the change in her mother's mood. "Angela. The most beautiful name for the most beautiful baby. Wait till your daddy sees you. Soon now, anytime now, Daddy is coming to get us. He'll be so surprised! Angela, my precious Angela."

Choosing the name had kept Rose's mind off her terrible predicament during all the months she had been confined to her room. Isolated, allowed to go out only where no one would see her, she had gone over names for boys, names for girls. She had concentrated on the growing baby in her body because it helped her feel not quite so alone, so totally rejected by not only her fiancé but most of her own family. But as though she had known in her heart her baby would be a girl, the boys' names were dismissed in favor of the girls'. And of those, only one was suitable for her baby. Angel. Angela. "I love you, love you, love you." She touched her cheek to the baby's.

Rose might have sinned, once, in love, but her infant was without sin. No matter what her mother thought, Angela was perfect, without sin.

Her own name, Rose, came from her mother Sybil's dead sister, Rose Marie. There was a photograph of Rose Marie, and it showed a beautiful girl with black hair and contrasting pale skin and blue eyes. Rose knew little about thinking who had died so young. Sybil wouldn't talk about her. Yet there must have been affection, or surely she wouldn't have chosen the dead sister's name for her own firstborn child. Rose had rather hoped her baby would look like Rose Marie, but

14

Angela's hair was as golden as fragile buttercups blooming along the woodland path, and her eyes as smoky dark as the coal in the basement bin. Like Harold's.

"Your daddy's eyes," she whispered. "My hair, and—"

The bedroom door opened with a faint squeak, too late for a warning that someone was coming in. Rose hurriedly smoothed her shirtwaist down, feeling that awful sense of shame that the entrance of her mother provoked.

Sybil stood for a moment in the doorway, her tall frame looking pinched at the waist, her corset holding her as stiff as the door her hand rested upon.

Rose got up, Angela pressed protectively against her bosom. Only the family had been allowed to see the baby, or know she existed. Rose's younger sister, Julie Sue, was the only real friend Rose had, now. Though Julie Sue was only fifteen, she seemed older, more understanding. Gertrude too had been allowed to see Angela, the day after she was born, which surprised Rose. Mama would want to protect Gertrude, who at age ten was too young to understand where babies came from, and that an unmarried sister could have one.

Papa of course had seen Angela, but he had only looked at her, he did not touch her or speak to her. He had not come to see her again.

But the hired help, even Beulah, who had helped in the kitchen for years, was not to know about Angela. Rose understood without being told. Their family name had to be considered. Their standing in the community must not be reduced by the scandal of a birth out of wedlock.

Rose saw that Sybil was holding something in her hand. It appeared to be a white gown or scarf, and trailed almost to the floor. But she held it half-hidden behind the folds of her skirt.

"Lay her away," Sybil said. "Put her into her cradle. I have something for her."

"Yes, Mama."

Rose laid the baby into the softness of the cradle. At least her mother had consented to having the cradle brought down from the attic for the baby. Even that had surprised and pleased Rose. She had also provided, sending it up with Julie Sue, a bolt of flannel, so clothing could be stitched. In the months of her confinement Rose had made diapers, gowns, bands, even a soft receiving blanket. Many times Julie Sue had helped her. And in the stillness of a winter afternoon they had sat together, their fingers freezing in the unheated bedroom, sewing.

Rose tucked the flannel blanket beneath Baby Angela's arms, and stood back for her mother. The baby had not been born until May, until warmth entered the room from the sun, and butterflies fluttered at times on the sill. Once, a cardinal had lighted there, and Rose had taken it as a good sign.

Sybil came forward. In the hall, watching in silence, Gertrude stood. The flickering flame of the lamp in the hall created shadows in Gertrude's face, and as Rose glanced at her it seemed for just a moment that Gertrude was not a child, but a very old corpse, mummified, whose face was sunken into shadows, whose eyes were holes of darkness. The light rose again, and Gertrude's cheeks rounded and became young once more. But her eyes remained hidden by shadows. Did Mama know she was there?

Sybil bent over the cradle, and now Rose saw what she had brought. Her heart's blood rushed warmly to her face. Had her prayers been answered? Was her mother softening toward Angela, accepting her? She was giving Angela the old doll, the one that had been kept in the cabinet on the third floor, the one none of Sybil's own children had ever been allowed to touch. It was an infant doll in a long, white christening gown.

It didn't matter that it wasn't a pretty doll. That its newborn face was pinched and thin, with only a touch of color in the painted cheeks. The grandmother was giving the grandbaby her own doll, one she had received in her own childhood.

"Mama," Rose said, moving nearer. "That's your doll."

"Yes," Sybil said. With no apparent warmth she laid the doll carefully at the side of Angela, arranging it so that the two faces, the real and the unreal, were close.

The doll's head was as large as Angela's head, but the face

narrower, the features far less perfect. When Rose was small, and had looked through the glass doors at the doll tucked into the back corner of the cabinet, it had not seemed as ugly as now. Now that it was beside an infant warm and real.

Once, Rose remembered, Gertrude had wanted the doll. She had stood with her small hands on the glass doors of the cabinet and cried because she couldn't play with the doll, and Mama had sent Rose to take her back downstairs and entertain her with other dolls. After that a wood fastener too high for a child to reach had been put on the door to the third floor. Rose had not seen the doll since that day, five or six years ago.

Baby Angela stared in silence up at the face of her grandmother, as if she recognized a stranger. How often, in her life, had Angela seen the face of her grandmother? It made Rose's heart ache. But maybe Julie Sue was right. "Be patient," she had said, so many times. "Mama will come around. Surely, Mama will come around. She'll grow to love Angela. Or, if not to love, at least to tolerate. *Surely.* Baby Angela can't live forever in this small room. Neither can you."

And Julie was right. Rose and Angela could not live their lifetimes in the confinement of the bedroom, allowed to go out only in the cover of night, and then only into the backyard and the meadows and forest behind the house. Perhaps this was the breakthrough. Instead of Sybil saying in words or smiles that she accepted Angela, she was giving to her the doll she hadn't even given to Gertrude, her own baby, her favorite child.

"Thank you, Mama. That's very kind of you."

"It's time you're going to bed, isn't it, Rose? Or you can go to your bath now, and I'll stay here."

Rose stared at her mother. She saw the thin, long face that was so much like Gertrude's, the only one of the three sisters who had taken after their mother. She saw the severity, the lips that hadn't smiled in a long time, and had smiled seldom before that, as if to be happy were wrong. She saw no outward sign of accepting, yet the action could not be denied. Sybil had brought something to Baby Angela that she had never given even to her own daughters.

17

"Are you giving your doll to Angela, Mama?"

Sybil sat down in the rocking chair. "Why don't you go on and take your bath? I can't sit here for long."

Rose hurriedly took her robe and her nightgown and went down the hall. One of the second floor bedrooms had been converted to a bath three years ago. Water, warmed in the basement at the furnace, came up a pipe and into the cast-iron tub, and it was like a miracle. A commode stood in one corner, so convenient, with a box overhead and a pull chain. The chain flushed the commode. It was so much nicer than having to go to the old outhouse, and certainly much nicer than having the old chamber pots that slipped out of sight beneath the beds. After three years Rose still delighted in slipping into the big tub and the warm water.

Tonight it was especially relaxing. For the first time, her mother was sitting with her child. For the first time, Sybil had brought Angela something. It was a beginning.

Rose leaned back in the tub, her eyes closed. It was a year ago, on a lovely warm night such as this, with the jarflies and the katydids making their comforting noises in the grass, and the frogs piping in the swamp, that she had walked home from the young people's meeting at the church with Harold.

He had drawn her off the road when the buggy passed, carrying Julie Sue and their father, who had come after her. It was he who had consented to the walk.

"Your father's not such a bad guy," Harold said, with that air of modernism that fascinated Rose. In the moonlight he looked taller and older than he had in the bluish gaslights at the church. He pulled her hand into his and Rose felt the tightening, the pressure, the sense of command.

Harold had been allowed to walk her home before, but tonight there was a difference, as if sometime during the past week he had matured, made some kind of decision.

"I'm going away, Rose," he said, turning her to face him, and Rose's happiness plummeted.

Life without Harold? How terribly, horribly dreary. Young people's meeting at the church would no longer be the exciting thing it was now. She had been in love with Harold since she first saw him in school; older, two grades ahead of

18

her, a handsome dark-eyed, dark-haired boy who looked at her in a special way. There was no one else for Rose.

"Why?" she pleaded. "Where? Where are you going?"

"I thought I'd try New Orleans, or Saint Louis. I thought maybe I could work on a riverboat. Be part of that business. I can't stay here. I don't want to work in my papa's store in this dinky little town."

"But—"

His scorn for the town, a town which her grandfather had founded and part of which her mother had inherited and her own father now controlled, was to feel scorn for her, too, to put her down as dull and unexciting, as stuffy as his own father's hardware store.

"Look," he said, giving her hand a hard squeeze. "I'll come back for you as soon as I can find a position. I have plenty of clerical experience. I shouldn't have any trouble. . . . I'll come back for you. Will you marry me, Rose?"

"What?"

"We're old enough to do what we want. You'll be eighteen next year, and I'll be twenty. If we want to marry, that's our business. It will be our secret until I come back."

"But—"

"But what," he whispered, and his lips came down to hers.

They had kissed before, under the dark eaves of her house, behind the holly bushes, along the road on the walk home, even beneath the mistletoe on Christmas Eve. But of course not when anyone was looking.

They had kissed before, but never like this.

They were going to be married. They would move to New Orleans, where life was abandoned and gay. They would spend their lives on a riverboat, traveling the Mississippi. *He wanted to marry her and take her with him!*

"Yes, yes, yes," she whispered, and it seemed the world around them changed, and a year had sped by and their marriage had come to pass. His dream was hers. His excitement was hers.

When he pulled her down to the soft bed of leaves, she felt wild and gay and abandoned. She was free from the bonds of being Rose Marie Madison, daughter of Sybil Wilfred Madison, whose ancestors founded the town and built the mansion on the outer land. She could feel the sway of the big boat on the Mississippi, and hear the lash of the water against the deck. That night Angela was conceived.

The water in the tub had cooled, and Rose struggled up from the memory of a night that happened a year ago. Over the months after Harold left she wept into her pillow and pleaded with him to write to her, to come and get her, to let her know what had happened. As if he could hear her, she had pleaded.

Once, before the rounding of her belly began to show and before she was confined to her room, she had gone to Harold's father's store. And she had asked, as casually as she could, "Sir, I was wondering if you'd heard from your son, Harold."

Harold's father adjusted his spectacles and looked over them at her. There was no resemblance between this pale-eyed, pale-skinned man and Harold, with the snapping black eyes and the dark hair. He had taken after his mother's side of the family, Harold had told her once.

"Harold," the man said, and snorted. "Worthless, just like his uncles. On his mother's side."

Stunned, Rose turned away. At that moment she knew. Harold would not be back. He had taken advantage of her. He was gone, and she was alone, to bear their baby in shame.

Still, never a day passed without thoughts of him. Never an hour, actually, although she had long since stopped seeing his face when she looked at the face of Angela. Angela was nobody's but hers.

Already, with the short absence from her little daughter, she yearned to get back to her. Her arms ached to take her up and hold her, rock her to sleep as always.

She dried her body rapidly and hung the towel back on the rack. With her robe pulled warmly over her gown, she went down the hall. At both the front and the end of the hall globes covered small, flickering gas flames. Next year, her father had said, they would convert the heat to gas, and the house would be warmer. Next year,

Rose thought, when Angela was walking.

Sybil was still sitting in the rocking chair, her head back, resting.

The room was quiet. Sounds from the frogs, the night birds and insects came through the open window, and the kerosene lamp on the dresser filled the small room with a dim, shadow etched golden glow.

Rose started toward the cradle, but Sybil lifted her hand, and Rose stopped.

"She's asleep," Sybil said. "Leave her alone. Go on to bed."

Rose stood still a moment longer, puzzled, feeling like a small child again, not a woman with a child of her own. Then she turned toward her bed in the corner, stepped up on the stool at the side of the bed, and sat on the mattress. She waited.

Sybil rose. "I'll turn the light down for you."

"Thank you, Mama."

"Good night."

"Good night." Rose watched her mother go to the door.

The door squeaked as Sybil opened it.

"Mama," Rose said quickly, "thank you for the doll."

Sybil said nothing. She hesitated slightly, her back toward Rose, and then she was gone, closing the door behind her.

Angela moved, reaching into the dark air of the cradle. Above was light. Somewhere in the room, out of sight of her searching eyes, her mother breathed. Angela's body stiffened as she tried to turn, to lift herself and go to her mother. The thing in the cradle bore down upon her. The strange, little human-like face pressed against hers. She struggled to turn onto her back, away from it. She tried to cry out, voice her need for her mother, but her cry was sucked away from her and silenced.

She knew her helplessness and fought against it. Her eyes searched for the light, but it was far away and very dim, and growing more distant and more dim with each attempt to reach it.

21

She wanted her mother, the warmth of her breast, the close security and comfort of her arms.

But the other infant in the cradle was drawing away all her breath.

Chapter 2

Julie Sue woke listening. Although the wall between her room and Rose's was thick, she had often heard the cry of baby Angela. She blinked into the darkness. The house was silent. If Angela had cried out, Rose must have taken her up to quiet her. In the beginning, when the baby was first born, Rose had slept with Angela in her arms. But then Mama had said the baby should have her own bed, and the cradle was brought down. Still, if Angela cried in the night, Rose took her into her bed, or sat and rocked her. She had told Julie so, but said not to tell Mama. There were so many things Mama didn't approve of. Especially anything to do with Rose's baby.

Julie remembered the night of the birth, and how it had continued on into the day, and Mama had ordered Rose not to cry out, not to let the hired help, Beulah or Moses, hear her. So they would never know a baby had been born here that day. But the day had passed too, and Julie had held onto Rose's hand and wept with her, and then had gone to plead with Papa to bring a doctor. She was terrified that Rose was dying, the birth was taking so long.

But Papa seemed then like a shadow of Mama, doing Mama's bidding, always. He removed himself from Rose's plight and sank into his work, as always. And Julie remembered that Papa had once been a mere clerk in the bank Grandfather owned, and which Mama now owned. It was Grandfather who had paid for Papa's law education, Beulah had told her, and it was Grandfather's law firm in which Papa went to work. When Grandfather died in 1895, the very year she was born, Mama became the employer. And it was as though Papa was still in Mama's employ even in matters of family.

Julie had bitten her tongue to keep back her angry revelations and had swirled away. Night came again while Rose suffered, struggling to deliver a baby that seemed reluctant to enter the world. Moses finished planting the spring garden and went home, and Beulah finished cleaning up from a supper no one ate and also went home. Then like a miracle the baby was born.

Yet when Julie held the bloody little thing in her hands she had gotten a strange feeling, a bad feeling that she could not have described in words. She had felt such sadness.

The sadness passed the moment the baby opened her mouth and mewed like a baby kitten, or lamb, and to Julie's surprise Rose laughed. Mama had been there, at the last, with water and towels and washcloths. She had worn a white apron over her dress, and had gotten it all bloody. Julie was shocked at the amount of blood a birth releases. In a way it was like a death, a terrible death.

But the doctor had never been brought.

Julie tried not to think about those painful twenty-four hours, and the winter before, in which Rose had been hidden away. She tried not to think how their parents had changed in her eyes and heart. She had always been a little distant from both of them. They had never babied Rose or her the way they did Gertrude, but at least she had felt safe with them. Until Rose's problem, until *the winter,* as she thought of it.

Her feelings about the whole house had changed. Even her feelings about her room. The house was no longer a safe haven, big and dark and quiet. It had become . . . a prison? No, not quite that. But something that had frightening things in the dark places.

Julie turned over and squeezed her eyes shut. She wanted to sleep, but she felt as if she had been awakened from a nightmare, and the very air around her was charged with it. She was suddenly Gertrude's age again, or younger, when she had imagined there were terrible, faceless, formless horrors lurking in the dark beneath her bed. She was not fifteen, in this moment of darkness and fear, matured from spending a winter of anguish with her older sister, and from standing by her as she had a baby their parents said was made of sin. She was a vulnerable, quivering, helpless being with that terrible sense of sadness she had experienced when Angela was first born.

And she was afraid.

She listened for Rose moving about in her room beyond the wall. She listened for the creak of the rocking chair, for the cry that had awakened her. But there was only silence in the room next door.

She pressed her hands against her ears and prayed for the night to end.

It was daily getting harder for Beulah to walk the two miles from her cabin to the Wilfred mansion. She was seventy-one years old now, and was proud to say she hadn't missed a day of work since her son was born fifty years ago. But still, it was getting harder to walk all that way. She had to get up earlier every year, feed her cat and dog before they woke up enough to get hungry. Milk the cow while the cow slept. Go out and feed her chickens while they were still on the roost in the henhouse.

Her company at that early hour, before the sun was even a pink streak in the eastern sky, was the old rooster, who'd been sitting up and crowing now and then while still on the roost and then tucking his head back under his wing for another nap.

Beulah went around in the early morning dark, carrying her lantern, its yellow light swinging back and forth on the ground in front of her. She'd find herself accompanied finally by her old dog, Buster, and the cat, Jenny, to the barn where she hung her lantern on a nail and then settled down on a stool at the side of Ginger, her cow, for the milk they all depended upon.

Then, the cow milked, the chickens, dog, and cat fed, Beulah fed herself. By that time dawn would be breaking, especially this time of year when the days were longer. She'd put on a fresh apron, adjust her wide brimmed hat on her head, fix the door just wide enough so the cat could get in and out, and make her way along the trail through the forest to the main road and along to the Wilfred mansion for her day's work as the cook, maid, housekeeper, or whatever else needed to be done.

Once, she'd had a horse, Sally. Dead now. Named after her dear old mother. Sometimes she hitched Sally to the buggy and rode to her job, turning Sally loose in the pasture behind the big barn where the Mister kept his horses. Sally was a young and lively colt when Rose Marie died, twenty-eight years ago. Beulah remembered well, that day after Christmas, the way the young girl looked in death, all color leached from her face. The young colt, born just a few weeks earlier, had seemed to Beulah to take on some of the gentle characteristics of the young girl, and in her mind they had become kin, in some way.

There had been snow on the ground the day Rose Marie died. Beulah recollected walking this same narrow trail, her hands cold, her feet colder, and thinking how strange that it would snow this far south. It was like the snow had come, silent and white, to mark the passing of the girl.

But why was she thinking of Rose Marie this morning? This morning the woodland flowers were blooming along the side of the road. Wild johnnie-jump-ups, which Sybil called violets, and lady slippers scented the air with a sweetness that made Beulah think Mother Nature wasn't all cruelty.

But then Sally too had died, just as almost everyone in Beulah's life had died. Even Freddie, her son, when he was still in the prime of life. Before he and his wife had any children, so that Beulah would be assured of having someone to call to when she got old.

Her husband had died, her son had died, and her horse. And now her family was the family she worked for, and her pet critters at home.

Lives had changed; families had changed; only the road on her way to work stayed the same.

The people she worked for had changed. The old mansion seemed to be changing too, slowly growing larger and darker,

26

colder in the winter, always cool even in the hot summertime. The trees in the yard grew larger. Thank God there was something that lived longer, on the average, than people, so you could always depend on it.

But why was her mind dwelling on death this morning? The sun was rising bright and hot in the east, streaking through the trees, turning the leaves golden. And the birds had roused and were singing. The day had begun, life was born anew.

Even at the old mansion, there was new life. No one had told her so, but she didn't have to be told. No one had said there's a new baby in the house. But she wasn't deaf and blind.

A few times she had heard its cry. And it had been months now since she'd caught a glimpse of Rose. And there were suspicious looking items in the wash. She had a hunch the baby's "didies" and gowns were hung to dry in the attic, because they weren't hung out on the line with the rest of the family laundry. Faye, the girl who did the wash, came out only twice a week, did her job, washed, starched, ironed, and then left. And during those hours she was there she wasn't sent anymore into the second story to bring down clothes. She went back to town with her pay. Julie Sue seemed to have taken on the duties of an upstairs maid, bringing the laundry down and taking it back up again.

If there was a rumor around town about the baby, Beulah hadn't heard it. She didn't go to the same church as the Madison family, so she didn't know what excuse was given for Rose's absence. She had been asked about Rose a few times and she'd said, "Rose is away now."

She wasn't one for spreading rumors herself. Especially not about the girls she had known and loved all their lives.

When she started working at the Wilfred mansion it was Sybil's father who was a young man in the house. He had married and started his family, two daughters. But then came the deaths. After Rose Marie died at age thirteen, it wasn't long before her mother, grieving for Rose Marie, also died. And then, when Sybil was twenty-five years old, her father had gone to his reward, as silently and unexpectedly as

27

his wife and daughter had gone. They left in the night, as if they had slipped away on the wings of something that flew into the old mansion only after the doors were bolted and the lights were out.

In those days it had been called the Wilfred mansion, and to Beulah it would always be the Wilfred mansion, even though the family name was now Madison, and the younger people of the town thought of it as the Madison place.

Beulah came out of the woodland road into the slanting sunlight where the road forked, the better traveled one angling off toward the south toward farmland, open and light. She began to walk faster. She had been the first one up and around on the premises ever since she had started working there at the age of fourteen. That was her job, to be the first one up and around in the house. The one who built the fires. Daily, except for when her child was born and the few weeks she spent at home with him before he was old enough to bring along. Daily except Sundays, it was the same routine. Open the back screen door, use the key she kept on a string around her neck, and unlock the back door.

Get the breakfast started. The wood she needed for the cookstove was in a box behind the stove, where she had put it the evening before. Do all the cooking as early in the day as possible, because the kitchen was connected to the main house, and even though she kept the door closed between the kitchen and the hallways and dining room, heat tended to seep through.

She walked fast along the road and reached the long front yard that lay between the mansion and the road. Trees shaded the neatly mowed grass. A row of shrubs along the front kept out dust that was occasionally raised by wind on the road, by horses and wagons, and sometimes by a motor car.

She went down the shaded driveway toward the house. It towered over her, dark and still. Yet she had a feeling, this morning, as she'd had so often lately, that she wasn't the first one up and around at this house. That somewhere behind one of those dark windows, in the cool and dim interior, someone else moved, unable to sleep.

She hurried faster, around the back of the house to the screened porch and up the steps. She reached into her bodice for the key to the back door as she crossed the porch.

She stopped, stiffening.

A cry? Perhaps even a scream, muffled by thick walls, or deep forests. But it had been so brief, it was like a remembered nightmare.

Many times lately she had imagined hearing that scream as she reached the mansion. Maybe it was the memory of cries heard here before, at the birth of a child. And at the death of a child.

She listened, and found the morning calm and still except for the songs of the birds, and the sound somewhere within the house of a door closing.

She was late. Mister Madison would be up and wanting his breakfast. If she didn't hurry along she'd be losing her job, and then what would she do?

Rose woke with a feeling of stark anxiety. Her heart raced, and for just a moment her mouth was dry with an unknown fear. Then she relaxed and lay still.

Sunshine slanted through the treetops outside the window, and the lamplight on the dresser looked sick and pale in its competition with daylight.

Rose turned onto her side, slipped her hands together beneath her cheek and looked at the cradle. It was in the corner of the room, shadowed so the baby would sleep. She had been warned by her mama, so many times. "Keep her quiet. Don't let her cry, Rose."

Yes, Mama. No, Mama.

Angela was such a good baby. When she was awake, her small arms waved in the air above the cradle, and if Rose didn't get up and immediately take her into bed and nurse her, she would start fussing.

But she so seldom cried.

Rose understood. Mama didn't want Beulah or Faye or Moses the gardener to know about Angela. While Rose ached to take her beautiful baby down and show her to

Beulah, who was like a grandmother, she had to wait.

Someday, Harold would come back. And then they would be married, and Angela would no longer have to be hidden.

She had so often imagined the day Harold would come. She would lead him upstairs to the cradle and say to him, "Harold, I want you to meet Angela, your daughter. Her hair is fair, like mine, but her eyes are dark like yours. Her lashes are long and dark and there's a dimple in her chin, like yours. Isn't she perfect?"

She would watch him pick up his daughter, and she would see the love in his eyes when he looked over their child's head at her. Together they would take her proudly out into the world.

The dream continued. Her mother would tell her she was sorry, and she would grow to love Angela very much, as would all the family. Beulah would hold Angela on her lap and tell her stories, as she had Rose, and Julie Sue, and Gertrude. As she said she had done with Sybil and Rose Marie.

Rose glanced at the clock on the dresser, and looked again. It was past six. Angela was sleeping longer than she ever had. Almost on the dot of six she had always nursed, eager and hungry. Wide-eyed and wiggly. Then, in Rose's arms, warm in her bed against Rose's breast, she would fall asleep again.

Rose got up, reached for her dressing gown and put it on, all the while watching the cradle. It was hanging so still this morning. There was no sway, no faint squeak as it swung on its springs.

Rose tied her robe at the waist quickly as she moved the short distance between the bed and the cradle. She looked down.

Angela's face seemed thinner, smaller, smothered in the shadows of the cradle. Her eyes were closed, her dark lashes even darker than usual on the pale cheeks.

But the doll's eyes were open and looking up at Rose. Its face looked rounder, less pinched and wrinkled, and there seemed now to be a faint smile on its lips. There was almost an *aliveness* in its eyes. There was something about it that made Rose wish her mother hadn't put it into the cradle with Angela. It took up too much room, now. It crowded her baby to the side.

Rose put her hand down to touch Angela's cheek, and the back of her hand brushed the cheek of the doll.

Rose drew her hand back slowly and stood still, staring down at the form of the baby, so small, so tiny beneath the blanket. Was it only her imagination that the cheek of the doll was warmer than the cheek of her baby? Angela looked as if she hadn't moved all night. The blanket did not rise with her breathing.

It did not rise and fall, that sweet, tender movement of life. Angela lay so still.

Chapter 3

Thank God, the night had ended. She had slept so little, it seemed to Julie Sue, after she woke with those awful feelings. As soon as she dressed, she was going to Rose's room to check on the baby. After that, and after her morning chores, she might walk to town and have a lemonade at the drugstore. Maybe she'd see some of her friends there. Maybe she'd stop in to see Sarah and talk some about school and beaus. Sarah's parents were allowing her to have beaus sit on the porch, and she was only three months older than Julie. She would ask her own parents about allowing fellows to stop in to talk, except this did not seem a good time.

Julie stretched one more time before she put on her corset. One last feeling of freedom before she stuffed herself into that tight thing and laced it up so her bodices would fit. She had tried to talk Mama out of making her wear corsets but Mama was plainly old-fashioned, that was all. Nobody could talk Mama out of anything.

And it was no use appealing to Papa.

Back in the winter when she learned about Rose being in the family way, she had tried to get Papa to send someone to tell Harold. If only Harold knew, Rose was sure, he would come to her. Julie Sue wasn't so sure. But at least they could try to find him. It wasn't as though Papa didn't have the money. There were such things as private detectives, didn't Papa know?

"Yes, of course, Julie Sue," Papa had said. "I know there

are such things as private detectives, but there are none in Wilfred. You'd have to go all the way to Little Rock to find one. And even then, we are not a family who would drag home a young man and make him marry one of the daughters. We are not shotgun wedding people, Julie Sue."

"But it seems we are the kind of family who intends to hide Rose from the rest of the world, Papa! And what are you going to do with the baby when it's born? Sneak it away in the middle of the night and have it raised by someone else?"

"Of course not. Rose's baby will not be given away unless she makes that decision herself."

"Then what does the family intend to do when Rose takes her child to church? Or does Rose never go out to church again?"

"Sarcasm is not becoming to you, Julie Sue."

"What about christening, Papa? Isn't the baby to be christened?"

Sybil spoke from behind her, and Julie whirled, unaware that her mother had entered the room.

"A child of sin is not christened, Julie Sue."

"How can you say that?" Julie cried, frustrated with her anger, her helplessness against her parents' beliefs and their stoicism. "The child can't help her mother not being married in the church!"

"Nevertheless, it remains a child of sin."

"I think that's terrible that you —"

"That's enough, Julie Sue!"

When her mother spoke to her like that, Julie knew to shut up. She had run out of the library that day and had not mentioned it again to her parents.

She could cry with her frustration, even now, every time she thought of it. The family name, ah yes, the family name. What would people think? The family name being of course Wilfred, her mother's maiden name. She was never allowed to forget that a great-grandfather had founded the town of Wilfred, had built the house in which she lived. And of course the Wilfred-Madison family had to set an example for the rest of the people, as if it were a kingdom.

She jerked her corset strings tighter, and let out a gasp for air. A sharp little pain angled across one rib. She stared at her image in the mirror.

Her hair was mussed, part of it falling out of the bun she had hastily pinned at the back. A corkscrew curl fell down toward one eyebrow. But all in all, she wasn't displeased with her reflection. She was darker than either of her sisters, and her skin looked as if she had been out in the sun without a bonnet to shade her face. She grinned a crooked grin as she recalled the time she had nearly sent her mother into convulsions.

"You know, Mama," she'd teased, "I do believe there is some Negro blood somewhere in our family. Look at my black hair, and these tight curls. Nobody else in the family looks like I do, and it had to come from somewhere, right?"

The look on her mother's face was enough to send her into spasms of giggles ever since. She had been very bold when she was fourteen. But that was almost two years ago, and she knew now she had to be careful about what she said. At least, most of the time.

She pulled her skirt on and left it hanging open until she had pulled her white bodice down and tucked it in at the waist. Struggling to reach behind, she fastened the bodice, then she fastened her skirt. Her waist looked very small, and her bosom filled out her bodice more than usual it seemed. Lordy, could she be in the family way? Who knew for sure exactly how babies were made? Perhaps she'd better not let Adam kiss her again. At least, not until she had talked to Rose, and found out exactly how a girl got in the family way.

She knew there was something very secret about it, and very shameful. But she also had a feeling it must be very exciting. Otherwise, why would it happen to a girl like Rose?

Rose had been so happy the day she told Julie her secret.

"Don't tell a soul, Julie Sue," Rose had whispered in her ear as they walked into the woods behind the house, "But last night when Harold walked me home from meeting, he asked me to marry him."

"You're engaged!" She forgot to keep her voice down.

"Shhh. It's a secret. Don't tell."

"Why not, for goodness sake? Don't you want parties?

34

Don't you want to start making plans for the wedding? Your wedding gown will have to be made, and all the bridesmaids' dresses! Will I be one of the bridesmaids, Rose? Please?"

"Of course you will, silly girl."

But Rose had looked over her shoulder to make sure they were alone in the woods. Above them, somewhere in the tops of the trees, a turtle dove crooned, and for a moment it had sounded as if it were moaning in sorrow. A bad feeling had come over Julie, just like last night, and when she first held Angela in her hands, smeared with blood.

She guessed now it was because she knew in her heart there was something wrong with an engagement that was secret.

She had watched Rose as days passed, and no letter came from Harold. She had watched Rose grow distant and staring. She had watched her grow quiet. Rose no longer wanted to take walks in the woods, or talk in secret about the wedding. She didn't want to hear about dress patterns for wedding gowns or bridesmaids' dresses.

Then Rose had gradually drawn away from the family, even from Julie. She had stopped going to church, or to town shopping. She had even stopped coming down to meals.

And Julie Sue could hear her sobbing, through the wall that separated their bedrooms.

"What is it, Rose?" she asked one day as winter hung dark and misty around the house. She had opened Rose's bedroom door without knocking and found her lying on the bed. She was still dressed in her robe, but even with that loose cover, Julie Sue could see the curve of her belly. And she knew. Instinctively, she knew, even though she hadn't seen many pregnant women in all her life, or knew very much about where babies came from.

She sat down on the bed beside Rose and stroked her forehead. When Rose looked up at her, eyes faded with tears, Julie said, "It doesn't matter, Rose. We love you. Don't cry."

"Not Mama," Rose answered, taking Julie Sue's hand tightly between her own. "Not Papa. They're ashamed of me, Julie Sue."

Julie sat with Rose after that, often. Especially after Sybil

35

told her, "If anyone should ask you where your sister is, Julie Sue, tell them she has gone away for a year. Do you understand? Not even Beulah is to know about this."

"Beulah would never tell!"

"Nevertheless—"

"Beulah knows Rose is still in the house! Why else does she fix the trays?"

"Julie Sue. Just do as you're told!"

Julie hated it when her mother spoke her name in that tone of voice, but all she could do was pinch her lips together in displeasure.

There were times when Julie loved Beulah far more than she loved her own mother, but she hadn't thought about it until now.

"She is not to be told anything, do you hear?" Sybil's voice was harsh and cold, yet Julie sensed the passion beneath it, and maybe even sorrow and grief. It was hard to tell, with Mama, exactly what emotions lay beneath the stiff exterior, the proper Sybil Wilfred-Madison.

Julie brought her thoughts back to the present. The day was going to be lovely, and perhaps she and Rose could take the baby outside into the sunshine in the afternoon. Angela hadn't even been in the sunshine yet. Mama and Papa had to learn sometime that Beulah had to see the baby, as well as Faye and Moses and others who came here to work.

The next step then would be to let visitors see her, and especially their minister, Reverend Culhane.

She brushed her hair out again and twisted the long rope at the back and coiled it. Holding the coil against the back of her head with one hand, she reached for the pins with which to secure it, but her hand poised abruptly in midair.

She saw her own hand, in that second just before the scream penetrated the walls, the darkness in the old house, the silences. She saw her hand, and it was clawed. As if it didn't belong to her, but to something evil and dark that had been freed to roam the halls and hide within the shadows.

The scream reverberated through the walls, sounding very close yet at the same time distant and thin and wild, coming from somewhere beyond. The third floor perhaps, closed off by a door at the foot of the stairs. Or the first floor, far below the high ceilings. Or next door, in the next room, where Rose and the baby lived day and night, night and day, month after month.

Julie didn't recognize the voice. Not at first. It had an animal sound. A sound of such terror, such helpless anguish, that it could have been the voice of a barnyard animal crying out in fear at slaughtering time.

And then she knew.

Suddenly, and horribly.

Rose.

Beulah carried the tray with the coffee steaming in the pot, and the plate with the hot bread and the jelly and butter through the swinging door into the dining room.

"How are you this morning, Mister Madison?" she asked.

He sat at the end of the table, papers on the table beside his plate. She had set places for the mister and the misses, and also for Gertrude and Julie Sue, although Mister Madison usually had finished his breakfast and was gone to town to his office before Sybil or the girls came to eat.

"Good morning, Beulah. Are you a bit late this morning, or did I get up earlier than usual?"

"I'm a bit late, sir. It won't happen again."

Rose's plate was on a tray in the kitchen. On it Beulah would later fix the hot bread, the oatmeal, the milk. Julie Sue would take the tray away. Sometimes Sybil would. No one had ever said to Beulah, "Don't bother with the tray for Rose, she isn't here." Beulah had fixed it for months now, and no one had told her not to.

She let the swinging door fall shut behind her and crossed the room to the table.

The scream reached her then, bursting through the ceiling in a distant and dreamy way that made her feel she was having her waking nightmare, hearing that scream in the house, piercingly heartrending and filled with pain.

A baby's birth.

A baby's death.

37

She saw, as if she were still in the nightmare, the Mister rise from the table. He floated phantom-like through the air, coming toward her, not seeing her. His arm hit the tray in her hand and she dropped it.

The coffee spilled, running in dark brown rivulets onto the rug, staining its patterns of red roses and green vines.

The dining room door into the hall opened at the Mister's push, swung back against the wall and banged noisily, and the scream filled the house. And at last, Beulah knew it was real.

Julie stumbled toward the door, one shoe laced tightly to her ankle, the other straggling around her toes. She kicked it away and ran on, like a crippled person with one short leg. Her shoe heel thudded against the rug, and on the polished wood floor between rugs, and her bare foot moved soundlessly between thuds.

In the hall, standing at the distant end without moving, Sybil seemed a part of the dark shadows there. She had turned out the gaslight. Her hand was still raised to the lamp on the wall.

Julie ran into Rose's room, fumbling for a moment with the doorknob, aware that Papa was coming up the stairs and that Mama still had not moved except to lower her hand. Coming behind Papa then was Beulah. And across the hall Gertrude's door was opening and Gertrude, still in her nightgown and nightcap peered out, her straw-colored hair circling the upper part of her face like a ruffle extending from the nightcap.

Julie felt the knob turn in her slippery hand, and she shoved the door back.

Rose stood between the cradle and rocking chair, holding the baby in her hands far away from her body as if making an offer. The baby wore a long white gown Julie had never seen before. Perhaps a christening gown. It covered the baby's feet and trailed toward the floor.

There was something strange about the baby. She was wearing a bonnet, too, as if Rose had gotten up early and dressed her to go out. Rose, though, was still in her dressing gown, her hair hanging down in its night braid.

"Rose! What's wrong?"

Rose did not hear her. She stared over Julie's head at the wall, her eyes wild, her face distorted. The scream continued on and on, with only short gasps of breath. Gradually she was extending her arms even further, with the baby, putting it so far away from her.

Julie's attention became riveted on the baby. Angela was too still. Her small legs and arms hung as limp as the long gown. There was no movement.

"The baby!" Julie screamed. "Something's wrong with the baby!"

She reached out toward Rose, while Papa shoved past her and put his hands out as if to stop Rose, somehow, or perhaps to bring her to him physically. Perhaps even to hold her, which Papa had never done to any of them since they passed the age of six. Julie took the baby from Rose's arms, and saw with part of her mind that Papa was actually holding Rose. Turning her to face him. Pressing her face against his suit, his hand on the back of her head. "There, there," he was saying, incongruously, "There, there."

And then all of Julie's attention settled on the baby.

She stared.

It was not a baby she held, not Angela.

It was a doll.

Chapter 4

Beulah trembled in the doorway to Rose's room. Her legs felt weak from the run up the long front stairs. Weakness radiated out from her heart, and the trembling reached into her arms and neck. She was aware of each member of the family. She saw the Mister holding Rose against his chest. She saw, as if she had eyes in the back of her head, that Sybil was still in the hall, and Gertrude still in her doorway peering out. But her eyes were held now by Julie Sue, who was turning toward Beulah, her face looking drained of color. As Rose now sobbed dryly against her father's chest, Julie Sue's voice rasped into Beulah's heart.

"It's a *doll*. It's not Angela, it's a *doll!*" She thrust the doll at Beulah and whirled away. "Where's Angela?"

Julie Sue ran to the cradle in the corner of the room and put her hands in as if to lift a baby, but then she drew back.

She turned slowly, her eyes meeting Beulah's.

"She's . . . dead. The baby . . . Rose's baby . . . *she's dead.*"

A hot poker of pain twisted in Beulah's heart. She hadn't known for certain there was a baby, although she had thought there was. But she hadn't known its name or even that it was a girl. Though it seemed right, that a gentle and lovely girl like Rose would have a baby girl.

Beulah hadn't known the name of the baby. But at this moment it was as if she had known this baby from the day it was born. That she had helped with the making of its clothes, and the planning for its occupancy in the family. That she had held the baby in her own arms and loved her, loved Angela.

Never before, in all the years Beulah had worked here, in all the years she had helped in her way to raise the children who grew up here, had a baby died. *Not a baby.*

It just wasn't right that a baby should die.

"She was so healthy," Julie Sue said, still staring with shocked and anguished eyes at Beulah, as if Beulah could tell her the answers. "Yesterday she smiled at me, and cooed. What happened to her?"

Beulah realized she was still holding the doll. It was made to look like an infant, with curved legs and arms, its face squeezed up like an infant's. Though as she looked down at it she saw it had a glow she hadn't remembered. An ugly baby doll, she had thought, years ago when she last looked at it. It belonged upstairs in the china cabinet in the hall.

She put it down on the foot of Rose's bed, and went to the cradle and looked in.

Before her eyes blurred with tears she saw a lovely small face, as perfect as Rose's face had been when she was three months old. As perfect as Rose Marie had been, and Julie Sue, and Gertrude. As Sybil herself, when she was an infant.

Angela looked asleep, yet there was a china doll look to her also, that stillness and coldness that comes with death.

Beulah reached down and touched her and was shocked at the icy feel of the smooth skin.

She looked up, turning, and through her tears she saw that Sybil had entered the room.

Sybil, straight as a board in her tight corsets, dressed for the day. Sybil's face, held tight against emotion, became more visible through Beulah's tears.

"I'll want to talk with you later, Beulah," she said, and her hand fell on Beulah's arm and guided her toward the door.

Beulah looked at the unmade bed, at the doll lying there

on the wrinkled comforter. Its eyes stared toward her, wide open, glass as blue as jewels.

In all the years since the doll had been in the house it had rarely been out of the china cabinet on the third floor. There was something wrong about it being here, in Rose's room, but . . .

"Beulah."

Beulah realized she had stopped and was staring at the doll. "Yes, Ma'am," she said, and moved out into the hall.

"Oh God," Julie cried softly, turning helplessly. She wanted to take Angela out of the cradle, but her mother was making them all leave the room. "What happened to her? Mama, Rose, what happened?"

Papa took Rose out into the hall, his arm around her shoulder, but Rose pulled away and tried to go back into the bedroom.

"My baby. Give me my baby."

"Your baby has passed on, Rose," Sybil said. "Go downstairs. Walter, take her downstairs. No, wait, she hasn't dressed. Julie Sue, get something for Rose to wear and help her get dressed. Take her to your room."

Julie whirled away and took a couple of garments from Rose's wardrobe. She returned to the door and found herself facing Rose. But Rose no longer looked alive. Her face had the look of a wooden puppet Julie had once seen.

Julie put her arm around Rose's waist and turned her away. "Come with me, Rose."

Beulah waited in the hall. She would be needed now, as she always had been when there was a death in the family. In the past, when a member died, word was instantly sent out, and neighbors gathered. Women and men waited, speaking solemnly and softly, in the parlors and in the dining room and library while the body was prepared for burial. In the barn behind the house the coffin would be built. Then burial would be in the family vault in the town cemetery. But it had been a long time since there was a death in the family. Now, probably, the funeral home in town would prepare the body.

Sybil came out of the upstairs family parlor where she had left Rose and Julie Sue, and indicated with a motion that Beulah was to follow her back into Rose's room.

Sybil closed the door.

The cradle in the shadowed corner looked as if it were shrouded by a cloud. It was stark, and bare, no blanket hanging over the side. Within, the baby lay, but it was out of sight, and Beulah had a terrible feeling that it was empty and had always been empty, its only occupant now lying on the foot of Rose's bed.

The doll. Sybil's old infant doll.

What was it doing out of the china cabinet upstairs, for the first time since . . . since . . . *since Charles Wilfred died.* Charles, Sybil's father. He too had died suddenly. Beulah remembered seeing the doll in his room that very morning. She had been the one to pick it up. She had found it on the floor by the high bed, slightly hidden by the comforter. The bed had looked, she recalled, as if there had been a struggle. The comforter was half off the bed. Charles Wilfred was sprawled crosswise on the bed, his face down.

And on the floor, beneath the bed, lay the doll.

Beulah picked it up, but someone had taken it from her and she had not seen it again until a month later when she was dusting on the third floor. It was back in its place in the china cabinet.

"Beulah, are you listening to me?"

Beulah jumped as if she had been caught sleeping. "Oh, sorry, Ma'am. I beg your pardon?"

"I said I'd like you to prepare the body for burial. I'll bring you clothing to put it in. Mister Madison has gone to Little Rock to bring back a casket, and he will bring men to dig the grave."

"To dig the grave?"

43

"Yes."

The baby would not be buried in the family vault, then. Beulah tightened her lips.

"And Beulah?"

"Yes Ma'am?"

"I'll expect you to say nothing about this."

"No."

"Not to anyone, even your family."

"No, of course not," Beulah said.

"Nor to anyone at your church."

Beulah shook her head and crossed the room slowly to the cradle. She reached in and lifted the baby. She felt the coldness through the flannel gown the child wore, and the stiffness of the body. Its arms were curled up toward its face, as fragile and brittle as if it were made of china.

Beulah turned with it and saw Sybil's glance touch it and move hastily away. Beulah looked for a sign of love and remorse, but Sybil's face was set with dignity. If there were emotions, they were hidden.

But hadn't it always been that way? No tears, not at the funeral of Rose Marie, nor the funerals of her mother or father.

It was not up to Beulah to judge her. After all, Sybil was like the daughter she had never had. She had held her and rocked her when she was as young and younger than the cold, still child she now held in her hands.

Sybil left the room, turning her back quickly, pulling the door shut.

Beulah laid the baby gently on Rose's bed. Someone had pulled up the comforter and the crocheted bedspread, but it was not neatly done.

She tried to remove the clothing from the dead baby, but could not pull the sleeves over the arms. She dared not pull the arms away from the body. To hear those small bones snap was more than she could bear. What caused this brittleness? As if all human characteristics had been removed from it. As if the small body had been changed into a. . . . Yes, a china doll.

It must be a disease that ran like a silent ghost in the Wilfred family. Now that she was faced with death again she remembered Charles Wilfred having that same brittleness, and so had Rose Marie. Rose Marie's mother had not. But hers was not a sudden, unexpected death in the darkest hour of the night. She had become ill after Rose Marie's funeral, and within months had taken to her bed, and lingered, finally dying one year after Rose Marie died.

Beulah turned away, wiping tears from her cheeks. This child, whom she had never known, was like her grandchild, or her great-grandchild. What caused these deaths in the family? As if death itself appeared only in the night, only while the victim slept. It took its soul and it left a body with all life drawn away.

Beulah found Rose's sewing basket and took the scissors. She was prepared to cut away the flannel gown when the door opened and Sybil stepped into the room.

Without looking at Beulah, she laid white, folded clothing on the bedspread. She left again in silence.

Beulah stood a moment, alone with the dead infant. Then she bent and began cutting the flannel gown. Up the front all the way to the neck, then down each sleeve. She removed all the clothing, the "didie," the booties, cutting them away with the sewing shears.

Sybil had brought an old christening gown, one that had belonged perhaps to an earlier child in the family. It was yellowed and old, but it was of good material, heavy Irish linen, with crocheted trim.

Beulah cut the gown down the back and put it to one side. Then she took the china basin from Rose's room and went into the bathroom and drew warm water. She returned to bathe the baby.

The smell of death now hung like a dark shroud in the room. That sweet, nightmarish smell that was so hard to forget. It would linger. Rose would be living with it, day and night, for the rest of the time that she remained in this room.

Beulah lifted the baby in her arms and went down the

hall to an empty bedroom, to finish the dressing of the child. To lay her on a satin pillow to await her casket.

The stairs to the third floor rose just beyond Gertrude's room, and Gertrude heard the footsteps rising, and waited, listening. Someone climbed the stairs, and their steps faded overhead. For a long time, at least ten minutes, Gertrude waited, listening for the steps to come back.

Sometimes in the night she heard footsteps going up those stairs. She would wake and lie cold and frightened, always afraid to go out and see who went in the dark to the third floor. The rooms above were never used except when there was lots of company, as at Christmas time, or Easter, when relatives came from other towns.

But this was daytime, and Gertrude waited. Mama, she thought. Mama had gone upstairs.

The steps came down again, and Gertrude heard the wooden button scraping into place, locking the door. She waited.

Her mother's footsteps faded along the hall toward the front of the house, and still Gertrude waited.

When the house seemed as if she were the only person on the second floor, she stepped out into the hall. The doors to Rose and Julie Sue's rooms were closed. Beyond the corner the hall turned, dividing, going around the balcony to the big bedrooms where Mama and Papa lived, and whose doors were hidden from Gertrude's view. The door to the third floor was, likewise, hidden from anyone who might be on the balcony, or who might come out of the upstairs parlor, or her parents' rooms.

Gertrude went to the door to the third floor. Now that she was ten years old she could reach the wooden button if she stretched tall. That had been like a birthday present to her, finding that now she could go upstairs whenever she liked, and no one would ever know.

She turned the button, and cast a quick glance over her shoulder to make sure she was still alone. Somewhere in

46

the house was the body of Rose's baby. She had never been around a dead person before, and she was a little bit afraid. But since the baby was so tiny, was she silly to be afraid, even though the baby was dead?

She had often listened to the sounds of the baby, when she was alive. Sometimes at night she could hear the baby cry, just a little, especially when she was first born. But only briefly. Mama wouldn't allow her to cry. Mama didn't want anyone to know she lived here. *And now no one would.*

She slipped into the dark tunnel of the enclosed stairway and pulled the door shut softly. She muttered under her breath a short prayer that no one would see that the button was turned, and then with one hand on the wall, she climbed the stairs.

The upper hall was lighted by a window at the end. It was a shorter hall than the one below, and its ceiling was lower. Near the end of the hall stood the tall piece of furniture that her mother called a curio hutch and Beulah called a china cabinet. It held a lot of interesting things, from tiny, faded china dolls, to little iron wagons and iron horses, to vases that were too fragile ever to be taken out and used. And on the bottom shelf, *the doll.*

She knelt and looked in.

Yes, the doll was there, again, where it had been all her life. There behind glass, beyond her reach.

When she saw last night that her mother was giving the doll to Rose's baby, she had felt something dark and mean within herself. She had thought she might take it away from the baby when she had a chance, because why should her mother give the doll to someone who wasn't even to be talked about to one's friends, when she wouldn't give it to her? Gertrude had always wanted the doll. It was a baby doll, and it would fit into her doll family as no other would. Besides, it was there. No one ever played with it. Why couldn't she have it?

Her mother had ordered her to stay away from it. She had even had the handyman put the button on the door so high she couldn't reach it.

47

She sat staring at the doll's face. It didn't look quite so wrinkled and ugly. There was a tiny bit of color on the cheeks, and it seemed there was almost a smile on its pouty lips. Its feet were hidden beneath its long gown, but she knew they were bare. She had seen its tiny toes. They were just like Angela's toes, small and real looking. But they weren't as plump.

Its hands lay at its side, curled fingers, with fingernails, tiny and narrow.

Suddenly she knew something. Her mother hadn't given the doll to Rose's baby because she liked her better. She had given her the doll for one night because she knew the baby was going to die.

Chapter 5

Rose and Julie Sue sat together on Julie's bed. All day Julie had held Rose's hand, had felt it limp and lifeless in hers, and was helpless to comfort her. Rose stared at the wall, her eyes dry most of the time. When a tear edged slowly down one cheek, Julie wiped it away.

She hurt for Rose, for Baby Angela. She couldn't imagine life now without Angela, and was awed at how much deeper Rose's grief must be. How could she stand it? She didn't ask Rose to talk, to try to explain how she felt. Though she wanted to ask, "What happened? Rose, what happened to the baby? Didn't she make a sound?" She remembered when she woke in the night, and now wished she had gone to see about the baby. Maybe she could have helped. Maybe she had heard her cry out, once. Just once.

She and Rose had made such plans together, while Rose sat in the rocking chair with Angela in her arms. "Perhaps we'll just move away sometime," Julie had suggested, "and I'll become a business lady, perhaps own my very own dress shop and make very fancy gowns by hand."

Rose had tipped back her head and laughed hilariously at that. "You?" she said, but not in a mocking way, only in a way that made Julie laugh with her. "You can't even sew a straight seam! You hate dressmaking!"

It was the last time they had laughed together. Julie remembered the wide smile on the baby's face, and the eager look in her eyes as she listened to their laughter. She had recognized it as a joyous sound, and had kicked her legs and waved her arms vigorously. She had been so alert, so healthy.

Just days ago. Just yesterday.

Shadows were filling the room. It seemed they had skulked behind the closed door of Julie's room recently, thickening and growing with the death of Baby Angela.

The door behind them opened without a knock, and Julie knew it was their mother. No one else would open the door without knocking.

"It's time, girls," Sybil said.

Rose didn't move, but Julie turned and looked at their mother. She was shocked to see that Sybil was dressed in her mourning black, the dress, shawl, hat and veil she wore only to funerals. Julie stood up.

"We're ready for the burial," Sybil said.

"The burial! But—"

"Come on, before it gets dark. Help Rose on with her shawl, the evening is cool."

Julie didn't understand. The sun had gone down. No one ever had a funeral this time of day. Then suddenly she understood that this would be a different kind of funeral.

"Aren't we going to the family vault at the cemetery?" she asked quietly, chilled by the lack of reverence over this baby's death. It reminded her of burying their dog last year in a hole in the ground near the woods where he loved to hunt. Though she knew her questions were useless, she couldn't stop herself. "Won't there be services with Reverend Culhane?"

"You know that won't be possible."

"It's too soon!" She heard her voice becoming more shrill. She was going to burst out crying, wailing like a banshee. "Mama, she only died this morning!"

"She probably had been dead most of the night, and its time to lay her to rest. Come now."

Sybil backed out of the room, leaving the door open. Her footsteps moved quietly down the hall toward the front stairs.

Julie stood fighting tears, her anger building. She felt explosive with it, barely able to contain herself. Her hands knotted into impotent fists at her sides as she looked out the door at the empty hallway, and listened to her mother's steps going toward the front of the house. She heard her go down the three steps from the hall to the balcony. She heard the steps cross the balcony and become muffled on the carpeted steps of the main stairway.

"How can they do this? *How can they do this!*" She spoke aloud, but only because it burst out of her. "It's like she was nothing! They don't even allow us a decent three days. There's not even to be a wake!"

"It doesn't matter," Rose said softly. "My baby's gone."

"Oh Rose!" She turned and put her arms around Rose's slumped shoulders. She hadn't meant her anger to spill out upon Rose. "I'm sorry."

Her anger had been present since she had learned of Rose's pregnancy. Having the baby alive and well in the house had helped alleviate it, but now it was back. She recognized it as a growing, bitter hatred for her parents.

"It doesn't matter," Rose said again, in tones so soft and low it was almost a whisper. "It doesn't matter where she's buried, Julie Sue. I knew they wouldn't bury her in the family vault. I knew they would not have a service for her."

Julie hugged Rose closely, and then she pulled two shawls out of her wardrobe, her old and her new, and she draped the new shawl over Rose's shoulder.

"Do you want a hat, Rose?"

"No. Angela wouldn't know me with a hat."

Julie paused, watching Rose. She didn't like the way Rose's eyes stared. She didn't like the tone of her voice, that lifeless, almost soundless, quality. These few words

51

were all she had spoken all day. They showed at least that she was aware of reality, but Julie was afraid. That she hadn't gone insane during the long winter before Angela's birth seemed a miracle. But, how could she survive this?

The house was silent and shadowed. Julie walked with her arm around Rose's waist, along the hall, down the front stairs. In the hall they saw Beulah. She motioned them to follow and turned, herself draped in one of Sybil's old black shawls, and a black scarf on her head. She moved ahead of them like a wraith of doom.

They went out of the house and saw beneath the trees, where the forest began, the small group of people. At first it looked as if mourners had been gathered, but as they approached, Julie saw it was only their mother and father, Gertrude, and three strange men.

Two of the men were dressed in workday overalls, and stood together away from the family. The other was wearing a black suit, and stood a short distance from Sybil and Walter.

Then Julie saw the grave. A small pile of dark soil marked it, and a shadowed hole in the ground that looked black and bottomless. On the other side sat a tiny box, a plain little casket, the lid closed.

"We are gathered here at the side of a grave," the strange man said, the Bible open in his hand, his voice serious and slow, "To lay to rest one who never knew sadness, nor sorrow, nor emptiness of spirit. We are gathered here to lay to rest one of God's innocents, who has been taken into His beautiful care to become one of His angels."

Julie listened, amazed. The preacher was talking as if the baby had been christened, as if she were free from sin. Julie felt satisfaction deepen within her, and knew it was partly a feeling of vindication.

She stood with her head bowed. In the silence after the preacher had closed his Bible, Julie heard the call of a whippoorwill in the distance, and then another, as if they were the choir for Angela's funeral. She heard the frogs singing in the pond out in the pasture toward the road. But darkness was moving like low black clouds from the forest and Sybil's face behind her veil was hidden by the gathering darkness.

Julie held her breath against the rush of sobs that were building in her. She glanced over at Rose, and saw that Rose's head was upturned. She was staring into the trees, not at the small casket.

The two men in overalls came forward and lifted the casket, and Sybil motioned for the family to leave.

"If you would like to view the body," the minister said.

"No," Sybil replied. "Thank you. We will go now. The casket may be put into its grave."

Rose remained behind, and Julie waited for her.

As Walter led the procession back toward the house, the minister nodded his head for the burial to be completed.

The two workers lifted the small casket and lowered it carefully down into the ground. It disappeared into the black hole, and Rose's gaze moved with it. She stood with her head lowered, then she yielded at last to Julie's arm and turned toward the house.

Rose sat in the rocking chair, rocking slowly, looking into the black night outside her window. She had lighted the lamp, but turned it very low. Behind her the cradle was shrouded in stillness and shadow. Such a safe and comfortable place for a baby. And in it, her baby was sleeping so well. Baby Angela hadn't stirred for more than an hour. Rose wanted to take the baby up and hold her, but she didn't want to disturb her rest.

Julie Sue had wanted Rose to sleep in her room, the way she had when they were very young and there was a storm raging outside and lightning flashed at the windows and cracked overhead like cannons in a war.

Julie should have known Rose would never leave behind her baby.

She was wearing a bonnet tonight, and a long christening gown. Mama had finally brought Angela a christening gown with a bonnet to match. It was so nice of Mama.

The door opened, letting in light that hurt Rose's eyes. Beulah came in slowly, bringing a tray. Her shadow fell across the floor toward Rose's feet. Along with the shadow and Beulah came the sickening smell of food.

"My goodness, child, why are you sitting in the dark? You need to turn your lamp up. Here, I'll do it for you."

"Beulah," Rose said, "You shouldn't be here. You should have gone hours ago."

"I'm here to see that you get something to eat, that's why I'm here, and I'm not leaving until you eat. Do you hear?"

She put the tray on the dresser, and then turned the lamp wick so high it began to smoke. She edged it down, until it burned smoothly. The soft yellow glow of the lamp reached Rose. She put her hand up to shield her eyes.

"But how will you find your way home in the dark, Beulah?"

"The Mister said that I could take one of the lanterns."

"But there are terrible things out there in the dark, Beulah."

"Mmm. Like what?"

Beulah placed the tray on Rose's lap. Rose turned her face away from the smell of the food.

"I can't eat."

"Yes, you can. You must."

Beulah held a spoon full of mashed potatoes to Rose's lips. Rose saw Beulah's eyes; it was as if they were behind a thin shield of rain. She saw the tears in Beulah's eyes, not running down her cheeks, but there, as they had been in Rose's heart before she understood about the baby. Beulah, the grandmother she'd never had. And often, the mother Sybil was not. She saw the love, felt it and remembered it, and her lips parted.

She ate, forcing it down, until Beulah finally said, "All right, we'll call that good. For tonight. Come now and I'll help you into your gown. You have to rest, Rose. I'll bring you some of my herbs from home tomorrow, to help you sleep. But tonight, you try. You understand? You do this for me, will you?"

"Yes." She would not be alone until she had assured Beulah that she would be all right. She understood that. Julie Sue had not been so persistent as Beulah would be. And Rose had to be alone. She had to go get her baby, and take care of her. She would be getting cold now. The baby needed her mother. It would be just the two of them, closed away from the rest of the world.

After Beulah helped her into her nightgown, Rose watched as Beulah turned back the covers of her bed.

"Thank you, Beulah."

"Will you rest now, Rose?"

"Yes."

Still Beulah did not leave.

"I'd take you home with me, Rose. I wish I had taken you away from here last winter. I'd give anything now if I had taken you home with me. You and the baby. Maybe . . ."

Rose was hardly listening. She wished Beulah would hurry now and leave.

At last Beulah turned away and pulled the door closed behind her. Rose sighed deeply.

Now, now she could go get Angela.

Chapter 6

Walter hesitated in the hall at the top of the back stairs. The two gaslights flickered and then burned steadily, small white flames within their globes. There was silence within the house. The grandfather clock in the lower hall began its resonate strike. He listened. When it reached twelve and then died away he sighed and walked quietly down the hall.

He was dead tired. As soon as he learned of the baby girl's death this morning he had gone out, hitched the horse to the buggy and gone to find a minister, grave diggers, and a casket for that tiny body. Of all the things in the world, he had not expected nor wanted Rose's baby to die. Twice when Rose had been out of the room he had gone in to look down at the baby. The last time he had touched her, and she responded. She had opened her hand and closed it around his finger, and in a kind of shocked surprise he had felt a lift in his heart as he looked down at his first grandchild.

He had decided he would have to talk to Sybil. The baby needed sunlight, he would tell her. They would have to make up a story about Rose eloping and her husband being killed, perhaps, by a runaway horse . . . or . . .

But now it was too late.

As he passed Gertrude's room, he saw the door was ajar. Across the hall and down one door was Julie Sue's.

Her door was closed, and there was no light showing beneath it.

The next door was Rose's room, and he was startled as it suddenly opened and Rose stepped out. She was wearing a loose robe over a long, white nightgown. In the room behind her the light of the kerosene lamp was turned so low the room was almost dark in contrast to the pale, white light in the hall.

"Rose!"

She stared at him, her eyes wide. Beyond her he saw the corner of her room, and gradually, as if it were coming out of a mist, the outlines of the cradle. The cradle should have been removed. No wonder she couldn't sleep.

"I'll take that cradle out of your room, Rose."

Her hand jerked up, palm toward him. "No!"

Walter ran his fingers through his hair. His hand was trembling. He looked down, and saw Rose was barefoot. Her feet looked small and pale on the dark floor.

"Tomorrow then," he said. "I've just come back from taking Beulah home. She was going to walk. She said she'd walked that road so many times she could find her way home in the dark."

Rose did not respond. She stood still in the doorway, the hand she had raised now resting on the door frame, still blocking him from entering.

"Well," he said, moving slowly past her. "I expect you were on your way to the bathroom. I'll go now. Good night."

"Good night, Papa."

He paused. Her voice sounded the way it always had. Soft, gentle, light. He looked back at her, but her face was in shadow. He wanted desperately to put his arms around her and hold her and tell her it was right and good to cry on his shoulder, but he only nodded instead before he went on.

57

In the front section of the hall he entered the suite of rooms where one small hallway connected his bedroom to Sybil's. The one bathroom, remodeled from a small bedroom, was down the hall toward the girls' rooms. Though he was too tired to walk the extra distance, he felt soiled with sweat and dusty from the long roads he had driven today. He'd get his robe, take a quick bath, get into his nightshirt and into his bed. The gaslight burning in the small connecting hall was all the light he needed to undress and find his robe.

"Walter."

Her voice was almost dreamlike, totally unexpected. For the first time he saw that Sybil's bedroom door was open. Although her lamp was not on, the light in the hall dwindled toward the large, dark bulk of her bed in the center of the west wall.

"Yes. It's I." He didn't move toward her room, but he peered in and could see her sitting against her pillows. They were stacked high and white against the dark headboard of the bed, and she lay upon them wearing something black and sheer.

"I know it's you," she said, and there seemed to be amusement in her voice. "Come in."

"Come in?" he repeated, feeling stupid the moment it was out of his mouth. He hadn't crossed the threshold of Sybil's room in over six months. The last time he had lain in her bed she had spent the time talking about Rose, and what they were going to do about her. She had suggested sending her away, and he had refused. He had finally left her bed without having had any satisfaction at all.

"Come in," she said again. She threw the sheet back, and uncovered her long, pale, shapely legs. He began to tremble.

He saw that one leg was drawn up, knee bent, the other straight but flung wide, revealing the dark fullness

58

of hair between her legs. Her nightgown was high around her waist. Without her corset, Sybil had a lovely, womanly body, with full hips and breasts and a small waist. Her skin was like pale satin. She was two different women, it seemed, the one emerging so seldom that he almost forgot she was there.

He stared at her with slow horror building. Tonight, with death like a cry from the tiny child, she was bidding him come to her?

He crossed her threshold slowly, as filled with fear, as self-conscious as he'd been the first time she invited him to her bed. So many years ago. He wondered suddenly if she ever thought of that time. Before matrimony, when they were in her father's house alone, she had suddenly excused herself. Several minutes later while he sat uncomfortably wondering where she was, she had called him. He had followed her voice to a bedroom upstairs, and had found her sitting nude in her bed.

He had made a fool of himself, that time, fumbling awkwardly. Finally she had helped him, giggling at times in his ear, at times breathing hot breath that threatened to drown him in ecstasies he had never even dreamed of. At the age of twenty-three he had never had an experience such as he had with Sybil that day, in one of the bedrooms down the back hall of this very house.

After he had succeeded in spite of all his fumblings and his awkwardnesses, she had whispered to him, "Now you'll have to marry me."

He had been delighted to marry her. He had imagined in his naivete that all his life with her would be filled with such delicious secrets as they had shared that afternoon. How wrong he had been. After their marriage Sybil's passion was rare, always surprising him after long abstention.

But tonight? Tonight after they had just buried their grandchild? It wasn't right.

59

"Come to me, Walter," she said softly. "I need you tonight."

Against his will he was drawn across that forbidden threshold into her room. His fingers worked at the fasteners on his trousers and his underwear, his body betraying him.

She reached out for him and helped him remove the rest of his clothing. He felt the softness of her bed, and a cool breeze moving through the window to touch him. She lifted her gown beneath her arms, and he sank upon her with a long sigh that was almost a groan.

He thought of nothing else, then, but of the girl who had called him to her bedroom, so many years ago, and whose need had risen again tonight. There was something obscene in its mystery, but he did not try to fathom it.

Rose stood as still as a statue in the hall, waiting, listening. She had long ago heard the closing of the door somewhere in the front of the house, which indicated her father had gone into the master suite, yet she waited.

The clock in the foyer below struck the half hour, and at last she moved along the hall, past Julie Sue's door, past Gertrude's. She went to the closed door of the third floor stairway and reached up to the wooden button and turned it.

Her hand rested for a long while on the doorknob before she finally turned it and opened the door to the third floor. She looked up into darkness.

After a moment she began to climb. The light from the gas lamp dwindled away as she slowly climbed the steps. With her hand sliding along the handrail, she went up into the third floor hall.

She stood without moving. At the distant end of the hall moonlight came through the window. Its dim glow outlined the sharp corners of the china closet.

Her footsteps whispered along the hall. She stopped in front of the large hutch and opened the door.

She went down onto her knees.

The baby's face was a pale blur in the edge of the moonlight, but she saw the welcoming smile on her face.

Why have you waited so long, Mama?

"My baby, my precious," Rose whispered and reached in. The baby's body felt warm to her hands, warm, soft, and so small. "My precious one. I looked for you in the cradle but you were not there. I thought I had lost you."

She held it against her breast and sat on the floor, facing the window and the moonlight. She held it to her breast and rocked her body back and forth, humming softly beneath her breath. She stood up and turned, carrying her baby.

Her baby was in two places now. Part of Angela lay in the dark hole in the ground, out in the edge of the forest at the back of the house.

But another part was here, alive, in her arms.

She quietly closed the glass door on the cabinet. In the silence of the house soft sounds, like the latch on the door clicking shut, carried far. She knew, because many times in the past she had heard that door click, and she would know that Gertrude, when she was smaller and less obedient, had come to play with the doll. And Mama never allowed Gertrude to play with the doll. So Rose would hurry and take the doll from Gertrude's hands and put it back before their mother found out. She'd lead her screaming sometimes from the third floor, and then not only Mama would know, but the whole household.

Then the button was put high on the door. And the soft click of the door closing was no longer part of the sounds in the house.

Mama had never allowed Gertrude to have the doll, nor herself, nor Julie Sue. She had been saving it for her first grandchild.

Except . . . this child in Rose's arms was really not the doll. It was Angela. Part of Angela. And its place was with her, in her room, in its cradle.

Her bare feet made little sound on the floor as she moved out of the moonlight and into the dark part of the hall where the stairs fell abruptly away, like the sides of a grave.

Rose felt cautiously down for the top step, and then began her descent, the doll held cradled in both arms.

When she reached the lower hall she adjusted her baby to lie on her shoulder so her right hand would be free to close and lock the stairway door.

Now she stood in the dim light that came from the one gaslight left burning at the junction of the back hall with the front halls. All doors along the back hall were closed except Gertrude's. Rose listened and heard nothing except the distant and sporadic piping call of frogs.

She went on, moving quietly but quickly, and sighed with relief when she stood in her room, the door shut between her and the rest of the world. The lamp on her dresser put out a soft, yellow glow, so different from the gaslight in the hall. Deep shadows hung over the cradle in the corner. That was good. The baby would sleep. She would be quiet and she would sleep, and Mama would know she was a good child and would not take her away.

Rose went to the side of the cradle and with her right hand spread the blankets smooth and turned back the top one. They were old blankets, used by earlier babies in the family. Herself, perhaps, and Julie Sue. Maybe even Rose Marie.

For a moment she held the baby against her face before she laid her down. She felt the cool cheek against her own. She felt the button nose pressing into her flesh. And it seemed she felt the nudging, the rooting, as if it were searching for her breast. But this was not her breast, but her face, this rooting for nourishment, the nudging for food.

She was suddenly very tired. Exhausted. A strange, deep weakness reached into her bones.

"I must sleep," she whispered to the infant against her face. "My precious Angela, I'm so tired. Mummy wants you to sleep, too, and be a very good girl."

She bent over the cradle, and felt herself sway. She steadied herself with one hand. The baby didn't want to let go of her, but she was so tired. She laid it down and pulled the blanket up to the chin.

She stood looking at the tiny face turned toward her, and the eyes that were opening wider, no longer swollen almost shut from birthing. She looked at the eyes and saw they were sky blue glass, not a smoky dark brownish blue. It was not Angela in the cradle. It was the doll.

The doll her mother had saved for the first grandchild.

For baby Angela.

Rose crawled into her bed and pulled her pillows to cradle her head. So tired. So very, very tired. There was something she should try to understand, something that had to do with her baby, and with the doll. And Mama. But she was so tired.

Julie stirred restlessly in her sleep. She woke abruptly and lay still. The room was very dark, with only the barest grey at the window, a lighter rectangle in a world without color. She listened, frowning into the darkness.

She had heard Rose singing a lullaby. She had heard

63

the squeak of the rocking chair. Just the way she had heard it two days ago, and the days before that, while Angela was still alive.

But the house was quiet and dark, the night deep and silent. Only an occasional frog piped somewhere in one of the ponds in the pasture. It was the hour when the world slept.

She got out of bed and went to her door. Without opening it she could smell death. She wanted to go to Rose, but after a moment she went back to bed. She shouldn't disturb Rose just because she had dreamed of hearing her singing and rocking.

She slept little the rest of the night, dozing, waking, hearing the squeak of the rocking chair in her imagination. Hearing Rose pace the floor as she had done those nights when the baby had been fussy.

At last, as the day broke with the songs of birds and the crow of roosters down in the barnyard, she went to Rose's room.

She knocked on the door lightly, and then opened the door.

Rose was sleeping, her face cupped by her left hand.

Pale, grey light seeped through the lace curtains at the window. The room felt chilled, although the window was closed. The odor of death was like a fog emanating from the walls.

She almost backed away, then her eyes touched the cradle in the shadowed corner. She went toward it.

Julie almost cried out in surprise. Surprise and joy, to realize yesterday had been a nightmare, nothing more. The baby was alive, and in her cradle. Her eyes were looking up at Julie, staring steadily and unnaturally.

Julie's hopes fell as swiftly as they had risen. It wasn't Baby Angela, it was only the doll. The baby doll from the old hutch upstairs. The doll that looked so much like a real baby, its face still wrinkled and ugly from

64

birth. It was wearing a bonnet, the fringe of lace white around the pale, pink face.

She started to take it out of the cradle to put it where it belonged, but as her hands reached down to touch it a sense of horror stopped her.

She drew back. The eyes still stared upward at her, and she felt scrutinized by them, as if there were something behind them that could see her. Though its eyes were blue orbs of glass that should have been closed, as doll's eyes always closed when the doll was laid flat, they remained open. The lashes were short, stubby, pale, and others were painted on, a few thin strokes of pale gold rising upward toward the almost invisible brows. Still, it seemed to her that the doll's eyes should have been swollen almost shut, the way a newborn baby's eyes really were.

Well, perhaps she was mistaken. They weren't shut now. And the doll looked less like a newborn. Judging by Angela, it was perhaps meant to be a one or two months old infant.

It didn't matter. Unlike Gertrude, she'd never wanted the old doll. It had interested her only because she knew it had been her mother's doll. And it seemed very strange that her mother had ever been young enough to have a doll.

Then she remembered a conversation with her mother about it one day after Gertrude had gotten in trouble once again for trying to take it for her own.

"I never wanted it," Sybil said. "I thought it was very ugly. I wanted a brooch, or a bottle of perfume. After all, I was twelve years old."

So it wasn't unreasonable to be unable to imagine her mother with that doll. She had not wanted it, and had never played with it. Why hadn't she let Gertrude have it?

And since Gertrude was never to remove it from the

cabinet, nor anyone else, what was it doing in Rose's room?

She'd talk to her mother about the doll being in Rose's room.

As she went quietly out into the hall she suddenly remembered it was the doll Rose had been holding yesterday morning.

She had been holding the doll, while in the cradle the real baby lay dead.

Chapter 7

"Excuse me, Mama, may I talk to you a minute?" Julie stood in one half of the library door looking into the large, shadowy room. On the opposite wall two long windows reached almost from ceiling to floor, and Mama's desk was in front of the one nearer the back of the room, where the book cases reached to the ceiling.

Her mother didn't look up. She finished writing something. Julie saw the back of her neck, with its lace collar, and her long auburn hair done up in a bun. No curl, no single hair strand was loose. For the past two days Julie's parents had seemed to be closing themselves into the library deliberately to get away from the rest of the family. Julie had not dared interrupt. But this morning Papa had gone to his office in town, and Mama was alone.

At last Sybil put down her pen and lifted her head. The chair turned, squeaking like a trapped mouse. "Yes, what is it?"

"Mama, did you know your old doll is in Rose's room?"

Sybil looked out the window behind the desk. It was one of two desks in the library. The larger one, which was Papa's, sat at the side of the room near the fireplace, and was hardly used except in winter. The small desk, exclusively Mama's, was in good light. During the day she made out her lists at that mahogany desk, wrote her letters there, and sometimes, when Julie peeked in, she saw her mother just sitting there, elbows on desk, chin in hands, staring out the window. She stared for a moment now out the window, then she faced Julie again.

"I put the doll away," Sybil said.

"But . . . why was it there?"

There was a long hesitation. Sybil picked up her pen again and began writing. Julie thought she had been forgotten and started to back out of the room.

Sybil said, "I gave it to the baby."

"*You* gave it to Rose's baby?"

"Yes. Don't concern yourself about it, Julie Sue. I put it away again."

Julie left the room, closing the door behind her. She stood in the hall. In the back of the house she heard a door close. The girl who did the washing was here again today, and Beulah was here as usual, and outside Moses, the handyman and gardener, was at work. It was almost like a normal day.

Julie went up the front stairs. She hurried around the balcony, up the short flight of steps into the hall, and down the back hall into the darker areas of the house. She wanted to go outside. Outside where the flowers were growing, the sun shining. There were so many things to do now that Rose could go with her.

Rose's door was closed, as always. She knocked, waited and listened, but heard no sounds within.

"Rose, are you here?"

Julie opened the door and looked in. The bed was neatly made. The rocking chair over by the window sat empty. The cradle still stood in the corner of the room.

Julie went over to look into the cradle.

The doll was still there, a blanket pulled up and tucked beneath its arms exactly the way Rose used to bundle Baby Angela.

The doll's eyes were closed today. In the shadows of the cradle it looked exactly like a very young infant.

Julie frowned thoughtfully. "I gave it to the baby," Sybil had said. And then, "I put it away again."

68

Did it really matter? At first Julie was afraid that Rose had gone mad. That she was treating the doll as if it were the dead baby. But last evening Rose had come down to eat dinner with the family, and today she was somewhere out of the house. So perhaps Julie was worrying needlessly.

She left the room, closing the door, glad to be out of the place that still smelled of death to her. And glad to have a door closed between herself and that room that held more than the memory of a live infant, and then death. There was something eerie and permanently shadowed in that room.

Rose should move into another room, she thought. Or go away to school, live in a dormitory with other girls, be surrounded by a different world so that this one would no longer torture her.

She ran downstairs to the kitchen. There Gertrude was at the table where the servants and sometimes the children had their meals, sitting with paper and scissors, busily cutting out a family of dolls. Beulah was trotting back and forth between stove and cook table. Smells of hot bread rose from the stove, and something sizzled on top in a big frying pan. It smelled tantalizingly like ham. The pot on the stove would probably hold the wild greens Julie knew Beulah picked herself.

"Umm, smells good in here!"

"I helped Beulah gather greens," Gertrude said.

"That she did," Beulah said, lifting her apron to fan her face after opening the oven door. "She did a good part of the work, she did."

"We're eating greens and cornbread for dinner. And fried ham. And of course there'll be potatoes for Papa later at supper, with more greens. Because we got lots of them, didn't we Beulah? A whole tub full. But Julie Sue, you wouldn't believe how they cook down."

"Where's Rose?" Julie asked.

Beulah closed the oven door. Heat from the oven swelled out into the long kitchen.

"All those greens boiled down to a mere pot full," Gertrude continued.

"Rose went out for a walk," Beulah said.

"Good. Maybe it will do her good to get out."

"That's what I thought. I didn't ask her where she was going. 'Just let her go,' I said to Gertrude. Maybe she'll walk up town and sit in the square for awhile where she can see some people."

"And watch the horses and wagons on the street and maybe even see a motor car," Gertrude said.

"I'll see if I can find her."

Gertrude called out as Julie closed the kitchen screen door and started across the porch, "Tell her she has to eat dinner with us, because we're having greens I helped gather and wash."

Julie went down the steps and along the old stone path. Grass grew between the stones, but Moses always kept it short and neat. Like Beulah he had worked here as long as Julie could remember, almost a part of their family. He was a black man, whose family lived in town, and he was gentle and quiet, and Julie loved him more than any of her uncles. She had no aunts or uncles on her mother's side, only her father's, and saw them sometimes as often as once a month. Today he was working on the side of the yard toward town, pruning roses.

"Good morning, Moses."

"Good morning, Miss Julie Sue."

"Have you seen Rose?"

She peered along the path toward town, but it was shaded, and soon curved out of sight.

Moses raised his head, and his eyes found a point toward the rear of the grounds, away from the open pasture where the five horses and two cows grazed. Julie saw he was looking toward the forest, toward the hidden grave. But of course it wouldn't have remained hidden from Moses. He was all over the place, from the roses in the yard to the horses in the pasture, to the woodland that reached miles away to the mountains of central Arkansas.

"She's there, Miss Julie Sue," he said, his voice low.

Julie turned away in silence. Had Mama really thought no one but the closest members of the family would ever know about baby Angela? She wondered for the first time what her parents had intended to do about Angela. If she hadn't died, what would have happened to her?

Julie passed behind the outbuildings where gardening tools were kept, and behind the buggy shed. She entered the trees.

Rose was kneeling at the side of the tiny grave. The soil still looked dark and raw, and slightly damp as if mixed with blood and tears.

Rose didn't lift her head, yet she knew Julie was close beside her.

"Bury me here," she said softly, her voice slow and tired. "Here, with my Angela."

"Rose."

Rose lifted her head, but there were no tears in her eyes. She looked up at Julie.

"Promise me, Julie Sue. Make me a true promise, that you will make Mama and Papa bury me here, with Angela, when I die. Not in the vault in town. I don't belong there anymore. I belong here, with my baby. Promise me."

"Rose!" Hot, rushing tears seemed to fill Julie's head with unbearable pressure before they burst forth. "Rose, you're not going to die!"

"I am. I'm dying. I can feel it, Julie Sue."

"No! I need you! Don't talk that way, Rose!"

"Promise me. Bury me here."

"You're not going to die. Come with me. We'll walk to

71

town. We'll go shopping. We'll buy pretty new material and make new dresses and go to meetings. On Saturday night we'll go to the square and listen to the band and have ice cream in the ice cream parlor just the way we used to."

"Promise me, Julie, please promise me."

"Yes, all right, I promise. Now will you come with me?"

Julie tugged at Rose's arm. Finally, pushing herself up with one hand like a very old person, Rose stood. But she walked slowly beside Julie, and when they reached the path to the house Rose pulled away.

"I'm so tired, Julie."

Julie used her sleeve to wipe tears from her cheek. She forced them to stop, filling her again with that awful pressure she hadn't understood until now.

She was scared.

She was terrified, but she wasn't sure of what.

Rose went on toward the house, but around to the side door where she could go up the back stairs unobserved.

Julie went toward the path to town, walking quickly. She had to get away. She had to think.

There must be something she could do to help Rose, but what was it?

She could not let Rose die.

Chapter 8

Rose closed her bedroom door. She wished for a lock, as she had many times in the past. Today she wanted desperately to be alone. She loved her sisters, especially Julie Sue, but when she went to her baby's grave, she wanted to be alone.

And now, here in her room, she wanted to be alone.

She stood by her door unable to think of what it was she had meant to do next. She was so tired, as if all sense of life's purpose had drained away with Angela's death. With her body being laid away in the grave.

She went to the cradle and looked in. The baby doll looked so real. Not like Angela had looked when she was newborn, but still it looked real. She had tried to make it real and had failed. Still, it was a comfort, in a way, to hold. There was in the straw-stuffed body a kind of warmth, a shape so like a tiny baby that it comforted her just to hold it. It seemed to Rose the small carved hands and feet and face were even warmer when she picked up the doll and held it against her. Its head put out the heat of a small animal's head, the warmest part of the body.

She sat down in the rocking chair and began softly to croon and rock. She cradled it in her arms and leaned her head back on the carved headrest of the chair and closed her eyes. She could imagine that the past week had been a bad dream, a nightmare of horrible, evil proportions, and she was holding her baby again. She could hear the soft breathing, the intake of breath, the exhale, as the tiny chest rose and fell. The sound of her baby sleeping, the most precious sound in all creation. It was that sound that put meaning in life, that gave existence a meaning.

"Lullaby, lullaby, and the sweet dreams will take thee . . ."

With her eyes closed, and the doll held with its face tucked in against her cheek and neck, she could imagine she could feel it nudging, coming closer, seeking nourishment as Angela had sought food from her breast.

She could feel a soft breath from its pouty little mouth, hear an intake of air, feel its lips against her skin in a feeble sucking motion.

"Goodnight, goodnight, my precious one . . . I'll rock thee through the evening sun . . . I've come to take thee far away, and keep thee with me all thy days . . ."

She stood up, to place her infant back in its cradle, but instead of going to the corner, she went toward her bed.

Mama did not want her to keep Baby Angela in her own bed, but she would lie there only to let her nurse before putting her in the cradle. They were so right together, she and the baby.

She slipped into bed and turned on her side, facing the baby. It lay on her arm, and she rested her chin against the top of its head. With her eyes closed it was Angela, her tiny baby. It was so easy to imagine that the past week had not happened.

So tired . . . so terribly . . . tired.

Julie left the cool shade of the woodland path and came out into the sun at the front of the church. It sat in a clearing that had been groomed into parklike beauty, with tall, spreading trees, evergreen shrubs, flowers, walks and benches. Even the cemetery behind the church looked parklike in its perfectly manicured grounds. Looking back toward the cemetery, she saw the keeper with his scythe, cutting grass. He was an old, stooped man who looked too fragile to keep the grounds so perfect, and he hadn't changed in her years of growing up. She didn't know his name. He didn't attend the church whose grounds he took care of.

In the distant corner, near the protection of forest trees, stood the mausoleum of the Wilfred family. It was like a small native stone house, with a tall door and a cross on the high-pitched, small roof. Inside were shelves made of brick and concrete and heavy beams, and on those shelves were the coffins of the Wilfred family. Rose Marie was there, and others, all the way back to Great-grandfather Wilfred.

Julie shuddered and turned her face away. She could understand why Rose would rather be buried in the ground near her baby. But to think of Rose being buried anywhere, to think of her dying, terrified Julie.

She increased her speed, almost running. Her long skirts tangled around her ankles, and she lifted them. The white, crocheted hem of her petticoat probably showed beneath the dark hem of her skirt, but she didn't care. The calf of her legs felt the caress of cool air, even through the black stockings she wore. She knew girls who went barefoot and barelegged in the summertime, and who waded in the creek and swam in the river, their dresses lying on the bank, their underwear clinging wet to their bodies. But her mother would be furious if Julie even asked for such privileges. Those people were the hillbillies, the trash, her mother had said when Julie told her they were allowed to take off their shoes and stockings in hot weather. Those people were the necessary evil of every town, every countryside. "We are not like that." Even so, Julie envied them.

Just beyond the church was the parsonage. White, like

the church, it was about the same size, but it had a porch and no steeple. The steeple of the church reached above the trees like a beacon. And beneath the steeple hung the bell tower. The bell rang on Sunday mornings, Sunday evenings and on Wednesday, for young people's meetings. It rang for funerals and weddings.

She thought of Angela's grave in the woods, and the silence of the church bell.

She passed three more houses, and then crossed the corner of the school yard. She looked at the three story brick building with yearning. It contained all grammar school grades and high school too. Life was far more interesting when the school year was in progress. There were more activities, more people to talk to. Less of the things she hated, like sewing.

She crossed the street to the square, another park with benches here and there and a bandstand in the middle. Flowers bloomed in tended beds. She followed the brick sidewalks and came out on the other side. Along the brick street horses pulling wagons or buggies made a comfortable clopping sound. A whip cracked in the air over a team's rump, and the horses broke into a gallop. Julie paused to glare at the driver, and saw a mountain man with a load of wood ties on the wagon bed. How like slaves they were, she thought, those poor horses made to do the man's bidding. Once there had been a war to emancipate people. Would there ever be a war to emancipate animals in slavery?

She stopped, and waited for a horse pulling a buggy to go by. The driver pulled the horse to a stop between Julie and the other side of the wide, brick street. A woman spoke.

"Good day there, Julie Sue, how are you?"

Julie searched for the face hidden beneath the brim of a bonnet and saw it was the minister's wife. Julie put a smile on her face.

"Goodmorning, Mrs. Culhane. I'm fine, thank you, how are you?"

"We haven't seen you at a young people's meeting in quite sometime. Is there illness in your family?"

"No, Ma'am. I'll be coming again, soon."

"Has Rose come home yet?"

Julie looked past the buggy, past the shadowed lady and the horse who was now resting with one foot on its toe and the tail switching at a persistent horsefly. Her destination was only across the street. She had desperately wanted to get there before the hardware shop closed for the noon hour.

"Yes, Ma'am, Rose is home."

"Then I expect she'll be coming to church and the meeting with you."

"Oh yes. It's been nice seeing you Mrs. Culhane. I'm running an errand, and if I don't hurry, the store will be closed."

"Yes, of course. Good day, Julie Sue."

"Goodbye."

Mrs. Culhane flicked her reins and clucked, and the horse moved lazily along. Julie ran around behind the buggy into the street and almost collided with a rider on a horse. He reined up and the horse whinnied. Julie reached a hand up to caress the velvet nose of the horse in a brief touch.

"Sorry!"

The rider, whose face she didn't look at, said, "Watch where you're going! Get yerself tromped on. Mess up my horse. Nervous fillies, both kinds, women and horses."

She could still hear him muttering as she ran on, and when she reached the sidewalk she looked back. He had a thin, dark face, set in a frown of displeasure, and his mouth was still working.

Julie felt a giggle rising within her, but it didn't reach expression. She had arrived at Lanning's Hardware, the

77

store that belonged to Harold's father. He hadn't closed for dinner yet.

A bell over the door jangled when she entered.

The store had an oily smell. Wood kegs near the door were full of nails of all sizes, and the counter held bolts, nuts, screws and countless other things boys might be interested in. Against the wall stood different lengths of boards and other materials for building. At the back of the store Mr. Lanning was waiting on a man.

Julie wandered about, waiting for the customer to leave. It seemed a long time before the man finished his purchase and went out, and the bell jangled as the door closed.

"Can I help you, Miss?"

He came in behind the counter, and bent over a soiled entry book to note the purchase. It had been charged, Julie saw.

"Mr. Lanning, I've come to ask if you know where Harold is, and how can I get in touch with him? It's very important."

He looked up. He had a long, thin face with deep wrinkles set vertically like the grooves in some of the boards against the wall. Julie didn't think there ever could have been anything pretty about him, even when he was a child. But his son, Harold, was dark and handsome, with fine eyebrows and daring eyes. Julie had understood Rose's attraction to him. A lot of girls giggled and fidgeted when Harold Lanning was nearby.

"You one of the Wilfred girls?"

"Madison. My name is Julie Sue Madison."

"Ah well, all the same, Wilfred, Madison. Your poppy the lawyer down the street."

"Yes."

"And your mammy still owns the old Wilfred mansion and the bank and part of the town buildings."

"Yes, I suppose so. I really need to get in touch with

78

Harold, sir, and I didn't know where else to go."

"And why this great need to get in touch with Harold?"

She looked away, wondering how much she dare tell him. "It's my sister Rose, sir. She's engaged to be married to your son, but she hasn't heard from him. She's pining away and I'm afraid she needs to hear from him. She's . . ."

"Engaged!" He smiled. It came and was gone in a flash. He closed the book in which he had written the purchases, laid his pencil aside and straightened. "Just happens a letter came from him not long ago. Have it here, somewhere."

Julie waited with fluttering heart, with hopes rising, while he rummaged through a drawer of stuff that looked as soiled as the credit book. Finally, he brought out a wrinkled envelope and smoothed it on the counter.

"There you have it. Some boardinghouse hotel in Saint Louis. He's working on the docks, trying to get a job on a boat. I don't know why he just doesn't come on home and get ready to run the store here. But he's like his mother's brothers and uncles, just like them."

"Sir, do you have an envelope I could buy? That is, charge? I could bring the money the next time."

"Oh, well, here. Just take it."

"May I borrow the pencil?"

"Of course. How else you going to write the address?"

"Thank you."

The pencil needed sharpening, and it was so short she could hardly hold it. The lead was hard too, and difficult to write with, but by printing and pushing hard she managed the address. She looked up. He sniffed.

"I suppose you want a piece of paper for your note?"

"Oh that would be very kind, sir."

"Well, I don't know how else you're going to send a note in that envelope. Got to have a sheet of paper."

He tore a sheet out of the back of another, smaller credit book.

With the pencil Julie quickly printed: Dear Harold, I'm asking you for my sister's sake to come home. It's urgent. Rose needs you. Please don't let her down again.

She signed it, Rose's sister, Julie Sue Madison.

She looked up to see that Mr. Lanning was reading what she had written. It didn't matter. She folded the note, put it into the envelope and sealed it. She pushed the pencil back across the counter.

"Thank you very much."

"How're you going to mail it?"

She looked at the envelope in her hands. The post office was right down the street. Of course she had not even a penny with her. She hadn't thought that far ahead when she'd started to town. She hadn't even known for sure why she was going to town.

"I can stop in at my father's office and—"

"And he'd want to know what it is you're mailin', eh? Maybe we'd just better keep this between us. Here, I've got a stamp or two. Have to send out bills every month, and most of the time it don't even pay. But here, here's your stamp."

He licked it, and stuck it on the envelope she held. She smiled at him. "I'll bring payment, sir, the next—"

"Now that smile was worth every bit of it," he said. "You don't owe me anything. Run along."

"That's very kind of you, sir."

She had reached the door when his voice stopped her again. She paused, listening.

"Don't hold your breath, Missy. I expect if it were known, there'd be a lot of young ladies who think they're engaged to my boy. Like I said, he's just like his mother's people."

Julie looked back at the storekeeper. "Thank you, sir."

The bell jangled as she closed the door behind her.

"Where is everybody anyway?" Beulah asked. She had stacked plates on the table where Gertrude was still cutting out dolls. On the stove the food simmered, and the clock struck half-past twelve. "Doesn't anybody want to eat today?"

"Do you know what, Beulah?" Gertrude said.

"What?"

"My mother is. . . . What's that word? You know, like being a medium? Who can look into the future and tell what's going to happen?"

"You mean fortune-teller?" Beulah forgot that the family was late for the noonday meal. Sybil a fortune-teller? It was almost funny.

"No, not a fortune-teller, but someone who knows things."

"Like God, you mean."

"No, not like God. Just like when you know someone is going to die?"

"Your mother knows when people are going to die? What makes you think that?"

"Well, her old dolly, you know. The one she always keeps in the curio hutch upstairs?"

"The china cabinet?"

"Yes. Well, you see, she would never give it to me. But the other night she brought it down and gave it to Rose's baby."

Beulah stared at Gertrude. The child was bent over her work on the other side of the table, cutting dolls carefully, cutting small dresses, hats, and shoes to fit the dolls. Her hair was the color of pulled taffy candy, and held back tight from her face in braids. Her eyebrows and eyelashes were pale and almost invisible. She was not pretty like Julie Sue, or Rose, but there was a sweetness about her face that Beulah loved just as dearly. Her hands were steady, small and smooth, and the scissors looked large for her. Still, she handled them well.

"Gave the old doll to Rose's baby?"

How very odd. Sybil had always been so selfish with that doll. No child had ever played with it in all the years it had been in the house. And she had given it to a grandchild she had never owned up to having?

"Yes," Gertrude said. "I saw her take it into Rose's room and put it right into the cradle with Rose's baby. And I thought she was just going to give her the doll forever. But do you know what I think now?"

"No, what?"

"I think Mama knew the baby was going to die, and so she wanted to do something nice for her. So she gave Rose's baby her very own dolly."

"Hmm, well. Why don't you clean your things off the table now and go wash your hands and face."

Gertrude spread her hands and looked at them. "But they're not dirty."

"I know. We've gone through this every day since the day you were big enough to come into the kitchen alone."

"All right!" Gertrude gathered her paper dolls and laid them on the top of the bureau, then went toward the washroom. Over her shoulder she called, "But don't you think it's interesting that Mama has that power? She's psychic! That was the word I wanted. Mama's psychic."

"Never heard the word, myself."

Beulah stood looking at the plate of cut cornbread and wondered if she should put it back into the warming oven. And then she thought of the doll. She had seen it, she remembered, and been surprised that it was in Rose's room instead of up in the old china cabinet.

There was something odd about Sybil giving the doll to Rose's baby, but she didn't think it meant Sybil had any special powers.

Chapter 9

Rose drifted between sleeping and waking, between dreams and reality. It seemed she was walking through the brown winter leaves and coming at last to the open grave in the woods. The grave was huge, large enough for many small caskets, and it reached down into the ground so far she could see no bottom.

Then she was in her chair, rocking her warm baby, but the baby began to grow cold in her arms. Though it was growing colder and colder, though it was dead now, it was moving. In a terrible way it was moving upwards, and she became aware it was climbing her. As if its hands had turned to small claws, it was climbing up her bosom to her face. It wasn't her milk it wanted, but something from her face. Kisses, hugs, and kisses. No, Mama wouldn't approve.

She was smothering. She gasped for air and found none. Someone in her dream had pressed a pillow over her face, and had closed off her breath.

No, it was her baby, Angela, coming to her face for kisses. So young, and yet how natural to seek the mouth, as if they were still of the wild, mother with baby, warm, caressing tongues.

Then she woke just enough to remember she was lying on her bed.

The doll was on her face!

She must have rolled onto her back, pulling it onto her face, though the strange, nightmarish dream of it climb-

ing unaided was still so vivid it seemed as if it had actually happened. She lifted her hand to move it, and found
her arm heavy and useless.

The doll had covered her mouth, her nose, and she
was pierced by a lightning charge of panic. *The thing on
her face was the thing that had been in the cradle with Angela.*

Her . . . *breath.*

It was taking her breath. She couldn't breathe. She was
suffocating. It was the doll. Its face pushed against hers,
its mouth, tiny and round, sucked at her mouth. Its
hands held to each side of her neck, clinging.

This thing had been in Angela's bed. It had taken her
baby's life.

The spirit of her child had not gone into this thing. It
was filled with something she had never dreamed existed,
something that went against all of nature, God, and love.

She tried to rise, but all strength had been pulled from
her. She tried with her hands to push the doll away, but
it clung. She turned her head back and forth, and flung
herself weakly on the bed.

"Mama!"

Help me. She had to get up and find her mother and
tell her what had happened. Tell her . . . about the doll
. . . before it hurt someone else. All . . . who lived . . .
in the house . . . were in . . . danger.

She was too weak to get up, to even tear it from her
face.

She closed her eyes again, to escape the nightmare of
this strange reality. In her darkened vision she saw the
cradle in the corner, and it hung still. She saw the grave
in the woods, holding her baby, her real baby, not this
horror she had tried to tell herself held Angela's spirit.
She saw her baby, lying sweet and serene in her grave,
and she yearned toward her, and at last sunk willingly
into oblivion.

Beulah had arranged the plates and food on the dining table, and Gertrude had brought her mother from the library, and they were seated. But the Mister might not be home today. He had a meeting in town with the town council, and he would probably eat with them. And Gertrude said she'd seen both Julie Sue and Rose go outside much earlier, and they were probably walking.

Cooking was getting to be a job, and Beulah felt as if it were all for nothing when nobody came to eat. She had said almost as much, but not quite out loud. After all, Sybil and Gertrude were there. But Gertrude could have eaten in the kitchen with her, and there was a time when Sybil might have eaten in the kitchen, too. In fact, sometimes when they knew the Mister wasn't going to be home, all of them ate in the kitchen, and asked Beulah to join them. Also, if it was wash day, Faye ate with them, and Moses.

Beulah had gone back to the kitchen when Julie Sue came through the backdoor. Her face was rosy, as if she'd gotten a sunburn, or had been running, and her hair windblown. But she was alone.

"Where've you been?" Beulah asked as she readied the places for herself and Moses in the kitchen. She could hear him in the washroom. He splashed water on his face and snuffled and blew, then he drank from the dipper. Beulah knew by the silence. Then came the sound of the metal dipper being hung on the nail above the sink.

"And where's Rose?" Beulah asked. "And Lord, look at your face. Why didn't you wear a bonnet?"

"I forgot."

"It's almost past dinnertime."

"That's all right, I'm not hungry. Who's eating?"

"Your mother and little sister, in the dining room. Me and Moses in here. Where's Rose?"

"I don't know."

"Gertrude said she saw the both of you outside."

"But I went to town. Alone. I think Rose came back inside. I'll go up and see."

"No, you go on and sit down. I'll go up and see."

Julie Sue went through the door into the dining room. Moses had come fresh and clean into the kitchen to the table by the window.

"My, looks mighty good, Miss Beulah."

"Well, set and eat, Mister Moses. I'll be back in a few minutes."

Years ago, when they both were young, Beulah had tried to get Moses to drop the Miss in front of her name, but he had stubbornly ignored her. "It just ain't proper, Miss Beulah," he'd finally said. "Well I don't know why not," she answered, "I don't call you Mister Moses." They had laughed together, but he had gone on calling her Miss Beulah, so she had started calling him Mister Moses. It had become a joke, and then a long-standing habit. Just because he was black and she was white didn't mean he had to treat her as if she were the employer.

She wiped her hands on her apron and went through the door into the side hall and from there to the back stairs. They were steeper and narrower, between two walls. They reminded her of the stairs to the third floor, and she rarely used them. Both sets of stairs made her feel trapped in a cave. There was a darkness that lingered even on the brightest day. Sunlight had never touched these dark places.

She came out onto the second floor on the back wing. It was an area closed off by another door into the central second floor hall. It held four bedrooms, all reserved for servants. When she first started working for the Wilfreds, while Grandmother Wilfred was still living, before Charles Wilfred married Alvia, the mother of Rose Marie and Sybil, Beulah had lived in the corner bedroom. But she wasn't happy there. Every night she had cried with homesickness. So her mother had let her come home and walk the two miles from the cabin she still lived in.

She went through the doorway to the wider hall where the girls' bedrooms were. Julie Sue's and Gertrude's doors stood open, but Rose's was closed.

Beulah knocked.

"Rose?"

There was no answer. Beulah put her ear to the door and listened. Her hearing was as sharp as when she was young, and if there was movement beyond the door it was so subtle nobody could have heard it.

"Rose," she called more loudly. "Are you there?"

Perhaps she was sleeping. And perhaps . . .

Beulah opened the door, and then unable to move or make a sound she stared at Rose, resting on the bed.

She held the baby in her arms.

No. It wasn't the baby, it was the old doll.

Oh Lord, the poor girl.

"Rose. Rose?"

Beulah went to the bed. Rose appeared to be awake. Her eyes stared steadily up at the ceiling. But her face looked oddly sunken and empty.

"Oh Lord," Beulah cried under her breath. Her hands shook as she tried to find a pulse in Rose's throat, on her wrists. The window was open, and the curtains fluttered in the warm breeze that came through but Rose was cold.

"Rose?" Her voice quavered.

With her hands shaking, Beulah pulled the doll from Rose's arms. It was lying face down on Rose's breast and neck, but when Beulah gripped it, the face seemed to turn on its own toward her. She was shocked at the healthy looking face. It seemed almost real in that brief glance, with a small pink mouth that looked moist, and pink cheeks that were rounding out like the cheeks of a growing baby.

Beulah dropped the doll onto the floor. She bent again

87

to Rose and lifted her head and shoulders into her arms. Then she raised her voice in a scream.

"Sybil! Sybil! Julie Sue!"

Julie was pulling out her chair at the dining table when it seemed she heard a voice. She paused, looking at her mother. Sybil stared at her a moment, then flung her fork down and was running before she reached the double doors of the dining room.

Julie followed her, hearing Beulah screaming, her voice sounding far away. Behind her came Gertrude, and then Moses. Moses came halfway down the front hall toward the broad entry and stairway, and stopped. A strange thought slipped through Julie's mind. Moses had never been in the front hall before. Yet he had spent more time here than she had. He had worked here since he was young, just as Beulah had. She motioned with a jerk of her hand for him to follow.

When she reached the top of the stairs, only steps behind Sybil, Julie had a terrible feeling that it was Rose.

Beulah, with her wrinkled face so white it looked drained of blood, came running out of Rose's room. She bypassed Sybil, as if she knew Moses was there too. Her eyes found him immediately.

"Moses! Go for the doctor. Hurry, Moses! It's Rose. Something bad has happened to Rose."

Julie slowed. Her last few steps to the bedroom were the most difficult she had ever taken in her life. She wanted to back up and run, she wanted to turn life back to a week ago when Angela was still alive.

When she finally came to the doorway she saw her mother bending over Rose. Sybil looked up and saw Julie.

"Julie Sue, help me. Bring pillows and let's get Rose up."

88

In a daze Julie brought pillows from her own bedroom and watched as their mother placed them behind Rose and forced her upright. But Rose's head slipped sideways to rest against her shoulder, and her staring eyes looked dull and lifeless.

Julie crumpled under that lifeless stare. She wanted to scream at Rose, Why didn't you wait? Why did you have to die too? Harold is coming. He's coming to get you, I know he is!

Too late.

Julie and Gertrude had been sent to wait in the parlor, just as Gertrude had been the night of Angela's birth. Gertrude had been crying off and on for the hours they had been there, but Julie felt unable to cry, now or ever. Images and thoughts swirled through her mind. What good had life been for Rose and Angela? They had been here such a short time.

Reverend Culhane had come and was with her parents. Mrs. Culhane had come, too. The doctor had gone home long ago. Rose's body had been taken away to the mortuary, carried in the black, closed carriage, that would later carry her coffin.

Julie wanted to talk to her parents about Rose's funeral, but she hadn't had a chance.

Night fell, and the sound of the whippoorwills was sad and melancholy. Even the katydids and the jarflies sounded as if they were playing a funeral dirge.

Was the whole family going to die now? This summer?

Sybil came to the parlor and looked in. "Girls, it's time you're going to bed."

Mama looked just like always, Julie thought as she got up from the chair she'd been sitting in for hours. At first, when Sybil had lifted Rose and put pillows behind her, Sybil's face had been pale, her eyes large and protruding, as if something in her skull were pushing them out. She had looked scared. Shocked. Just as Julie had felt.

But now she seemed back to normal. Her eyes, always a little protuberant, looked calm. But they also looked washed out, as if she had been crying. It seemed strange to think of her mother crying. In all of Julie's life she had not seen her mother shed a tear. And perhaps she hadn't even now. Perhaps the paleness, the washed-out look, was from something else.

"Mama, I need to talk to you and Papa."

"Not tonight, Julie Sue. Take Gertrude and go on to your rooms."

"No!" Gertrude cried. "Not up there! Two people have died up there, and I don't want to sleep there anymore."

"And exactly where are you going to sleep, Gertrude? Julie Sue, do as I say."

Gertrude cried out, tears freezing on her face. Julie saw the fear in her little sister's eyes.

"Mama! Open up the other wing, Mama! Let me sleep there!" Gertrude begged.

"My dear, you will be very safe in your own room. Relatives are coming. We need the extra wing for them. Now go on. Your room is perfectly safe. I'll be up to check on you later."

"Mother," Julie said. "Please, I need to talk to you and Papa. It's about Rose."

"Tomorrow, Julie Sue, not tonight. We're exhausted. Can't you appreciate that we're exhausted?"

She was gone then, slipping quietly away to go wherever it was she had to go. Julie thought the Culhanes might still be here, somewhere in the house. And if word had already been sent out to relatives, they'd start arriving tomorrow.

"Julie Sue, can I sleep with you?" Gertrude asked in a thin voice.

"I don't know. We'll see." But Julie wanted to be alone.

The thought of Gertrude cuddling up against her in bed tonight made her feel trapped. "Maybe I'll sit with you until you go to sleep."

Julie walked with her hand on Gertrude's shoulder. In the hall she heard low voices coming from the library, and knew there were more of the church people than just the Culhane's there. Perhaps even Papa's partners in the law firm were there too. She wondered where Beulah was.

"Did Beulah go home?" she asked, but Gertrude was crying again, softly. "No, you wouldn't know, would you?"

"No, she didn't," Gertrude sobbed.

"How do you know? You've been with me all afternoon and evening."

"I know she wouldn't go. She just wouldn't."

"But she has chores at home."

"Then she would come back."

They went up the stairs and around the balcony to the hall to their bedrooms. Their footsteps on the bare wood between rugs sounded loud and echoing to Julie, and the upstairs so quiet now, and the gaslights dim and distant tonight, like stars. It was, Julie thought, like going into the mausoleum, that place where Rose did not want to be laid away. She wanted to be buried with her baby, in the ground, in the woods. Julie had to tell her parents.

"I don't want to take a bath," Gertrude said.

"You don't have to."

"Are you going to sleep with me?"

"I'll sit with you."

"But then when I go to sleep, you'll sneak away." Gertrude's face, turned up toward her, reminded Julie for the first time of their mother. There was the same tapered chin, the thin cheeks, the large, rounded, slightly bulging eyes. The tears that filled them spread a film over the blue, making them look lighter than normal, even in the shadows of the hall.

"If you wake and find me gone, I'll only be across the hall. There's nothing to hurt you, Gertie, baby." But even as she said it, a deep, terrible dread filled her. Perhaps there was something to hurt Gertrude. As Angela had died, so suddenly, and Rose, perhaps Gertrude, too, would die.

"All right," Julie said. "I'll sleep with you, tonight. At least for tonight."

She went into Gertrude's room and lighted the kerosene lamp on the dresser. She helped with the unfastening of Gertrude's bodice, and lifted the thin, short-sleeved summer nightgown over her head. She helped her up into bed, and arranged the curtains at the window so the summer breeze would drift into the room. But Gertrude pulled up her comforter.

"I'm cold, Julie, close the window."

"Then we can't hear the frogs, and the jarflies. I'll lie down on the side by the window, so you won't be cold."

She turned the light low, and lay on the top of the thin comforter with her clothes and shoes on, her ankles crossed. She stared up at the ceiling and closed Gertrude's hand into hers and held it tightly. Gertrude lay with her head on Julie's shoulder, and long after Julie thought Gertrude had gone to sleep, after her sobs had stopped and her breathing was soft and deep, Gertrude spoke.

"There's just the two of us now," she said in tones close to a whisper.

"Yes."

"Julie, don't die."

"Of course I won't, don't be a silly." But she knew how Gertrude was feeling. She clung to Gertrude's hand as hard as Gertrude clung to hers.

They had never been as close as she and Rose. Gertrude was the spoiled baby sister, the one she and Rose had been forced to see after, to take care of, to give up to. If Gertrude wanted something of their's, they had to give it to her, at least as long as their mother was around. When she was gone, they could take it back, and threaten Gertrude if she cried or told.

Gertrude was their mother's baby. The family baby. And there'd been times in Julie's life when she wished Gertrude had never been born. But tonight she knew she loved Gertrude, and she didn't want to lose her, too.

"Why did Rose die, Julie Sue?"

"The doctor said apoplexy, probably."

"What's that?"

"I don't know. A blood vessel bursting in the brain, I think. Shhh. Go to sleep. Don't think about it." She died, Julie thought to herself, of a broken heart. But the doctor hadn't known that. He'd never known about Angela.

"Julie Sue, did you know that Mama can always tell when someone is going to die?"

"No, of course she can't. How could she? Why would you say that?"

"Because. She only gives her doll to someone who's going to die. She gave it to Rose's baby, the night she died. She knew, and she was being nice. She would never give it to me. She wouldn't even let me touch it."

Julie stared at the lamp globe until it became an orb of soft formless light. There was something about what Gertrude was saying that made her feel scared and blinded, as if a dark curtain hung between her and the truth. Instead of telling Gertrude she knew about the doll, she said, "Really?"

"Yes. And then she put it away. But then she must have gotten it again to give to Rose."

"No, Rose—"

"But I saw it. It was in the cradle, in Rose's room. So Mama knew like a person who can look into the future. What do you call it? I keep forgetting."

"A fortune-teller?"

93

"No! The other, the real kind."

"A clairvoyant?"

"Yes, a clairvoyant. She knew Rose was going to die, too, so she must have gotten the doll again from the hutch and given it to Rose."

Julie stared hard at the ceiling. She didn't for a minute believe what Gertrude was saying, but there was something very strange about the circumstance of the doll being in Rose's room.

Memories flashed into her mind one after the other, crossing and recrossing, becoming muddled.

Gertrude, only two or three years old, screaming and hanging onto the doll the day she had first gone up to the third floor and helped herself to it. Gertrude, pulling on their mother's dress when Sybil had taken it away from her. The look then on Sybil's face was one Julie had thought she'd never forget. She had gone white as the lace that trimmed her collar, and snatched the doll from Gertrude's plump little hands. The doll was something that she and Rose had peered at through the glass a few times, giggling that their mother had ever been young enough to play with dolls.

One day Sybil had found them there, and she'd taken them both each by an ear and guided them back toward the stairs.

"That doll," she said firmly, "is not for playing. Do you understand? Don't ever come near it again."

"But why?" Julie had screamed, her ear hurting, her feelings hurt. She had dolls, several of them, but not one that looked so much like a little baby. That doll in the cabinet was so much like their papa's niece's little tiny baby, both she and Rose had wanted it. It even had eyes that were kind of swollen, like the little brand-new cousin, and creases on its forehead and chin.

"Because I said so!"

So they had never touched it. Not once.

But Gertrude hadn't learned so easily. Finally, when Gertrude was four or five years old, Sybil had Moses fix the door so Gertrude couldn't open it.

Another memory, of taking the baby from Rose's arms, that morning a week ago, melded with all the older scenes. Rose, screaming, the baby in her arms. Julie had thought it was the baby.

She had taken it from Rose, as others entered the room, and then she had looked at it and seen it was the doll, not Angela. Not Angela, but the doll.

The doll that was never taken out of the cabinet on the third floor.

"Gertrude," Julie said, feeling suddenly so very weary. "I guess Mama just finally decided to let someone have her old dolly. It doesn't mean that she knew the baby was going to die."

"I think it does, Julie. Mama knows."

Julie squeezed Gertrude's hand. "Of course not. Anyway, she didn't give the doll to Rose. She told me she put the doll away."

"Then how did it get there? In Rose's room?"

"Rose took it, I guess."

"Why?"

"Because . . ." Julie sighed. "Because Mama gave it to Angela, maybe. And Rose wanted to keep it. Let's go to sleep now, Gertrude."

As Gertrude grew still beside her, Julie could not close out her thoughts, her feeling that something was horribly wrong. Maybe Mama had been sorry she had not acknowledged Angela, and had tried to make up for it by giving the baby her old doll. Maybe that was the reason.

Yet if that were true, why hadn't she allowed Angela to be laid to rest in the family mausoleum?

Instead of alone in the edge of the woods like an animal?

Chapter 10

"Mother, Papa, I have to talk to you." Julie stood in the partly opened library door looking in. Her papa sat in the chair by his desk, but it was turned so he faced the room. Her mother stood by the fireplace. The voices Julie had heard from the hallway were low and muffled. Her Aunt Alison and Uncle Victor, Papa's sister and brother-in-law, sat in chairs grouped near the fireplace. They both rose.

"We'll go to the parlor," Uncle Victor said. He was a short, portly man, with a smooth face that showed none of his years. Only his white hair linked him with the older generation. Julie liked him, though she hadn't seen him since she was nine years old. Back then he had liked to hold her on his short lap and tell her stories. When he went past her now, he touched her cheek with his hand. "Such a pretty girl."

Aunt Alison looked nothing at all like her brother. While Papa was tall and slightly stooped, reminding Julie of Abraham Lincoln, Aunt Alison was short and almost as portly as Uncle Victor.

She, too, touched Julie's cheek, and murmured agreement with Uncle Victor.

Julie closed the door.

"That was very rude," Sybil said, though the expression on her face didn't change, and Julie suspected it didn't really matter to her. She knew her mother had never been very fond of Aunt Alison or Uncle Victor, and was glad they lived three hundred miles away and didn't visit any more often.

"I've been trying for two days to get you to listen to me," Julie said, tears coming to her eyes and making her angry at herself for her weakness. Almost every time she uttered a word, the tears came. "I wanted you to know that Rose made me promise to have her buried beside her baby, in the woods, in the ground. She didn't want to be put away in the vault. Papa, you must listen. Mother, she begged me to promise. I think she knew she was going to die."

Sybil sat down in the tall-backed chair near the fireplace. Julie heard her sigh. It filled the quiet room as if the house itself had taken a deep, slow breath. She leaned her head back and closed her eyes.

"Of course that is the most ridiculous thing I ever heard. She said nothing of it to me, which must indicate to you, Julie Sue, that she knew it was a ridiculous request and would not be even considered. What on earth would the family think? Not even mentioning the people in the neighborhood."

"Papa?" Julie appealed to him, and he shimmered beyond her tears as if he floated beneath water in the river. She remembered once when she and Rose were small and were playing in the creek, Rose had lain down beneath the water and looked up at her. She had pushed her cheeks out and pursed her lips, and her blue eyes had stared through the shallow depth upward at Julie. And Julie had been afraid Rose was really drowning. "Papa? Please?"

He said, "Your sister's body was taken to the mortuary yesterday, Julie Sue. The funeral services will be tomorrow. At the cemetery in town. Just think about it."

"Then," Julie cried, her voice ringing in the room,

"then her baby should be taken out of the ground and put with her!" She raised an arm and pointed toward the woods and the lonely little grave. "How can you do this to Rose?"

"Julie Sue—" Sybil's voice echoed some of the hysteria of Julie's, and Julie whirled toward her.

"You're mean! You mistreated her! You did! And you know you did! And I—" *Hate you for it.* She bit her lip, knowing she had almost gone too far. Through her blurred vision she saw that Sybil had risen from her chair, and had raised her own arm and was pointing toward the door.

Julie ran, not waiting for her mother to order her to her room.

In the foyer Beulah was letting in more company, an older man and woman who Julie didn't even want to speak to. She whirled toward the rear of the house, the hallway toward the service entrance, and up the back stairs.

In her room she lay down on her bed, her face buried against the comforter, her world black behind closed eyes. Yet she saw Rose's face, the day she had begged Julie to make her parents bury her beside the baby, and she saw Rose's face in death, and shimmering beside her was the small, perfect face of baby Angela.

She wanted to bawl her eyes out now that she was alone. Cry out all her anguish. But her tears dried and became like empty hulls behind her eyes and in her heart.

She sat up and looked at her room. Once she had loved the pale blue wall paper with the roses and vines. She had felt comfortable here, all her life, where her window looked out into the trees beside the house and down upon the driveway between the rows of trees. She had felt safe and happy, if not especially well-loved by her parents. They were there, and her sisters were there, and Beulah and Moses were there.

But now she felt trapped, and she had a sudden, terrible feeling. If she didn't leave, she, too, would die.

Beulah had chosen to walk home from the funeral services. The Mister had offered to have Moses drive her to and from the funeral services in one of the buggies, but Beulah told him no. It was less than half a mile, and she preferred to walk the path through the woods.

She had sat at the back of the church, where she would be one of the first to pass through to view the body. She had sat there, because she wanted to leave as quickly as possible. She had not wanted to view Rose in her coffin. It was something she could not bear to do. It was like viewing that tiny baby girl of Rose's, after she was dressed in the long, yellowed gown that had been the christening gown of other children, a century ago.

She wanted to walk alone through the woods and try to piece together the truth of what had happened. She remembered, as if it were happening now, Julie Sue coming to her with tears in her eyes and that old pleading on her face that had always wrung Beulah's heartstrings. Only this time Julie Sue hadn't wanted Beulah to help her cut out a new dress pattern, or help her fasten her bodice. This time she had said, "Rose begged me to promise that she would be buried next to her baby, Beulah, and they won't listen. They won't even consider it!"

Beulah put down her dishrag, wiped her hands on her apron, and pulled Julie Sue into her arms. Julie Sue was too tall now for her head to rest against Beulah's chest, but Beulah hugged her as if she were still small.

"Honey," she whispered against the girl's smooth

cheek. "It doesn't matter. They're both dead now, and if there be a God, then they're together, and the earthly bodies are put away and the spirits are free."

"Oh Beulah, do you really believe that?"

Julie Sue's voice had begged for reassurance. Through her own doubts Beulah had told her yes she believed. As once she had told Julie Sue she believed in Santa Claus, she now told her she believed in heaven and God and humans living on in spirit in a perfect, happy land of God's making.

The scene in her mind changed. Gertrude was sitting at the table in the kitchen cutting out paper dolls and paper dresses. Gertrude was saying, "Mama knew Rose's baby was going to die . . . She gave her the doll . . ."

Beulah found she was hurrying. The path through the woods was not a source of peace and comfort today. She had to hurry back to the house. There was something there she had to see, to understand.

And it had something to do with the doll.

Julie moved with the crowd, following the pallbearers with the closed casket. After the mourners had each paused by the coffin while it was still in the church, they had gone out the door at the back of the church and waited. The family was the last to leave. The veil Julie wore made the day seem cloudy and dark, the way it had been when Angela was buried. The way the woods had been, shadowed and still.

Young people from the church's Young People's Meeting had been chosen to carry the flowers, and they walked behind the coffin and the pallbearers. Though Julie walked among dozens of people, she felt alone. Ahead of her she saw her papa and mama, and Gertrude, with her hand in Sybil's. There, too, were the relatives that had come from other towns. Others who

100

lived nearby and whom she saw often. All of them come to mourn with Papa and Mama.

In the throng behind her it seemed as if the whole town had come. She saw faces she had seen only in the town square on a Saturday afternoon when the band played. Some of the faces of the younger people had been part of the faces at school, but were not friends or even casual acquaintances. Yet she felt grateful. "Thank you for coming," she said to each person who told her they were sorry. She had never known she would feel gratitude that people would take time to come to a funeral.

But she had failed. Rose was being put into the family vault, not in the soft, cool soil near her baby. She wished she could believe Beulah, about the spirit going to a beautiful world beyond. But who could be sure?

"Julie Sue."

The voice was at her shoulder. It was the voice of a man, soft, deep. She turned and glanced up.

"Harold!"

His hand touched her elbow, and he walked beside her, his head up, his eyes following the casket.

"I got your letter," he said. "What happened?"

Julie wanted to talk to him, but she was afraid to speak. Though her veil hid her face and would conceal any tears, she didn't trust herself. Not yet.

The pallbearers reached the door of the small family mausoleum, and Reverend Culhane opened the door. The crowd paused, some milling nearer to hear the last words. Julie turned away, facing the line of trees just beyond the cemetery.

"She didn't want to be laid to rest here," she said, and was surprised that her voice was clear and her eyes almost painfully dry. "Not here."

"What happened to Rose?" Harold asked, his dark eyes squinting, as if he tried to see through the veil.

"Why did you leave her?" Julie asked, then saw some of the people were listening and watching. She clutched Harold's wrist and drew him away from the crowd, toward tall tombstones with angels, toward the trees. "She said you had asked her to marry you, and you were going to send for her, or come back, and you didn't even write!"

"I did write! She didn't answer. I wrote as soon as I had an address. Three times I wrote, and got no answer. I thought maybe she had regretted being with me. I was going to come back. As soon as I could afford to. When I got your letter I came right away. I got into town just an hour ago. I didn't even know she was sick. What happened to her?"

Julie stared up into his face, and unable to see him well, jerked her veil up. "You wrote?"

"Yes, I did."

She believed him. The mail carrier delivered the mail every day to the box out by the road. In the summer, Julie went to the mailbox. But during the winter, when she went to school, the mail would have been picked up by Moses and taken to her mother.

"Mama must not have given it to her," Julie said. "Oh Lord, if only Rose had known! Don't you know what has happened? Of course you don't know! Come with me, Harold."

She flung her veil back over her hat and got him by the wrist again; then she remembered. She looked toward the gathering by the mausoleum and saw she was in plain sight of most of them, including her mother, whose face was shrouded in a black veil.

"I have to ride home with my parents and sister. But you come later. Just before sundown. I have something to show you." She started to leave, to go back to the crowd, then faced him again. "Come to the backyard. I'll find you."

He nodded. She saw his gaze drift past her toward the stone mausoleum where Rose's body now lay, and knew his love for Rose had been true. She saw in his eyes the sorrow, perhaps built of pain suffered during a long year in which he had thought Rose no longer loved him. Julie wanted to tell him Rose had never loved anyone else, but now, she had to go back to her family. She couldn't take Harold by the hand and lead him through the path in the woods to Angela's grave.

There were proprieties she had to observe.

"Mama," Gertrude tugged on Sybil's hand, and Sybil bent down toward her young daughter.

"Yes, dear?"

"Who's that man with Julie Sue?"

Gertrude raised one white-gloved hand and pointed off toward the woods on the west side of the cemetery. Sybil turned. Julie was now coming toward the mausoleum, and the man with her was slowly following. But he was a dark shadow, without features or distinguishing characteristics.

"I don't know him, dear," she said, glancing around to see if anyone else had noticed that Julie Sue had gone off to one side with a strange man. She lifted her veil, and a sudden burst of recognition caused her heart nearly to stop.

Harold Lanning!

She dropped her veil. She could feel the tightening of her lips, her cheeks pulling as her muscles tensed. Harold Lanning, the father of Rose's bastard baby. The man who had literally sent Rose to hell.

Rose hadn't told her who'd fathered the child. Sybil would never have known if it hadn't been for the letters. Three of them, the first of which she'd opened, read, and then burned. She had burned the other two without opening them. The first told her all she needed to know. Rose was preparing to disgrace the family by running away with a nobody. His uncles on his mother's side had bad reputations. Harold Lanning was not the kind of man she wanted her daughter to know, much less correspond with, and certainly not to leave home for. That Walter had allowed Harold to walk Rose home from Young People's Meeting had infuriated her, and the letters were only an added insult.

That first letter had come from Saint Louis.

I think I'm going to get a position in a shipping firm, and as soon as I have a place to stay, and enough saved, I'll send for you. I am sustained night after night by remembering how you felt in my arms. And our nuptial bed, in the sweet leaves of the forest, is in my dreams nightly.

She knew when she read that letter that Rose had known Harold Lanning, intimately. The Good Lord only knew how many times.

And now after destroying Rose, here he was again, with Julie Sue. Probably eyeing her with thoughts to the same bed of leaves.

She must not let Harold Lanning so much as talk to Julie Sue. Julie Sue who was budding into a beautiful woman. A much prettier girl than Rose had been. Julie Sue, who tended to be outspoken and rebellious anyway.

Sybil started walking through the crowd that had gathered by the open door of the stone mausoleum. Julie Sue and Harold were coming together through the cemetery, but it looked as if they were talking as they walked slowly. Harold's head was down, as if he were listening to Julie Sue. Sybil saw the girl put her gloved hand up and touch his arm. They stopped.

A hand gripped Sybil's arm, and she almost gasped,

she had been so unaware of those around her. She looked into the face of a church member, a woman whose aged eyes were pale with sorrow.

"Sybil, my dear. There's no pain like losing a child. I have lost two husbands, both my parents, of course, at my age, a brother and two sisters. But the worst was the losing of my daughter, many years ago—"

"Yes, I remember, Helen. I know you understand. If you'll excuse me, I must talk to Julie Sue."

She moved on, away from the crowd, but now Julie Sue was coming near, and she was alone.

Sybil stopped.

Harold Lanning was walking away. He was almost to the cemetery gates over near the church.

"Julie Sue!"

Julie Sue paused, looked at her, and changed directions. Still, she stopped several feet away. Sybil had an urge to reach forward and jerk her fifteen year old daughter's veil up so she could see the expression on her face, but she knew it would be set with fury.

"Julie Sue, you were talking to Harold Lanning, weren't you?"

"Yes Ma'am."

"I want you never to speak to him again. Do you understand?"

Julie Sue stared through her veil at Sybil in silence, then she turned and walked back the way she had come.

Sybil hurried after her and grabbed her arm, careful not to jerk her around, careful not to make a scene. She kept her voice low.

"And where do you think you're going!"

She felt Julie Sue try to pull away, but Sybil held more tightly to her arm.

"I'm going to walk home through the woods."

"No you're not. You're going to come with me, ride home with the family, and be there to say goodbye to our company throughout the rest of the afternoon."

At first Julie Sue resisted, then Sybil felt her yield.

With her hand dropping away from Julie Sue's arm, but touching her for guidance, Sybil joined the crowd, seeking out Walter and Gertrude to walk with them back to the carriage.

Chapter 11

Beulah went into the kitchen, took off her hat and laid it on the fireplace mantel. Both tables were covered by food that neighbors and church people had brought. She must hurry, and arrange it.

Breathless, she hurried into the service hallway and opened the door to the enclosed back stairway. She went up in the shadows of the stairway, leaving the door at the bottom open to give her light. The house seemed too quiet when she reached the second floor. On the second floor landing the stairway turned and went on up to the third floor. But it was never used, the door at the top of the stairs had probably rusted shut by now.

She went out onto the second floor and paused, breathless. The only sound in the house seemed to come from herself, from her racing heart, the pulses in her temples, the thundering of her blood. She felt as if she were doing something wrong. As if she were preparing to sin in a bad way, as she never had before.

But she had to know. Was the doll with Rose when she died?

She went to Rose's door and turned the knob. She pushed the door back slowly and heard a low, rusty whine as if she were being warned not to enter.

Someone had closed the blinds, and the room was shadowed and still. The bed was carefully made, as she herself had left it.

The cradle was still in the corner, a dark, bulky reminder of a tiny girl who had never been out into the sunshine in all the three months of her life.

Beulah went slowly around the foot of the bed, past the rocking chair, and to the cradle. She looked in. It was empty except for the bedding. The featherbed in the bottom was still indented where a small body had lain. It was covered by a flannel blanket, with a thin summer comforter pushed back near the foot. It held the smell of death.

She started to reach in for the bedding, and then drew her hands back. She couldn't touch it. She looked around the room. The doll was not here.

Someone must have put it upstairs in the china cabinet where it belonged. Behind the closed, latched doors made of glass and dark wood.

She sighed with relief. What had she had in mind? That whenever the doll came out of the cabinet someone died? Silly old woman, she chided herself.

She went to the door, and then turned again for one last look at the room.

She stepped over the threshold and pulled the door, and heard a low cry. She stopped, a long, slow chill coming up her spine.

She had thought it was the door, the first time, but now she knew it was something else. She had heard that sound before. An infant's voice, so much like any infant animal, a squeak, half-cry, a sound asking for attention.

The room was haunted. Haunted by the voice of a dead child whose voice she had never heard during its short life.

She stood still, her head turning, her eyes covering the room again, carefully. The cradle, the large bed centered against the wall, the dark crocheted bedspread that hung almost to the floor.

Almost to the floor . . .

There was something white beneath the bed.

Beulah bent down. She saw a white gown, swelling over something small, a curved leg, a foot. The tiny toes on the foot looked like buds.

She reached for it and drew out the doll.

Its eyes had the swollen quality of a newborn infant, but its face looked less wrinkled than she remembered.

She had handled the doll only once before. The morning the baby had died, Julie Sue had thrust the doll into her hands.

Staring intently down into its still face, Beulah went out into the hall where there was more light. She listened, but there was no sound yet of the family returning from the church.

She went toward the stairway to the third floor, lifting the long gown of the doll as she walked slowly, examining its body, its clothing, its legs and feet. The body was cloth, and had a tight, crisp feel, as if it were stuffed with straw. But its legs were composition, or some such material, though the skin seemed almost real. The legs were curved at the knee, like a real baby's, and the feet were narrow and small, with the little budlike toes. It was wearing a band around the middle of the round belly, and a "didie" made of white cloth and pinned with safety pins.

She pulled the gown down over its feet.

The upper part of its body was composition. It rested like an armor over the top of the stuffed body, and the head and arms were connected to it. The arms were curved too, like the legs, and the hands open, fingers extended as if reaching.

The head had golden curls painted beneath a bonnet trimmed in narrow lace and tied beneath the wrinkled chin. Its nose was budlike too. And it had the face of a. . . . No, not a newborn infant, not now, though she had always thought it had. When she had wiped the glass doors of the china cabinet, she had looked at the contents. And she remembered well the day she first saw the doll within the doors.

It was the doll Sybil's father had brought her from somewhere far away. South America, she thought. Yet the doll was well made and had looked so much like a baby just born that she had been stunned at first glance.

Sybil had not liked the doll. "A doll! A baby doll?" Her voice was petulant. Harsh with disappointment. "Why didn't you bring me a grown-up doll like Rose Marie's if I must have a doll, Papa? I wanted a brooch, like Mama's."

And her mother's voice speaking with false cheerfulness, "But isn't it realistic? It's a very interesting doll, Sybil, and Papa knows how you enjoy playing with dolls."

Sybil answered, "That was last year."

The next morning Rose Marie was found dead. She had died in her sleep.

Beulah had forgotten the doll until she went up to the third floor to dust a month later, and there it was, its face screwed up, its eyes puffed almost shut, but looking out at her from behind the glass, and its small, realistic hands reaching as if asking to be taken up.

The eyes, Beulah noticed, were not painted on. They were made of glass, but they were a clear sky blue, instead of a deep, smoky blue like a real baby's eyes. And they were looking at her, staring.

They were not puffed like she remembered. And the face was fuller, rounder, as if it were slowly growing.

She frowned, touching its bonnet with a rough finger. She was not one of these old women who no longer trusted their memory just because they had passed a certain age. She knew what it had looked like, and she saw what it looked like now, and the difference disturbed her. This doll was with Rose when she died. It was with the baby, and it might have been with Rose Marie. And it was changing. But what did it all mean?

Rose's body had the same brittleness that her baby's had. It wasn't she who had prepared the body for burial, but she had touched her arm and hand and found it stiffer and more brittle than most dead bodies. It was like all that had been alive in her had been drawn out.

A sound drifted up to her, reaching her consciousness abruptly. Voices, doors, people entering the front door, going into the parlor and library. Distant and muffled by high ceilings and thick walls.

Beulah opened the door to the third floor stairs and hurried up. There hadn't been enough overnight company to use the third floor. The guests had been put into the front bedrooms on the lower portion of the second floor.

Beulah opened the door on the china cabinet and laid the doll in the corner, its feet near the little iron horse and wagon.

She closed the door and latched it, then she hurried away.

What had she thought she would find? What silent message of death could a mere doll hold? Well at least it was back where it belonged.

She went down the stairs carefully, closing the door to the third floor, turning the button that had kept Gertrude from climbing the stairs when she was a too curious youngster, then entering the service stairs and going on down. She had to get the food on the table, mix the lemonade, make sure Moses put the flowers in the right places.

What had she thought she would find? What could there be about the doll that portended death? Was it just a coincidence? Or, did it have a poison dart or something of that sort in it?

It was possible. Weren't the natives of those backward countries the kind of people who used poison darts? She had read about them in some of the magazines Sybil's father had kept. When she had more time she would examine the doll more carefully.

Rose Marie had died the night the doll first came into the house. For years glass doors separated it from family. It was removed from the cabinet, and Rose's baby died.

Rose had died, and the doll was still in the room, on the floor beneath the bed in which she had died. It might have been on the bed earlier.

And now, as she remembered, the doll had been in the room with Sybil's father.

She stopped short, remembering. It had jumped into her mind unbidden, as if her brain were trying to make connections she hadn't consciously thought of.

Sybil's father, dead in his sleep before he grew old.

Beulah lingered in the service hall and stared back in time at the scene of Charles Wilfred's death. How odd, how much a coincidence. She had never thought of it before, but she remembered clearly the morning she had come to work and Mister Wilfred had not come down to breakfast at his usual time.

Sybil, a young woman, the mother of three year old Rose and infant Julie Sue, flat as a board as if she hadn't just had a baby two weeks ago, had sat alone at the dining table, waiting. Her young husband had gone on to town to the law office, and Mister Wilfred was strangely missing. Perhaps he had gone out for a walk. Except his knees bothered him, and he had to walk with a cane. But still, he might have gone out.

"Beulah, go upstairs and call Papa. He's getting so senile lately."

She had said it with a sneer. Sybil, a young woman, contemptuous toward her father, who had worshipped her even more after Rose Marie's death. Lately, Beulah thought, Sybil had been treating the elderly gentleman as if he were a servant. Ordering him about, lifting her nose whenever he had tried to talk with her.

Sybil, who was dear to her, still needed talking to

about the way she was treating her father. But who was going to do it? Beulah didn't dare. She needed her job. She had no one to help her now that her son had been killed in the sawmill accident. She could only mutter it under her breath as she climbed the stairs and went to wake Mister Wilfred.

"He's your papa. Treat him with respect. He's not an old man yet, he's not feeble yet. Just his knees, rheumy and knotted. He still runs his business."

But his hands had begun to tremble, and his chin shook when he tried to talk. And Sybil had never been really respectful to anyone, had she?

But perhaps it wasn't Sybil's fault. She had known sorrow early. Her own sister Rose Marie had died, in the same room where Sybil slept, when Sybil was only twelve years old. And less than a year later Sybil's mother had died. She had sickened and grown thin and pale, coughing her life away in two short weeks. The doctor had said it was pneumonia, but Beulah thought it was a broken heart. She had loved Rose Marie so much.

Beulah reached the door to the master bedroom suite where a short private hall joined two large bedrooms and a sitting room. The door to Mister Wilfred's bedroom was closed.

Beulah knocked on it, and listened for an answer. She heard nothing but a gust of wind outdoors. The weather had chilled her on her walk this morning. It was February, and the day cloudy and dark.

"Mister Wilfred?"

There was no answer. Puzzled, worried, she opened the door, calling out as she did to avoid embarrassing herself or him. "Mister Wilfred, Sybil asked me to see . . ."

He was sprawled face down, half off the bed, his right arm dangling. Later, when she could think, it seemed as if he had tried to get off the bed, that he had struggled, and lost.

113

She hadn't thought much of it then, she had been so shocked by his death, but the doll had been on the floor beneath his hand. On its back, it had gazed up at her like a helpless baby, waiting to be picked up. She had taken it back to the cabinet upstairs, when nothing was needed of her for awhile.

She had only briefly wondered, at the time, why the doll was there. Today, fifteen years later, she felt the first dark clutch of fear.

Chapter 12

Julie slipped away from the people who sat in the parlor, briefly joining Jonathan Gilbert and his wife Bessie and their daughters Grace and Ellen as they left. She stood with her mother at the door to tell them goodbye and thank you for coming, listening one more time to murmurs of sympathy. Then as Sybil went back toward the parlor and the other guests, Julie uttered her own murmurs, asking to be excused.

Julie slipped through the halls hoping to be invisible among the company. She saw that Beulah was in the dining room replacing pitchers of lemonade. She had a sober, pinched look to her mouth, as if she were studying something seriously. When Julie reached the service hall and kitchen door, she ran.

She had sat for hours in the parlor where she could watch the driveway, and she had not seen Harold. Would he treat her like Rose, and not come back?

She went across the back porch and out the screen door. Shadows were lengthening across the backyard between the garden shed and the house. Behind the shed, the smokehouse, with the hollyhocks blooming in front of it, looked darkened by the trees beyond. Wild grapes and chinquapins bloomed in the woods, but there was the dank, musty smell too of the mausoleum. Julie had never seen inside that burial place before. The shelves were made of stone, like the exterior, and looked deep and dark. Rose's coffin had been placed on one of those deep, stone shelves, to be closed into the darkness with all the other coffins. Yet, how could she smell it here, through the woods?

She strolled, her hands clasped tightly in front of her, against the tightness of her corseted waist. She went along the path to the garden shed, and then around it to the smokehouse. Within the smokehouse there were corpses of animals hanging, hams, salted, smoked, strung to the ceiling by wire around what once had been a living leg.

She edged away from the building. She hated the smokehouse, especially in the fall when the hogs had been freshly killed and hung there.

"That's just the way it is," Beulah had told her once when she was ten years old and had screamed and cried in revolt when she saw the killing of the animals.

"Why is it?" she had screamed, tears almost choking her. "Why? Bertha knew her name! She'd come to me when I called!"

"You made a pet of her. You should never make a pet of a pig that's going to be butchered."

"*Why?* I'm not going to eat her! She knew her name!"

"She was a dumb animal, Julie Sue."

"She was not dumb! I'm not going to eat her! How can the rest of you? Why can't we just eat vegetables? And fruit and stuff? Not my Bertha!"

Her mother had heard her screams and had sent her to her room. She had cried for days, and had refused to eat any of the meat that might be Bertha, and eventually to eat none of it. After nagging her for three years, Mama had quit, allowing her to eat as she chose. But she had heard her mother tell her papa, "That is the most headstrong child that ever lived. I'm afraid she's headed for a brief, unfortunate life." She had said it very angrily, as if she didn't care.

Julie stopped, staring into the growing dimness of the

116

forest a few yards beyond.

She hadn't thought of those words before, not really. At the time, when she was thirteen, she had only tossed her hair back, gone upstairs, and spitefully torn off her corset.

Now it seemed her mother had made a chilling prophesy, and it might come true. She might die like her sister. She was suddenly sick with fear. She wanted to run, but where? To town? She really had no best friend, none whose parents would take her in and keep her. To Beulah's house?

"I was afraid you weren't coming." The deep voice seemed to emanate from the woods.

She whirled, her heart pounding. Harold stood in the shadows behind the smokehouse, almost hidden by the vines that grew on the greyed boards.

He reached out and steadied her. His large, strong hand squeezed her arm reassuringly, and she felt like throwing herself against him for protection.

"And I thought *you* weren't coming, Harold."

"I've been here an hour. I didn't go to the kitchen because I was afraid your housekeeper would tell your folks, and I knew they'd probably not let me talk to you."

"We should hurry. It's going to be dark soon. I want to show you Angela's grave."

She walked quickly on, to the thin path Rose had made through the trees to the grave.

"Angela?" he asked.

She could hear his steps, just slightly off the path. Beneath his boots twigs snapped and leaves rustled. She hurried faster and came to the tiny clearing in the trees where the dirt of the grave was still fresh and mounded.

On the mound were the remains of flowers. They were brown now and limp, lying across the grave as if they were a kind of woven cover.

Harold stopped behind her, looking down.

"A baby," he whispered.

"Yes. Angela. She died just a week ago. She was Rose's baby. And yours."

"Oh God. I didn't know. I thought a girl couldn't get in the family way on the first . . . you know . . . the first . . ." His face looked drawn anguished. "Why didn't she write and tell me?"

"Why didn't you come back?"

"She could have gone to my mother and asked her, and she would have given her my address! She could have gone to my pop! He's not real fond of me, but he would have given it to her."

"I don't know, Harold. Maybe she felt ashamed. Rose was very happy after you left. First she told me you two were engaged, but then she got very unhappy when she didn't hear from you. I heard her sobbing at night. And she stopped going out of the house. Then I found out she was going to have a baby. And Mama and Papa wouldn't let her go out into public, even downstairs where she would be seen by Beulah, though Beulah would never have told."

"What happened to the baby? She was born . . . April?"

"How did you know?" Then Julie thought of why he would know, and she felt her cheeks grow hot. But he wasn't looking at her, he was looking down at the tiny grave. "Yes," she said. "April fifteenth."

He slowly bent down to one knee, and put his hand on the grave. "Then she died when she was three months old."

"Yes. She was beautiful, Harold."

"Was she sickly?"

"Oh no! She was very healthy. She—"

"What happened then?" Harold demanded, as if she were in some way responsible for the death of the daughter he had never seen.

118

It tore at Julie's heart, as if somewhere within herself she had actually been responsible. As if she could have stopped both the death of Angela and of Rose, if she had only done the right thing.

He stood up, and took her hand. He cupped it between his own hands. They were large and warm, so much warmer than hers.

"I'm sorry," he said. "It's just that they were everything I wanted. I didn't even know how much until I came back and found nothing but death."

Julie eased her hand out of his. She bent and began cleaning the brown, wilted flowers off the grave.

"I don't know what happened, Harold. She died in her sleep."

"What did the doctor say? Could he tell? If Rose died of apoplexy, was it the same with the baby? Or do doctors just say that when they don't know what it is."

Julie smoothed the soil of the grave with her hand, slowly, wiping away small pebbles. "No doctor ever saw her, Harold. No one ever saw her but me, my little sister Gertrude, and our parents. She lived her whole life in Rose's room. No one ever knew she was here."

"Like she didn't exist."

"Yes. Like she didn't exist."

"What kind of people are your parents? To do a thing like that to Rose and our baby?"

Julie stood up. "Oh, no, you don't understand. They're really not bad at all, or cruel. They're just proper. You know a baby born without a father—"

"Goddamnit she had a father! Me!"

"But they didn't know that."

"Well, I think they did. I wrote to Rose, and never heard from her. Those letters stopped somewhere. They didn't come back to me."

"But my parents are really very good. Papa brought down the old cradle and put it in Rose's room for the

119

baby. Mama brought material to make the baby clothes. She even gave the baby a gift she had never given to any of us, her own children. She gave her a very special doll that had been given to her when she was a child. It wasn't that they didn't love Angela. It wasn't that."

She turned her face away, unable to look at him. She was trying to convince herself as well as Harold.

Harold started to walk away, but only turned a circle and stopped again, frustrated.

"Rose wanted to be buried here, but of course that wasn't possible either," Julie said.

She felt Harold's eyes, staring at her. It was a long moment before he spoke.

"And why is *she* buried here? Angela? Not even a stone with her name on it, or the date of her birth, or death."

"Well, she'd never been christened, you see, and—"

"Good God! Well, I'm getting out of here."

She mustn't let him go; she had to make him stay.

"Wait! Where are you going?" she asked. "Back to Saint Louis?"

"I've lost my job."

"Lost it! But why?"

He stared at the ground, his hands still in his pockets. "I couldn't get time off. So I just left."

"Then are you staying here? Perhaps work in your papa's store? I know he wants you to."

"No, good God, I'd rather die. My younger brother can take the store. Being shut up in that place. . . . I'd rather dig ditches."

"But you can't leave. Not yet."

He shook his head. "Nothing to hold me, now."

"But, where will you go?"

"Saint Louis. Maybe even New Orleans. Not Little Rock. I want to work on a riverboat on the Mississippi. It doesn't matter. I've always liked the water."

She stopped. He wasn't going toward the house or the

driveway beside the house. He was walking through the trees, away from the almost invisible path that led to the backyard.

He looked back, then stopped. A brief smile touched his lips.

"Thanks Julie Sue. I'm glad I came back, anyway. Goodbye."

"Goodbye Harold."

She watched him walk away. She saw him dodge limbs and duck beneath a low hanging tree and blend into the deepening darkness of the woodland that reached all the way to the churchyard.

Somewhere back in the woods came the call of a whippoorwill, and its call sounded sad and lonesome.

She went along the path to the yard. Carriages and buggies were leaving, taking the guests. The last buggy, with its one horse standing half asleep, was being untethered at the hitching rail beside the driveway, and the people were leaving.

Tomorrow, probably, her aunt and uncle would leave. There would be no visitors. The house would be so quiet without Rose and Angela. Julie didn't know how she could stand it.

She went up the steps to the porch and into the kitchen.

Beulah was putting on her bonnet, tying its black ribbon beneath her chin. A black shawl hung over her shoulders.

"Are you going home?" Julie asked.

"Yes."

The look Beulah gave Julie was warm, almost like a caress.

"Do you have to go?" Julie asked. "You could sleep here."

"But I have my animals. I have to feed my animals."

Julie wanted to say, "Then can I go with you?" But she

didn't. She watched Beulah open the door.

Beulah looked back at Julie. "Take care, Julie. Close your door tight. God will take care of you."

Julie swallowed something hard that had formed in her throat. Let her believe. Let her be comforted by her beliefs. As for Julie, she'd never forget the look on Rose's face when she lay dead.

"I'll see you tomorrow, Julie Sue. You go up and take a hot bath and go to bed. Keep your light on tonight." She hesitated again, then said, "Whatever you do, Julie Sue, don't touch that doll. Let it stay where it is, safe behind them glass doors."

The door closed behind Beulah, and Julie stood in the silence of the kitchen, wondering. Poor Beulah. What had she meant, the doll "safe behind glass doors"? The doll was still in Rose's room. She had seen it there, the day Rose died.

A gaslight had been turned on in the big hall, and its pale, white glow partly pushed away the shadows in the service hall. But the stairway up was almost totally dark.

Julie climbed carefully, her hand sliding along the handrail. She sighed with relief when she came out onto the second floor landing.

She opened the door out onto the wider second floor hall. A gaslight had been turned on here, too, helping to dispel the shadows. Beulah would have done that, before she left for the night.

She opened Rose's door. If Beulah wanted the doll put away, Julie would put it away, though it seemed Beulah's concern was peculiar. The room was closed and dark, even with the hall light spreading a path from the door to the bed. There was a lingering odor that caused Julie to hesitate. Ghosts of voices and sounds still lived in the room. She could almost hear the faint creak of the rocking chair, and Rose crooning, "Lullaby, lullaby, and good night . . ."

122

Today the rocking chair sat still by the closed and curtained window, and there was no young mother to sing to her infant.

Julie walked slowly into the room. The bed was smoothly made, bedspread tucked beneath fat pillows. The tops of the dresser and chest were dusted and neatly arranged.

Julie went around the foot of the bed, passed the rocking chair and looked into the cradle. The bedding the baby had used was still there, but the cradle was empty. Where had she last seen the doll? It had been on the floor, while Rose lay on the bed, looking in death old and haggard. Not Rose, but a shadow of Rose.

Julie got down on her knees and looked under the bed, but it wasn't there, either. The doll was not in the room. Beulah must have put it away. Yes, "safe behind them glass doors."

"Julie Sue!"

Julie screamed softly before she slapped her hands against her mouth. She whirled.

Her mother stood in the doorway, the light outlining the pile of hair on her head, shining through its outer fringes so that it looked like a halo. Julie couldn't see Sybil's features, but her voice had sounded cold with anger.

Julie felt as if she faced a stranger. She was not afraid of the doll. But she was afraid of her own mother.

Chapter 13

"Would you come out of Rose's room, please?"

Sybil backed up. Still the light only outlined her, and her features were blurred with shadow. Julie went slowly toward the door. She thought of Papa, briefly, and realized she was afraid of him too. He was one with Mama, the two of them stood together as one. Their closeness had always made her feel secure, until now. Now it left nowhere to turn. She didn't understand her fear, but it was there, closing off her breath, placing a tight band around her chest.

"I was only . . ." *Looking for the doll.* She must not say it. Something deep and instinctive told her not to reveal why she had entered Rose's room.

"What were you doing in the woods with that young man, Julie Sue?"

"What?"

Then it had nothing to do with Rose's room after all. It had to do with Harold.

"You heard what I said, Julie Sue."

"I was only talking to him, Mama."

"I hope you weren't foolish enough to take him to that grave."

"I thought he should know. He was, after all, the father."

"The child had no father! What are you trying to do, totally disgrace us? Rose is dead. Don't sully her reputation!"

Julie stared briefly at her mother and then avoided her eyes. Rose was dead, but all her mother cared about was Rose's reputation. She closed the door, and backed against the wall. It felt solid and cool. She put her hands back and flattened her palms on the wall.

"You tell one, you tell all, Julie Sue. That man killed Rose, do you want him to do the same to you? If it hadn't been for Harold Lanning's attentions to Rose, she would still be alive. Don't you realize that? Let's just pray you haven't already spread the news of Rose's travail. I demand you not so much as talk to anyone else."

"Yes, Ma'am. May I please be excused?" she asked. "Beulah said I should come up and take a hot bath and go to bed."

"Beulah is not your mother! I'm telling you for the last time. You are never again to speak to that man."

"He has left. I won't be speaking to him."

Sybil nodded, her eyes boring into Julie. Though her head was lowered she could see the narrowed slits, the blue-green color, the pale lashes, the crinkles caused by the intensity of the stare.

"You may be excused," Sybil said, and turned away, going down the hall, and down the three steps to the lower balcony in the front wing of the house.

Julie heard her speak to someone who was somewhere out of sight, and her voice was now polite and soft. Julie ran into her room and closed the door. She stood in the darkness of her room trying to breathe normally. She wished, for the first time, that her door had a lock.

Julie lit the lamp on her dresser. With the soft glow of the kerosene light pushing shadows deeper into corners and behind furniture, she began to undress. She unfastened her skirt and bodice and let them fall to the floor, then began untying her corset.

There was a time, she remembered, not long ago, when her greatest concern had been her hated corset. But now, as she folded it and laid it on the cedar chest at the foot of the bed, she wondered at the innocence of that girl.

She slipped out of her stockings and bloomers and was for a moment naked in her room. She hurried, and pulled a nightgown over her head. Then she stood hugging her arms across her stomach. Beulah had told her to take a hot bath. She wanted to. But she was afraid to leave her room.

She turned the light low, opened the window wider, and got into bed. Then she lay in a knot facing the door, staring at the white porcelain knob.

She listened to footsteps in the hall. Gertrude's, and her mother's. She heard the muffled, distant sound of water running in the bathroom.

Then Sybil's footsteps went back toward the front of the house and the large bedroom suites on the lower level of the second floor.

From somewhere in the woods the whippoorwills called to each other. From the ponds in the pasture the frogs peeped. She heard a dog bark, and heard the distant mooing of a cow. And she heard the steady buzz of the jarflies and katydids. A soft, cool breeze wafted in at the window, touching and chilling her. She pulled her sheet closer beneath her chin but was afraid to move to pull up the summer comforter she had folded back to the foot of the bed.

She heard no footsteps, but saw the white knob of her door turn. She stared at it, unable to move, knowing only that the horror of death was coming for her now, as it had come for Angela and for Rose.

The door opened, but it wasn't death. It was only Gertrude. She looked small and thin in her white nightgown, the dim light of the gaslight at the end of the hall making her look featureless and ghostly. But Julie was so glad to see her she could have wept.

126

"Can I sleep with you?" Gertrude asked.

Julie held out her hands to help her little sister up into the bed.

She slept, her arms wrapped around Gertrude. She felt the warm cheek against her own, even in her sleep. In some way, they protected each other. They were in a safe cocoon. The night seemed more silent. The whippoorwills farther away. Sounds drifted on the soft air of the night, fading. Gertrude's breath blended with hers.

Then she was suddenly and abruptly aware of someone standing over them. She cried out as she was waking, her fear making the real world seem like a nightmare.

"Shhh," the specter that bent over the bed whispered, and Julie recognized her mother. "Don't wake Gertrude."

Sybil reached down and lifted sleeping Gertrude and carried her through the open bedroom door and away.

Julie lay tense and staring at the door, seeing the contrasting light, the pale white moon glow of the gas against the yellow of the kerosene. All that had comforted her had been taken away.

After a while Sybil passed her doorway, going down the hall, her arms empty. She did not pause to close Julie's door, or even to glance in. She was not wearing her black dress now. She wore a flowing robe, the hem brushing the floor.

Long after she passed the door Julie heard the sweep of the robe against the floor, the whisper of its passing, and yet its staying, so near, just beyond her view.

Finally she slipped out of bed and went to the door and looked into the hall.

No one was there. The hall looked long, like a tunnel, with a small light at the far end. Julie closed her door and went back to bed.

But this time she stayed awake, afraid to close her eyes.

Beulah stared at her dark ceiling. She hadn't been able to sleep at all. Something was growing in her mind, but it was as if it grew behind a curtain. A black curtain that had been drawn there a long time ago, when Rose Marie died.

Where was the doll the night Rose Marie died? Exactly where?

She turned over on her straw mattress and stared at the pale rectangle of her window.

And where was the doll when Rose died? Exactly where?

Her bones ached, she had held them in such tension for such a long time. She tried to relax, but couldn't.

She listened for a suggestion of early morning, and heard none. The night was dragging. On the floor beside her bed the dog snored. And on the foot of her bed the cat snored. But Beulah stayed awake, and her thoughts kept returning to the doll.

It was only a doll, but the strange deaths had started when the doll was brought home from South America by Sybil's father. He would not have given his beloved daughter something that might hold a deadly danger. Not if he had known. But Sybil had not died. Nor Julie Sue nor Gertrude, thank the Lord. Not yet.

She could stay in bed no longer.

She got up, and felt her way to the lamp. She heard the snoring of both her pets stop, and knew they had raised their heads to watch her.

She struck a match and lit the lamp. She looked at the clock and saw it was only three-thirty. Another hour before she had to rise.

"I hope," she said aloud, "That Bossy doesn't care if she's milked in the middle of the night."

Both the dog and cat got up and stretched and yawned

as Beulah began to dress. She went into the kitchen and lighted the lantern, then took her milk bucket and went out the backdoor, the cat and dog with her, both of them slow and sleepy.

In the barn she hung the lantern on a nail and put out a cup of grain into Bossy's manger. As the cow ate, Beulah milked. When she had finished she poured part of the milk into a pan, and the cat and dog drank a few laps. Beulah turned the cow out into a dark pasture, and when Beulah went away with the lantern swinging at her side the cow stared after her, puzzled.

Beulah took the milk back into the house and strained it through a clean, white cloth. Then she rinsed the cloth and hung it out on the clothesline. With the milk in the crock, she put the lid on to cover it and took it out to the springhouse where it would stay cool. The cat and dog followed.

When she got her bonnet and left the house, lantern in her hand, the cat and dog watched her from the small porch.

She reached the long driveway up to the old Wilfred mansion long before daylight. Light glowed dimly in one window at the front, like one narrowed eye, watching her. She stopped, lifted her lantern and carefully turned the wick as low as it would go without going out. She didn't want to be seen.

With the lantern on her left side, away from the house, she went into the driveway where tall, old trees lined both sides, and the lighted window at the house blinked off and on beyond tree limbs and leaves.

When she reached the backdoor she dug the key out of her pocket and opened the door and went in. She closed the door quietly. Though she was a long way from the bedrooms on the second floor, she felt as if someone were listening and watching and hearing.

But of course that was ridiculous.

129

It was the deaths that were bothering her. She was an old woman losing her mind, after all.

She took a candle from the candle drawer and found a holder and lighted the candle with a kitchen match. She raised the globe on the lantern and blew it out. Then with the candle held carefully in front, she went upstairs. She used the service stairs and walked softly, avoiding squeaky stairs, opening and closing doors softly.

On the third floor she was careful to make as little sound as possible. There were no rugs to silence her footsteps. Like a thief in the night she tiptoed down the hall to the china cabinet.

She lowered the candle.

The doll was still there.

She stared through the glass door at it. Oddly, it seemed to be asleep, its puffy eyes closed, the crease above the eyes and below there again, as if it had returned to being a newborn.

Beulah opened the glass door and reached in.

The doll's straw-filled body felt almost like the body of a real baby. The straw had a soft feel that she hadn't noticed before.

She wished she had brought up a butcher knife from the kitchen so she could open the cloth and see what was really stuffed within the body. She had a sudden, horrible vision of slicing it open and entrails falling out, unwinding like thin snakes or worms, bloody red and filled with poison.

She tucked the doll in her bent arm and used one hand to push herself up from the floor. Holding the candle carefully she went to the stairs and down to the second floor landing and paused.

Rose's room . . . or the kitchen?

She wanted to sit and think where she wouldn't be disturbed.

Of course all the family was asleep. The Mister

130

wouldn't be rising until daylight, and there would be no work for him today. Today there would be breakfasts cooked for guests who were sleeping in the guest rooms at the front of the house.

But Moses might come in early. He came and left in the kitchen as he needed, but he would not go beyond unless asked.

Beulah opened the door into the second floor hall, closed it quietly behind her and, holding the candle carefully, went along the hall to Rose's room.

She put her candle on the bedside table between the bed and cradle and went back to close the door.

She sat down in the rocking chair, and heard its faint squeak as she sat back. With the doll held where the candle light fell upon its face she looked at it. She untied the bonnet and hung it on the chair arm. She removed the long gown, and unpinned the "didie."

She began to feel foolish. What was she doing, sitting here in a dead girl's room, taking the clothes off a doll that had been in the family nearly thirty years? It was an ordinary doll. Except it wasn't pretty, like most dolls. But there were no secrets beneath the clothes.

She had no knife with her to see what was beneath the cloth of the body.

But what would Sybil do when she found her doll had been slashed apart? She would have to bring up her sewing basket and make sure she put it back together.

Rose's sewing basket was sitting on the floor at the side of the rocking chair, and in it was a pair of scissors. Beulah leaned over and reached for the scissors.

The baby cried. It was the soft, mewling sound of a newborn, brief and chilling.

Beulah sat back in the chair and stared at the doll.

Its eyes were open, staring through the slitted, puffed lids. Its mouth pouted, lips pursed as if reaching for a nipple.

Of course she hadn't heard a baby cry. It was the chair, she told herself. The chair had squeaked.

Without looking into the bright, glassy eyes, Beulah began redressing the doll. She pinned the "didie" back on, and pulled the gown down over its head. She tied the bonnet back on, the ribbon in a bow beneath its creased chin.

She leaned back, resting her head against the chair, and closed her eyes.

The doll lay on her lap, its head near her knees, its feet with the tiny, perfect toes against her belly. Her hands rested folded together on the stuffed body.

With her eyes closed, half asleep, she imagined she felt it moving. She felt the toes dig in to her stomach, as if she held a real baby. She could imagine herself sitting here with Rose's baby, taking care of it while Rose was out. She could feel it squirm beneath her hand.

Chapter 14

Julie lay still, listening. She could hear the sound of the rocking chair in Rose's room, and once she had heard the baby cry. The way she had cried when she was first born, a bleating, like young lambs or baby goats. She wanted to get out of bed and go see. If Rose and the baby had come back, she wanted to see them, even though she didn't know what she would see. But she was terrified.

The world outside her window had grown silent, and she knew it was close to dawn. Beulah would come soon after daylight.

Beyond her wall the chair squeaked as it rocked, and then it, too, was silent.

She couldn't live here anymore. But where could she go? Could she perhaps go with her aunt and uncle, by using the excuse that she wanted to go to school in the city instead of here in Wilfred?

No, her parents would say she was too young yet.

How could she stay here three more years until she was eighteen and perhaps allowed to go away to a university?

Could she run off with Andrew or Claude and get married? Each of them had asked her to be his girl, even to be engaged.

She turned in her bed, facing the window. Such a black night beyond her room, beyond the pale glow of her lamp.

Of course neither Andrew nor Claude could get married. Andrew was only sixteen, a few months older than herself. And Claude seventeen.

Could she leave on her own? Just pack her bag and go, hoping to find a job somewhere.

Maybe Harold would help her.

As she stared at the window she began to perceive a distant light, grey and ghostly. But within it dark leaves formed, and she knew the long night was approaching day.

Beulah's dreams were jumbled, like pieces of a cardboard puzzle knocked off a table. She slept restlessly, her head back against the high wood back of the rocking chair. Even in her sleep she was aware that she was in Rose's room, yet at times she was out in the woods by an open grave. When she stepped forward and looked down, an infant was lying uncovered in the bottom of the grave. Lying on the wet dirt, with no blanket, it wore nothing but a long, yellowish christening gown.

Then she saw it wasn't a real infant. It was a doll.

She saw its face clearly and was repelled by its ugliness. The face was wrinkled as if very old skin had been used to make it; real skin, taken from an ancient crone, used to create the doll. It stared up at her through slitted eyes, the wrinkles above its colorless eyebrows and beneath the lashless eyes framing an evil that held her stunned and unable to move.

She turned her head, unable to get her breath. She was back in Rose's room again, and there was a sound that slowly brought her back to reality. She listened, her eyes closed, thinking she was still more asleep than awake.

It was a soft, grunting sound. A sound she had heard before, which at one time in her life had filled her with happiness. But now drew terror into her heart.

134

It was the sound of an infant at the breast, breathing, grunting faintly as it nursed. As it drew nourishment.

She couldn't breathe.

Her hands grasped the arms of the chair and she opened her eyes. A grey dawn filtered through the lace curtains at the window. The candle on the table had gone out. Something was in front of her face, pressing against her.

She saw the edge of its bonnet, felt the weight of it against her face, and in a sudden burst of terrible fear knew that somehow it had crawled up her chest and was against her face. She felt the hard porcelain of its mouth, pushing into her soft, human flesh.

A long shudder passed over her body.

She struggled to raise her hands, but it was as if they had become part of the chair arms. Only her thoughts were capable of movement.

Sybil . . . the children . . . the Mister . . . here, helpless, not knowing . . . this thing, this horror, free in the house, out of its glass cage . . . *Oh God, she had to get up and go warn them* . . .

Sybil's father, Mister Wilfred, lying half off the bed. And beneath the edge of the bed, the doll . . . Gertrude, saying, "Beulah, Mama knows when someone is going to die. She gave the doll to Rose's baby . . ."

Beulah had to get to Sybil and tell her . . . I have opened the cage, Sybil . . . it's free in the house.

"Mama knows." *No, no.* Beulah did not believe Sybil knew about the doll. But Beulah had to tell her.

Her hands trembled as she forced them up. Her arms shook weakly as she raised her hands to pull the doll away from her face. She reared forward and up, and found her legs boneless and trembling and uncooperative. She felt its hands in her hair, clinging, and its terrible face sucking against hers as if they were glued together. She stumbled forward and bumped against something that rocked, and saw it was the cradle.

The doll came away at last in her hands and she dropped it into the cradle and then turned. The door was too far away.

She was falling. The grave with the wet, dark dirt in the bottom opened for her and the infant doll opened its arms to accept her.

The sound of something heavy falling in Rose's room caused Julie's heart to pound. She sat still listening, and heard no more. At last she got out of bed and pulled her robe on and went into the hall.

Across the hall Gertrude stood in her doorway. The room behind her was dark, and pale Gertrude looked like a ghost.

"What was that?" Gertrude asked in a loud, harsh whisper.

"I don't know."

But Gertrude's presence gave Julie courage, and she went to Rose's door and turned the knob. She pushed it inward. The door opened a couple of inches, and then came against a barrier. Julie hesitated, looking back at Gertrude. Gertrude came into the hall, her eyes large and frightened.

"What is it?" she asked.

"I don't know."

Julie pushed the door a bit harder, and felt it yield, then a hand fell into the opened space.

The hallway filled with screams. Julie wasn't sure who was screaming. Gertrude, herself, or the ghost of Rose and Angela beyond the half-open door of the bedroom, or the person whose limp hand had fallen into sight.

Julie stumbled back and screamed again as someone touched her. Then she saw it was her little sister, and she reached out and drew her into her arms. Gertrude clung to her, and Julie was aware of the trembling of the small, slim body. The hand lying in the open doorway looked at first like Rose's hand, grey with death. Lying palm up, its fingers curled, it seemed to be waiting. Then Julie saw it was not young and smooth like Rose's hand. The nails were not pink and tapered, but short and work worn, and she began to understand somewhere beneath her terror that the hand was real. Someone lay on the floor. Someone, real and alive, had fallen in Rose's room.

It was not a ghost. *It was real.*

She knew she should help. But all she could do was stand with Gertrude. Adults came in dressing gowns from the front of the house, hurrying. Papa, with his hair mussed, as Julie had never seen it, and Mama with braids down her back like a little girl. Aunt Alison and Uncle Victor came following. Julie saw widened, questioning eyes. She saw that adults, too, felt fear. She saw it in her aunt's eyes, and her papa's.

But her mother was never afraid. She seemed annoyed, impatient at the sight of her two daughters clinging together like frightened children in the hallway.

Then she saw the hand in the partly opened door, and whatever she had been going to say to Julie was never said. She hesitated only briefly, then she placed one hand on the door and bent to lift the hand.

She looked over her shoulder at Walter. He stood staring at the hand, his mouth open.

"I think it's Beulah, Walter. Help me."

Together they eased the door wide enough so they could enter the room, and Julie was able to see that it was Beulah.

Uncle Victor rushed forward to help Papa, and Mama directed them to lay Beulah on the bed. Julie heard breathless remarks about heart failure and apoplexy. Just as there had been with Rose.

Julie turned her face away, burying it in Gertrude's

137

hair. Beulah couldn't be dead. God couldn't be so cruel.

Sometime during the morning Sybil ordered Julie to her room to dress, and she obeyed listlessly as if she were two beings: one mental, one physical. Her hands trembled constantly, as did her chin. She kept her teeth clenched to hold her chin still, and she held her hands to steady them.

She brushed her hair and coiled it, pinning it on the back of her head without looking in the mirror.

She sat in the parlor then, her hands clutched together. They had trembled when Baby Angela and Rose died. But not like this. Now they shook as if palsied. She thought constantly of Rose's room, of the deaths there. It was as if the room had suddenly taken on a curse. Whoever entered, died.

How could she go upstairs tonight and sleep next to the room where three people had died within the past two weeks?

She had to leave the house.

In the afternoon Julie slipped unnoticed out of the house. The sun was shining, and the flowers were blooming just as always. Hours ago the enclosed carriage from the funeral home had come for Beulah's body and had taken it away. She hadn't seen, but she had heard the whinny of the horses, and she had heard her parents talking. Then Papa had sent Moses out to Beulah's house to take care of her animals, and on to her preacher to tell them what had happened. Her mother had already arranged for a temporary housekeeper, Faye's mother.

Julie left the house by the service hall and door. She had slipped out as if she were sneaking out to meet a lover, and she didn't even know where she was going.

She followed the path toward town, walking quickly. She reached the church and the cemetery, tried not to look at it.

A voice called, ghostly and distant, "Good afternoon, Miss Julie Sue."

She almost cried out. The caretaker of the cemetery was kneeling beside a tall tombstone near the front wall. He had clippers in his hand and was clipping grass. She swallowed, and found her throat dry. He stood up.

She could not speak, only nod, but she slowed.

"I hear there's been another death at your house, Julie Sue. Your housekeeper, Beulah. She used to stop by when she'd go in for groceries. We'd pass the time of day together. I'm going to miss her."

Julie nodded. "Me too."

Her voice was barely a squeak, as if it had long been unused.

She hadn't wanted to see the family mausoleum, at the back of the cemetery where the forest trees grew, but her eyes found it. The green vines that had grown across the door in the long years it hadn't been opened were now dying. Someone had cut and torn them down, and they hung limp, wilted and turning dusty brown.

She turned her face and eyes toward town and walked on.

She heard the caretaker say, "It's almost like a curse has hit the old Wilfred mansion. It's like it was years ago when Rose Marie died, and then her mother. Two deaths, like that, except there was more time passing between the two than this time."

She glanced back and saw he was working again. And she began to run.

Not until she came to the beginning of the brick street that surrounded the square and crossed it to the grassy, tree shaded park, did she know why she had come to town.

She had to find Harold.

Find him and beg him to take her away when he left.

* * *

Sybil stood quietly looking into the cradle. The doll lay sleeping, its cheeks pink and rounded, one curved hand up by its face. Beulah had brought it down from the cabinet, without asking. Perhaps it was just as well.

Sybil turned away. The room was neat, the bedspread smooth, the crocheted cushion in the shape of a heart carefully placed upon the pillows. She had told Beulah not to bother, but Beulah had tidied the room anyway.

At the door Sybil looked back at the cradle, almost lost in the shadows in the corner of the room. Then she stepped out into the hall and pulled the door closed behind her.

Chapter 15

Julie passed two women sitting on a park bench. She stopped running, aware under their gaze that she'd been holding her skirt almost to her knees. She let it drop and walked with as much grace as she could muster. She heard them grow quiet and knew they were still watching her. When they thought she was out of hearing they started talking again.

"That's the Madison girl, the second one. You know Walter Madison, the lawyer, has his offices over there on the corner."

"Her mama's Sybil Wilfred. The old man Wilfred owned most of the town at one time, but I hear this smart lawyer husband of hers ain't smart enough to keep it. They don't own so much anymore. They still have the land to the original place, though, and still live in the old Wilfred mansion. I hear that place's got about a hundred rooms, all the way up to three floors and an attic. Who needs that much house?"

"It's her sister that died. And the way I hear it there's a grave in the woods . . . not no animal, either. A little grave, no bigger than a baby's grave."

"Had another death there this morning. The old lady who did their cooking and mothering since she was a child herself."

"What's going on, you reckon?"

"A grave in the woods? I hadn't heard that. Don't they bury their dead in that big tomb . . ."

141

Julie began to run again, pinching her full skirt between her fingers and carefully lifting it only to her ankles.

The wide street was clear. A few horses stood tied to various posts along the edges of the brick sidewalk, and here and there a buggy with its horse standing half asleep took up a long space.

An automobile started up somewhere and chugged along. Any other time Julie would have stopped and looked at it, because automobiles were not a common sight. But today she had no curiosity, only fear.

She reached the sidewalk, passing a horse tied to the railing. She paused on the sidewalk and put her hand out, her eyes taking in the people who wandered about. The horse put his nose to her hand and she caressed him. She saw three girls and a woman looking in the department store window. Two of the girls looked familiar, but she didn't want to be seen by them. They stood between her and the Lanning hardware store.

To avoid them she went into the nearest store. The owner glanced up at Julie, then stared. And Julie knew from the stare that she recognized her and knew all the rumors that were around town about the old Wilfred mansion, the deaths, and the grave in the woods.

She left, unable to face her or anyone she knew.

Out on the sidewalk again she found her way clear to the Lanning hardware store. The woman and her daughters were going into the department store. Somewhere down a side street a horse whinnied, a man shouted, and the automobile chugged closer.

Julie opened the door of the hardware store and heard the familiar little clang of the bell that hung overhead.

There was no one in the store but Mr. Lanning, and Julie hurried toward him.

He was cleaning an upper shelf with a feather duster. He glanced at her, then turned another long gaze on her

as he stepped down off the short ladder.

"What can I do for you, miss?"

"Mr. Lanning, is Harold still here?"

"Don't know. I think he was on his way off somewhere again the last I saw of him."

He stood with the heels of his hands on the counter, the feather duster pointed into the air. His sharp eyes stared at her.

"I was sorry to hear about your sister," he said.

Julie looked down and blinked back a sudden need to start crying. "Thank you."

What was she going to do? She had no money, nowhere to go, yet she was afraid to go home. Home, where death lived now more than life. Gertrude? She could take Gertrude with her, perhaps, or come back for her as soon as she had a job, or send for her. But Gertrude was only ten years old. Mama and Papa would never let her go away.

"You got problems, Miss Julie Sue?"

She looked up. "Sir . . ." She bit her lip. She'd been going to ask him for a job. But she couldn't humiliate her parents by doing that.

"I'm sorry," he said, "that Harold ain't here. If I ever see him again I'll tell him you were in."

She left the store and went the long way around toward home, to avoid the street where people she had known all her life might see her. Instead she took a side street, and carefully skirted the town square.

She crossed a street that was rutted and rocky and headed for the woods on uncleared land between town and the road that led past her house. Somewhere on the road behind her came the ring of a metal horseshoe against a rock, and she began to run.

"Julie Sue!"

Harold!

She whirled, and saw a black horse with its rider just

143

around the bend. She ran back to meet them, aware that a woman who had been weeding in her yard was standing with her hands on her hips watching.

Harold reined his horse in. The saddle creaked under his weight as he twisted toward her.

"I thought you had left town!" Julie cried, so relieved she was trembling.

"Not yet. Tomorrow, probably. I was just on my way up town when I saw you. Where're you headed?"

"Home. Harold, Beulah died." She saw a slow frown gather on his face as he listened to her. She had reached up, she noticed vaguely, and was holding the edge of the saddle with her hands, as if it would keep him from getting away. He was her only hope.

"Beulah?"

"Beulah, our cook. Our sort of Grandma. She died. In Rose's room. In the night. Harold, I'm scared."

"Hell, kid, I don't blame you. What's going on at your house?"

"I don't know. The doctor said it was probably her heart. She was old now, you know, but she wasn't sick or feeble. I—"

"Yeah, but it could've been her heart all right." Harold looked off through the trees. He turned farther in his saddle, hooking his knee over the saddle horn. "I had an aunt, looked healthy, acted healthy, and one day at the dinner table she just fell over. It was her heart, the doctor said."

"Harold, when you leave . . . take me with you."

"*What?*"

He stared at her again, frowning, and she saw how dark his eyes were, and was reminded of Angela's eyes and her death and how the inner light had gone out so suddenly.

"Harold, help me. You're my only hope. I have to get away. I'm scared to stay there, Harold."

144

He shook his head. "I can't take you, Julie Sue. How old are you? Fifteen?"

"I'll be sixteen in two more months."

"I think there's some kind of law against a guy like me taking a kid like you across a state line. Where did you want to go?"

"I don't know. With you. Saint Louis? New Orleans? I look older than I am, don't I?"

His eyes swept her hastily. "Yes, I reckon so, you might pass for eighteen, even twenty. It's not like you're flat, or anything like that, the way some girls are at fifteen. But, look, Julie Sue, I go on my horse. Just me, and this horse I got from my brother. I may wind up no telling where."

"Please."

He was silent, looking at her, the frown gone. "What are you afraid of?" he asked gently. "I know you've gone through a lot. But here you've got your folks and a little sister. There, in the big cities, you'd have no one. It's not easy out there, Julie Sue. Especially for a young girl like you. Who would you have? What would you have? I mean, you could get a lot of men, but that's not good for you. Do you know what I mean?"

"Harold, please. I'm not asking you to be responsible for me. I just beg you to help me get away. I'll take care of myself from then on."

"You could take a train, Julie Sue."

"How? The closest depot is twenty miles away! How am I going to get there?"

"What are you afraid of? At home?"

"I don't know, I just am."

He patted the leather and blanket that lay on the horse's back behind the saddle. "Get up here and I'll take you home." He put his hand down for hers.

She backed away.

"Oh no! My mother . . ."

145

"Oh yeah. I heard that stuff from Rose, too."

He drew a long sigh and stared ahead, turning to sit straight in the saddle.

She stood at the side of the road looking up at him. She had almost gone down on her knees. For the first time she saw herself from his point of view. A man in his twenties taking with him a girl of fifteen, and then having to be responsible for her. She remembered she had no money. What would she do for food?

She said, "I can sew, so I could work in a factory. And I can certainly read and write and do arithmetic. It isn't as though I can't do anything."

He suddenly smiled down at her. "Hey, you've convinced me. I think you're wrong, but that's your business. I'll pick you up tomorrow about sunup and we'll be on our way."

An unexpected new fear gripped her. She was desperate to get away, yet suddenly she was afraid of what lay ahead.

"I have no money," she admitted.

He shrugged. "I didn't figure you'd have much cash lying around. I'll grubstake you, all right? You meet me at the cemetery gate. That's not far from your house. Don't bring much. Not any more than you can carry."

She nodded, backing away step by step into the woods at the side of the road. She looked up the street and saw the woman who had been watching them was weeding flowers again, no longer interested. For a few minutes she had forgotten they were being watched by someone who might spread the word. But it didn't matter who talked or what they said, she was leaving.

Harold tapped the end of the rein against the horse's neck and made a soft sound with his tongue. The horse began to walk, then suddenly Harold pulled him to a stop again.

"If you're not at the gate by sunup, I'll know you

changed your mind, all right?"

She started to tell him she wouldn't change her mind, but only nodded her head. She would be there.

"You think it over, okay? I've got a little sister about your age, and I'd hate to see her take off with a guy like me, or anyone. You promise me you'll think it over tonight."

She nodded again, and then turned and ran into the cool shadows of the woods.

She came into the woods behind the church and saw the cemetery with its spaced trees, its sunny and shady areas, and the iron gate and fence at the front. She went around it at the back, keeping to the woods, then turned to her left and found the path. She ran, swatting at a small cloud of gnats that swarmed across the path in a low, damp place. She dodged low limbs that caught at her hair.

At the edge of the yard she stopped, looking. The windows of the tall house seemed like dozens of eyes, dark and small and staring. If there were other eyes behind them, they were hidden.

Moses was not in sight either. The house and yard seemed deserted. The woodland crowded close against both side and backyard, opening out farther beyond into the fields and pastures where the cattle and horses grazed.

She tried to smooth her hair with her hands so it wouldn't look as if it were a rat's nest, as Beulah always called it when it was mussed. She took a deep breath and walked with as much dignity as she could across the yard to the back of the house. She went up the steps to the screen door and across the porch to the kitchen. The door stood open.

The unfamiliar woman in the kitchen looked up. She was stirring batter in a bowl at the cook table. She was nothing at all like Beulah, and seemed like an intruder in

147

Beulah's kitchen. Where Beulah had been thin and lanky and quick in movements, this woman was plump and slow, and there was flour and a mixture of other things on the front of her apron where she had wiped her hands.

As Julie entered the room, the woman put down the wood spoon in her right hand and wiped her hand on the apron.

"Are you Julie Sue?" she asked.

"Yes."

"Your mother has been looking for you."

Julie nodded. The new woman picked up the wooden spoon again. The smell of food cooking made Julie feel sick to her stomach. She dreaded facing her mother. Her papa would be there too, which only doubled the problem.

"I think she's in the library."

"Thank you."

Julie went into the inner halls. Gaslights had been turned on, and she realized how late it was getting. She went down the halls to the library. Both doors were closed. She hesitated, wishing with all her heart she could just run on up to her room and start choosing the clothing she would take with her, wishing she was out of this house forever.

She knocked.

"Come in."

It was Sybil's voice, calm and even. Maybe she wasn't mad after all.

Julie opened the door.

She saw Sybil first, sitting in the chair with the high, straight back. Over at the desk her father moved, getting up, turning slowly, coming to sit on the sofa. Gertrude sat like a much younger Sybil, as if she wore a corset that did not allow her to slump.

Her aunt and uncle were not in the room.

148

"Where's Aunt Alison and Uncle Victor?" Julie asked. "Where have you been?"

There was a moment of silence, then Walter said, "Your aunt and uncle had to go home today."

"Before Beulah's funeral?" Julie cried, and then remembered that she, too, would be leaving before Beulah's funeral. But it wasn't because she didn't love and respect her. It wasn't that. She hoped Beulah, if she knew, understood.

"They would not be required to remain here for the funeral of a servant, Julie Sue," Sybil said. "I asked where have you been all afternoon?"

"Beulah wasn't a servant! Beulah was *family*."

"Julie Sue," Sybil said, "You will please go to your room! I think you will not come down for dinner tonight! I've had enough of your lack of respect for the rules in this house, one of which is not to talk back to your parents, and another is not to run off to town just anytime you feel like it! Now go to your room!"

Julie whirled away, almost running by the time she reached the door. She had an urge to slam it, but knew she didn't dare agitate her mother any more. She closed it carefully and then on tiptoes ran to the foyer and the stairway.

In the upstairs storage room she grabbed an old carpetbag that had belonged to an earlier member of the family and hurried with it to her room. She dropped it on the floor and struck a match to the kerosene lamp. She carefully closed the door and then began searching through her wardrobe.

Her hands shook as she chose the bare minimum of clothing. Skirts and bodices of dark material, white bloomers and black stockings and one pair of white stockings. A hated corset, because without it her waist was too large for the waistbands of the skirts. A nightgown, and then, into the edge of the carpetbag, which was growing

149

tight with clothing, she stuffed a second nightgown. She would need a shawl, too.

She turned to the open doors of the wardrobe again when she noticed that someone had opened her bedroom door and was standing quietly watching her.

Fear flooded into her throat like vomit rising, and her hands flew to her mouth to stifle the scream that threatened the silence.

Chapter 16

The shadowy figure at the door separated from the shadows behind it and stepped into the room.

Gertrude! Julie's feeling of faintness diminished. How strange, she thought, that Gertrude looked so different now with recognition. Her figure in the doorway at first had seemed huge and threatening, ghostly, throwing a long, enveloping shadow; but now looked so small and fragile. She was dressed for bed, wearing a white nightgown that touched the tops of her bare feet.

Julie grabbed her and hugged her. When she released Gertrude, she saw her young sister staring at the open carpetbag.

"What are you doing?" Gertrude cried. "What is that thing? A valise! Where did you get that old thing?"

"Shhh." Hastily Julie went to the bedroom door and looked out into the hall. Lights had been turned on hours ago, but the hall had a strange dark quality. It looked long, tunnel-like, and the opening onto the steps down to the balcony at the other end looked distant and endless. The hall was empty except for its occasional chairs and tables.

She carefully closed the door. When she turned, Gertrude was at the carpetbag and had lifted out the corner of the last nightgown Julie had stuffed into it. Gertrude's face turned toward her, shadowed by the lamp on the table, looking almost like a skeleton with darkened holes for eyes and a dark open hole for the mouth.

151

Julie closed her eyes for a moment to reorient herself. Everything around her now seemed nightmarish. Even her little sister.

She opened her eyes, but Gertrude's face was still shadowed. She saw that fear glistened in her eyes.

"What are you doing?" Gertrude whispered shrilly. "Where are you going? You're running away, aren't you?"

Gertrude began to weep. She dropped the nightgown and turned her back to Julie.

Julie rushed to her and took the trembling little girl into her arms. Gertrude sank against her.

"Hey, don't cry. It's all right, Gertie, honest to God. It's all right. Gosh, baby, no wonder Beulah was always after you to eat. You're just skin and bones, like she always said."

"Don't leave, Julie Sue. What will I do without you?"

"You'll wait for me, because it won't be very long before I'll come and take you with me."

"But I don't want to leave, Julie! And I don't want you to leave!"

She raised her face, and the soft, dim light fell fully upon it. Julie could even see the brown freckles that lay in a diamond shape across her nose and out onto each cheek. Her lashes were pale, tipped in gold, and teardrops clung to them like crystal beads.

Julie pulled her handkerchief from her pocket and gently wiped the tears away, but more came, and Gertrude pressed her face against Julie's shoulder and hugged her tightly around the neck.

"Rose's baby, and Rose, then Beulah, and now you, Julie Sue. Please, don't go away."

A sudden tremor shook Julie. "But it's not the same. Leaving to go somewhere else to live is not dying, Gertrude."

"Where will you live?"

"I don't know yet. But listen to me. Stop crying and

listen to me. It's important."

Julie waited as Gertrude grew still, her body jerking in silence with the sobs she couldn't control. At last, as Julie patted and rocked her back and forth, Gertrude lifted her head. Her eyes were dry, her body jerking with a sob only spasmodically. Her eyes looked dark in the dim light.

"I'll be back. But it's urgent that I go."

"Why?" Gertrude whispered.

Julie looked beyond Gertrude at the window, and tried to find a clear definition for her fear, not only for Gertrude but for herself.

"I'm afraid here, Gertie. I've lived in this room all my life. All my memory. I don't remember ever being a baby in the nursery. And I was happy here until . . . last winter. Then I saw the way Mama and Papa treated Rose just because she was going to have Angela."

"But you're not supposed to have a baby if you're not married. It was for Rose's own good that Mama made her stay away from people who knew her. So they'd never know and Rose's reputation wouldn't be ruined. If people knew, no young gentleman would ever want to marry Rose, and then what would she have done?"

Julie stared at Gertrude. "Who told you that? All that stuff about nobody wanting to marry her?"

"Why . . . Mama did."

"She talked to you about it?"

"Yes."

Julie felt surprised, and then wondered at herself for being surprised. Mama and Gertrude had always spent more time together than Mama had with either Rose or herself.

"Well," she finally said, "I can't sleep here anymore. The head of my bed is against the wall of Rose's room, and I could always hear Rose moving around in there. I could hear her rocking Angela. The chair squeaks just a little. And I could hear her singing lullabies to Angela. I can still hear those sounds, Gertrude."

"Do you think her room is haunted?"

"And then Beulah died in there, just like Angela and Rose did. So, yes, there's something about the room. I don't want to be here anymore."

"You could get another room, Julie Sue! There are lots of empty rooms."

"No. I just have to get away."

"You mean like for the summer? Like going home with Uncle Victor and Auntie?"

"They're gone."

"Then who're you going with? Who's going to take care of you?"

Julie looked down, bit her lip tightly, and then decided she owed it to Gertrude to trust her. "I'm going with Harold. He'll help me until I can get a job. Now I've told you something I wasn't going to tell anyone. That means I trust you more than anyone, Gertrude, now that Rose is gone."

They sat in silence, looking into each other's eyes.

Julie moved, lifting Gertrude by her hands.

"You must go to bed, Gertie," she whispered. "But you must promise me something."

"What?"

"That you will not tell. When Mama asks you where I have gone, you must tell her nothing."

Gertrude continued to stare into her eyes, saying nothing.

"Promise me. It's very important. It might be the very last thing you will ever do for me."

Gertrude's face puckered. "Don't say that."

"It's important, Gertie."

Gertrude nodded. "All right. I promise." She raised her right hand and made a cross over her heart. "Hope to d . . ."

154

Julie walked to the door with her, her arm around Gertrude's shoulders. At the door she hugged her, and then waited until Gertrude had crossed the hall and gone into her own room.

Julie hurried back to the carpetbag, pushed into the corners a handful of combs, pins for her hair and a brush, some handkerchiefs and another pair of stockings. The bag would hold no more. She closed it, snapped its latch, and shoved it under the bed where it should have been when Gertrude came into the room.

She hadn't even wanted Gertrude to know she was leaving. Later, after a couple of weeks, she had planned to write to them and tell them she was fine and would see them again. And even later, after a year or so, she would have come home for a visit. But she didn't think she would ever be able to come back here to live.

She undressed, although she didn't want to. She hung her clothes in the wardrobe as she always did when they weren't put into the laundry, and put on her nightgown. But beneath it she pulled on her corset and her clean stockings and bloomers.

She turned the lamp low and climbed into bed, then lay staring at the ceiling.

It was hours yet before daybreak, but she didn't want to go to sleep. She must be waiting for Harold at the cemetery gate at sunup. As soon as dawn began to break, she would slip into her waist and skirt, get her carpetbag out from beneath the bed and go quietly down the back stairs and out of the house.

Why had he chosen the cemetery gates?

She understood the reason, in one part of her mind. It was close to her house. There was a path through the woods leading right out to the road and along the side of the road past the gate and churchyard. But the fearful part of her mind saw it as an omen.

She was so afraid.

155

There were noises in the house she had never heard before. Her brain felt invaded by a fine, thin sound that was pitched so high it was felt more than heard. It lasted a moment and was mercifully gone. It was replaced by the rocking chair creaking softly and rhythmically, and the faint, lingering strains of a haunting lullaby. The sounds chilled Julie. She pulled up her quilt and curled into it.

She was so very tired suddenly. She closed her eyes, unable to stay awake.

Gertrude lay in bed listening. She heard sounds now, too, like Julie Sue had said she did. There was the slithering movement in the hall, and she was no longer sure it was her mother's soft night garments swaying and brushing the polished floor. She heard the notes of something like a song, and a voice, distant and thin, crying, or perhaps laughing in hysteria. She wished she had told Julie, then maybe Julie wouldn't run away, if she knew someone else heard the sounds and would stay nights with her. The sounds made Gertrude afraid, too, but not so afraid that she would run away from home.

She got out of bed and went to the hall. Julie Sue's door was closed. Closed too was Rose's door. But all along the hall in both directions other doors were open on the spare rooms, and framed darknesses that made Gertrude think of open mouths.

Walking silently Gertrude went along the hall to the balcony, but she stopped at the top of the steps. The foyer below was dark, and the gaslight that burned on the right side of the balcony near her parents' suite of rooms only made the foyer look like a bottomless black pit.

She wanted desperately to go talk to her mother, but was afraid of the black pit, even more than she was afraid of the black mouths.

She hurried back to her room and got into bed and listened for her mother's footsteps.

She listened for Rose's footsteps too, those ghostly movements across the hall in Rose's room, and those steps up and down the stairs to the third floor.

She listened for Julie Sue's footsteps. When was she leaving? In the dark of the night? At midnight or past when the owls screeched in the woods, and the wolves howled far away?

Mama had told her there were no wolves, not anymore. People had killed them because they were afraid of them. But Gertrude could hear howlings that didn't sound like dogs. Especially since Angela died, and Rose, and now Beulah. She could hear those distant howls in the dark of the night, and sometimes they seemed not so distant.

She heard steps in the hall outside her door, and they had the quality of her mother's steps, which always sounded as if she were slipping on tiptoes along the halls. She could hear the rustle of her skirts, the taffeta she wore in the daytime.

The door opened, and her mother came into the room. Smiling, she came toward the bed. Her cool hand touched Gertrude's forehead.

"Are you still awake?" she asked in the whisper she always used at night when she came in to check on Gertrude.

Gertrude nodded.

"It's very late, you know. Past eleven o'clock."

Gertrude saw her mother was not wearing her black taffeta daytime dress, she was wearing a long robe tied at the waist, and her waist looked almost as small as it did when she was wearing her corset.

"Mama, I have something to tell you."

She felt terribly guilty, but it had to be done. Her

157

mother and father had to make Julie Sue stay at home. It was frightening out there in the world. Mama had already told her that. She knew she would never leave.

"Yes, dear, what is it?"

"Julie Sue is going to run away."

Sybil's smile disappeared. She waited a moment before she said, "How do you know this?"

"I went into her room, and I saw her with an old valise from the storage room, and she was putting clothes in it. She said it would be all right, she's going with someone who'll take care of her, but I don't want her to go."

The hand on Gertrude's forehead slid down the side of her face and gently gripped her chin.

"Who, Gertrude? Who's she going with? And when?"

"I promised not to tell."

"That's all right. I'm your mother. You must tell me everything."

Gertrude sighed, then blurted, "Harold. I guess sometime tonight." She felt relieved that she no longer had to keep such a terrible secret. Mama would stop Julie Sue from leaving. And Julie Sue would be glad, someday.

"You're my good girl, Gertrude," Sybil whispered. "You'll always be my good girl, won't you?"

"Yes, Mama."

Sybil leaned down and kissed Gertrude's forehead, and Gertrude felt surprised and pleased. Though her mother hugged her sometimes, and often patted her, she had seldom kissed her.

"Good night, Gertrude. Close your eyes now and go to sleep."

Gertrude closed her eyes.

It was all right now. Mama wouldn't let Julie Sue leave, and someday Julie Sue would forgive her for breaking her promise.

Chapter 17

Julie watched the figure in her frightened, restless dreams. The world she looked down upon, as if she were part of the air, was dark and without form. The figure emerged through the darkness, taking shape only by becoming a thin, tall, darker shape moving upon the night. The figure terrified her, yet she couldn't look away from it. She watched it move through the dark to the grave in the woods, and bend down. When the figure straightened, it was holding the baby from the grave.

No, it wasn't the grave in the woods from which the figure had taken the baby. It was the cradle, in the quiet, dark corner of Rose's room. But it wasn't Rose who had taken baby Angela from the cradle. Where was Rose? She must find her and tell her something terrible was going to happen.

Julie's sleep lightened, and sounds of footsteps entered her awareness. She heard the footsteps in the hall as if they were created in the darkest depths of her brain, as she had never heard them before. The intensity of the sounds, echoing, coming closer and closer, disturbed her sleep but kept her paralyzed in her half-dream state. They came to her room and the door opened.

It was her mother, bringing baby Angela to her bed.

Sybil stood in silence at the side of the bed for a long time, and Julie could hear the short gasping breaths of the baby, but nothing else. Baby Angela was impatient for her mother's breast, but didn't Mama know Julie was not the mother? Rose . . . Rose was dead. That knowledge hit Julie with a newness that caused her to cry out silently in her anguish. Rose was dead. Perhaps that was why Mama was bringing Baby Angela to her for nursing. Julie tried to move, to wake and tell her mother she could not nurse the baby. The baby needed her mother.

Still she couldn't move, or rouse herself from her paralyzing nightmare.

Then Sybil bent down and pulled back the sheet from Julie's chin and laid the baby across her breasts.

Then she was gone, going out the door, closing it in that same slow, soft way. Her footsteps echoed along the hall, and the hems of her taffeta skirts swept the floor, rustling.

Baby Angela lay upon her. Julie could feel the small face turning against her neck. She could hear the infant's breaths, the intake of air, the short sucks of air that Baby Angela always took just before she was given Rose's nipple.

But everything was wrong.

She wasn't the baby's mother. Why had Mama brought the baby to her for nursing? Couldn't she see that Rose was waiting, standing outside the mausoleum with her arms outstretched and her mouth frozen in a silent and endless cry for her baby?

Julie woke slowly, leaving her nightmare with difficulty.

Her room was dark. Even the window was lost in the darkness of the room. Had she only dreamed her mother entered the room and came to her bed? As if to tuck her in. The way she tucked Gertrude in at night.

She became aware that something moved upon her. The darkness in her room was caused by this thing above her eyes. As consciousness cleared, she felt it, the weight of it. She felt its movement as it positioned itself upon her face.

Panic surged into her and she lifted her hands and gripped it. She felt the firm, stuffed body, the hard composition head, the curved arms and legs. She couldn't see, she couldn't breathe. Her body arched as she sought air, as she fought to tear it from her. The thing gripped her face tightly.

"Whatever you do, Julie Sue, don't touch that doll. Let it stay where it is, safe behind them glass doors."

For many years the doll had stayed behind the cabinet doors. Then her mother had given it to Baby Angela, and the baby died. It had been with Rose, and Beulah. Mama knew about the doll. And now Mama had laid it on her chest. It was not a nightmare from Julie's own tortured mind. In her sleep she had known.

Mama! Oh Mama, what have you done?

She couldn't breathe, but the terrible fear, the wild panic, sent her into silent, screaming madness. She stared upward, past the ruffle on the edge of the doll's bonnet, and she heard the suckling sound it made as it drew her life away. But she was powerless to stop it, as she had always been powerless against her mother.

Gertrude heard footsteps in the hall and opened her eyes. It was daylight, and birds sang outside. The lamp on the dresser still burned, and shadows lingered at the end of the dresser. She had slept, but hadn't known it until now. The footsteps she had heard in the dark of the night were just like the footsteps she heard now.

Her mother was there, coming to her room.

No, not to her room. To Julie Sue's, across the hall.

Julie Sue! Had she run away after all? Mama was going to see if Julie Sue had run away.

Gertrude threw her sheet back and ran barefoot to the door and into the hall. It was still dark in the hall, the gaslight made little shadowy darknesses dance behind the chair and table, behind the pictures hanging on the wall.

Julie's door stood half-open, and Gertrude went soundlessly to stand just outside the threshold.

Her mother, still dressed in her nightgown and robe, was

161

leaning over Julie Sue's bed. Beyond her Gertrude could see the bulk of Julie's body on the bed. She was still here. She hadn't run away. Mama had made her stay at home. She was still sleeping, lying very still. She looked long and slight beneath the sheet drawn up over her.

Sybil straightened, and Gertrude saw she had something in her hands. She was holding it out from her, as if she didn't want to touch it.

Gertrude's first joy at seeing that her mother had stopped Julie Sue from leaving evaporated under doubt. Something was wrong with Julie. She was lying too still. Gertrude caught a glimpse of her face and saw it was very white. As white as Rose's face had been, as white as Beulah's. As drained of life and blood as Baby Angela's had been.

Gertrude drew back, pushing up against the end of a glass-fronted bookcase that stood between Rose's closed door, and Julie Sue's door.

She watched her mother come out of Julie's room, and she saw the thing in her hands was the doll. *The old baby doll.*

Gertrude watched as her mother went to the door to the third floor and unbuttoned it, carefully holding the doll away from her. She disappeared into the darkness of the stairway.

Gertrude ran into Julie's room and stood at the side of the bed.

Julie Sue's beautiful dark eyes stared upward at the ceiling. A dark eyelash had fallen to her cheek. It looked long and thin, like a tiny worm. Her mouth was twisted all out of shape. It hung open, the lower lip drawn to one side, as if it had been permanently mashed into that ugly shape.

Gertrude backed away. Julie Sue was dead. She could see it in the way Julie stared upward, in the way the eyelash lay on her white cheek. In the way her mouth twisted.

She wanted to scream and couldn't.

"Gertrude."

Gertrude whirled.

Her mother stood in the doorway, one hand reaching out toward Gertrude.

Chilled and slow with fear, Gertrude went woodenly toward her.

"Go back into your room dear," Sybil said. Her hand on Gertrude's shoulder was cold and heavy. "You're my good girl. You won't ever disappoint mama, will you?"

"No, Mama," Gertrude said, and her voice trembled.

Gertrude moved with stiffness during the days of Julie Sue's wake and funeral. She felt like the puppets that she had gotten for her birthday, dolls made of wood with painted faces and carved limbs, yet her mind wouldn't be still.

She kept going over and over how Mama had stopped loving Rose when she grew up and had Baby Angela, and how she had stopped loving Julie Sue, too, because she was going to run away. And she vowed to herself at night, when she lay stiffly in her bed staring at the walls and thinking about everything, that she would never grow up and have a baby.

She vowed she would never disappoint her mama.

As she had promised she wouldn't.

After the funeral was over and they came home, Gertrude went upstairs to her room.

She sat on her bed, thinking. But now it seemed like her mind was filled with broken pieces of puzzles. All together in one thought was Baby Angela, Rose, Beulah, Julie Sue. And in the center of it all was Mama's old baby doll.

Gertrude slid off the bed, putting her feet, so tightly encased in the black shoes that buttoned high on her ankles, first on the stool at the side of the bed, and then on the braided rug.

She stood up.

163

She tried to separate her thoughts, and could not. But slowly, the doll was pushing away the other images, the faces of Rose, of Rose's baby, even of Julie Sue. Julie Sue who had lain so still and white in her casket, her dark hair fixed in a way Julie had never worn it, smoothed back with none of the curls falling forward. Her forehead had looked like something made of wax, and her dark eyelashes, closed forever, looked like black brushes on her white skin.

That face, so recently seen, was being replaced by the face of the doll. Tiny, ugly, wrinkled in a strange way that wasn't like old wrinkles, but very young wrinkles. A face that hadn't filled out yet. Eyes that were almost closed, puffy with birth. Like Baby Angela's eyes had looked the first time Gertrude saw her.

Gertrude went into the hall and stood for a long while near the door to the third floor. It was closed, the button crossed, locking it.

But she was taller now, and she stretched and her fingertips touched it. She pushed against it and watched it turn. The door swung slowly open.

She entered the dark stairway, and pulled the door closed behind her. It didn't latch. She thought of her mother, and that her mother would be disappointed in her. But her mother was downstairs with all the people who had come home with them from Julie Sue's funeral.

She went up slowly. When she reached the upper hall she stood still. Dust motes danced in the sunlight that fell through the window at the end of the hall, as if there had been movement here.

Yet there was stillness and silence, as if the world outside didn't exist.

She heard her own footsteps as she went down the hall to the china cabinet.

She went down on her knees and stared through the glass.

The baby doll stared back at her, its eyes open and glassy blue. Its face looked rounded, as if it had grown as old as

Baby Angela, and there was color in its cheeks and lips. The corner of its lips turned up slightly, in a kind of strange, secret smile. It wasn't ugly anymore. It had a round, pretty face with glossy skin.

She no longer wanted to touch the doll. She was glad glass separated her from it. A frown of concentration settled on her face as her thoughts grew more fragmented. The doll . . . Angela . . . death . . . Rose . . . the doll . . . death . . . Julie Sue . . . Beulah . . . the doll . . . *death. . . .*

"Gertrude!"

Gertrude cried out in terror and whirled.

Her mother stood at the top of the stairs, her long, black taffeta mourning dress touching the tops of her sharp-toed shoes. Her hair was drawn severely up and smoothed away from her face, the way Julie Sue's had been. Gertrude was more frightened of her mother at that moment than she was of the changing, growing doll.

"Get away from there!" Sybil said through her clenched teeth, her voice angrier than Gertrude had ever heard it. "Don't ever touch that doll!"

Gertrude stood up, and moved away from the china cabinet. But she had a strange feeling all of a sudden that an invisible thread connected her mother to the doll.

She remembered that her mother had not cared when Baby Angela died. Gertrude knew. In her heart she knew. And she had not cared a lot when Rose died, or Julie Sue.

Her mother, and the doll, had in some way caused all the deaths.

But no one must ever know.

Gertrude's voice came out of her throat, surprising her that it wasn't torn and twisted, like the images in her mind.

"No Mama. I'll never touch it."

She offered her hand to her mother, because her mother must never know that Gertrude knew, and together they went down the stairs.

Book Two

The Revival

Chapter 1

1950

I don't want to go in there.

Annie couldn't politely voice her feelings, say aloud how scared she was to go into the shadowed bedroom to see Grandmother Sybil. But when her mother pushed Annie held back. She felt her mother's soft hands enclosing hers as Jenny bent down and whispered to her. But even the closeness of her mother, and her daddy already gone into the room ahead of her, didn't make her feel better.

"You have to, sweetheart. Just this once, I promise you. It's your daddy's mother, your only grandmother. And she wants to see you."

Annie pulled her mother closer and whispered, "Why? She never wanted to see me before." Annie remembered once, when she was about three or four, they had been in town and Aunt Gertrude invited them for Thanksgiving dinner. Grandmother Sybil hadn't even spoken to Annie. And Annie understood that day that they weren't welcome because of her, that Aunt Gertrude hadn't known that Grandmother Sybil did not like Annie. So why did Grandmother Sybil want to see her now?

"Because, Annie," Jenny whispered very softly close to Annie's ear, "Your grandmother is dying."

Mama didn't want Daddy or Aunt Gertrude to hear, Annie thought. They would be sad, because she was their mother. But Annie was afraid. The house was so big and so dark, and the smell was bad.

Annie saw Jenny's profile between her and the high ceiling of this big, shadowed place. Her mother's face was a soft glow of safety in a dangerous world. She had seen Grandmother Sybil, that distant and mysterious person, once before in her eight years, but would never forget it. Grandmother Sybil had sat at the end of the long dining table so straight and stiff, her hair streaked white and brown and puffed up on the top of her head with a jeweled comb at the back. Her face was long, her nose long, her ears long, and her neck long, and when her eyes looked at Annie they shriveled her and made her feel tiny and helpless. Grandmother Sybil didn't seem to have any lips at all, just a line of darkness between her pointed nose and pointed chin. She never smiled.

When Annie later whispered to her mama that Grandmother Sybil looked like a witch, Jenny had clamped her hand over Annie's mouth. But then she laughed. Only it was a very short laugh.

Annie didn't think Grandmother Sybil hated her because of what she had said about her looking like a witch, because they were getting ready to leave then. And her grandmother hadn't liked her the moment she entered the house.

She had thought she would never have to come see Grandmother Sybil again.

Back down the long stairway, where there was a large hall, a picture hung among dozens of others. Daddy, who thought she couldn't remember Grandmother Sybil, had pointed it out to Annie when they first arrived just a short time ago. He told her that was his mother, and her Grandmother. It didn't look like the woman she remembered seeing. In the picture was a pretty woman who resembled Aunt Gertrude, with high cheekbones and a less pointed chin. There was even a smile on her face, just

170

enough to lift her cheeks. Mama said Annie had high cheekbones, too, like her own, but their faces didn't look like Aunt Gertrude's or Grandmother Sybil's.

Annie felt her mother pull slightly, and Annie looked up. Her mother's blue eyes held a sadness that made Annie worry. Was she going to cry? Annie didn't understand. Her mother was usually happy. She didn't want to add to Mama's unhappiness, but she couldn't, go in there where someone was dying.

"Please, Mama, no," she whispered.

Aunt Gertrude stood farther along the balcony, at the door to the room of death. She was waiting for Annie and Jenny.

Jenny put her cheek to Annie's. "Listen," she whispered, her hands cuddling Annie's with a special tenderness. "It would hurt your daddy's feelings if you didn't go in to see Grandmother Sybil. You don't want to hurt his feelings."

"No."

"Then, why can't you go in?"

"Mama . . . she's *dying*. I'm scared of dying."

"Oh. But honey, she isn't dying at this moment. She's living so she can see you. She's very ill, and she can't get up. But she wants very much to see you. That's why we came all the way from Washington, so Daddy could be with his mother, and Grandmother Sybil could see you."

"Why?"

"Because . . . because you're her only grandchild. You're your daddy's child. And he's in there with her, waiting for you."

She began a steady tug on Annie's hand, and Annie moved. She was wearing her prettiest new dress. Her mother had taken her to a store especially to buy this pink dress with the full skirt, the layers of lacy petticoats that held it out like an umbrella around her waist. It felt scratchy, but she didn't want to tell her mother, because she knew Jenny had saved tips from her waitress job for a long time to buy this dress. Annie would rather be wearing her jeans and sweater.

When they reached Aunt Gertrude, the lady smiled down at Annie and laid her hand for a moment on the curls Jenny had so carefully coiled. She bent and whispered, "What pretty hair you have. Just like your mother's."

Annie tried to smile. But through the doors she glimpsed dim figures at a high bed, and smelled a subtle odor that made her feel like she might throw up.

Don't go in there.

The warning was like a whisper in the back of her head. But Aunt Gertrude gently pushed Annie across a small inner hall and into the bedroom on the left.

The lady on the big, high bed looked nothing at all like Aunt Gertrude, or the portrait in the hall of Grandmother Sybil, and very little like the lady she remembered seeing. She didn't even look like a witch anymore. Annie recognized a very sick person, and she was sorry.

Grandmother Sybil's hair was not white, but many shades of grey, and looked as if it had been combed out into a fan around her head. The hair was long, and thin, and fell out of sight over the pillows. In the center was her face, a heap of bones, the eyes so pale and shimmery they looked coated in something slimy. All the flesh had sunk in, so that her face looked more like a skeleton than a real person.

At first Annie felt sorry that she'd ever said Grandmother Sybil looked like a witch, but then those sunken, floating eyes found Annie and stared, and Annie felt the terrible pressure of them. She wanted to extricate herself from Grandmother Sybil's eyes, and was trapped instead.

Annie was so afraid of her she couldn't move on her own. She stood on legs like stumps, unable to go closer even under the gentle push of Aunt Gertrude's hand. She could hardly breathe in the airless warm room where on

172

the hearth a small gas heater spit and burned. Annie felt smothered.

Grandmother Sybil suddenly moved upward. Her head lifted from the large stack of white pillows. Her thin hair pulled from the pillows and streamed forward against her face. From the shadows in the corner came a woman dressed all in white. She adjusted the pillows behind Grandmother Sybil and asked her something Annie couldn't hear.

Grandmother Sybil put out her hand. Annie shrank back and felt someone behind her. Her daddy stood at the foot of the bed, his hands gripping the carved, dark wooden footboard. His head was hanging, and his dark mustache drooped.

Aunt Gertrude moved quickly to the outstretched hand, took it and bent forward to hear Grandmother Sybil's faint voice.

Then Aunt Gertrude asked, "Do you want Annie to come nearer?"

Annie cringed.

"No," Grandmother Sybil said, in a weak, faltering voice. "Just adjust the light so I can see her better."

Aunt Gertrude tilted the shade of the lamp on the bedside table and its light glared full on Annie's face. Annie blinked. She could see the outlines of her grandmother's face beyond the glaring light, but she couldn't see her eyes anymore. Annie looked up from beneath her lowered brow to keep the light from hurting her eyes. She felt abandoned.

Help me. She doesn't like me.

Her plea was silent, to her mother, to her daddy. But neither of them could hear a cry that was only in her heart.

Couldn't they see Grandmother Sybil didn't like her? That her feelings moved like waves of something rotten in the air between the two of them?

173

She wants to kill me. She wants to make me die in her place.

Grandmother Sybil reared up onto an elbow, bringing her face closer to Annie's. Annie pushed back against her mother, and felt her mother's steadying hands on her shoulders. She dropped her chin and stared at her feet, her pretty white slippers and pink stockings.

She heard a long sigh from the bed as Grandmother Sybil sank back. Annie blinked up under her lashes to protect her eyes from the glare of the lamp bulb.

Grandmother Sybil looked at Aunt Gertrude, and back at Annie. But not in the same, glaring way. It was more as if her glance skimmed Annie, and skimmed Aunt Gertrude before her eyes closed. She spoke clearly.

"She's yours now."

Annie had a feeling Grandmother Sybil meant her, somehow, someway, in that short message. As if she were giving Annie to Gertrude.

The room was very still, as if no one breathed. Then Annie heard a long sigh. It ended in a rattle, coming from Grandmother Sybil's chest. She seemed to sink into the featherbed and stacked pillows. Her eyes slipped half-open and stared steadily toward the foot of the bed where Annie's daddy stood.

The silence lasted a long time. Then Aunt Gertrude began to weep.

Annie didn't move. Her daddy straightened, came around the bed and took Aunt Gertrude into his arms. He hugged and patted her shoulder, and his face twisted and tears slipped down his cheeks. He stared at his mother's face sunk into the softness of her pillows.

Annie looked up at Jenny.

"What's wrong?" she whispered.

Jenny stooped and whispered to her as she turned her toward the door and led her out of the room, "Your Grandmother Sybil just passed away, sweetheart."

In the hall, hearing the awful sounds of Aunt Gertrude's

sobs, Annie asked, "Is passed away the same as dying, Mama?"

"Shhh. Be still."

Yet of course Annie knew in her heart what passed away meant. It meant died. And Annie felt the coldness of death within her. She wanted to leave the dark old house, and the smell of death, and go outside into the sunshine. But her mother stood on the balcony, waiting, her warm hand holding hard to Annie's.

Finally the sobs subsided, and Daddy came out of the room and began talking in a low voice to Mama, about the funeral and staying with Aunt Gertrude. Together they all went down the long, curving stairs to the big hall below, and then through double doors to a narrower hall and on back to a big kitchen.

When Daddy began making a phone call to the doctor, Annie wondered if the doctor was going to try to bring Grandmother Sybil back to life.

"Mama . . . ?"

"Shhh."

Annie waited, but she had to know. She tugged on Jenny's sleeve. "But Mama . . . ?"

Jenny looked at her, just as Daddy was hanging up the kitchen wall phone. Even though Annie whispered, her voice seemed to echo in the high ceiling of the kitchen.

"Mama, is the doctor going to bring Grandmother Sybil back to life?"

Her daddy touched her head. "No, baby, that's not possible."

Annie breathed a sigh. Part of the tight, scared feeling went out of her. "Then, can we go home?" Back to Aunt Carol's, because they didn't really have a house of their own yet. But they had been looking for one, and Annie enjoyed looking at the apartments and houses and imagining living in them.

"Not yet. We have to stay with Aunt Gertrude for

awhile." Her dad turned back from looking out the window, and patted Annie's head again. "You just find something to stay quiet with, a book maybe. We won't be leaving for several days."

Annie saw the look that passed between her mother and father, over her head. She didn't understand. There were a lot of things she didn't understand.

"Daddy, what did she mean when she said to Aunt Gertrude, she's yours now? Did she mean me?"

"Of course she didn't mean you, sweetheart. You're ours. I don't know what she meant. Why don't you go outside and look around? But stay out of the driveway. The doctor and somebody from the funeral home will be here soon."

He helped her into her coat, and kissed her cheek.

Annie obediently went to the back door and across the porch. Leading off the porch were old steps made of wood, and they creaked when she stepped on them. She went down into the backyard and found a spot of sunshine.

"She's yours now."

Not even Daddy knew what Grandmother Sybil meant, but it seemed she had meant her, because she had been looking at her. Grandmother Sybil had been talking about her, she knew, in some way. And even though she was outside the huge house, still she felt afraid. Would her mama and daddy go away and leave her with Aunt Gertrude?

She stared into the dark trees at the back of the house, and pulled her coat closer against the chill of the winter day.

Daddy had said they would never leave her, but she was afraid she would die here too, in this big house, just like Grandmother Sybil had.

Chapter 2

Gertrude slept restlessly, turning in her bed, waking with an anxious, frightened start. She rearranged her pillows to lift her head higher, and tried to go back to sleep, but drifted with the vague, undefined sense of terror that had lived with her most of her life.

The body of her mother had been removed from the house, and the funeral was over, but in the nights since her death Gertrude felt as if Sybil were still in the room on the other side of the connecting hall. Often she'd rise out of a deep sleep with that awful pounding of anxiety, and have her feet on the floor before she remembered her mother no longer needed her.

Sometimes she wept.

She lay tense staring up at the dark ceiling and thought of living alone in this huge old house. She couldn't do it. Ted had brought a comfort into the house she hadn't known since the night he left to marry Jenny. Little Annie was precious, the child Gertrude had never had. A lovely little girl, her niece. The years were gone now, but still she felt a deep sadness for all she had missed. All Sybil had missed in never knowing her grandchild.

The night Ted told Mama he was marrying Jenny returned, as it had almost daily in the past nine years. Sybil, who had seemed literally to worship the son who was her change of life baby, born when she was forty-five, had turned to stone when Teddy brought her the news.

"Of course you won't marry that girl."

"And what in the hell is wrong with Jenny?"

Gertrude stood in the hall outside the library doors, her hands tightly clenched, knowing she should not eavesdrop. But she couldn't move. Jenny had moved to a room in the servants' quarter when her daddy died. She was sixteen. Two years earlier, before Jenny's mother went away with another man and took Jenny's sister, Carol, with her, Sybil had hired Jenny to help with the cleaning once a month. The money was running out, and they couldn't afford help more often. Gertrude did the laundry, and most of the cooking and cleaning. She liked Jenny. She was a very pretty girl with a wide face and large, luminous eyes like deep water that reflected the distant blue of the sky. She didn't look like Julie Sue, but with Jenny in the house, it was almost like having Julie back again. Jenny sang when she worked, and laughed a lot, and to Gertrude's surprise Sybil didn't stop her. She had a liveliness about her that was much like Julie Sue.

Gertrude had seen Ted looking at her as Jenny grew taller, more fully developed. And she had seen the nervous excitement Jenny displayed when Ted came around. It was no surprise to her when Ted began dating Jenny. On her twentieth birthday, he had given her an engagement ring.

Up until then Sybil had said nothing. Ted had dated a lot of girls. Through it all Sybil had humored him. Ted didn't have to dig in and try to keep the money from going down the drain. He wasn't interested in following in their father's footsteps and becoming an attorney. After being in and out of college for a few years, he had worked here, worked there. Couldn't Mama see that Jenny might be the stablizing influence Ted needed? Did she want him to be a bum all his life? Chasing off on a whim to God knew where, showing up three months later, happy and carefree and with no responsibilities? At

178

age twenty-six he had finally stopped chasing and had decided to marry Jenny. And Gertrude had thought all was well. But the voices in the library shocked and disappointed Gertrude.

"Jenny, in case you've forgotten, Ted," Sybil said in that voice made of rock that Gertrude had never heard her use with Ted before, "*works* for us. She is hired help. In my father's day we would have called her a servant."

"So what the hell difference does that make? You ought to be used to having her around then. Having her live here shouldn't bother you so much. You've known the girl for six years, and lived with her for four!"

"*Live here?*"

"Certainly! Where else? This is my home, isn't it? You've got room for me and Jenny, and our kids."

"Kids!" Sybil spat the word as if he'd said *worms,* or some other such loathsome creatures.

Gertrude held her breath, fearing her mother might have a stroke. Her health had been deteriorating lately. When Sybil climbed the stairs she had to stop and rest. Often, Gertrude had gone up to help her mother. Hadn't she always helped her mother, been here for her, always, denying herself a life apart from her mother?

"Yeah, Christ, Mom, you don't think I want to die without having a kid, do you? You didn't think I'd be like poor old Gertie and just be here, a permanent kid all my life?"

Hearing what her younger brother thought of her made Gertrude feel as if she had been stepped on and ground into the earth. But he was right, she had continued to live the life of a daughter and nothing more, even at age forty-one. She was fifteen when he was born. A sober, quiet girl who didn't have any friends, she was delighted to have a baby brother. At first she had been so afraid, so afraid, because death had seemed such a close com-

179

panion, taking away Rose's baby, Rose, Julie, and her beloved Beulah. But he had grown and thrived, and she, with her mother and father, adored him.

Sybil asked, "Is she . . . ?"

"No, she's not. Yet. I have more love and respect for her than that. But I plan to get her that way as fast as I can as soon as we're married."

"Oh Lord."

Gertrude started to knock on the door. Her mother's voice had sounded as if she were going to faint. But then Sybil was talking again, and her voice was strong and commanding, a strength drawn from somewhere in the past. Gertrude felt ten years old again as she stood with her hand on the knob listening.

"We'll talk about this tomorrow, Ted. After a good night's sleep. Come along, dear."

Gertrude heard their footsteps and pushed back into the shadows at the end of the hall. They came out of the library, Ted holding Sybil's arm gently. As they went up the stairs, Gertrude could hear her mother's voice, talking of something that had happened at church, as if the conversation about Ted marrying Jenny had never occurred. Gertrude stood with her hands behind her, pressed flat against the wall. She became aware of her trembling, and of the slipping back into the past when one early morning she had stood in Julie Sue's doorway and saw that she would never rise from her bed, that she would not run away from home, ever. She saw her mother straighten from bending over Julie Sue and come toward her. She was holding something in her hands, but Gertrude couldn't remember what it was. Something . . . her mother had used to stop Julie from leaving home.

The house had grown silent around Gertrude. Ted had not come back downstairs.

Gertrude went toward the stairs. The old gaslight was still on the wall, but the balcony above was lighted by electric wall lights. The one by her mother's suite had been turned off.

She climbed the stairs and went down the hall to Ted's room. His door was closed. Gertrude knocked softly, two taps. She looked over her shoulder toward the balcony, but her mother didn't appear.

"Yeah?" Ted answered.

Gertrude opened the door. Ted had not changed from his trousers and shirt, but he was lying on his bed, his arms beneath his head. He stared at her, then sat up.

"What's wrong, Gertie?"

"Ted, you must leave. Take Jenny, and go."

"I plan to. If Mother doesn't change her mind, I'm out of here tomorrow."

"No, I mean go tonight, Ted."

The barest suggestion of a frown settled on Ted's face. His stare didn't waver. "What's wrong, Gertie?"

She couldn't tell him, there will be no tomorrow. There was no tomorrow for Julie Sue, and there won't be a tomorrow for you and Jenny. It would mean explaining things she didn't understand and couldn't explain.

"She's going to stop you, Ted. Please go, tonight. Don't sleep in this house tonight. Get Jenny and go. Mama won't change her mind."

He smiled and leaped off the bed, suddenly exuberant with life. He was the old Teddy, her beloved little brother. It made her happy to see him happy. He came to her, kissed her cheek.

"Okay, you've convinced me. I'm gone. Tell Mother I love her, anyway, even though I don't trust her!"

Jenny and Ted left that night and never came back.

The house grew large and silent around Gertrude, like a terrible tomb. The dust gathered. She had never handled the money and she knew very little about her mother's circumstances. But each week Sybil gave Gertrude a check which she took to the bank and withdrew household money. And gradually the size of the check decreased, while the estate's shrubbery increased and grew wild.

No word came from Ted, or Jenny, not even a Christmas card. Gertrude didn't even know where they lived. World War Two seemed to linger forever, and Gertrude prayed nightly that Ted would survive it. An army camp went up not far away, and men in uniform were a more common sight around town than men in business suits or work clothes.

The war ended.

One windy day in November Gertrude was in the supermarket when she met Ted and Jenny face to face in an aisle.

She stared at them, and they at her. In the grocery cart seat was a little doll of a girl with pale silky hair and the same large luminous eyes that had been Jenny's best feature. She was three or four years old. Her lovely blue eyes stared at Gertrude even before Gertrude spoke, as if the child had a premonition.

"Gertie!" Ted cried, and his face turned on that old light that Gertrude remembered.

He stepped around the cart and grabbed her up in a hug. Then Jenny hugged her, and Gertrude held the precious baby and kissed her soft, smooth cheek. She hadn't kissed a baby's cheek since Ted was a baby, and the weight of the child in her arms brought a pain to her heart that was born both of happiness and sadness. She could hardly hold back the tears.

They all talked at once.

"Where have you been? How old is she? What's her name? Where do you live?"

"How've you been, Gertie? How's Mom? Is she still angry?"

"She's fine. All's well. Why haven't we heard from you?"

Jenny said, "Ted was in the war, and the baby and I've been living in various army camps, mostly. We've been all over. California, Texas, Washington, Alaska, Florida."

"My mother went to Washington, when she took Carol and left Dad. She's dead now, but my sister married and lives in Spokane. That's sort of our home base. But Ted wanted to come home this fall, now that he's out of the army and free to roam."

"There's no place like Arkansas. It's great to be home." Ted squeezed Gertrude around the waist.

Gertrude invited them out to Thanksgiving dinner. Surely Mama wouldn't mind now that Ted had married Jenny, and there was a child. If she saw Annie, she would adore her.

Happily Gertrude spent an extra ten dollars and bought a small turkey. It would be the first Thanksgiving dinner she had cooked since Teddy left home. "Don't bother," Sybil always said before. "Don't bother, just for us. We don't need the meat anyway."

She didn't tell Sybil that Teddy and his little family were coming for dinner. On Thanksgiving morning she had hummed as she stuffed the bird and put it into the oven. Sybil didn't come into the kitchen until she smelled it cooking, and then she came leaning on her cane, and looking with suspicion at Gertrude.

"Something's not quite right around here. What is it?"

"Oh, Mama!" She almost giggled. She was happy, yet she was so nervous her hands were shaking uncontrollably. She was afraid to tell her mother.

"Don't tell me you're in love, after all these years," Sybil said, and there came a tiny smile on her thin, stiff lips.

Gertrude's eyes filled with tears. She couldn't stop them. Her whole body began to tremble. She had never even had a date. She had stayed close to her mother's side because . . . because . . .

She couldn't remember anymore. It had something to

183

do with Rose, she remembered, and with Julie Sue. And with the baby that was buried in the woods. But she didn't want to remember.

"It's Teddy, Mama! I saw him in town and I asked him to come to Thanksgiving dinner."

Sybil stared at her, and leaned more heavily on the cane.

"He's come home?" Sybil said. "After all this time? He's never been away so long before, Gertrude."

"I know that, Mama. You don't mind that I asked him for dinner, do you?" Why couldn't she say *them?* Sybil had to know he would not be alone.

"Mind?" Sybil smiled again. "It's about time he came back! Do you have his room ready? Fresh linens on the bed, towels on the rack. He always used so many towels when he bathed. It's about time he came home!"

When she left the room she walked straighter and stronger. Hope actually could make the frail stronger, Gertrude saw.

During the rest of the meal preparation Gertrude's hands shook. What would their mother do when she saw Jenny and Annie? Would she fall in love with Annie the way Gertrude had?

Baby Angela's hair had been softly fair, and her face round and pretty. She was developing an intense interest in life, her eyes watching with curiosity every movement. Baby Angela had died. But that was all so long ago. She had made herself forget. She must not start remembering now.

Gertrude was glad Ted didn't arrive until the table was set and Sybil was already at her place. She had set three places, but the two extra plates and silverware were waiting on the sideboard. She hoped Sybil wouldn't notice.

When the doorbell rang Sybil sat back in her chair, her eyes on the dining room door. "Well, bring him in, Gertrude."

Gertrude hurried to answer the bell.

Jenny was lovely in a pale blue suit, and Annie, who Gertrude now knew was three years old, was dressed in a blue and white dress with the full ruffled skirt held out by layers of white petticoats. Ted's face had lost its happy eagerness, and he looked as scared as Gertrude felt.

Gertrude led the way, little Annie in her arms.

The look on Sybil's face cut them down, held them in the doorway of the dining room. Her cheeks turned alabaster white, her lips tightened until all color was gone. She stared at the four of them, her glance ripping through them, again and again.

Then she lifted her chin, and said, "Well, sit down. I see Gertrude has brought in plates for all of you."

The ice was only partly broken.

It was the most strained dinner Gertrude had ever sat through. Sybil said nothing more. Annie didn't make a sound. Jenny spoke only occasionally, and long silences crept in between Ted and Gertrude's attempt to have a conversation. After dinner Sybil rose, said, "It was nice seeing you. Do come again." And then excused herself.

Ted, his face white, took Jenny and Annie and left immediately afterwards.

Gertrude was afraid she would never see them again. She stood on the front walk and watched them drive away, and the sickness of spirit that overcame her and sent her back into the house reminded her of her dark months after Julie Sue died.

During the next four years Ted's name was not mentioned. Gertrude went weekly to the supermarket, but little Annie's face was never there, except in glimpses of other children who resembled her.

Sybil was no longer able to leave her bed, and finally, as Gertrude sat beside her and the night grew still and dark around them, Sybil spoke.

"Bring them to me," she said.

Startled, Gertrude sat forward. The cushion she'd been resting her head on fell into the chair at her back.

"What?" she said. Then, "Are you all right, Mama?"

"Listen to me. I want to see her."

"Who?"

But in her heart she knew. *Annie.*

"The child. Bring her here. Bring them all. I'm dying, Gertrude. My last wish is to see that you're taken care of."

For a moment Gertrude couldn't speak. "My last wish is to see that you're taken care of." What did her mother mean by that? Did she mean to give her family, someone to be with her, to care about her?

"Have them come home. I want to see her. The child."

"Yes Mother! Except, I don't know where they are."

Her mother lay back, exhausted. Her breathing rasped.

"Shall I call the doctor, Mama?" Gertrude asked frantically. She was terrified of losing her, of being left in the world alone.

"No," Sybil whispered. "Call . . . Jenny's . . . sister."

Gertrude rushed to the telephone in the kitchen, the only telephone in the house now that they had been forced to economize. She struggled to remember what Jenny had said Carol's married name was, and failed. Then she remembered that Jenny had distant relatives not far away, and called them. As it happened, one of them still communicated with Carol at Christmas, and had her telephone number. Gertrude placed the call.

A female voice that sounded nothing like Jenny said, "They aren't here now, but I'll give them the message."

Gertrude went back to her mother's bedside. Climbing the stairs that night was a long, lonely way. There was little hope in her heart, but she couldn't take that message to her mother.

"They'll be here soon, Mama," Gertrude said, settling in her chair to wait for her mother's death. Perhaps the

186

hope of seeing them, and closing the long gap that separated them, would keep her mother alive.

She sat in the chair, unable to sleep, through the rest of the night, the next day, the next night. She left only to do what she had to do.

Then, to her utter delight and surprise she answered the doorbell and they were there, on her doorstep. Ted. Jenny. *Annie*. The little girl still looked much as she had five years ago, only larger, taller. Her eyes still were luminous and wide. She hung back with shyness.

Gertrude brought then in and guided them upstairs, as if they had forgotten the way. A nurse had been sent to help the last time the doctor visited, and Gertrude felt more free to take her time. She went into the room while Ted and his family waited in the hall and told her mother.

"They're here, Mama."

She moved only her head in a slight nod. Gertrude returned to the balcony and Ted went into the bedroom. Gertrude wanted to hug Annie to her, but she kept her distance. The child was terrified.

Poor little mite. Gertrude ached to ease her fear, but didn't know how. Gertrude had a terrible feeling that Annie was afraid of her, too. *Her*, who wouldn't hurt a mouse.

Tears eased from Gertrude's eyes as she lay in the softness of the bed, unable again to sleep. Life had a way of replacing. Her mother was gone, but Teddy, Jenny and Annie were here. And God willing, they would stay.

Chapter 3

"Ted, we're not going to be living here!" Jenny whispered against his face as she snuggled toward him in the bed.

"Sure, it's half ours, and Gertie wants us to stay. Finally you have a house of your own, Jen."

"Couldn't we take your part of the inheritance and go buy a small house? Just a cottage. Two bedrooms is all we need. And a small kitchen. The dinette could be in the kitchen. We could have a fenced backyard, and in one corner we could grow vegetables. And we could have a flower garden. Annie would love that. And we could get her a puppy and a kit—"

"You're dreaming, Jen."

"But why?" she cried. "If you want your sister to live with us, we could get three bedrooms, or even four—"

"Jen," his hand felt for hers and clasped it so tight her wedding ring hurt her finger. "Jen, there's no money. Just the house and an allowance from a small trust. And that is Gertrude's, to keep the house running."

Disappointment hit her with its usual heavy fist, right in the pit of her stomach. That fist was getting harder to take in recent years. She should have grown used to disappointments by now, but each one only made her more vulnerable.

She had never liked this big old house. When she had first come here to work at age fourteen, she had been terrified. But she needed the job. Her mother and dad

188

had separated, after years of hard times. She had wanted to go with Mom and Carol, but she didn't think it was right that her mother went off with another man, and she couldn't bring herself to leave Pop alone. But his ability to work and bring home money had gotten worse, and he spent even more of it on booze. So she had gone to the big house she passed every morning on her way to school and gotten nerve somehow to ask for a job. If she wanted any school clothes at all, she had to earn the money for them.

Being in the upper part of the house to dust and sweep in those days, always feeling as if something were watching her, always feeling a need to look over her shoulder, was exactly the way she felt now. Even though she was closed into a bedroom with Ted, warm and snug in a big, soft mattress, she still felt that old nervousness. She couldn't believe her mother-in-law had really meant for her to live here, even though her will had left half of the property to Ted. And as Ted's wife, Jenny inherited also. If Miss Sybil wouldn't even allow her to enter the house after her marriage to her son, why on earth would she want her to share it now as a home?

"Ted?"

But Ted didn't answer, and she heard him breathing deeply and slowly. He had gone to sleep.

Jenny lay still for a while longer, then she slipped out of bed and went barefoot to the door. She remembered how some of the doors used to creak and squeak when they were moved. But tonight this door was silent.

In the hall she found total darkness. Not even a light from a window helped orient her. If this was going to be her home, she'd damn well fix that. She didn't like darkness.

With her hand trailing along the wall she felt her way toward Annie's room. They had put her next door, on the same side of the hall.

189

From out of the darkness a voice said, "Who's there?"

That harsh voice, loud in the stillness, came at Jenny from all directions.

A light came on suddenly in the hallway from a bulb overhead. Jenny blinked and stared. The woman who had turned it on stood several yards away, where the three steps dropped down to the balcony. She was wearing a long white nightgown that covered her from her neck to her wrists and fell to the floor, and on her head she wore a nightcap. The face was Sybil's, as she had looked when Jenny came to work so long ago.

Then the face smiled. She looked as relieved as Jenny felt.

"Oh. Jenny. Lord, girl you scared me."

Jenny went toward Gertrude. She had never disliked Gertrude, although she had always felt intimidated by her. But her obvious affection for Annie brought out another part of her personality that was less intimidating.

"I'm sorry," Jenny said. "I was just going in to see about Annie."

"And so was I," Gertrude said. "It just occurred to me that Annie didn't have any light in her room and she might want one. I have a small lamp here."

She was carrying a tiny blue lamp Jenny hadn't seen before.

"They burn one of those little four watt bulbs. If it's all right with you, I'll take it in and tell her good night again."

"Sure," Jenny said, though she had wanted to hug her daughter one more time herself. She backed up instead toward her own room.

She left the hall door open, following the slanting trail of light from the door to her side of the bed. Jenny heard the murmur of voices in the next room. Gertrude's, and Annie's answering.

Jenny lay staring at the ceiling until the light was

190

turned out again. Even in the dark her eyes retained the image of falling ceiling paper, hanging down several inches in places.

The house had deteriorated markedly in the past nine years. Wallpaper had loosened, wood had darkened. The rugs looked old and dark and threadbare.

If she had to live here, she was going to repaper and paint if she could find any money to do it with.

Gertrude turned in her bed. The feathers had knotted beneath her and she was sorry she had tried to use the old featherbed. What had there been about her mother's death that she thought her old featherbed could help?

She reached for her lamp and turned it on, then got up and remade her bed, dragging off the featherbed and replacing the sheets on the mattress. She dragged the featherbed over to the corner and left it.

"Until morning," she whispered, as if she still needed to explain her every movement to someone.

She went back to bed and turned out her light. She didn't mind darkness now, but when she was Annie's age there had been times when she appreciated having a nightlight.

The thought of the little girl over in the bedroom wing gave her a feeling of both happiness and anxiety. She wanted so desperately for Ted and Jenny to stay. She had even offered to turn over all of the trust fund money to Ted if he would promise to stay.

"Gertie, I can't do that," he said, his hand warm on her shoulder. "That part is specifically yours."

They had just come out of the attorney's office after the reading of the will. She was delighted the house and land were half his, but she was willing to give him the money, too, if he would just stay. She couldn't face going back out to the old house alone.

"I can get a job of some kind," she said.

"No, the money's yours. It's to take care of your needs. I'll get a job, Gertie. I'll look around and see what's available in a few days. But we're not leaving. I planned all the time to move in on you if you think you can stand us."

"Oh, Teddy, are you sure?" Her relief was the deepest emotion she had ever felt, other than fear.

"I'm sure."

"What about Jenny?" She felt guilty for being so selfishly happy. A young woman would want her own house.

"I'm keeping her. We ought to be able to find enough room for her, too."

They laughed. It was the first time they had laughed together in many years.

"I mean, do you think she'll want to live there? After the way Mama treated her and Annie?"

He shrugged. "Why not?"

But in the dark of her room Gertrude felt anxious and uneasy. She could see that Jenny didn't feel at home. She had moved about in the house like a servant or an awkward guest.

Time, she thought. Maybe time would take care of that.

She closed her eyes, and for a long time small lights danced in the darkness behind her eyelids.

Then she was seeing long tunnels of darkness and at the end of the tunnel something was moving. Gertrude felt the cold terror of déjà vu, though she didn't understand. She knew she had been here before, in this tunnel, and that figure had come toward her. Or was it a hallway? And the figure was . . .

She tried to see through the darkness. A misty grey light was beginning to fill the tunnel. She was in a very long hall. And the small figure at the other end was a child. No, not a child, but something resembling a child, a baby. It was crawling toward her. She wanted to turn and run, but she couldn't move.

Abruptly it was closer and she saw through the dim light that it was the old baby doll. Somehow it had gotten out of the cabinet and it was waiting for her to come to it. It had risen from its belly to its hands and knees, and it looked large and threatening. She tried to run from it, but the distance between them kept diminishing.

Gertrude woke, her heart pounding.

She groped for her lamp, and touched nothing. In horror she realized she was not even in her bed, she was standing, her bare feet on a cold wood floor.

A dim light revealed a window not far from her, and moonlight suddenly broke through clouds and fell across her feet, and shone through the glass of the china cabinet.

Moonlight touched the features of an infant, enclosed within the glass of the cabinet near her feet. She stared in horror at the small face.

She was in the third floor hall, within reach of the cabinet that held the old baby doll.

She stumbled away, and tripped over her long gown. Falling, she threw out her arms. She went down on one knee, then hurriedly pulled herself up. Behind her the glass door swung slowly open, and the baby doll turned and started crawling toward her.

She didn't want to look back, but couldn't stop herself.

She stared. The door hadn't opened after all. It was still closed, and the doll was still lying on its back.

Gertrude ran, the bottom of her long gown gathered up into her hands. In the hall below she turned the latch on the stairway door and leaned for a moment getting her breath. Then she went down the hall, pausing at Annie's door.

She opened it and looked in, then went in to stand by the child's bed.

She longed to touch her, to lean down and put her lips against the softness of the young cheek, but she was afraid it would scare her.

"God keep her safe," she whispered.

Chapter 4

Annie lay very still. At first she thought the figure bending over her was Grandmother Sybil. Feeble light from the little blue lamp on the dresser outlined the woman and made her look like a ghost. Annie would have screamed but she couldn't move or speak.

Then she heard a whisper. It sounded like, *God keep her safe,* but she wasn't sure. Warm breath touched her forehead. Annie cringed inwardly even as she recognized her visitor.

Aunt Gertrude. Knowing her visitor wasn't the ghost of Grandmother Sybil didn't take away Annie's fear. Why had Aunt Gertrude slipped like a ghost back into her room? She had already told Annie good night. She had brought the little blue lamp and kissed Annie on the forehead. So why had she come back, now, after Annie had been asleep a long time?

She closed her eyes and hoped Aunt Gertrude wouldn't notice that she had woke. The tall woman in white lingered at the side of her bed, not moving, for what seemed to Annie a long time.

Finally, she walked away, and Annie peeked out from beneath her lashes.

She was glad Aunt Gertrude was gone, even though she was very nice. Now that Mama and Daddy had both promised they weren't going to give her away to Aunt Gertrude, Annie didn't mind being here. She remembered what Daddy said, "When I was a little boy, I thought the house went on forever. There were so many rooms to have fun in, and I was all over every one of them," and it made her feel more at ease.

She turned over and got comfortable on her side, and reminded herself that Mama and Daddy were close.

"We're right here, through the wall," Mama had said at bedtime when she and Daddy left Annie in the room alone that first night after Grandmother died. "You don't have to be afraid."

"Why on earth would she be afraid?" Daddy asked Mama, frowning at her. "There's nothing to be afraid of. I grew up in this house, remember? My room was just down the hall. Remind me to show it to you, Annie. I'll bet you all my old trophies are still there, right where I left them."

It comforted her to remember that her daddy was a little boy in this house. It helped take away the fear, just knowing that.

Yet she lay facing the door, afraid to close her eyes. She stared at the door until it blurred and blended into part of a strange scene.

She was looking through a very dim light, and could barely see the figure in bed at first. Then she saw the skeleton where the face once had been, and the hair that reached out from it like thin wires, or very long, slender worms. No, not a skeleton, but a person. A real person, her head lifted by fat pillows. The eyes were alive and burning at her. She couldn't get away from the eyes.

"She's yours now," a wispy, low voice said.

Annie pulled the covers over her head and squeezed her eyes to shut out the vision. She didn't want to have bad dreams or thoughts about her Grandmother Sybil, but sometimes they entered her head and wouldn't go away.

* * *

196

"This I won bowling," her daddy said. "And this is a Boy Scout trophy."

Annie had never seen anything so pretty. "Is it real gold?" she asked. They were in his old bedroom.

"I used to think it was gold." He leaned down and gave her a prod with his elbow. "But gold doesn't tarnish, eh?"

"Sure it does. My friend, Betsy, you know, back in school in Oregon? She had a gold ring, real gold, and it turned black and made her finger green."

"Wow, what a combination of colors. Do you suppose she only thought it was real gold?"

Annie giggled. She remembered she'd had some doubts, even back when she was six years old and pretty dumb.

"How about going outside now?" Daddy asked.

"Okay."

When they went into the hall they heard a long ripping sound.

"Sounds like your mom's up to something. Let's see what it is."

They went along the hall to Annie's room, and there was her mother, wearing her old jeans, standing on a board that reached between two tall ladders and ripping down old ceiling paper.

"Ye Gods, woman, what are you doing?" Ted asked.

Jenny looked down at them, and Annie laughed. Her face was speckled with black.

"I'm going to repaper Annie's room."

"I thought you had gone shopping with Gertrude."

"Well, we're back. We picked out the prettiest paper. It's still downstairs. Go down and see it, Annie." She climbed down one of the ladders and pushed Annie and her daddy out of the room. "And stay out of here."

"You're going to kill yourself when you fall off that scaffold of yours."

"No, I won't. Get."

She closed the door and left them in the hall. But Annie was worried now.

"Daddy . . . ?"

He rubbed her shoulder and then dropped his arm in a loose embrace around her neck. "Aw, it's okay, pudding pie. Your mom's pretty agile. And remember, she worked for awhile with some paperhangers back in Nevada. She knows what she's doing.

They went down the long hallway to the front of the house where the balcony encircled the open area above the foyer. Three steps led from the hall down to the balcony. Annie could see the open door into the suite where Grandmother Sybil died.

"Daddy, where does Aunt Gertrude sleep?"

"I don't know anymore, pudding. I think she took the room next to my mother's, so she could be near her. It used to be my father's room."

"Where is your father?"

"He died years ago, when I was still a little boy. I was younger than you are."

She thought of being without her daddy, and reached out her hand for him. The warmth of his hand around hers only barely comforted her.

"Daddy, you're not going to die, are you?"

"Hey, you better believe I'm not! I'm here forever, just like you."

She looked up into his face, and saw the sparkle in his eyes and the wiggle of his mustache and eyebrows. He could make her laugh and forget all her worries.

In the kitchen they found Aunt Gertrude baking something that smelled really good. She was wearing an apron over her dress. There was a smile on her face as she leaned down to be on level with Annie, but Annie involuntarily drew back against her daddy. Aunt Gertrude didn't seem to notice.

"What's your favorite dessert, sweetheart?"

198

"I don't know."

"What? You don't know? What goes best with ice cream?"

Annie twisted uncomfortably. What did Aunt Gertrude want her to say? "Everything," she said, and Aunt Gertrude laughed and went back to cleaning flour off the cook table.

"I think you're going to be easy to please, Annie."

Ted sniffed the air. "Smells like cake baking."

"What flavor do you think it is?" Gertrude asked Annie. "It's especially for you, and for your mommy and daddy. I remember how Teddy used to like this flavor, so we won't let him guess."

"Chocolate!" Annie said. She knew Daddy's favorite cake.

Aunt Gertrude laughed again. She sounded so delighted that Annie laughed, too.

"Not only chocolate, but chocolate fudge. Which means very dark chocolate. Do you like chocolate, Annie?"

"Oh yes."

"Well, you come back to the kitchen in about thirty minutes and I'll let you lick the frosting pan."

"We'll be back," Daddy said. "Won't we Annie?"

As they went out onto the porch Annie kept looking at her daddy. There was something different about him, but at first she couldn't figure out what it was. They went down the steps and across the yard, and stopped beneath a big tree where a swing hung from one of the lower limbs.

Then she knew what it was about her daddy. It was the look in his eyes, the near smile that came often to his face. He was glad to be back to his home.

Maybe that was why they had never bought a house, or stayed in one place very long, as Mama had talked about doing. Because Daddy wanted in his heart to come home.

199

Jenny tore the old curtains down. They were dusty and rotten, and came apart in her hands. Breathing this dusty stuff would probably give Annie pneumonia.

She struggled to push up the window and finally heard it break loose from the frame. Pushing and straining, she opened it a couple of inches. The air that came through was cold, but at least it was fresh air.

She didn't have curtains for the window yet. First she'd have to finish papering the ceiling, which was very difficult. The ceiling was high, and she'd had to fix a makeshift scaffold. A couple of tall stepladders Gertrude had helped her bring upstairs, with a board across the tops. Meantime, she had moved Annie across the hall to another dreary old room.

There were times when she felt a little angry that Ted didn't help her. He was back to being a child with Annie, it seemed. Well, she loved him sometimes as if he were an older child. She'd give him a chance to be a boy again, then he'd have to go look for work. She didn't know exactly what the monthly income was, but whatever it was belonged to Gertrude, and she and Ted needed money of their own.

If she couldn't get him to move, she at least could get him to look for work. He had never been lazy, just mostly hard to please. He had worked at everything from construction to sales, and not long at any of it. They had never settled long enough even to lease a house. They were lucky to rent from month to month. And every few months they had gone home to spend a few days with Carol and her husband before they had taken off again.

Jenny couldn't really say she had hated the life. She had looked forward to new places, too. It had been more difficult when Annie got old enough to go to school.

Which reminded her. Annie had to be enrolled in

school. The school she had gone to had been enlarged and modernized, and Gertrude had mentioned that a couple of new schools had been built.

As far as work went, she might be able to find herself a job. She could clean houses and work in cafes at anything from cooking and cleaning to doing waitress work. Gertrude would probably not mind watching Annie after school, taking care of her while Jenny worked.

But first she wanted to fix Annie's room really pretty. A pretty bedroom all her own was something Jenny had wanted desperately when she was a child. She hadn't had one, and Annie hadn't either, yet. But soon she would. The paper she and Gertrude chose had little blue birds and pink daisies on a white background, and she would get ruffled curtains and a pink bedspread. It would be the kind of bedroom she had once dreamed of.

Chapter 5

Annie sat in the big library with her daddy, her elbow on his thigh just above the open picture album.

Another day had passed since Grandmother Sybil's funeral, and still Daddy hadn't made Annie go to school. Next Monday he would enroll her, he had told Mama this morning. Next Monday's soon enough. Annie counted on her fingers the days she had left before that frightening experience of going to a new school, and it was . . . five, six if she counted today. Grandmother Sybil's funeral was last week, and Mama had wanted Annie to go to school this Monday, but the day had passed and she didn't have to go.

Next Monday. Her stomach tightened into a sick knot just thinking about it. Remembering other schools she had gone to only made it worse. She hardly ever stayed long enough to make friends. Only that once in Oregon.

Her daddy's words filtered through her worries.

". . . sisters. Rose and Julie Sue . . ."

She leaned closer and looked at the photograph in the middle of the page. It was larger than most of the others, and pasted on thick cardboard that was black and trimmed in those squiggly little vine-like lines. These were gold. But the girls in the pictures seemed to stand out because of what her daddy had called them. Sisters. She didn't know he had anyone but Aunt Gertrude.

In the picture were three girls. Two of them grown-up,

and one only about nine or ten. The little one had light hair pulled back from her stern face. A few little ringlets edged her wide, high forehead. Another girl, with light hair in a pompadour with curls hanging by her ears as well as on her forehead, was sitting in a chair. She wasn't smiling either.

But the one standing up, with her hand on the back of the tall chair, was smiling. Just a little, just enough to show a dimple. Her hair was dark, and her face was beautiful.

"*Whose* sisters?" Annie demanded.

"Mine."

"Yours?" Annie looked for Aunt Gertrude, and decided she must be the youngest of the three. Yes, now that she really looked at her, that was Aunt Gertrude.

"How old was Aunt Gertrude?" Annie put the tip of her right index finger on the photo, gently.

"She was about ten then, I guess, or nine. The date is on the bottom of the frame. What does it say?"

"It says . . ." Annie squinted. The figures were black on black, and hard to read. Daddy wasn't wearing his glasses, she noticed. He didn't wear them unless he had to because he hated them. They kept falling off, he complained when he got them three months ago. "It says eight-four-nineteen nine."

"Almost forty-one years ago," Ted mused, looking beyond the album, beyond Annie. "I'll bet this was the last picture taken of Rose and Julie Sue."

"They were pretty, weren't they?"

"I guess so. It looks that way, doesn't it? Especially Julie Sue."

"Where are they? Why didn't they come to Grandmother Sybil's funeral?"

He put an arm around Annie and hugged her briefly. "Lord, child, I've never told you much about my family, have I? These two sisters died before I was born."

"But they're so young," Annie cried. "Young people shouldn't die."

"I know, but they do. Especially back then when there was no penicillin or other medications to cure such plagues as flu and typhoid fever."

"Is that what they died of? Typhoid or flu?"

"I don't know. I never asked, I guess. I do know they both died the same year, within weeks of each other, so it must have been something like flu. Flu was very dangerous in those days."

"But Gertrude didn't die."

"No, thank God."

"Nor Grandmother Sybil. She died from old age, didn't she daddy?"

"Wherever did you get that idea?"

"Well, because she was old."

"I guess that's as good a reason as what the doctor said."

"What'd he say?"

"Heart failure. She had gradually developed a weakened heart. The last few years of her life she had to stay in bed."

"Why didn't you come home to see her, Daddy?"

Her daddy looked more serious than she had ever seen him, except for the day of the funeral.

"Just one of those things. Here, let's find a picture of Papa. There's a wedding picture somewhere, of my mother and father." He turned the album page. He pointed at a baby in a newer looking photograph.

"And guess who this is?"

The picture of the baby sitting on a photographer's tall stool, wearing a long white dress that hung down halfway to the floor, made her laugh.

"That's you! I can't believe you were ever like that! Wearing a long dress, too, like a girl!"

"Well, what did you think? I popped full grown into

204

the world? And don't you make fun of my dress. It was the last one they let me wear."

"Why?"

"They decided along about then that I should be a boy. So I could grow up and be your daddy."

"I don't think that's really you. You just didn't exist until there you were, my daddy." She laughed up at him, teasing. He had taught her to tease, and she loved their teasing times.

"So nothing in the whole wide world existed until you were born, eh? Princess of the world. You wake up one day, and there's the sun and the moon, the grass and birds, dogs and cats. And lo and behold, a mom and dad!"

They laughed. But she was only half serious, because that's exactly the way it had seemed to her.

"Well, Daddy, where were all of you before I saw you?"

"Now that is a deep question, and I'm going to need some thinking time. You don't suppose that we were here all the time, just waiting for you?"

She sighed. It was her turn now. "But nothing existed, see. And, when I die, nothing will exist again."

"How do you know that?"

"Well, I asked Aunt Gertrude if Grandmother Sybil could hear us and see us now that she is dead, and Aunt Gertrude said that for her nothing exists anymore."

"Yes, Annie, consciousness is a strange and wonderful thing. Nobody understands it." He turned a page. "See, here I am on my first day of school, got my little lunch pail. I even remember what I had that day. A peach, a sandwich made with hardboiled egg and pickles and sandwich spread, and a piece of cake. And guess who made the cake?"

"Aunt Gertrude!"

"Right! And guess what flavor it was."

"Chocolate fudge! With lots of frosting."

"Right again."

They laughed and hugged and looked through more of the album and found the wedding picture of a young couple that had been her daddy's parents. The man wore a mustache and beard, and not much of his face showed. Grandmother Sybil's face had looked much rounder then, when she was so young.

"I guess people never smiled in those old days," Annie said. "And that's why Grandmother Sybil grew to look so much like a witch."

Her daddy gave her a quick, sharp look. "A witch, huh? I wish you could have seen her through my eyes, sweetheart."

The tone of his voice, low and sad, made Annie sorry she had called Grandmother Sybil a witch.

"I didn't really mean that, Daddy. It was just that her nose was long, and her chin long and . . ." She bit her lip. She was only making it worse. She didn't want to hurt her daddy's feelings.

Annie saw more pictures of Ted growing up. He posed in his baseball outfit, holding his bat and pretending to be ready to hit the ball. He posed in his car, and waved a funny cap. Then there were no more pictures. The rest of the big album was blank.

"What happened, Daddy?"

"Well, there was the war. And I married your mother, and we were all over the country during the war. She stayed with you in Washington with Aunt Carol while I went overseas. When I came back you were a big little girl, almost three years old. And we just weren't around here anymore, so there were no more pictures taken."

"But there's no pictures of anyone. Not Aunt Gertrude, or Grandmother Sybil, or anyone."

"No, well . . ."

"There's no wedding picture of you and Mama, and no

206

picture of me. Why didn't you ever send her a picture of me, Daddy?"

He looked at the blank pages of the album as if he couldn't think of anything to say.

Annie watched him closely. "Grandmother Sybil didn't like me, did she Daddy?"

For a moment his face looked filled with something that hurt Annie. Then he was smiling again, his eyebrows and mustache wiggling in that funny way to make her laugh.

"How could anybody not like you?"

He slid the album off his lap onto the sofa, and grabbed Annie up.

"Let's go see if your mother and auntie have supper ready for us. We need to eat a bite or two of vegetables so we can get to that fudge cake."

At that moment, being carried in her daddy's arms, her head almost reaching the top of the high doors they passed through, she was glad they had come home.

Gertrude stood looking down at Annie. She slept deeply and soundlessly. She wanted to lean down and kiss the precious forehead, the pale, silky bangs, but was afraid of waking her.

Annie had been a poor child all her life, Gertrude guessed. She had very few toys. Maybe it didn't take a lot of toys to make a child happy. She certainly was blessed with love. Both of her parents adored her. And, though it mattered less, so did her auntie.

Yet Gertrude felt sorry for her. Didn't most children sleep with a favorite stuffed animal or doll? Gertrude had seen Annie playing with a small lady doll, the kind that has a wardrobe. The wardrobe of Annie's doll looked like it all came from the rag bag. Gertrude had offered to

207

wash and iron the clothes for Annie, and at least now the wardrobe was clean.

But she needed a doll, and Gertrude's thoughts kept going to the doll upstairs.

The more she thought of it, the more she wondered if her mother had been talking to Annie when she said, "She's yours now." And if she had been talking about the old baby doll.

Sybil had given it to her first grandchild. Was it logical that she might, on her deathbed, give it to her second grandchild? Perhaps it was her way of trying to make amends for her neglect.

Annie would love the doll. Just as Gertrude had remembered loving it when she was a child, and wanting it so much she had cried for it. She remembered how puzzled and hurt she had been when she saw her mother give the doll to Rose's baby, when Gertrude herself had never been allowed to touch it. She remembered, too, the foolish notion she'd had that her mother could foretell death. Simply because Baby Angela had died. In Gertrude's ten year old mind had lived many fears that she only dismissed now with a shrug of her shoulders. Her mother remained a puzzle, and always would, but of course she had not been able to foretell death. No mortal had that power.

Gertrude remembered even being afraid of her own mother for awhile. As the years passed that old fear was forgotten. Until now, when Gertrude considered bringing the doll to Annie.

She had seen her mother finally as a person weakened by illness and age. A pathetic person who had been too proud, too determined to hold on to some idea of what was proper. Then at the end giving in, and calling for her exiled family to come home, her pride gone. It was the child she had wanted to see, at the last. Ted's child.

But to her mother there was something special about

the old baby doll. And perhaps, for only the second time, Sybil had given it to a child.

Both were Sybil's grandchildren. It was one of the perplexities of her mother that Gertrude didn't understand.

Gertrude left the bedroom, pausing to look back. It was a dreary old room, but Jenny was working hard on the bedroom across the hall. The ceiling was papered in fresh blue, and she had started on the walls. They had picked out the curtains, the bedspread, and had even bought a couple of white throw rugs.

Jenny's concern about the cost was touching. Gertrude didn't tell her how small the trust was getting, how the monthly income no longer stretched over the added cost of living. But she had a feeling Jenny knew. Or maybe Jenny's cautiousness about spending was a way of life.

Gertrude closed the bedroom door.

She looked at the stairway door, and thought she should obey her mother and bring down the doll. But a tightness like the corsets she wore when she was a child shortened her breath and made her feel as if she needed air.

She turned away, going quickly toward the front of the house, putting distance between herself and the door to the third floor. Only she suspected the meaning behind her mother's last bequest, and only she was in a position to carry it out.

Perhaps she would buy Annie a doll instead.

Chapter 6

Gertrude stood by her mother's bed, looking down upon the skeletal face in the shadows of the pillow. Her mother's hands were clasped on the blanket at her chest, and her fingers seemed now to have lost all flesh. "Mother," she tried to say, "what's wrong with you?"

Then the mists shifted, and Gertrude saw that Sybil was young, her hair pulled up into the pompadour she remembered from her childhood. Sybil rose in bed, her eyes unsmiling.

"She's yours now," she said clearly, and Gertrude heard the words even though she hadn't been able to hear her own.

"Thank you, Mama." She had wanted the doll so badly, and now her mother was giving it to her.

But then Gertrude saw Sybil was looking beyond her, and Gertrude turned to see who was there.

She woke suddenly, her heart pounding in terror. The comfort of her bed was gone. She turned, her arms at her side, frigid air enfolding her.

She was standing in total darkness, and she sensed a narrow confinement. She was afraid to breathe, to make a sound. It seemed she was not alone, and the other presence was evil, and was able to see her in the dark. Where was she?

She had gone to bed, and to sleep, and remembered no more.

She blinked. A dim light seemed to be reaching toward

her from somewhere above. Suddenly the light increased and outlined the top of the stairway above her, and she knew where she was in the narrow stairway leading up to the third floor.

She put out her hand and touched the wall and the railing. She could breathe more easily now knowing where she was, but she felt out of control.

Was this new habit of sleepwalking going to become a part of her life? The thought of such a thing terrified her. The inability to control one's actions while asleep seemed to her the ultimate in horror. What if she fell over the bannister?

She turned, her hand on the railing by the wall, and started back downstairs. She remembered her dream suddenly. The doll, her mother saying so clearly, "She's yours now."

It had been one of the most frightening dreams of her life, as if her mother knew that Gertrude had not obeyed her dying wishes, and had returned in her displeasure to force Gertrude to do her will.

She turned back toward the third floor and climbed until the moonlight in the upper hall became a soft, dusty light at her feet.

The old doll would make a perfect gift for Annie. Why was she reluctant? Was it because she had wanted it for herself, and if the child she had been couldn't have it, no one else could?

She didn't think back, to her own lost opportunities to marry and have a child. She had never even gone out with a man, never been touched by anyone. Yet there was a hollow place in her heart and a shadow over her life in those rare moments when she let herself *feel*. Annie was her last chance to fill the emptiness.

She went to the cabinet and unlatched the door. How long since it had been open? Perhaps Sybil had opened it occasionally and dusted the contents of the cabinet, but

Gertrude knew it hadn't been done in the last ten years. Sybil, with painful arthritis, climbed only those stairs she had to climb.

Gertrude heard a faint creak of hinges as she opened the right side of the cabinet. She had to get down on her knees. The doll lay on the bottom shelf.

As she pulled the doll off the shelf, she felt the elastic tug of a spider web. As the doll's face turned more fully into the moonlight, she saw it was covered with dust.

With the doll lying surprisingly heavy in her hands she went to the window where the light was better. She began cleaning the webs off the bonnet. The doll's eyes opened as she tilted it.

They caught the moonlight and glittered. And that feeling that she was not alone came over her again. She tilted the doll's head down, and its eyes closed.

It occurred to her that this was the first time she could ever remember touching the doll. Perhaps when she was a very young child . . . ? She had a vague memory of one of her sisters taking the doll away from her. But no, she was sure this was the first time she had actually held it.

She would have to wash its clothes before she gave it to Annie. She must take the doll downstairs and clean it up where she had better light.

Suddenly the moonlight was gone, and she stood in darkness. A memory forced itself into her mind. She was ten years old again, and had heard her mother come down the stairs and go along the hall, her long skirts whispering. She went into the hall, but stood quietly, watching.

She looked into a room lighted only by a kerosene lamp. Her mother was in the room, bending over a cradle. Gertrude could see small hands moving above the cradle, and then they disappeared. The cradle stopped swaying.

Her mother was putting the old baby doll into the cradle with Baby Angela.

The scene changed only slightly. The bedroom became Julie Sue's.

Gertrude stood in silence watching her mother. She was carrying the doll again, into Julie Sue's room. No, she was bringing it out. Julie Sue had been going to run away, but she couldn't now, because, like Rose's baby and like Rose, like Beulah, Julie Sue was dead.

The doll in Gertrude's hands grew heavier. She stared out the window at moonlight that was moving away from her, moving farther and farther away, and leaving her in a narrow, deep darkness that was filled with dust and spider webs and something else. Something that brought cold terror into her soul.

She turned slowly in the dark hallway. She could barely see the glass display cabinet, the edge of the door she had left open. It seemed the doll's head wobbled, as if it were a real infant she held in her hands.

She had to get rid of it, put it back into the cabinet. She could never give it to Annie. *Never.*

Next month, when the next check came, she would take Annie to the store and let her pick out her own dolly.

But this one, this old unnamed doll, she had to close away again in the cabinet.

She stooped to put the doll away.

Suddenly she was standing in her own room. Misty, grey dawn filtered through the dingy old lace at the window. She could see the dark bulk of dresser and chest, and the white quilt thrown back over the foot of the bed.

"Oh God," she whispered, her hands against her mouth.

She stood still, her heart pounding. What had happened? She had been upstairs, putting the doll away. There had been some moonlight. That must have been two or three hours ago. *Where had she been?*

So weak she was afraid she might fall, she felt her way along the side of the bed to the lamp, and turned it on.

She was wearing the nightgown she had dressed in at bedtime, but it was smeared with dust and cobwebs.

Her last memory was of holding the doll and preparing to return it to the cabinet, hours ago. Where had she been since then?

What had she done with the doll?

Her hands shook so hard she could hardly pick up her robe and tie it on. One end of the tie trailed close to the floor as she got her flashlight and went out onto the balcony.

Barefoot, she followed the trail of the light as it bounced ahead of her. If she turned on the lights, it might disturb Ted and Jenny, and she didn't want them to know the problems she was having lately walking in her sleep.

She climbed the three steps to the back hall. The door to Ted's room was closed, but Annie's stood open a couple of inches.

With the light pointed at the floor and muted to a rosy red with her fingers, she quietly entered Annie's room. She went to the bed and looked down. Annie's angelic face was almost hidden in blankets. She was a curled little knot in the middle of the big bed.

Gertrude leaned over and gently pulled the covers away from her chin and felt for the doll. She stood back with a long sigh of relief.

She hadn't put the doll into bed with Annie.

As she turned away from the bed and the sleeping child, she knew she would never put the doll close to Annie.

She was afraid of it.

And that, she thought, was probably why she'd been having these odd experiences. Something inside her subconscious had been drawing her both to and away from the doll.

The doll was an agent of death, somehow. She didn't understand, but she knew she wanted no more of it.

She didn't want to go upstairs to see if by chance she might have put it back into the cabinet, but she had to. Her hand trembled on the wooden door button. She turned it, and freed the door.

She climbed the stairs, the light beam ahead of her. Daylight brightened the upper hall, with a hint of a rising sun beyond the window. But Gertrude kept the flashlight on.

She shined it into the lower shelf of the cabinet.

The place where the doll had lain for so many years without being moved was clean and empty. A dusty rim outlined what had been the long gown, and the round head.

Quickly Gertrude shined the light on the other shelves. Little dusty iron horses pulling dusty wood wagons, and on the seat rusty, dusty little men sat with tiny leather reins in their hands. She swung the light over all the stuff that was crammed into the cabinet, but there was no doll.

She whirled, feeling an urgency to find the doll. *Where could she have put it?*

It must be down in her own room. It must be.

She hurried down the stairs, tripping once on the hem of her robe. She grabbed the railing and kept herself from falling, then moved more carefully on down and out into the warmth of the second floor hall. Carefully she buttoned the door to the third floor.

She went back to her room and turned on all the lights. For almost an hour she searched her room. But the doll was not there.

She went back down the hall, searching every corner in the angling passageways, even those never used. She looked into rooms long closed.

Finally she stood at the closed door of Ted and Jenny's bedroom. But she couldn't disturb them.

What would she say? Something as inane as, "By the way, did I by any chance drop off my mother's old doll here?"

Of course she would not have opened Ted and Jenny's closed door and gone into their room. Why would she put the doll in there?

Finally she turned back toward her own room, to search it again.

Chapter 7

Jenny woke, disoriented. At first she thought it was raining, the wind blowing hard and steadily. It was barely daylight, with a sick light coming from somewhere. And somewhere out in that dreadful storm someone was making a sound that cried wordlessly for help.

She sat up abruptly, blinking. There was no storm. It was only the remains of a distant dream, lost beneath the reality of waking. Wind whistled, but not loudly. As it steadied to a whisper, no longer part of a dream, she heard the other sound.

Ted was having trouble breathing. His breath rasped in with difficulty, long and slow, like a child with the croup. Jenny was suddenly terrified he was dying.

She lunged at him. He lay on his left side, hunched away from her. She grabbed his shoulder and tried to turn him onto his back, but his curled position held him frozen.

"Ted! Lord, Ted!" What would she do without Teddy? What would she and Jenny do? For one instant she saw their future before them, living without Ted. No more mountains to roam. No more exploring old ghost towns. No more love.

"Ted!" Her scream echoed back from the high ceiling. Her hands on his shoulder pulled and rocked him at last to his back.

His eyes blinked open and he drew in a long, harsh breath. Leaning onto his right elbow, helped by Jenny, he teetered upward against her, into her arms.

Jenny wept against his shoulder, her arms tight around him.

"Teddy, what's wrong?"

He sounded hoarse, as if his throat were inflamed. "What a dream, Jen." He put his hand to his throat. "I dreamed I was being smothered. No, not exactly that. I thought something was pulling all my insides out, starting with my breath."

"You have to go to the doctor. Today."

"No, it's okay now. Just catching cold, I guess. I'm okay now. Hey, you crying?"

Jenny wiped her eyes on her sleeve and smiled at him. "No, silly, why would I cry? I only thought you were dying, that's all! You sure sounded like it."

"What time is it? I suppose I might as well get up."

He turned away from her, while she sat with her knees up beneath the covers and her arms resting on them to support her head. Her neck felt as if it had lost every bone that held her head upright.

"What the hell's this?" Ted's voice was both annoyed and amused.

Jenny looked over his shoulder. He was holding something in his hands that at first glance looked exactly like a baby. She stared over his shoulder, seeing a small face with round cheeks and a pouting mouth. It's eyes were closed. It was dressed in a long white gown and a matching bonnet.

"It's a doll," Ted said in disbelief. He twisted and handed it around to Jenny, as if it were a baby who needed its diaper changed. "What the hell was a doll doing in my bed?"

His laughter was a questioning snort.

With the doll in her hands, recognition came.

"Oh," Jenny said.

"I didn't know anybody around here pulled practical jokes. But if I had to pick anyone, it'd be you, Jen. Is this a hint of some kind?"

"Isn't this the old doll that was always in your mother's cabinet upstairs?" Then it dawned on her what he had said. "A hint? What do you mean?"

"About two weeks ago, remember? Just before we came back here."

"Oh." Yes, the baby. She'd had an urge to settle down, buy a house, get steady jobs, and have another baby. "I'd forgotten about that. As soon as I mentioned it I noticed you were packing the station wagon and getting ready to move on."

"We had to come home, Jenny. I had a feeling it was time to come home. You wanted to be settled so we could have another baby, and I thought, why not? But when settling time comes, it's home. Home where most of our friends and relatives are. Well," he added, "where the heart is, anyway. We don't have very many of the other two left, do we?"

Jenny held the doll across her lap. Her hands untied and retied in a nicer bow the faded ribbon beneath the doll's chin. One finger dug out the dust that encrusted the creases in the face, the almost invisible wrinkles across the forehead, around the eyes and on each side of the button nose.

"Babies have such precious noses," she said, beginning to feel a new contentment. "Could we, Ted?"

"Well, we're home, aren't we?" He was still stretching, every muscle in his body growing taut against the underwear he had slept in.

"But it's not as though we have friends here anymore," she said. "And no family we're close to, either, except Gertrude."

"That's enough. And we can make friends. New ones. And there might be a few old ones left somewhere around town."

"I wish my mother and dad were still living. Still together, and owned that little farm Pop always wanted. I wish Carol weren't so far away."

"That would be great. We could go over for Sunday dinners. But you've got us, Jen, Annie and me and Gertie."

"Thank God."

Jenny separated the tiny fingers, and found them surprisingly flexible, though the doll was not made of rubber or plastic.

Ted reached over and tugged her toward him. Bed clothes wrinkled between them.

Jenny felt bathed in warmth. She could give in on where they lived, give up on a small house of her own, and try to make this old house her home, too. Especially if they could have that new baby.

"Annie would love it," she said softly.

"Yeah, she's kind of short on dolls and toys. Maybe she can be like other kids now."

"I mean the baby. She'd love a new baby sister or brother."

Ted propped his head up with crossed arms. "I thought you were talking about the doll."

"No, silly," Jenny giggled. Their conversations could get so twisted, with neither of them being able to follow the thoughts of the other the way most married couples seemed to. "Well, that too, probably. She's never had a doll like this. Isn't this a real old doll, Ted? I remember seeing it in the bottom shelf of the glass cabinet upstairs. But Miss Sybil always told me to leave the cabinet alone. She said it didn't need dusting, even though it was filled with cobwebs and dust that filtered in through the cracks. I had a hunch the doll hadn't been moved in fifty years. But if she didn't want it cleaned up, that was all right with me. I had enough with the first floor and the bedrooms on—"

He grabbed her suddenly, pulled her over onto him and started nuzzling her neck. She giggled hysterically, her neck the most ticklish part of her body, and his tongue like

220

a finger searching out the most sensitive spots. She pulled the doll out from between them and dropped it behind her on the bed.

"Let's make that baby," he whispered against her mouth.

"Really?" she breathed.

"Yes."

As deftly as ever he had somehow managed to get her nightgown up beneath her chin without her being aware of it. She felt cold air on her nude body, and the warmth of Ted's bare skin. She drew a long sigh, and wrapped her arms around his body, pushing his undershirt up to expose his back. Her hands began a slow caressing motion down his back to his buttocks.

Ted's arms trembled with a weakness he had never felt before. He didn't even have the strength to make love to his wife. What the hell was wrong with him?

"Honey?" she whispered. "Sweetheart?"

He rolled over and covered his eyes with the arm he should have been hugging her with. Panic rolled through him like distant thunder.

"What's wrong?" she asked, alarm lifting her voice. She leaned on her elbow over him. "Teddy?"

"I'm just tired that's all, babe."

He listened to the slow pounding of his heart. It felt as if he'd had some kind of attack on waking, and his heart was struggling to do its job.

Jenny leaned down and kissed his chin. "Then you rest, lover, and I'll bring you up a tray."

He felt the bed shift slightly as she left it. The rustle of her clothing as she dressed lulled him.

"Jen," he said after a minute, "did you put that doll in our bed?"

She didn't answer, and he moved his arm from his eyes to see that he was alone in the room. She had left so quietly he hadn't even heard the door close.

For the first time in his life he thought of death in connection with himself, and he was scared. Oh God, to leave Jenny and Annie?

His family had a history of sudden, unexplained deaths. He had asked his mother about the two sisters who had died before he was born and she had not wanted to talk about them. He remembered her shaking her head.

"How did you know about them?" she asked.

Surprised, he shrugged, as if he'd been caught smoking behind the barn. The look on her face made him feel guilty. He was thirteen that summer, and had lived all his life without even knowing there'd been more kids besides him and Gertie.

"Gertie told me."

"Her name is Gertrude, Teddy."

"Well, is it true or not?"

"Yes, of course. If she told you, it must be."

"I saw their picture in the old album."

She said nothing more that he remembered. His curiosity led him to take down the older albums and look at the faces of his dead sisters until he knew them almost as well as he knew Gertrude's. But it was Gertrude who told him, "They just died in their sleep, Teddy. Nobody knew why. Other people in our family have died that way. Our grandfather, for instance. When I was a little girl we had a housekeeper. She was like a grandmother to us girls. She had helped rear all of us. She told me my grandfather died in his sleep. Then Rose and Julie Sue. But she also told me that Mama had a sister named Rose Marie, and she, too, had died in her sleep."

Ted remembered his flip answer. Typical of a thirteen year old. "Guess I'd better not sleep. The next time Mom wants me to go to bed, I'll tell her. It's dangerous to sleep around here, and I'm going to stay awake."

Now he had a feeling he'd just missed becoming another

222

member of the family who mysteriously died in his sleep. He'd ask Gertie to be sure, but he didn't think there had been any deaths of that nature since early in the century.

He sat up, feeling that strange weakness through his muscles. Leaning forward with his arms and head on his knees he rested. Then he remembered. Jenny had said she was bringing breakfast up to him.

He sat a while longer, his eyes pressed tightly shut against his arms. He heard soft rustling of the bedding, and felt the slight pull of the sheet. Jenny had come back. He didn't smell the food, and he hadn't heard the door open, but he knew she was standing at the side of the bed looking down at him.

He flopped back on the bed, ready to greet her with a smile. And found himself lying on something decidedly lumpy.

Reaching behind his back, he dragged it out.

That damned doll again.

"Jenny!" he chided, figuring she had tossed it there out of the way as she straightened the sheet. Then he saw she wasn't at the side of the bed after all. With an odd sense of fear trickling up his spine he threw a quick glance around the room, from the half-closed drapery to the closed door.

She was nowhere in the room.

He'd only thought he felt the tug of covers.

For the first time he took a good look at the doll. His mother's old doll.

He thought of Annie. She had a couple of dolls, but none like this. An antique, it was probably worth a lot of money.

Was that what his mom meant when she looked at Annie just before she died and said, "She's yours now?"

He liked thinking so. Tears came unexpectedly to his eyes. Did it mean that his mother had accepted his daughter after all?

223

He had never gone against his mother's wishes until she refused to accept his marriage to Jenny. They had been close, as only a mother and son can be, and no matter where he went in the years he was away, he had wanted to come home to live close to his mother. He wanted her to love Jenny and Annie, and be an old-fashioned, pampering grandma to Annie.

He lay back on the bed, the doll across his chest.

With his eyes closed, his hand on the body of the doll, he dreamed of presenting the doll to Annie and saying to her, "Your grandmother loved you after all, Annie. She wanted to see you before she died, so she could give you this very special dolly."

Of course, he'd have to ask Gertrude first.

Chapter 8

"Let me help you," Gertrude said. "We'll fix it on this old tray, it's one of the biggest. I'm larger than you, so I'll carry it upstairs for you."

"Oh you don't have to do that."

"But I want to. I'll have eggs scrambled in a minute. If you want English muffins, you can toast them and butter them, and I'll dish up a bit of my blackberry jam. Teddy used to love blackberry jam. He'd even help me pick the blackberries." Gertrude laughed. "Until he was about fourteen, then he thought he was too big. He'd still eat it though."

Jenny was a little puzzled at Gertrude's mood change, from an almost frantic anxiety to joviality. As soon as she entered the kitchen just a few minutes ago Gertrude, all seriousness, had demanded to know if they were all right. And when Jenny told her Ted was a little tired and she was going to take his breakfast up to him, Gertrude seemed to get even more concerned. "What's wrong with him? He's not sick, is he? Maybe he's catching cold. Does he have a fever?"

"I'll just take a slice of toast," Jenny had murmured. "He's okay, really he is."

Gertrude went through a total change. From anxious nosiness she was suddenly happy and laughing and wanting to help Jenny with the tray.

Jenny toasted English muffins and spread them generously with butter. She put on the tray tiny salt and pepper shakers Gertrude brought down from a cabinet above, and added napkins and old silver that needed polishing. She made a mental note to take care of it when she had time, because it had a nice design.

Gertrude placed a bowl of yellow scrambled eggs laced with bits of onion and sweet peppers on the tray and added a sprig of parsley.

"For goodness sake, Gertrude," Jenny said. "So much? Fit for a king, too."

"But he is, isn't he? Our king. And there's enough for the queen too. You two have a nice breakfast, and when Annie wakes I'll bring her down to eat with me. How does that sound? I'll carry the tray up."

"Oh no, I can."

"I will. Up the stairs at least."

Ted gasped, reaching for air to fill lungs that felt as if he had been underwater a long time. He was smothering to death, gasping for air.

He turned his head, and felt the doll, still in his hands. He had been holding on to it as if it were his lifeline.

He reared up, feeling a little sick.

Leaning over, he put the doll down on the floor beneath the side of the bed.

He'd dozed back to sleep for a minute, and had somehow held the doll to his face. He'd probably been dreaming it was Jenny. There wasn't anything wrong with him, except he was trying to smother his silly self.

He knew now how a fish felt when it was taken out of its natural world of water. That silent, awful gasping. He knew how it felt. He had done his last pleasure fishing, as of now.

He pulled over Jen's pillow to add to his own and was just fluffing the both of them when the door opened.

Jenny held the door wide for Gertrude, who came in

226

with a big smile on her face and a ladened tray in her hands.

The smell of the food, a mixture that seemed to include onions somewhere, made him feel nauseated. But he could see on Gertrude's face that she had enjoyed making the kind of eggs he had liked when he was young and healthy as a colt.

"I'll just set it right here on the bedside table and then I'll go." She looked critically at Ted, a long, searching gaze. But her smile didn't falter.

Jenny made room on the table for the tray, and Gertrude put it down. Then she reached over and put her hand on Ted's forehead.

Before he thought, he jerked sideways.

"Just testing," she said apologetically.

"Sorry, Gertie, your hand was cold. If you want to know if I'm getting pneumonia, the answer is no. I'm fine."

"You're sure?"

"Hell, can't a guy be lazy anymore?"

Gertrude left the room with a final remark to Jenny. "He sounds just like he used to. I'm not going to waste my time worrying about the lazy twerp."

But once out of the room, with the door shut behind her, the smile left her face. She hated having to smile when she didn't feel like it. All her life, when Mama had visitors, Gertrude had been forced, from something within herself, to smile politely and listen politely, though in reality she was bored half to death and would rather be in her room reading.

This morning her happiness at learning that Ted and Jenny at least were still alive had instantly been dampened by hearing that Ted didn't feel well enough to get out of bed.

227

She had to go up and see for herself. And he had looked all right, and he had sounded just like he used to. But Gertrude went to Annie's room with a heavy dread in her heart.

She was so afraid of losing them.

The door to Annie's room was halfway open. Jenny must have looked in on her, and surely Annie was well. But Gertrude had to see for herself.

She pushed the door farther open and looked in, and Annie's bright eyes met her movement.

"Good morning, sweetheart," Gertrude said, going to the bed to kiss her little niece's forehead. For one precious moment Annie's soft arms hugged Gertrude's neck.

"Did you bring Daddy his breakfast?"

"Yes. Your mama and I did. Are you ready to get up and go down and eat with me?"

"Just the two of us?"

"That's right."

"Oh Good! That'll be the first time in all my life I've had breakfast with just you."

"And maybe we can find some more adventures. It's cold outside, and there are some icicles on the eaves. We can count them from the window."

As she helped Annie dress, as she listened to the child's chatter, her eyes searched the room. As she made the bed, she carefully pulled the bedspread even all around, and on her knees looked into the twilight world beneath the bed. She looked into the dresser drawers, all of them empty, and into the closet where a few of Annie's dresses hung, while Annie ran across the hall and came back with jeans and sweater from the chest in the room Jenny was redecorating.

The doll was not in Annie's room.

She even looked into the room being decorated. The stepladders were there, the board still lying across them even though the ceiling paper was now hung. One strip of wallpaper was up, and it was a bright track of small birds and flowers in a dull, dim room. The doll was not there either.

Forget the doll, Gertrude told herself. It was mixed up with old nightmares and frightening visions that were only the figments of a young child's imagination. She reminded herself she'd been only ten years old when her sisters died, when Baby Angela died.

In the brighter light of day she could almost put aside her recent compulsion to get up in her sleep and go to the doll. The death of her mother, her last words, all of it had tangled in her subconscious to create a small hell for her.

But it would pass.

This too shall pass.

"Let's think up something really happy to do today, Annie," Gertrude said brightly as they went from the stairs to the lower hall. *Think happy, be happy.*

"Okay. What?"

"How about us going to the big toy store and picking out a nice new doll?" She could float a check. The bank would cover for a few days until the next trust payment was due.

She listened to Annie's happy response as the child danced at her side.

"Really, really, Aunt Gertrude?"

"Really, really."

"When are we going?" Annie asked for the sixth time as she stood at Gertrude's side.

Gertrude had read to her, played tic-tac-toe with her, and a game of checkers, as they waited for her parents to come downstairs. It was almost eleven o'clock. They sat in the small sitting room; it was Gertrude's favorite room.

"As soon as your mom and dad come downstairs," she

229

answered, as she had answered before.

"We could go up."

"We might do that if they don't show up soon."

"And can we eat out, too, like you said?"

"Certainly."

She'd have to go to the bank and get the cash, she had decided. If she spoke to one of the clerks who knew her, she knew it would be all right.

At times she wondered what had happened to the money over the years. After her father died it seemed to disappear slowly. Of course, in truth, she knew. One hundred thousand dollars in trust back in the twenties had been a lot of money. In the thirties it had shrunk from bad investments until it was cut in half, and the income from that wasn't much. However, it was all she had. It paid the utilities, if she was very careful, and used only what light was needed, and only a minimum amount of heat. Her mother's bedroom had the burner in the fireplace, which had helped keep the room warm. And most of those last years had been spent in Mother's bedroom.

"Aunt Gertrude . . . Aunt Gertrude."

She realized she'd been staring at the wall.

"Oh. Sorry, sweetheart. What were you saying?"

At that moment there were footsteps in the hall. The door opened and Jenny and Ted entered. Annie ran to meet them. Gertrude started to speak, then she saw what Ted carried in his hand.

The old baby doll.

The white gown trailed down toward the floor, just the way it had when Gertrude saw Sybil bringing it from Julie Sue's room.

Chapter 9

"Daddy!" Annie squealed, jumping up to run to her parents. She reached her arms up for the doll. "Where did you get it? Is it for me?"

Gertrude stared in horror at the doll. Its open eyes had shifted, like a real baby who attempts to take in strange faces and surroundings. She wanted to ask where they had found it, but couldn't speak. She stood up, her hand out too late to stop Ted from putting in into Annie's arms.

Annie's face glowed with love and pride like that of a new mother who was seeing her infant for the first time. Her face reminded Gertrude of Rose's, so long ago, when she had looked down at the tiny, creased face of her baby Angela, and Gertrude was horrified by it.

Gertrude clumped forward, her legs feeling stiff and ungainly, her practical shoes too heavy to carry.

"Here, please," she said, taking the doll from Annie.

Annie looked up at her with all her hurt feelings displayed. Her eyes grew large and sad and questioning, as if she were seeing her aunt from a point of view she had not dreamed of before. Now Aunt Gertrude was not the generous aunt who was going to take her to town to buy a doll, she was the ogre who had snatched away the old one.

Both Ted and Jenny stared at Gertrude in silence.

Gertrude forced a smile. She put out her right hand to lightly brush Annie's hair and cheek. Her heart ached

231

with love, but fear iced around it.

"Don't you remember, Annie? We're going shopping to buy you a new doll."

Annie looked at the doll in Gertrude's hand and nodded her head. But her face was solemn, the pleasure gone. Ted noticed this immediately.

"But why bother spending the money, Gert? She's not going to hurt the old doll, is she? Why can't she play with it? Do you think it might fall apart?"

Jenny said, "Ted, Gertrude would rather keep the doll as a treasure. It might even be a valuable antique by now."

Gertrude returned to her chair.

"It was Mama's doll," Gertrude said lamely.

Jenny said, "Of course, Ted, she would want to keep it safe. See, Annie, it belonged to your Grandmother Sybil. She got it when she was a little girl, perhaps about your age."

Annie nodded. "Yes Ma'am. But I wouldn't hurt it."

"Oh no," Jenny answered quickly, "We know you wouldn't, baby, but it is old, and it might just fall apart. I'm sure if Aunt Gertrude buys you a new doll it's going to be very special, and it will be your very own."

Ted grunted. "I don't see the point. Annie likes this one. Besides, Sis, did you hear Mother's last words?"

Gertrude kept her head down and waited.

Ted continued, "She said, 'She's yours now.' And she was looking right at Annie. I didn't know what she meant. But this morning it occurred to me she meant her old doll. What better gift could she leave Annie to let her know she loved her after all?"

Jenny said quickly, "I thought she was looking at Gertrude, Ted."

"I'd bet she was talking to Annie."

Jenny said, "But I was on the same side of the bed as Annie and Gertrude, and it seemed to me—"

"Huhuh," Ted persisted, grinning at Jenny. "Annie."

Gertrude lifted her head, forcing laughter. Ted had teased and argued with Jenny in the early days, she remembered suddenly, before he had started dating her. He was not really serious, now. But Gertrude wanted to put an end to the thing about the doll. She looked at it on her lap, a very real looking doll. It was so exquisitely made, but it was only a doll, with a stuffed body and composition head and limbs. *Only a doll*. Why shouldn't a little girl enjoy it?

"It doesn't matter who she was looking at. I don't want to disagree with you, Jenny, but I came to the same conclusion that he did. And let me see. Does it need to be cleaned up?"

Using that for an excuse, she began to look the doll over. She untied the bonnet and looked at the head, with Annie eagerly at her elbow, watching every movement. How little it took to excite a child. How little they asked for.

She had to put aside her silly old fears, and give the doll to Annie. Maybe that would allay her bad dreams.

She turned the doll in her hands, feeling its oddly soft body, and hard little feet and hands. The body was made of cloth, strong, stained brownish, probably from moisture in the cabinet where it had lain for so many long years. Yet there was something different about it. She remembered it had looked somewhat squished up in the face and wrinkled, with puffy eyelids, just like newborn babies who hadn't filled out yet, but now its cheeks were pink and full. There was only a trace of wrinkles across its forehead and beneath its eyes.

It had gone into Baby Angela's cradle with a little, wrinkled, puffy face, and had come out of Julie Sue's room with round cheeks and bright eyes. Gertrude tried to push away the horror of remembering. Yet she was lost in the twilight of the hallway, long ago, watching her

233

mother carry the doll, its white gown trailing, and seeing that it had changed.

Annie's voice brought her back to the moment.

"Why is it wrinkled?" Annie asked, her fingers tracing a faint crease that remained on the forehead. "Because it's old?"

Ted and Jenny laughed, and Gertrude explained, "I think it just looks that way because whoever made it tried to make it look exactly like a newborn baby. Isn't that right, Jenny?"

"It looks just like you did when you were a couple months old, baby," Jenny teased, reaching over to tweak Annie's ear.

Annie giggled. "Oh, Mama."

"Funny thing," Ted said. "This is the first time I ever saw that doll out of its cabinet. How do you suppose it got into our room?"

Gertrude looked up and said before she thought, "Was that where it was?"

"That's where it was. In bed with me yet. I knocked it out on the floor. Lucky it didn't get broken."

"Well," Gertrude tried to laugh, as if sharing a secret with Annie and her parents. "Maybe it gets around all on its own, right, Annie? Searching for its little mother."

But as she said it she knew it was less a joke than she had intended. She suddenly wanted to be rid of the doll. She pushed it away and Annie saw her movement.

The child looked up at Gertrude with sudden hope in her eyes. "Her mother? You mean *me?*"

Gertrude smiled at Annie as she pulled the long gown down over the doll's feet and tucked it under. "This is an old christening gown," she explained, delaying the moment Annie would take possession of the doll. Memories flashed, like pictures buried in her brain.

"Did Grandmother Sybil christen the doll?" Annie asked.

Baby Angela, dead.

"I'm sure it must have come this way."

Sybil, coming from Julie Sue's room, the doll in her hands, and saying to Gertrude, "Don't ever touch this doll, do you understand?

"What's her name?" Annie asked.

Julie Sue, dead.

"If it ever had a name, I never heard it," Gertrude answered, her voice tight, her breath shortened, reality shifting from long ago to now. It could not have happened the way she thought it had. Her memory was faulty. She had to believe that in order to release the old doll to Annie.

"Can I name her?"

Gertrude said, "I understand how you feel, Annie. When I was a little girl, younger than you, I used to cry for this doll. But Mama would never let me have it. She bought me another doll. But my feelings were very hurt. I couldn't understand why I couldn't have the doll. After all, Mama didn't play with it, and as she later told me, she never had. She was twelve years old when her papa brought it home from one of his business trips to South America, and she was insulted because he had brought her a baby doll."

Ted asked, "You mean she never liked the doll?"

"It sounded that way."

"I guess she thought it was for a child younger than herself," Jenny said. "She was probably wanting perfume by age twelve."

Rose, dead. The doll still in the room.

"I wouldn't," Annie said. "I'd want the doll. I like dolls."

Beulah dead. And then Julie Sue.

Gertrude had made sure she stayed away from the doll, just as her mother had warned, and so she had lived. The deaths ended. Later, when Ted was six years old, their father died, but he had suffered a heart attack at work and died in the hospital. The curse of the doll had not affected him nor other members of the family. It was never removed from the cabinet after Julie's death that Gertrude knew of. Not until now.

She had been a frightened child, that summer of the deaths. Only in her mind was the doll in some mysterious way connected. In reality it was not possible. Unless of course, some lingering disease had clung to the doll. Was that possible? Ted would laugh at her if she mentioned her fears, tried to explain why she didn't want Annie to have the doll. There was no way to keep it from her.

"Then," Gertrude said, holding the doll out to Annie. "I don't know why you shouldn't have it."

God protect Annie.

"Really?" Annie cried, the light back in her face. She took the doll very carefully, holding it as if it were the most fragile thing in the world.

"And you can name her whatever you want."

"Give me some names Mama and Aunt Gertrude. Girl names."

Ted said, "I'll give you some boy names. Thermon, Orville, Roscoe—"

"Oh Daddy," Annie giggled. "I want girl's names."

"Oh all right, if you insist. Considering I'm the grandpa I ought to be able to name it. So, how about Clementine?"

"No! Mama? Aunt Gertrude?"

"Funny thing," Gertrude said, "I used to be afraid of that doll. Not so funny to me then."

Ted and Jenny laughed. Jenny sat on the sofa and drew her legs up. She kicked off her shoes and pulled a cushion over to lean against.

"Why on earth," Ted asked, "were you afraid of a doll? I thought you used to cry because you couldn't have it to play with."

Gertrude's smile faltered. "That was earlier. Later,

when I was ten years old I grew afraid of it. The year our housekeeper, Beulah, and my sisters died. And the baby, too, in her crib. She was the first."

She bit her lower lip, hoping they wouldn't notice what she had said. But Ted caught it immediately.

"The baby? What baby?"

Gertrude stared out the windows above Annie's head. From the corner of her eye she could see Ted's face. He wasn't going to let this pass.

What baby, Gertie?"

"Well, I don't suppose it matters much to Mama now. Poor Baby Angela. She belonged to Rose."

"Oh yeah?"

"Well, you know, Rose wasn't married. She was just eighteen when she had the baby. It was a little girl, and Rose named her Angela. Julie Sue—" Gertrude looked at Jenny and explained, "They were my sisters, Julie Sue and Rose, and they died within weeks of each other back in 1910. They were so young. Eighteen and fifteen."

Jenny murmured, "That's terrible. What was wrong?"

Gertrude shrugged. "I don't know. One day they were fine, and the next morning they were dead."

"This baby Angela?" Ted asked. "What about her?"

"She was the first to die." Gertrude looked down. "And that's what frightened me, made me afraid of the doll. Rose's baby and Julie's death. In both cases Mama . . ."

Gertrude stopped. She couldn't finish her sentence. *Mama gave them the doll.* Only now she realized the truth of that. Because if Mama hadn't put the doll in Julie's room the night she died, how had it gotten there? After all these years, why had she mentioned the baby? She thought of its grave, in the woods, almost lost now in the undergrowth.

"What do you mean?" Ted asked. "In both cases what?"

"Well, Baby Angela had a cradle. The old cradle up in the attic. It's never been used since. You had a brand new nursery set, do you remember?" She changed the subject, leading them off onto a tangent. "Of course you don't remember. But when you came along, very unexpectedly, Mama kept herself so well hidden that I didn't even know I was going to get a baby brother. Anyway, when you were born she and Papa had the nursery redone completely. I was fifteen years old and had no idea Mama was going to have a baby!"

"What about the baby who died, Gertie?" Ted asked softly. "I'm thirty-five and never knew Rose'd had a baby."

Gertrude tried to think of a way to escape. "Well, we weren't allowed to talk about the baby. Mama and Papa felt like . . . in those days especially, you know . . . you know how it was. You must have an idea. An unmarried girl?"

She glanced at Annie, but saw that Annie seemed absorbed in the doll.

"So poor Rose was a disgrace to the family, hmm?"

"Yes."

"But the baby?"

Gertrude drew a deep breath. "She was a lovely baby, only three months old. She slept in the cradle. In Rose's room."

Gertrude paused. Perhaps, if she did explain her fears about the doll, Ted would make Annie put it away. And then Annie would be in no danger, imaginary or real.

"What happened?" Ted asked. His persistence made Gertrude feel trapped.

"Mama brought down the doll from the cabinet and gave it to Rose's baby. I watched her from the hallway. She took it into the room Rose hardly ever left. She wasn't allowed to take the baby out. No one knew about the baby at all, not even our housekeeper knew. I was only ten, and I was very hurt that Mama would give the doll I had wanted all my life to Rose's baby."

"I watched her put it into the crib with the baby. And

the baby was hardly old enough to want a doll, you know. She was only three months old. But Mama had given her the doll. The next morning the baby was dead."

"Oh my God," Jenny murmured.

Ted asked, "Do you think the baby was smothered, or something?"

"I don't know. The doll was in there. Of course, I didn't start being afraid of the doll until much later, after Julie Sue died. Before that, though, Rose died, and our housekeeper, Beulah. But the doll had been in Julie Sue's room, too, as it had been in Rose's. So at first I had an idea that Mama could somehow foretell death. And she'd give the doll to whoever was going to die. Then sometime afterward, I became afraid of the doll, rather than . . ." She swallowed with difficulty. ". . . than Mama."

Gertrude saw the frown on Ted's face smooth away, and the birth of a grin. "How old did you say you were?"

"Ten, that summer."

He shook his head and he and Jenny exchanged a long look that made Gertrude feel as if they had made some kind of decision about the state of her mind.

Ted got up and stretched. He patted Gertrude's shoulder as he passed by her chair.

"No wonder you associated death with the doll, Gertie, I can see that, can't you Jen?"

Jenny nodded, her smile wavering. "It was a terrible time for you, Gertrude." The smile was sympathetic, Gertrude saw.

"But," Ted continued on his way to the door, "that was a long time ago, sis, and you were a kid. You're all grown-up now. You can stop being afraid."

Gertrude understood. Something a child of ten might fear was not acceptable in a woman of fifty.

"Gertie, I've been in the family vault a couple of times over the years, taking flowers and whatnot. Mom used to insist, you know. But I never saw a plaque for the baby.

Why?"

"She's not in the vault."

"Why the hell not?"

Gertrude felt as if she were to blame. Not only were Jenny and Ted's eyes on her, but Annie had lifted her head and turned, and all three were waiting.

"She was buried elsewhere." Gertrude got to her feet hastily. "If I don't get back to the kitchen I'll never get through with my work."

Jenny rose also.

"And I have to finish Annie's room," Jenny said. "Come on, Ted, I'm hiring you as my right hand man."

Gertrude looked back to see if Annie were following her parents, but the little girl sat as if she didn't know she was alone in the sitting room now. The sun turned her hair to pale, lovely, diaphanous gold as she bent over the doll.

As Gertrude went down the narrow hall that was always dark even on a sunny day, she could hear Annie's voice as soft as a whisper of wings, singing a lullaby.

The child would be fine, she told herself when she entered the kitchen. *Annie was happy now.*

"No," Annie whispered to the doll, bringing her up against her shoulder the way she had seen mothers do their very young babies. "It wasn't your fault. You're not a bad dolly. You're a very good dolly."

She crooned, making up the song as she went. "Good baby, good baby, Annie's baby, sleep on Mommy's shoulder. I'm your mommy now, baby."

She laid the doll down on her knees again and bent to kiss the rosy little face. And then she laughed.

"Do you know what you look like sometimes? When you look up and your brow wrinkles? One of those apple dolls. But I'll feed you and make you grow."

She brought the doll up to her breast and put its face against her. Humming she rocked back and forth, thinking names.

"Julie Sue. Rose. Baby Angela. Angela. But those names have been used already."

The doll crept upwards, rising from her breast to her neck, to her cheek. It nuzzled against her, and she felt the cold, hard, tiny nose poking into her flesh. She giggled softly. It tickled. It seemed, with her face against the doll's, that she could hear it breathe.

Chapter 10

At night Gertrude sat reading in the silence of her room until the house grew very still and quiet. Then, walking silently, avoiding the loose boards, she went through the halls to Annie's room.

They had started leaving a tiny nightlight plugged into a hall socket. It made it easier for her to slip into the room, look down at her niece sleeping with the doll cuddled in her arms. Working slowly, she removed the doll.

The first night Annie woke, her arms tightening around the doll. With her blue eyes wide and startled, she stared up at Gertrude, and Gertrude stared back, her heart pounding. She hadn't meant to frighten the child. But then Annie closed her eyes, released the doll, and turned over again, sleeping soundly.

She didn't take the doll from the room.

Slipping it quietly out of the bed, away from Annie, she held it. The pull of the upstairs was strong that first night, the cabinet open and beckoning. But to take the doll and put it back in its dusty old spot would raise too many questions. Ted would think Gertrude herself didn't want Annie to have the doll. It wasn't that, she told herself. The truth was, she was still afraid of the curse, or whatever it was.

So she laid the doll on the dresser across the room.

No one mentioned to her about the removal of the doll from the bed. Not the first morning, nor the second. By the third night Gertrude was beginning to feel more at ease. Annie had been playing with the doll for three days now, and nothing bad had happened to her. She hadn't even stubbed her toe.

Gertrude dozed off in her chair, waking suddenly at the distant dong, dong of the old clock on the mantel in her mother's room next door.

She looked at the clock on her dresser. 3:15 A.M. The doll had been in Annie's bed five hours too long. She hadn't realized she had slept so deeply or so long.

Gertrude hurried down the hall, her robe sweeping the floor, like her mother's robes once did. Was she becoming her mother? She tied her belt to lift the hem from the floor.

Annie had turned away from the doll, and it lay at her back. It was facing her, as if snuggling up to her.

Before Gertrude could remove it Annie groaned and flung her arm back over the doll. She moved her head, back and forth, as if struggling against a dream, and Gertrude saw the back of her hair was damp.

Gertrude waited, looking down at the child.

Annie turned again, toward the doll, and then rolled onto her back, her arms up over her head. Gertrude watched her more closely, worry seeping in. Something was wrong with Annie. She had waited too long to come and remove the doll from the bed.

Gertrude lifted the doll and laid it on the foot of the bed, her eyes still on Annie.

She would call Ted and Jenny to see what was wrong with Annie. Perhaps to take her to the doctor.

But then Annie took a long breath and settled into a deep sleep.

Gertrude remained at the bedside, watching. Annie was sleeping peacefully, as she usually did.

Gertrude picked up the doll and put it on the dresser, then quietly left the room, closing the door.

Annie stirred at the sound of the door closing. She heard footsteps in the hall, and the squeak of a board. Every night Annie heard Aunt Gertrude, but tonight it was like part of a nightmare.

The room she was sleeping in seemed unreal. The ceilings were so high it was like there was no ceiling. The little light Aunt Gertrude had put on the bedside table did not reach the ceiling. The light was like a cap the table wore. It didn't shine anywhere else.

Something by the dresser thumped, and Annie knew the doll had rolled off the dresser again. The first night she had gotten up and picked up the doll, and put it back onto the dresser, because that was where Aunt Gertrude wanted it to sleep. But when morning came she found it on the floor again, right under the edge of her bed. So last night she picked up the doll when it fell and put it into the drawer. She made it a bed in the drawer, and left the drawer open just wide enough so it wouldn't be afraid.

"That's all right," she had whispered as she kissed it good night. "You have your very own crib, right here in the drawer. When I was a little baby like you I had a crib by my mama's and daddy's bed." She kissed it again, and she could feel its face yearning toward her.

She knew she should get up and pick up her baby, make sure she wasn't hurt, and put her into her crib. But tonight she felt made of lead. She couldn't move. How long would it take her baby doll to crawl to her? Maybe she never could.

She hadn't named her doll yet. All day long she went around asking for names. She asked Aunt Gertrude for all the names she could think of, and she wrote them down on her paper. She had gotten all the names Mama and Daddy could think of, too, but none of them seemed just right for her baby doll.

It had to be very special. She was considering calling it Angela, after the dead baby. The dead baby who wasn't buried with the family.

But every time she thought of that little baby, something happened to her stomach, something that kept her from naming her doll after it. Poor little baby.

She felt the tug of the bedclothes, and she was suddenly wide awake and very cold. Something was beneath her bed, pulling on her covers, and she was scared.

Then a tiny hand appeared, reaching up at the corner. Its fingers curled and grasped the star in the quilt and sunk into the material.

The ruffled sleeve appeared, and the edge of the bonnet, then the face of the doll.

Annie stared.

The doll was on top of the bed now and coming toward her, slowly, laboriously crawling, the sound of its approach like the soft rustle of something unseen in the walls or in the dark beneath the bed. Annie was torn between a yearning love that made her want to cry and reach out for her baby that was trying so hard to get back to her, and the most awful fear of her life. She hadn't really thought her doll could move by itself. It had fallen off the dresser because Aunt Gertrude laid it too close to the edge. She had only pretended that it could really crawl, that it could climb her bed and reach her all by itself.

She had only pretended. And now she was so scared she couldn't move.

It came closer, its tiny fingers stretching out, gripping the quilt, squeezing. Annie could see the quilt wrinkle in the grasp of the doll, as if the strength in the hands was enough to rip the quilt to shreds. The doll had reached her tightly drawn legs, her feet. She felt its touch. It was coming to her, it needed her, but she shrank back from it. It moved like a real baby, not a mechanical doll, but it

245

wasn't a real baby. It shouldn't be able to move all by itself. Yet it was closer and closer.

She heard its soft slide across the bed. It touched her leg, and its eyes watched her steadily, never blinking like a real baby. She was getting sick to her stomach because she was so afraid.

"Daddy!" Annie screamed. *"Daddy! Mommy!"*

Ted's feet hit the floor with the second call. On the other side of the bed Jenny was getting up, too. He heard her kick something with a soft thud, and a low curse.

"I'll go," Ted told her, searching the lamp for the light switch.

The light came on, and Ted blinked at the sudden change from dark to light. Jenny was already going out the door, her hands out as if she were still stumbling through the dark. Ted hurried to catch up with her. Across the hall and down three doors, Annie was calling again, her voice sounding far away.

When he reached Annie's room, Jenny was already holding their child in her arms. She sat on the bed, and her soft reassurances had a singsong rhythm.

Annie was crying hysterically and clinging to her mother. "Take it away! Take it away!"

Jenny reached for the doll. "No, see, sweetheart? It's just a dolly, that's all. Your Grandmother Sybil wanted you to keep it for your very own, and Aunt Gertrude gave it to you."

Jenny gave Ted a penetrating look over her shoulder, but he didn't quite understand.

"A bad dream?"

"No, no, no," Annie cried. "It was crawling. It's a bad thing, it's not a dolly, it's a bad thing."

Ted took the doll from Jenny and laid it carefully out

of sight at the foot of the bed.

"You just had a dream, pudding," he said.

Jenny held Annie, stroking the back of her head. "It's all right. We're with you." Then to Ted, as Annie relaxed and stopped crying, Jenny whispered, "I think what Gertrude was talking about when she was a child? I think Annie picked it up."

Ted squeezed in between the table and the bed, to sit on the edge. He patted Annie's back, and it seemed to him he could feel the heat of her small body through the material of her nightgown.

"Just a nightmare, baby, just an old bad dream."

Annie shook her head. "It was crawling, it was, it was!"

"Is she all right?" Ted asked. "Do you think she has fever?"

"Yes, she might. I'll go get a thermometer. Here, sweetheart, Daddy will stay with you. I'll be back in a minute."

Jenny stood up and Ted took her place. Annie relaxed against his chest, her eyes closed. She seemed to be sleeping again, almost before Jenny was out of the room.

He held Annie, patting her back, pushing her hair off her forehead.

The flu coming on, or just a cold?

He pushed the old doll out of the way, nudging it with his elbow toward the foot of the bed. He laid Annie back, plumping the thick pillow around her small head.

"Daddy," she whispered.

"What, baby?" He had thought she was asleep.

"Don't leave me alone."

"No, of course I won't."

Her forehead felt hot. There was no perspiration there now. It had burned away with the fever that was growing.

Fever is beneficial, he reminded himself. Fever eats up the bugs in the body that make us sick. But still, fever scared him. It meant there was a bug that didn't belong there. His baby was sick, and it was 3:30 A.M. and the hospital was across town. He didn't even know the name of a doctor. Of course Gertrude would know their mother's doctor, but what would he do tonight except tell them to keep her warm and give her plenty of liquids? And if she didn't improve tomorrow bring her to the office. They'd had these experiences before. Why do children always get sick at night or on the weekend?

Jenny came back and slipped the thermometer into Annie's mouth. In her sleep Annie turned her head and tried to get rid of it, but Jenny murmured encouragement, and put her hand on Annie's chin.

Annie lay still, her eyes closed.

When Jenny removed the thermometer she held it under the dim light to check it.

"Just slightly over normal, Teddy. Not really high enough even to be called a fever."

"I think I'll sit with her awhile," Ted whispered.

"Don't you think she'll be okay alone? She seems to be sleeping good now."

"She asked me not to leave her alone."

"Maybe we should just take her to our bed."

"No, that's okay. I'm not very sleepy right now. You go back to sleep, I'll stay awhile until I know she's settled down. She had a bad dream. She may have a little upset stomach."

Jenny smiled faintly. "I don't doubt that. I'm surprised you don't, too, the way Gertrude feeds you cake every night." She yawned. "Well, at least, it doesn't seem serious."

"I'll be in later."

"Okay."

Jenny pulled the door only halfway closed. He heard her bare steps on the floor in the hall, and then the faint squeak of their bedroom door.

He crossed his arms on the edge of the bed and put his

248

head down, his face turned toward the dresser. The mirror looked old and dingy, and reflected the dark rise of the headboard, and the shadow it cast on the wall. He breathed deeply and closed his eyes.

Thank God her temperature was only slightly elevated.

Chapter 11

Daddy, take me away. Daddy, Mommy, let's go away. I don't want to stay here anymore in this house. The doll is bad, Daddy. Daddy, please hear me.

She was sunk into a big, deep hole that was black and without any light, and she was burning up. Was this hell that she had fallen into? Had the bad doll pulled her down into hell?

Daddy, tell Aunt Gertrude we have to leave. Tell Aunt Gertrude to come with us. The doll is bad.

She struggled to breathe. All around her the sounds of the night were magnified. She could hear the rustle of her bedding, as the doll crept closer again. Her ears rang with the sounds of creeping, and she struggled to scream. *The doll.* Couldn't Daddy see the doll was moving again?

"What is it, baby?"

Her daddy's voice sounded like a distant drum, thundering and echoing through the deep, dark well she had fallen into. But somewhere in the darkness came the doll, steadily closer, closer.

Daddy's hand touched her forehead again. It felt as rough as sandpaper against her hot skin. She tried to reach up and grasp it. The hand would lift her out of the darkness, away from the bad doll.

"It's not long until daylight, baby. I think we'll hunt

up a pediatrician. Maybe the old family doctor. You'll be fine."

She could feel him staring at her, but it was as if he leaned over the top of the well looking down at her, far, far beneath him.

Daddy. Take me away from this house.

Her voice in her own ears sounded hollow when it broke through. "Daddy, the doll . . ." She stopped, exhaustion pulling her down again.

"What? Your doll? Here, Sweetheart. Daddy'll put your dolly to sleep right beside you."

She felt the touch of the doll's face against hers. It was cold, as cold as her fear, as cold as darkness and depth and never seeing light anymore.

Daddy, no . . . no . . .

Gertrude tapped lightly on the door before she opened it. The light was on, she had seen it shining in a narrow strip beneath the door.

"Did we wake you, Gertrude?" Jenny asked.

"I thought I heard someone crying." Gertrude took a quick glance around the room, hoping she didn't look as if she were snooping. Jenny was sitting on the side of the bed, but Ted was not there.

Jenny said, "You must have heard Annie. She had a nightmare, and she's got a slight fever. I didn't think it was enough to get alarmed about, but Ted is such a worrier where Annie is concerned he stayed with her. She's okay now, Gertrude. Sorry we disturbed you."

Gertrude's heartbeat accelerated so much she felt it throbbing in her temples. She resisted an urge to run to Annie's room and see for herself that Annie was all right. "Maybe I could sit with her, so you two can get your rest."

"Ted wouldn't hear of it. They'll be okay."

Gertrude stepped back out of the room and closed the door. She waited, and the ribbon of light shining beneath the door turned dark as Jenny went back to bed.

Walking quietly and slowly, Gertrude went on down the hall to the room Annie was occupying while her room was being redecorated. The door stood a few inches open.

She could see only a tangle of curls on the pillow, beyond Ted's shoulder. But Annie lay very still as if she were sleeping comfortably now, whatever terrors she'd had in her sleep salved. Gertrude felt vastly relieved that Ted was with her.

Ted looked over his shoulder. He sat on the chair at the side of the bed. He had been leaning forward, his head down.

"Can I bring you something?" Gertrude asked in a loud whisper without entering the room. "Hot cocoa? Coffee?"

Teddy shook his head.

He looked sleepy, his face long and serious, the dark mustache drooping at the corners. At that moment, with his face shadowed, he looked just like some of the old portraits of family men from earlier times.

"You need to get some sleep," Gertrude whispered.

He nodded. "I'll take a nap here."

"If you need me . . ."

"Sure," he whispered.

The child lay so still. Gertrude watched her, and felt uneasy.

"Is she asleep?" Gertrude whispered, leaning farther into the room.

"Yes. Finally."

Gertrude nodded and backed away, pulling the door slowly closed.

As she returned to her own room it occurred to her she had not seen the doll on the dresser where she had put it earlier. She stood still, closed into her room, and tried in her memory to picture the dresser exactly as it was minutes ago when she had leaned into the room whispering to Ted. She could not recreate the dresser with the doll lying on the old scarf. She was sure it was not there.

What did it matter? Ted was with Annie.

There was no curse. No South American voodoo curse, or any such thing. Only a weird series of coincidences.

She went to her dresser, poured a glass of water from the pitcher and rummaged about in the top drawers for one of the sleeping pills left over from her mother's supply of medicine. She had brought a couple or three pills into her room, hoping they would help stop her sleepwalking. She must have taken them, or she had lost one.

For the first time since the day the bedding had been removed from her mother's death bed, she went back to Sybil's bedroom. Entering her mother's room she felt lost, like a lamb separated from its flock. How had she lived all her life in a house that now felt too large, too dark? Tears filled her eyes and made the room shimmer when she turned the light on. The light was dim, and shadows heavy. The large, high bed dominated one end of the room, the canopy shadowing the bed where Mama had lain. Over by the windows stood the chair with the cotton throw, and the small table with magazines that Sybil had read months ago. For the first time in Gertrude's life it occurred to her there was no Bible in her mother's room. Although they had continued to go regularly to church as long as Sybil was able, Gertrude could never remember seeing her mother read her Bible.

"Gertrude."

Gertrude stopped, weakened, feeling her legs tremble and almost fold beneath her. She turned slowly and looked at the bed, at the deep shadows that lay on the pillow. She could almost see her mother there. She had heard her voice, as clearly as ever.

"She's yours now. She's yours now. She's . . . She's . . . yours . . . yours . . ."

Trembling, afraid to approach closer to the bed but afraid not to, she stumbled to the bedside table and picked up from among the bottles the one that held sleeping pills. Turning, she ran from the room. As she crossed the threshold into her own room she let out a long breath of relief.

She swallowed a capsule and went to her bed, curling up in her cold blankets, hiding her face in the smothering darkness beneath them.

She would sleep now, and not worry anymore. The door was closed between her room and her mother's, and Ted and Jenny would take care of Annie. The fever was something children got, and Ted was with Annie.

The doll was only a doll.

Ted's neck hurt. Sleeping with his head on his arms had put such an unnatural strain on his shoulders, arms and neck that it was about to kill him, yet he couldn't move. But he had to. He had to lift his head and see what Annie wanted. He could feel her tugging on the quilt, trying to wake him, or trying to get more cover. He was good at pulling covers. Jenny had told him that many times.

He breathed shallowly, feeling the pull of the blanket. It was a frisky tug of war game with him and Jenny, but tonight, tonight his little girl was sick, and she was pulling, pulling . . .

He lifted his head and blinked eyelids that felt glued shut.

Annie lay still, her face half buried in the blanket beneath the quilt. Pale hair lay over the top of the blanket, on the edge of the quilt pulled taut. The small hand that held the edge of the quilt was strangely reduced in size, distorted, somehow, as Ted tried more clearly to see it.

What was wrong with him?

What was wrong with Annie?

The doll lay between them, its face pressed close against Annie's. And the hand that clenched the quilt was not Annie's but the doll's.

He stared, trying to rise. Annie's face was too still, her eyes half-open and lifeless.

He wasn't awake, he was dreaming. It wasn't real, none of this. The light in the room was too dim, the air too frigid. Annie's eyes were too lifeless. And the doll, lying between his face and Annie's, was a real infant of some kind, not human, not animal, but something horrible, and in its way, alive.

It was moving, its hand gripping the quilt, its head turning from Annie's to his, its face so close to his. He couldn't breathe or move. He saw the eyes of the doll gleaming. The unreality of dreams. How true were they? A world where life was transferred so easily from one's child to her doll. He saw its cheeks, rounded and red, as if it had absorbed not only Annie's life, but her fever. As if the fever had animated it, the doll rolled onto its stomach and fastened its hands onto the quilt and pulled itself closer and closer to his face.

He saw the swollen cheeks, the cold eyes, the opening mouth as it puckered for nourishment. Its face came between him and all else, closer and closer, filling his nightmarish dream with the reality that lived beyond human understanding.

Chapter 12

Jenny felt alone. She lay on her right side, her hands beneath her cheek on her flattened pillow. A sickly grey daylight had replaced the darkness, but the house felt strangely empty. She lay still, beginning to sense that she had slept a lot later than usual. How quiet the house seemed this morning. But it was always quiet. What was different?

She turned over and reached out for Ted, but his side of the bed was cold and empty. She sat up, remembering Annie's cry in the night, and the slight fever that had kept Ted with her. But that was hours ago. Jenny felt as if she were alone in a huge house encapsulated by the cold of winter. She was surrounded by an ominous silence.

Something was wrong.

She whirled, looking for the alarm clock: 10:10 A.M.

"My God," she muttered and flung back the covers. Cold air struck her bare legs. She reached for her old robe across the foot of the bed, and as she pulled it on she went to the window to push the curtains back and let in more light.

The world beyond the window looked lifeless, frozen in cold winter. Tree limbs stretched naked toward the grey sky. Icicles hung down from the top of the window frame. So unusual for Arkansas, icicles that had slowly been growing longer over the past several days, frost that rimmed the glass.

There was a gas furnace in the basement, but the thermostat setting had not been turned up this morning. Where was Gertrude? Gertrude always got up early and turned up the thermostat. Annie would die of pneumonia in this cold.

She ran down the hall and opened the door to Annie's room.

She stopped, staring toward the bed.

The room seemed refrigerated. The blind hadn't been opened. The light on the bedside table looked as dim as a candle, throwing a small cone of pale yellow onto the table and barely touching the edge of the bed. It touched Ted's left shoulder and the wood back of the chair in which he sat, and dwindled to deep shadow beyond.

Annie lay still on the pillow, only the top of her head visible, and Ted slept with his head on his arms. But there was no movement, no sound of breathing, and Ted's jaw and chin, the only part of his face Jenny could see, looked made of sharp bone and taut skin. It didn't look like Ted.

Jenny stood, willing movement in the room, willing warmth and life as within her everything froze.

"Ted?" she ventured, and her voice sounded hollow and echoing in the room as if it had turned overnight into a cave. "Annie?"

The stillness remained in the tremoring wake of her voice. She tried to laugh, to bring a touch of humor to a scene that was becoming increasingly frightening.

"Hey, sleepyheads, wake . . . up . . ."

She went forward, hardly aware of herself or her actions. She saw Annie's face, with the half-open eyes, and Ted's, staring in cold isolation at nothing. She saw the reach of Ted's arm, as if he had tried at the last to touch Annie. She saw the crumple of the blanket beneath the edge of the old star quilt. But as her scream ripped the cold air all she saw was the changed faces of her

258

loved ones. The horrible thinness, the sunken cheeks and hollow eyes.

She might have touched them. She might have jerked back the quilt because later it was found hanging over the footboard of the bed. But as she realized that her child and husband were dead, her reality became a jumble, never to be pieced securely together again.

She heard her voice crying, screaming. She must have tugged on Ted without realizing what she was doing, because he had fallen to the floor, and she was with him, her arms trying to lift his shoulders. She felt the awful skeletal thinness, and heard herself crying, "What's happened? *My God what's happened to them?*"

Gertrude tried to wake up, but her brain was so heavy. She felt half removed from the world, growing aware yet unable to lift herself from bed. The house was terribly cold. The thermostat hadn't been turned up yet. The weather had changed from cold to frigid, and no one had turned up the heat. Even at its best, not much heat came into the upper stories.

She was dreaming that somewhere far away someone was crying. But she couldn't reach them because she was in another world. She felt as if she had been drugged.

Then she remembered she had taken one of Mama's sleeping pills last night.

She pulled herself up in bed and blinked at the clock.

Good Lord. Past ten in the morning. She had never gotten up so late in her life.

Ted . . . why hadn't Ted or Jenny turned up the . . .

The crying penetrated the thick walls, the long hallways, her closed door. It was a child, or a woman in terrible anguish.

Jenny! *Annie!*

She flung open her bedroom door, and the sound of

cries took on even more desperation and agony.

Now she recognized it as a woman's voice, not a child's.

"Jenny!" Her voice almost failed. She ran around the balcony and up the three steps into the rear hallway.

The cries continued, on and on, rising and falling, with words occasionally distinguishable. "Annie . . . Ted . . . Ted . . ."

Gertrude followed the sobbing voice to Annie's room.

In the twilight the horror unfolded. Ted lay on the floor, half on his side, twisted, his hollowed face gaping up at the ceiling. He looked, in that first terrible moment, like a century old person, all flesh sunken away.

Jenny was in the middle of the high, antique bed on her knees, and Annie was stiff in her arms, her small face shrunken to bones. The quilt had been thrown over the foot of the bed and hung to the floor. Pillows were tossed haphazardly as if Jenny had been trying to throw away this thing that had happened.

Memories of other deaths flashed vividly through Gertrude's mind. Beulah, looking strangely ancient and hollowed in death. Rose, thin, sharp bones protruding. And worst of all, the round, pink and white face of Julie Sue turned grey and sunken. Her pink lips flattened against her teeth, her cheekbones sticking up and the roundness of her cheeks gone as if her very flesh had been drawn out of her.

Gertrude felt split suddenly into two people. The panic and terror remained inside, and a strange calmness took over.

She went to Jenny. Jenny needed her.

Gertrude pulled Jenny toward her, and took Annie out of her arms. The child felt as light as if all substance had been removed from her. Beulah's words, buried just beneath the surface of her daily thoughts, returned. "There's a strange disease in the family, Gertrude. It

260

makes people die suddenly, like your aunt, and now your sister and her baby. It drains something out of them. Their vital fluids. It's like all of it is sucked out."

But then it had happened to Beulah, too, even though she was not blood related.

Now Gertrude could tell Beulah. *Not* a family disease, Beulah, but *the doll.* Something about the curse of the doll. She had left the doll on the dresser, but it was not there now, and it had not been there last night when she checked on Ted and Annie.

Dear Lord, why hadn't she asked about it then? Because she hadn't allowed herself to really believe. And now her whole world was being absorbed, consumed. *Eaten.* There was only her and Jenny, and she had to get Jenny out of here.

"Jenny, come with me, dear. Come downstairs. We'll call a doctor."

"Oh God, it's too late."

"Come with me."

To Gertrude's desperate relief Jenny allowed herself to be led out of the death room and downstairs. Gertrude took her to the kitchen and sat her on a kitchen chair. Jenny had grown very quiet. Gertrude dialed the only doctor she knew, her mother's doctor, Old Doc Highland.

Gertrude heard her voice saying now to Jenny in a shrill monotone, "It's the family disease, Jenny. There's something in the family that causes sudden death, and the loss of vital fluids. It's like they just evaporate."

Her voice repeated what Beulah had told her, while inside the terror was raging louder and louder. It hardly mattered what she said. Jenny wasn't listening. She was lost in her own world of disbelief. As she hung up the phone she assured Jenny, "The doctor is coming."

Jenny shook her head. "It's too late." She hugged her arms against her body and bowed her head. "It's so cold."

"Jenny, where was the doll?"

261

Jenny didn't raise her head.

"The doll, Jenny, was it on the bed? What did you do with it, dear?"

Jenny shook her head and answered, "I don't know. What doll?"

"The old baby doll that Mama—"

"What difference does it make? Why do you care about an old doll when my baby . . . my husband . . . both lie . . ." Her voice grew suddenly shrill as she lifted her head and looked at Gertrude in anguish.

Gertrude put her hand on Jenny's shoulder and the girl calmed again. She was shivering.

"I'll go turn the heat up," Gertrude said. "You let the doctor in. He said he'd be here in a few minutes."

She left the room, afraid now to enter the long dark halls beyond the kitchen. Afraid to go upstairs. She turned on the lights, and turned the thermostat up to seventy-eight. Mama had gotten where she demanded more warmth, but even at eighty degrees the upper hall would remain closer to sixty.

All the lights bloomed ahead of her as she found the switches and pushed them. She climbed the stairs slowly, her eyes taking in every shadow on the stairs and along the halls. She hadn't seen the doll on the bed or on the dresser. She had to find the doll and put it away again before it claimed Jenny for its own, too. Jenny and . . . herself.

Her footsteps sounded hollow on the upper hall. The darkness stayed in the corners, the lights inadequate. She was afraid. Each step brought her closer to panic.

Jenny was in the house, unprotected, unsuspecting. She would lie down to sleep, and the doll would take her, she reminded herself.

She had to find the doll and lock it away in the cabinet.

In cold terror she crossed the threshold into the room

where Annie lay on the bed and Ted on the floor. She turned on the ceiling light, but it seemed only to increase the twilight of the darkened room, and the shadows that lurked like black monsters everywhere.

Gertrude walked slowly around the foot of the bed, kicking aside the quilt, hoping to uncover the doll. Aware for the first time that she was still barefoot, that she wore only her long flannel nightgown, she started back to her room to dress. She must not be in her nightgown when the doctor arrived. Mama would be horrified. Then instead of going to the door she changed her mind and went to the window instead and put the blind up. The grey daylight penetrated the room only a few feet.

She began a search of the room. She looked under the bed, under the bedding. She looked into the drawers. She pulled them out and let them fall. She searched, growing more frantic. The desperation that had remained within her bursting forth like madness.

The doll was not there.

But she continued her search, looking again through the bedding, beneath the bed, muttering under her breath, "Oh Lord, have mercy."

Chapter 13

Jenny remained in a strange state of numbness through the doctor's visit to the house and through the three days preceding the double funeral. The doctor's words went through her mind over and over, but told her nothing.

"Your husband must have had a heart attack. Your daughter had a fever, you say?" He shook his head, puzzled. "Sometimes deaths happen for no reason that we can see. There's history of sudden death during sleep in the Madison family. It comes through Ted's mother's side of the family. We could send the bodies down to the State Medical Examiner if you want."

"No."

Dear God, they were dead. If she had known this would happen when she married Ted, would she have married him?

She wept into her pillow at night, asking herself that question. Had the years of love and happiness been worth the anguish she now suffered? Then the disbelief and numbness would return and save her. They were in the house, or outside, playing almost like two kids, instead of a father and child. Ted was showing Annie around the home he had grown up in. Or they were in Ted's old room looking at all his boyhood treasures. Sometimes Jenny went into his room, and sat with the ghosts of her husband and child. She could see them, diaphanous, their heads together over something that had been important to Ted.

Sometimes she went into the room she was redecorating for Annie and tried to get to work. But the moment the wallpaper rustled in her hands the spell was broken, and she was cast back on the black waters of reality.

Gertrude went silently about the house, looking almost as wan and sunken as Annie and Ted had looked before the funeral director plumped their cheeks again. Even in the darkest hour of the night Jenny could hear her, footsteps slipping along the hall.

"What on earth happened here?" the doctor asked when he first entered the room where Annie and Ted lay dead. And Jenny looked at the drawers pulled out of the chest and the dresser, empty drawers tossed aside. She looked at the bedding pulled off and scattered about on the floor.

No one answered him. Gertrude picked up the bedding and put the drawers back where they belonged.

Later Jenny thought that Gertrude must have been looking for the doll. The goddamned old antique baby doll that had belonged to her mother. Lying in her bed, staring into the dark, Jenny clenched her hands at her side in bitterness. Was the doll more important to Gertrude than Ted and Annie?

But the next day her bitterness faded. Gertrude was to be pitied, not censored. She was suddenly a shadow of herself.

Her child and husband were buried side by side in the family mausoleum. There was room for two more. Gertrude and Jenny herself. Then the vault would be locked forever. To Jenny the best burial place was the ground. To return to earth, to become part of the growing earth.

But she had not argued with Gertrude about the burial place.

Very few people had come to the house before or after the funeral. The doctor came, bringing his wife, who Gertrude didn't even know. The minister and his wife came every day, and sat for a long hour talking about the virtues of heaven and God's love, until Jenny thought she would scream. On the day of the funeral the women of nearby churches came bringing food. Jenny wondered what would happen to all of it. There were only two of them, and after today there would be only one. She could not stay here with Gertrude in this big, shadowy house where every movement and sound made her think Ted or Annie would step out and greet her.

She couldn't bear it.

She had to leave.

In the silence of her room at night she was packing, slowly, to keep herself busy. She was packing not only her clothes but Ted's and Annie's. She would be taking away with her all that she could of her child and husband.

She would go as far as her few dollars would take her, then stop and get a waitress job. And by that method make her way back to Washington where Carol lived.

She stood at the window looking out at the setting sun. Streaks of blood red tinged the sky, beneath turquoise and rose. She thought with longing of her childhood here before her mother took Carol and left. Life hadn't been easy at home. Pop had a drinking problem and a problem keeping a job. But at least they had been together. He was her family, and he's gone. Ted and Annie were her life's pleasure, and now they had passed away.

God takes home his loved ones, it is not for us to question why.

Why! WHY?

She could scream the question at the sinking sun, at the memory of the minister and his wife, sitting there so smug, as if they had an inside track to God. One which she would never share.

Jenny turned away from the window and pressed the button of the light. Three suitcases sat on the floor at the foot of the bed, ready to go, bulging at the seams. The two large ones were hers and Ted's, the smaller one was Annie's.

She wanted to leave tonight. She had spent four nights in this room without Ted, and she could spend no more.

You can't leave Gertrude.

Yes.

No.

You have no money to leave.

She was hearing voices in her head. She would go as crazy as Gertrude seemed to be these past three days if she didn't get out of here.

At the dresser she looked through her purse and Ted's billfold. Fifty dollars. Thank God, enough money to buy gas to get her all the way to Washington if she took some of the food the ladies from the church had brought. Enough to get her to Carol's if she didn't have car trouble. Or enough to rent herself a room somewhere between here and there and work for awhile. It would probably be good for her to work, to listen to the noise in a busy cafe, to walk her legs off trying to keep people served.

She snapped her purse and pulled on her coat. And stopped, listening.

The movement was in the hall again. The footsteps.

267

As they had been every day, every night since . . .

Then, as she listened, a door closed and drawers slid from old, tight bureaus and slid back again.

Jenny picked up a suitcase. It felt as if it would pull her arm out of its socket, and she swung it to the front and gripped it with both hands. At the door she let it thump to the floor while she turned the knob. She shoved it out into the hall and went back for another.

When she turned she almost screamed.

Miss Sybil stood in the shadows of the hall glaring at her through eyes that were like large, dark holes. She moved, edging into the lighter doorway.

Jenny sagged in recognition. It was not Miss Sybil. Gertrude, thank God, it was Gertrude.

"Jenny," Gertrude whispered, and the sound was like an accusing hiss. "You're not *leaving?*"

"I have to, Gertrude. I can't stay here where they died. Please understand."

Gertrude had begun shaking her head the moment Jenny started speaking, but Jenny knew it was not in agreement. Then she saw, as the outdoor light faded and the lamplight replaced it, that Gertrude was not staring out of accusation, she was afraid.

"Gertrude, you can come with me." She felt an instant lift of spirits. Why not? Gertrude was not so old that she couldn't start a new life. "Why not, Gertrude?"

"Oh no. Don't you see, Jenny, I have to find the doll."

"For God's sake, Gertrude, are you still worrying about that damned doll? Why do you need the doll? You could just lock the house and drive away with me, and stay as long as you like. See the country. That's what we could do, Gertrude, we could see the country! That's what Ted liked."

"But Ted had come home. He told me he had wanted to come home for a long time. But, perhaps it is better if you leave, Jenny. At least I'll know you're somewhere safe . . . somewhere out there."

Gertrude came into the room, stepping past packed suitcases. She only glanced down at the other two.

"You can leave, Gertrude."

"No. I can't go. I have to find the doll, Jenny. Have you seen it?"

Jenny stared at Gertrude.

"Think carefully, Jenny," Gertrude urged, her hand closing on Jenny's arm and pulling her back into the room. She cast a worried glance toward the hall before she closed the door. "You found Ted and Annie. You were the first one in the room. Where was the doll?"

Jenny shook her head. It was so important to Gertrude, even though she didn't understand why. She tried to think. "I don't remember. I don't think I saw it at all, Gertrude. I'm sorry."

"I have to tell you," Gertrude said, bringing her face closer to Jenny's. "It was the doll that killed Annie and Ted. And I have to find it and put it back in the cabinet before it gains so much strength that it can't be stopped."

Jenny wanted to pull away, to tear her eyes away from the madness in Gertrude's, but she couldn't.

Gertrude's hand clutched both of Jenny's arms and shook her.

"Do you understand, Jenny?"

Slowly, to humor her, Jenny nodded. A long chill shivered over her body. The madness of Gertrude brought to Jenny a fear she had never known before. She knew she couldn't walk out tonight on this poor woman. Perhaps she could get Gertrude to a doctor tomorrow.

"I understand, Gertrude," Jenny said, hearing a

quiver in her voice. She cleared her throat and put her hands up to grip Gertrude's elbows. Gertrude wore old-fashioned dresses, all long sleeved, all in a somber material. And beneath the fabric Jenny felt the bones of Gertrude's sharp elbows.

"It worries me, Jenny, when you're not with me. Who knows what the doll can do now?"

"I'll stay with you. Maybe now you should go to your room and try to get some rest."

"Oh no, now that I've told you, now that you believe me, we have to search together for the doll. You do believe me, don't you, Jenny?"

Jenny sighed. "I think you're upset about all the deaths. Your mother, not long ago, and now Ted and Annie. I think you're overwrought."

"Then you don't understand." Gertrude shook her head in a way that seemed almost sane. "You must listen to me. I didn't want Ted to give Annie the doll because it seemed that whenever the doll was given to anyone they died, and—"

"No," Jenny interrupted. "What about your mother, Gertrude? Wasn't it first given to Sybil? She didn't die. Not then. She lived to be old."

Gertrude paused as if considering that. Her steady gaze wavered. Softly she admitted, "That's true."

"Don't you see. Maybe it's just like the doctor said, there's some kind of disease that runs through the family on your mother's side."

Gertrude sagged as if she were going to fall. Jenny helped her to the bed, where she sat. She put her arm up and pressed it against her forehead.

"I don't know. Maybe you're right, Jenny. Do you suppose I'm going crazy?"

Gertrude glanced up with an attempt at a smile and laughter. The laughter sounded like a croak.

"No, of course not." The lie slid easily from Jenny's tongue.

"But Jenny, there's still something unexplained here.

"What? The disease?"

"No, Jenny, the doll. Please, listen. When Annie went to bed, where was the doll?"

Jenny could hardly bear to think of the last time she had kissed Annie good night. She could see again that lovely little face, and beside it, the face of the little baby doll.

"It was there. She was cuddling it."

"Yes. And later, when she was asleep, when I thought you and Ted were asleep, I did what I had done every night since Ted gave Annie the doll. I took it out of her bed and laid it on the dresser."

"On the dresser," Jenny repeated numbly. Again she was reliving that night, as she had a thousand times in the days since. She had gone in to answer Annie's cries, she and Ted, and as she thought back she remembered the doll.

"Yes, on the dresser," Gertrude urged, her eyes getting that burning look again.

"Then she must have gotten up to get it," Jenny said, "because it was in bed with her."

Gertrude whispered, "Are you sure?"

"Yes."

"It wasn't on the dresser?"

"No. On the bed."

Gertrude let out her breath. "I knew it wasn't on the dresser. Later, when I got back to my room, I remembered it wasn't on the dresser. But I thought Ted was there, and it would be all right. I never dreamed Ted, too—"

"Gertrude, why don't we go downstairs to the kitchen where the lights are brighter?"

271

Gertrude seemed not to hear her. "Remember back, Jenny. When you went in and found them dead, where *exactly* was the doll?"

Jenny found herself recalling the room, the scene, again and again. She hadn't wanted to. But now in her mind she was touching Ted's shoulder again, and he was falling slowly.

And Annie . . . a small skeleton, her face sunken, her eyes sunken, the flesh molded close to her bones.

Jenny shook her head. "No doll," she said. "The doll was not there."

Chapter 14

"What happened to it?" Gertrude asked. "I have looked and looked, and I can't find it."

"Why is it so important you find it, Gertrude? I understand it was your mother's doll, and of course you don't want it lost or destroyed, but it's somewhere around. You'll find it."

Gertrude said, "It's important that we put it back in the cabinet, and lock the door to the top floor. I don't know what else to do."

"All right. Tomorrow I'll help you look."

"You're staying then?"

The look on Gertrude's face was not completely relieved. Jenny saw concern, too, and fear, that wild-eyed look she had seen in animals that were afraid.

"Yes, I'll stay."

"Then, Jenny, I want you to use my mother's room. It's closer, right next door to mine. That way, I'll know you're safe."

Jenny smiled. "I'm not a family member, Gertrude. I'm not a Madison."

Gertrude didn't smile in return. "Please. Humor me? You don't mind sleeping in Mama's room?"

Jenny said no, even as she was thinking of the large, dark room, filled with so many pieces of old, large, unnecessary furniture.

Gertrude visibly brightened. Her face smoothed, not quite into a smile. "We'll get fresh bedding from the bureau, and make the bed. I'll get her medicines off the bedside table, and maybe we can even open the window to let in some fresh air. The weather is so much warmer. Is this your suitcase?"

Jenny nodded.

Gertrude picked it up and went down the hall with it bumping against her leg. Jenny gave one last look around the room, then turned out the light and closed the door. With the other two suitcases she followed Gertrude, but she left Ted's and Annie's things on the balcony above the stairway. Ahead of her Gertrude turned on lights, entering the small hallway that branched to both Sybil's room, and to the room Gertrude had occupied for the past several years.

Gertrude went about in the room turning on all the lights. The head of the bed reached more than halfway up the high wall, a dark, solid wood headboard with carved high relief figures lumpy with dust in the depressions. Gertrude swiped at it perfunctorily with one hand.

"We couldn't afford someone to clean in later years. No one worked for us after you left, Jenny. Mama missed you very much."

Jenny doubted that. Miss Sybil had never been a friendly person. Mrs. Madison, not Miss Sybil. And never just Sybil. Even in her thoughts her mother-in-law's name did not come easily.

The featherbed lay in the corner, like a great blob of lint. The mattress was so old it was colorless. Two fat feather pillows had been tossed into the middle of the bed.

"You will want the featherbed," Gertrude said, going toward it. "It's so much warmer."

"No," Jenny said quickly. She could still see Mrs. Madison sunk into that softness, and it pillowing up around her. "No, just something on the mattress."

She wasn't staying long, she thought firmly to herself.

Only long enough for Gertrude to relax and feel more at ease.

"Then we'll make it up with blankets. They're right here in the bureau drawer."

Gertrude's attempt at cheerfulness and bravado failed. She grew silent as she helped Jenny make the bed. It seemed such a waste of energy as Jenny worked, spreading, smoothing, tucking. It was like making a table, it was so high. On the right side of the bed a miniature stairsteps, standing like a footstool, afforded access.

Something pecked at the window. Jenny looked out and saw white sleet piling up on the window sill like grainy snow.

Gertrude said, "I guess our good weather is over. I'm so glad it was nice and sunny for the funerals."

"I hardly noticed," Jenny answered. Then spoke her thoughts. "This seems such a waste, Gertrude. Why don't I just sleep in my own bed?"

"It's safer here, Jenny."

She had forgotten. Gertrude wanted her next door because she was afraid. It was so easy to forget everything but Annie and Ted, as her thoughts constantly sought the days when they were living. When Annie was warm and soft in her arms, and Ted her rock of security.

"How awful it must have been for you all these years, Gertrude, being alone," Jenny said.

"Oh I wasn't alone. I had Mama."

"Oh, sure. I'm sorry. I was just thinking of Teddy and Annie, and how important they were to me. And you without . . ." She bit her lip. And you without ever having a husband and children? How cruel could she be? "I'm sorry."

During the past long days and nights since she had found her husband and child, she had not slept. She had lain awake nights listening to the house, to the screaming of her soul against this loss, and to the movements of

Gertrude, searching, searching. Although at the time she hadn't known what she was looking for.

"I have flashlights we can use," Gertrude said. "The house has so many unlighted places. It wasn't wired, you know, until I was a grown girl. Before that we used natural gas for light as well as heat. With flashlights we'll be able to see under furniture and into places, otherwise so dark."

"Tonight?" Jenny asked in surprise. "We're going to look tonight?"

Gertrude's large eyes looked hollow, and for a moment as empty as Ted's had been.

"Why yes," Gertrude said. "Of course. It's at night that it happens, you know. The deaths. We have to keep active. We have to find it."

Jenny shivered and hugged her sweater closer. A cold draft had entered the room. Gertrude had slipped back into her madness. Just as Jenny thought she was past it, she was gone again.

"Yes, well," Jenny said, "Let's go then. There are so many rooms." Humor her, humor poor Gertrude, even if it takes all night to find the old doll.

"I've looked through all the rooms on the first and second floor, and even the third. I've closed all the doors so it can't get in those rooms."

"Can't get . . ." Jenny repeated in astonishment. Gertrude was talking as if the doll could get around on its own. She made herself stop just in time. Poor Gertrude. *Humor her.*

Gertrude collapsed suddenly onto the chair at the side of the bed, lowering her head to her hand. "Oh God, Jenny, what am I thinking of? A week ago I would never have said such a thing. But, if there was only some explanation of what happened to it. I can't find it anywhere."

"Yes," Jenny said, relieved that Gertrude had become

lucid again, if only for a few minutes. "It was in the room. Could the doctor have taken it? He was there, too. And then the people from the funeral home . . ."

Gertrude looked up. "Why would they want it?"

Jenny shook her head. She didn't give a damn why they took it. "If they didn't, it's got to be there, Gertrude. Sometimes it's easy to overlook things. Let's just go back and see."

Humor her. Then get her to bed, and tomorrow to a doctor. It might even help Jenny herself, give her something to do, to help her get through these horrible days and nights with the ebbing and flowing of her grief like a fresh bleeding wound. Sometimes the wound would burst open, and her heart's blood would spill as she realized Annie and Ted were gone.

No, it was better to keep busy. And maybe, deep inside, that was one of the reasons Gertrude felt such an urgency to get the old doll and put it back in the cabinet. Just something to keep her busy.

With flashlights they went back to the bedroom where Annie and Ted had died. Even with the overhead light turned on, the flashlights helped.

Jenny laid her flashlight on the dresser, its beam angled upward and making a bright spot on the wall. She picked up the quilt with the star design and folded it and laid it in the corner. A blue blanket on the bed was crumpled and kicked to the foot, and Jenny folded it.

Gertrude tore the sheets from the bed, and the mattress cover, and folded them.

They worked in silence together.

Gertrude pulled out the drawers again, and then replaced them.

Jenny stood watching her, hands on hips. She couldn't bear to look at the bed.

"It's not here, Gertrude. We have to assume somebody moved it. We could go see your doctor tomorrow, and

277

ask him. Perhaps he could take a look at you, too. How long has it been since you had a good physical?"

Gertrude didn't answer. The worried look on her face intensified. She turned her head sideways and stood listening.

"Gertr—"

"Shhh. Listen," Gertrude hissed.

Jenny took a deep breath and held it.

Outside the window a whispering sound of something softer than sleet fell. Snow, perhaps.

Gertrude suddenly grabbed Jenny's arm. "Hear that?"

"I think—"

"Shh. Not out loud, Jenny. Listen."

Jenny heard the soft falling of snow at the window. She looked, and saw the window black and reflecting only the room, like a watchful eye.

"It's upstairs," Gertrude whispered. "It's gone back upstairs."

"Gertrude, I—"

"It's crawling. Hear it crawling, Jenny?"

"Oh Gertie, for Christ's sake. It's snowing. That's snow you hear. Look out the window."

Gertrude came with her to the window. Jenny felt the cold air inches away from the glass. Bits of heavy, damp snow were beginning to pile up on the sill, held in place by the glistening sleet that had packed onto the sill earlier.

"See, Gertrude? Annie would have loved the snowfall. Ted would have too. In the west, as soon as the mountains had a fresh snowcap, we'd go up as far as we could drive, and play in the snow. Then what an appetite!"

"No," Gertrude said, her voice low but no longer whispering. "That's not what I heard. It's upstairs."

Good, Jenny almost said. Maybe it can put itself back into the cabinet. Then she felt sorry for being so sarcastic, even in the silence of her mind. Poor Gertrude.

278

"Let's go up and see," Jenny said, taking her flashlight from the dresser.

Gertrude at first seemed reluctant.

"There's no light up there," she said. "It was never wired with electricity."

"We have our flashlights. Come on."

As they climbed the steep stairs into the third floor Jenny wondered, for the first time, what had actually happened to the doll. Had Ted himself put it away? It was a possibility she might mention to Gertrude, later, after they found it.

As they climbed and then came out into the third floor hallway it suddenly seemed to Jenny the one logical answer. Ted, remembering what Gertrude had said about the doll, had taken it in the night and returned it to the cabinet with the glass doors. As Jenny went toward the cabinet, the beam of her flashlight guiding her, she had no doubts they would find it in the cabinet.

Chapter 15

The bright, narrow flashlight beam jerked over the contents of the cabinet, settling on the bare place on the bottom shelf. Dust outlined an area that once was occupied by the doll. Behind Jenny, Gertrude aimed her light down the hall to the window at the end, then upwards toward the ceiling.

Jenny stood up.

Gertrude opened a door. Standing on the threshold, she looked into the room. She closed the door and stepped back.

She whispered, "I heard it."

"I thought perhaps Ted had brought it back up here and put it away."

"No."

Jenny started to suggest they go back downstairs. Not only was there no light up here, there was no heat. The cold penetrated her sweater as if it were made of gauze. But if they went downstairs without searching the whole area, Gertrude would continue to think the doll was here.

"Come with me," Jenny said, taking Gertrude's arm. "Let's look into each room."

The rooms were small and in most cases furnished with the bare necessities of bed, dresser, and a lamp table. Old curtains hung limply at the windows. Spider webs coiled in the corners of the rooms and beneath the beds. Dust faded the patterns of the rugs. Jenny was glad there were only five such rooms. The rest of the area was taken up by a storage room. She stood in the doorway aiming the flashlight beam over the clutter that filled the room. A couple of small tables, a few old chairs, two grey lumps in the corner that might be featherbeds. Boxes were stacked neatly against a wall, and beside them three trunks balanced precariously in another stack, leaning between boxes and wall. There was a musty, old smell. Old wood, old fabrics. Perhaps the tiny dens of comfortably established mice.

Jenny stepped back and closed the door.

"Of course it wouldn't be in there, Gertrude," she said gently. "The door was closed. Shall we go down now?"

Gertrude's eyes hovered deep in shadow, her cheeks sunken, her mouth pursed at the corners. Slowly, she nodded.

Jenny checked once more to be sure all the doors were closed, then she led the way downstairs. She turned the button on the stairway door. It fit snugly, as it always had.

Gertrude went with her in silence as Jenny led the way down to the kitchen. The lower hall lights were on, but the high ceilings seemed to absorb them, and shadows hung heavy in every corner, every doorway. Jenny turned her flashlight on again, and looked into the small sitting room where they had gathered since Miss Sybil's death. She looked over the room, behind the furniture, on the mantel of the cold fireplace.

When she turned, she saw that Gertrude was waiting in the doorway.

"You should eat, Gertrude. You'll feel better." When Gertrude didn't answer, Jenny offered, "I'll eat with you."

They entered the kitchen where linoleum brightened the floor, and the builder hadn't been so stingy with windows. It had always been Jenny's favorite room. Maybe because she felt more at home in it. At one end was the sitting area, with the rocking chair where once she had rested. A small radio still stood on the library table beneath the windows. In the middle of the room was the informal dining area, with a big round table and chairs, and a china cabinet against the wall. On the east end was the cooking area.

Gertrude turned the gas on under the coffee pot, and got cups and saucers while Jenny uncovered a couple of platters. They ate in silence. Jenny forced her food down, slowly, watching Gertrude. Gertrude swallowed hard, she saw, and knew the food was no easier for her to eat than it was for Jenny. But if they each could pretend for the other . . . they would survive.

Survive. It seemed odd that survival should be important. Though she had lost her whole world, still she sought survival.

"I heard it," Gertrude said. "But perhaps it was down below."

"Below? You mean down here?"

"Yes. Or the basement."

The basement. Lord, she had forgotten that horrible place. She hoped Gertrude didn't insist on a search of the basement, where water stood in pools you were never sure were shallow, where spiders ran rampant, and rodents made nests and dug holes.

"Gertrude, what did you hear?"

At first it seemed Gertrude would not answer. She chewed, looking down at her plate. Then, with a long sigh she said, "I know you think I'm crazy, Jenny. I'm not."

"I don't think you're crazy, Gertrude," Jenny said. She was so tired, suddenly, that she didn't feel like lifting her fork.

"I heard it . . . crawling."

It was Jenny's turn to sigh. Gertrude had heard the snow at the window. That soft whispering, that almost

282

silent movement of snow. She had to ignore Gertrude's remark if she were going to spend any more time in the house with her.

"The only answer," Jenny said, "is that someone moved the doll. I think Ted did."

Gertrude looked at her. "Ted? Why?"

"I think he got to remembering what you said about the . . ." Jenny stopped. The doll, given to the baby they had never known about before. And the baby dying. And then the doll given to Julie Sue . . . ?

Jenny said aloud, "It does seem very strange that so many of your family died that summer."

"It was the doll," Gertrude said. "I knew, when Mama took it out of Julie Sue's room, that the doll had caused the deaths. And when Mama looked at me, the way she gave me orders never to touch the doll, I knew. The doll . . . killed."

Oh God, it couldn't be possible. And yet, Annie and Ted had died. Jenny tried to recall the scene of death. Where was the doll? Annie, her face half buried in her pillow and the blue blanket, swam in her eyes and sharpened. Jenny saw the bed, and Ted leaning on it, his head resting on his arms.

That was wrong. He was reaching. One hand was out, fingers coiled. As if . . .

Jenny stood up.

She didn't know what the death scene meant. But she was sure of one thing. The doll had not been in the room then.

"It wasn't there, Gertrude. The doll wasn't there. I know. I was the one to find them. I think Ted put the doll away somewhere. I'm ready to look into the basement, Gertrude, if you are."

Gertrude led the way to the basement door. It was a

part of the house easily forgotten. The basement door opened off a narrow hall that joined the back stairway to the laundry room. Set into the wall like a secret opening, it would be easy to pass by if one didn't know exactly where to look for it.

Gertrude was torn in her thinking. Maybe Jenny was right, and Ted had removed the doll, putting it somewhere it might never be found. He would not have chosen the basement. If he had ever gone into the basement, she didn't know of it. As a child he was not expected to do chores, such as seeing to the lighting of the furnace pilot. Those chores were hers. Nor had he ever been sent to the basement with a box of canned fruit or vegetables.

And the doll—could it have gone on its own? She had heard movements that were like the movements her mother had made, material sweeping the floor as she silently walked. She had seen the doll, in her mind, moving, pulling itself along like a worm, humping, flattening, inching forward, its long gown trailing and making the sounds her mother had made. Could it go on its own? She was terrified that it might.

At times when a certain lucidity overcame her fears, she would stop, shocked at herself for even thinking that a mere doll was the source of her fear. A doll that moved and drew something vital from humans, destroying them in the process, and thereby strengthening itself. But then, a deeper lucidity would bring back the fear. *She knew.*

She looked back at Jenny, and saw her close behind, the flashlight in her hand lifted to trace the outline of the basement door. Jenny's face looked sharply white, her cheekbones more prominent, her full lips tighter and thinner.

Gertrude opened the basement door.

Rusted hinges squeaked.

"I oiled these," Gertrude said, hearing her voice drop into the hollow beneath. "Twice a year when I go down with the gas man to tend to the furnace, I oil these hinges, but it doesn't seem to last."

She must try to sound normal, so that Jenny would be less afraid. Whatever she had to do, she must keep Jenny with her. She couldn't bear the thoughts of being alone in this house, surrounded by the smell of death, with the doll.

Jenny was the only person she had left in the world. Relatives that once had come to visit had drifted away. Cousins, she had known vaguely when she was a child, no longer communicated with her. She couldn't even remember their names.

She felt the tension of Jenny's arm, as if she were trying to pull away. But Gertrude couldn't let her go.

"Be careful," she said, finding an excuse for holding to her. "The basement stairs are very steep. And there's no handrail."

The cold air lifted in a wave, carrying musty odors of rats, mice, old wood, unidentifiable odors. It singed her nostrils almost like extreme cold.

Gertrude slid her flashlight into her pocket to free her hand, and felt along the rough wood of the wall for the switch.

"We'll have some light here in a minute," she muttered for Jenny's sake.

The light blinked on, one bulb near the furnace about thirty feet away.

Gertrude released Jenny's arm and went slowly down the steps. On the basement floor she picked her way between pools of water, shining her light ahead, finding the solid, red clay paths.

On the right were the shelves of fruits and vegetables, some of it too old to eat now, turned greenish black in the jars. Boxes were stacked on the floor, the bottom ones rotted by the moisture. Piles had fallen.

Gertrude swept her flashlight beam to the other end of

the furnace and saw the stone wall, and the pillars that held up the floor of the house.

"It's not here," Jenny said, her voice a shock to Gertrude, causing her to jerk convulsively. "If Ted had brought it down, he would have just laid it here. Close to the steps. He wouldn't have walked on that floor, Gertrude."

The doll was not in the basement. And that meant it was still upstairs, somewhere, hiding.

She climbed the steps, going back up to the lighted hall. She turned off the basement light and closed the door, and checked it to be sure it was firmly closed.

Then she began a search of the unused rooms on the ground floor, even though she had searched them before in the long hours past. She had to find the doll.

Chapter 16

Jenny climbed the small three-step ladder to Miss Sybil's bed and dropped in exhaustion. She was almost too tired to change into her nightgown. It seemed a useless waste of energy to get off the bed, search through her suitcase for a nightgown, and put it on. At least she would probably sleep, dreamless, too tired to do anything but let her body rest.

The night was very dark. She had looked out only briefly as Gertrude insisted on checking the front door and looking out onto the step. The snow had stopped falling and was replaced by a light rain, peppering softly down into the snow and turning to ice.

She pushed herself up from the bed. The table lamp was burning, casting a dim light toward the corners of the strange room. But she was so tired she didn't care that she was going to spend the night in Miss Sybil's bed, or that if Miss Sybil knew she would be horrified.

Jenny lifted the lid of her stuffed suitcase and dug out a flannel nightgown. She dropped it over her head and then undressed beneath it, using it as a shield against the cold. There was an open vent in the floor, which was supposed to allow warm air from the lower floor to rise, but Jenny felt none of it. Over on the hearth of the fireplace, which didn't look as if it had been used to burn wood in a long time, was an electric heater. But Jenny didn't bother to plug it in.

She climbed into the bed and settled back, closing her

eyes. Then she remembered she had left her light on, and she reached out to turn it off.

"Jenny . . ." It was a mournful wail, and might have been a wind from the netherworld mocking her. And then again, *"Jenny."*

Jenny sat up in bed. The voice was real. It had sounded far away, but it had to be Gertrude, even though it hadn't sounded like her voice.

"Jenny."

Again, the low cry, and Jenny realized Gertrude was calling her in hushed desperation. Oh God, was the poor woman never going to sleep?' They had been searching the house for hours. Jenny hadn't realized the house was so large, nor contained so many stairways. Or she had forgotten since the days she had cleaned it.

"What is it, Gertrude?" Jenny called. Thinking to herself, I've got to get out of here. Tomorrow, or the next day. I can't stand this.

"Jenny, listen, come here. Please."

Jenny slid out of bed and walked through the tiny hallway and to the threshold of the other bedroom. The outside door to the mezzanine was closed. Gertrude had insisted on that when they went to bed.

Gertrude was sitting up in her bed. Her table lamp cast a dim light on the side of the bed and down onto the floor, reminding Jenny of the light in the room where Annie and Ted had died. Five nights ago. Was it that long ago? How had she been able to sleep so many nights without them? Was that how one survived the death of a loved one? One night at a time? Too sick in the heart, too exhausted in the body, but to sleep?

"What, Gertrude?"

Gertrude hunched forward on the bed, her eyes staring and filled with terror, her mouth open. She was listening, her head angled.

"Shh," she said, her voice low and whispering. "Hear

it? It's in the hall, Jenny. It waited until we stopped look-ing, and now it's in the hall outside our rooms. Listen!"

Jenny sighed. "It's all right, Gertrude, nothing's out there."

"Yes! Listen, Jenny, *listen*."

She listened.

She heard the whisper of rain at the window, louder than the fall of snow, and she heard something crawling in the walls. A mouse making its bed, or perhaps even a rat or chipmunk crawling up between old boards.

Gertrude hissed, "There!" She pointed toward the wall. Her eyes sunk into madness, her mouth opening and closing, "Do you hear it? Now do you believe me?"

Jenny licked her lips. They were dry and cracked. How long had it been since she had put moistening lip-stick on? How should she handle Gertrude? Try to bring her back to normal, or pretend to agree that the sounds were in the hall? That it crawled along the halls toward their door?

"It's mice in the walls, Gertrude, and rain. Rain at the window, mixed with snow. There's a thin layer of ice coating the snow, and the roads will be very slick tomor-row." Get her mind onto something else. The roads will be very slick tomorrow, too slick to drive, even to take Gertrude to the doctor. Oh God.

"Then you *do* hear it."

Jenny hesitated. The sound continued, louder now. But couldn't Gertrude hear it was in the wall? The inner wall, between the room and the balcony as it was usually called.

"It's in the wall, Gertrude." The noise was a soft, steady movement, a pause, then movement again. "A chipmunk, Gertrude."

She shook her head. "No. It's the doll. It's crawling now, Jenny. We have to be very careful. It's coming along the hall just outside the room. I hear it, you hear it, too.

Lock the doors, please, Jenny. The key is there, on the wall. I wanted you to hear it, so you'd be more careful."

"We'll see if it's in the hall, Gertrude," Jenny said. She turned toward the closed, outer door and reached for the knob.

"No! Don't open the door!"

Jenny heard a loud thump and looked back. Gertrude had fallen. She lay on her hip, leaning on one hand, the other hand reaching down to her leg. There was a twisted grimace of pain on her face. In her hurried attempt to get out of bed and rush to keep Jenny from turning the doorknob she had tangled in her blankets and crashed to the floor. Jenny rushed back to her.

Gertrude groaned, her hand down to caress her ankle. It had twisted beneath her, almost doubling back on itself.

"Oh Gertrude, did you break it?"

Gertrude pulled herself up against the bed. Her ankle was already beginning to swell, but her face turned toward the door, watching as intently as she had listened.

Jenny said, "I'll get something—"

"No! Don't leave the room, Jenny, please. I'll be fine. Just help me back into bed, please."

"Are you sure? I could go down and get some ice—"

"No, please. Lock the door, Jenny. Promise me you won't open the door until morning."

"I promise. Now, lie down and try to rest, okay?"

She helped Gertrude back into bed, and then she took the old, long key down from the hook on the wall and inserted it into the keyhole in the door in the connecting hall. She had to use both hands to turn it, and at first it seemed it would not turn. She exerted more effort. The key cut into her fingers, and she took the hem of her gown for padding. The key turned, slowly, and the lock thumped into place.

When she returned the key to the hook on the wall,

Gertrude lay back, her head on the pillows, her eyes closed.

Jenny remembered seeing a pitcher and a wash basin on the dresser in Miss Sybil's room. From one of the crowded drawers she removed a terry cloth towel with crocheted trim, and a larger one for bandaging. The water in the basin had a thin layer of ice. She carried it into Gertrude's room and made a cold compress from the small towel for Gertrude's ankle.

"You shouldn't go to so much trouble, Jenny. I'll be fine."

"Sure, I know, but this will help keep the swelling down."

Jenny wrapped Gertrude's ankle in the cold wet cloth with the ice from the basin melting within, and wrapped the dry cloth around it. Gertrude's bare toes looked almost blue with cold. Jenny pulled the heavy nightgown to cover the bandage and arranged the bedding so it wouldn't weigh so heavily on her foot.

"I'll go down to the kitchen and get you a hot water bottle."

"No, please. Don't leave the rooms, Jenny. Promise me."

Jenny sighed. No hot water bottle. Gertrude's baseless fear was going to do them both in. Especially now that Gertrude couldn't walk. Not for a few days, anyway.

Jenny hoped it was only a sprain, but still Gertrude wouldn't be able to get around without help for several days. Leaving loomed farther and farther away. It was as if she were trapped, Jenny thought as she went back to the other room and to bed. It was as if some evil power had brought her here and was going to keep her here, in this house, for the rest of her life.

She slept briefly and woke with a snap. The doors between her room and Gertrude's were open, and the only light at the windows. She stared toward the dark connecting hall between the two rooms.

Had Gertrude gotten up? It sounded as if something were dragging on the floor, softly, slowly, coming gradually closer to her.

Her heart pounded hard and slow, thundering in her temples and threatening to obliterate the sound of the other. She put her hand over her heart and willed it to relax. To *listen.* She was like Gertrude, irrational in the dark of the night. Fear closed over her, holding her as if she were encased in ice.

The extreme fear brought her stomach up until she felt she would start being sick. She had to have light. She had to change the atmosphere in the room, this terrible feeling of having someone creep upon her in the dark, someone who could see without light while she was blinded.

"Gertrude?" she said, her voice ringing loudly in the dark world that surrounded her. At the same time, as if her own voice broke the icy paralysis, she reached for the lamp.

"Yes?" Gertrude answered, her voice distant and muffled and slow, as if she had been sleeping.

Jenny sat up in the bed, staring toward the connecting hall.

No one was in her room. Gertrude was not dragging herself closer and closer.

The sound of movement had stopped.

Jenny got up and went to Gertrude's door. Light from her own room illuminated faintly the bed against the far wall, the tall headboard, and Gertrude. She didn't look as if she had changed position since Jenny had wrapped her ankle and said good night to her. She blinked at Jenny and started to sit up.

"No," Jenny said, "Don't get up. It's all right. Do you want your light on?"

"No, thank you."

Jenny stood in the tiny connecting hall, listening. She put her hand out slowly and touched the knob. The door was still locked, and she was glad. The cold porcelain of the knob gradually warmed in her hand as she stood still, listening.

The silence was broken then by that soft movement she had heard from her bed, but now she could tell it was beyond the door, on the mezzanine.

She jerked her hand away from the knob and stood holding her breath, listening. The movement stopped on the other side of the door, and Jenny had a feeling that whatever it was could see her, or sense her, and that it knew she was just beyond the door.

A long scratching sound was followed by a couple of short ones, like a dog or cat wanting through a door. Yet she knew there was no animal, no pet in the house.

She stood staring at the doorknob, thankful the door was locked. *Something* was on the other side of the door. As Gertrude had been so sure earlier, she was the one who heard it now.

Unless she, too, had gone as mad as Gertrude.

Chapter 17

Jenny stood listening to silence. Whatever it was had not moved in a long time. The snow and rain seemed to have stopped, too, except at times she could hear something hard rattle the window pane, as if sleet still occasionally fell.

She slept fitfully. Miss Sybil's bed enveloped her and deadened the soft sounds beyond the walls of the room. In the bed she could tell herself she had been a victim of imagination when she had heard something at the door.

She had sunk into her first restless sleep when the sound of her name brought her back. The call sounded far away, and she couldn't tell at first if it was a woman or a child.

Annie, she thought, and felt the sharp, raw pain of loneliness. Annie would never call her again.

Gertrude. Yes, Gertrude was calling.

Daylight had penetrated the windows, and she could see the warming light of the sun shining on the bare limbs of the trees beyond the windows. Gertrude was calling, her voice sounding lost in a cave. Jenny remembered she had closed Gertrude's door.

She grabbed a robe from her suitcase and rushed through the dark connecting hall to Gertrude's room.

"Jenny, thank God."

"What's wrong, Gertie?"

She went straight to her sister-in-law, and felt the thin arm go around her shoulders.

"If you would just help me stand up . . ."

"Sure. But, can you balance?"

"Oh Lord, I never meant to be such a burden on you, Jenny. I'm sorry. I don't think I can get to the bathroom without you."

"Let me open the curtains first, okay? We need some light. The sun is up and shining, thank God. I could use some sunshine."

"I think there are some old crutches somewhere, Jenny. If you could find me one. Mama's walking canes are in her room, in the closet. If you would get me one, please?"

Jenny went into Miss Sybil's closet and searched among the old, dark clothing until she found the walking canes.

When she returned, Gertrude had managed to get out of bed and was standing, one hand on the post at the foot of the bed. Jenny saw a grimace of pain on her face, and the look of utter helplessness as she looked at Jenny.

Jenny gave her the cane, and then took the key down from its hook on the wall. She unlocked the door into the outer hall, and opened it.

She looked both ways along the mezzanine. Light came through windows at the front of the house, and from a window down the bedroom hall at the rear. There was nothing outside the door, in either direction. And no sign that anything had been there in the night.

The trip to the bathroom and back was exhausting, for both Gertrude and Jenny. Gertrude kept apologizing, and Jenny kept reassuring her.

"You'll get well, Gertie," Jenny said. "In another week, you'll be running up and down the stairs like a spring chicken."

Gertrude said, "Even at my best, I wasn't that spry."

"I'll bet you were once."

At least, Jenny thought as she helped Gertrude back to bed and propped her swollen ankle up on a pillow, it helped to keep their minds off the deaths of Annie and Ted.

And of course there was Miss Sybil's death, too, which would still be very painful for Gertrude. Poor Gertrude, who wouldn't let Jenny call a doctor to look at her ankle. Gertrude, who was beginning to look so old and thin.

"I'll get you a nice, hot breakfast," Jenny promised.

"No, please don't bother."

"Of course I'm going to bring you breakfast, and I want you to eat. You're going to be sick, if you don't."

To her surprise Gertrude cooperated, and even smiled a little, as Jenny returned and arranged the tray on her lap. Jenny sat in a chair nearby with her own bowl of oatmeal and forced down a few mouthfuls.

When she took the tray away, she offered to bring up books from the library, but Gertrude shook her head.

"I don't see well enough to read anymore," Gertrude said. "I have to be in very good light. I've grown far-sighted."

"Then you need reading glasses."

"There hasn't been money for extras for quite a while now."

Jenny paused in the doorway, the tray balanced in her hands. "Then we'll just get jobs, and get you some reading glasses."

"Me on crutches?"

"Well, you aren't really poor, Gertrude. Not really, even if there isn't much cash. You have this huge house, and the land. Sell it. You don't need such a large house. And you need only a small yard."

"Yes, you're right."

"Why don't you sell it, Gertrude? And buy a small house in town? And all this furniture. I'll bet it would bring a mint at auction."

"Sell?"

"Yes. You should get a lot of money for this house and land, say nothing about the antiques."

"No. I could never sell. It's going to be all yours, Jenny. Everything."

Jenny hadn't thought of that. Not once had it entered her mind that with Annie and Ted's death, she was the only one left to inherit what remained of the Wilfred family fortune, if she survived Gertrude. What irony. She a poor girl from the wrong side of town, a former maid in the house. Poor Miss Sybil. It was good that such a thing had never occurred to her.

Then suddenly a thought brought Jenny up short. She stood staring at the wall. Perhaps Miss Sybil had thought of that. Maybe Gertrude was right about there being something strange and dangerous about the doll, and that was why Sybil had given it to Annie.

"Gertrude," Jenny said with a calm sanity that surprised her, "You said your mother never would let you play with her old doll. You said she told you to leave it alone, and never touch it."

"Yes. She did."

"Then you saw her give it to Rose's baby."

"Yes."

"And the baby died."

Gertrude said nothing. Jenny felt her staring. But Jenny went on.

"Then you knew she had given it to Julie, too, because you saw her take it from the room, and she warned you about it again. Julie was dead, too."

From the corner of her eye Jenny saw Gertrude nod.

"Maybe she gave it to Rose, too, and your housekeeper?"

"I don't know," Gertrude said slowly.

"Then, when she felt she was close to death, Miss Sybil had you contact Ted."

"She wanted to see . . . Annie. She didn't say anything about seeing Ted. Just the child."

Jenny began to feel hollow. She felt something cold filling that hollowness, filling, filling, until the coldness began to seep through to her skin. She couldn't stop the piling of fact upon fact, of seeing the past as Gertrude had presented it to her, or the feeling that she had been blind.

"She wanted to see Annie," Jenny said. "And her last words were, 'She's yours now.' "

She paused for so long that Gertrude, sitting still in her bed, staring at Jenny's profile, murmured, "Yes."

"Gertrude, you knew all the time that she was talking about the doll. Didn't you? You tried to make us see things you didn't think were possible. Miss Sybil didn't give the doll to Annie because she loved her, as Ted had hoped. But because she wanted her dead."

Gertrude said nothing. Jenny felt as if her mind had shattered. What was she thinking about? What kind of craziness?

Gertrude said, "No, I never thought Mama wanted Annie dead. She'd only met Annie once. She wanted to see her. I didn't know what she meant about that. Her last words. I didn't know any more than the rest of you. It was Ted who thought she meant the doll. If I had ever thought Mama wanted to hurt Annie, I would never have called you to come home. *Never.*"

Jenny looked at Gertrude and saw her face strained and on the verge of tears. She had upset her, and was sorry. She should have kept that sudden and unexpected flow of thoughts about Miss Sybil to herself.

"I'll be back soon," Jenny said as she went out with the tray.

She didn't want the property, she thought as she went down the stairs. She was sure Miss Sybil hadn't intended for her to survive Gertrude. Survive? What was life without Annie and Ted?

There was a rotten board about halfway down the steps. She could feel the softness of it when she had inadvertently stepped on it earlier when she carried the breakfast tray up to Gertrude.

She didn't want the damned property.

She wanted Annie and Ted back. She wanted them back so badly that she felt as if the pain were growing, expanding to more than she could ever bear.

In the afternoon she went back into the room she had been repapering for Annie. For the first time in several days she pushed the door wide and stood in the doorway looking in. The ceiling was lovely and fresh, the blue paper dotted with silver and gold stars, and tiny silver angels. The angels flew happily among the stars.

Tears came to Jenny's eyes as she looked at the paper. Annie had loved the paper. Angels among the stars. How prophetic it had been.

There was something on the floor beneath a sheet that had been used to protect the bed from ceiling dust. She saw old, yellowed cloth contrasting with the white sheet, and the bulge of something that hadn't been there when she covered the bed.

299

The doll?

She crossed the room and picked the doll up, murmuring under her breath, "I'll be damned." So this was where Ted had put the doll. Gertrude must have looked into this room. But it would have been easy to miss seeing the doll, hidden as it was beneath a fold of the sheet.

In the light of the sun, filtered only by the window and the leafless limbs, nothing had ever looked more benign. It was just an ordinary old doll made in the shape of an infant, wearing a long christening gown and a bonnet, the material of which had turned dingy and yellow. Ted, for his own reasons, must have laid it in the room that was being redecorated for Annie.

That she had gone along for one moment with Gertrude's old fears about the doll now seemed ludicrous to Jenny. How nutty could people get?

Slanting sunlight fell like black lace on the doll as Jenny held it in her hands. It had a soft body, and felt oddly heavy, like a young baby. But it looked different from her memory of it. Hadn't it been about the size of a three month old baby, with rosy cheeks and a puckered mouth? With little creases on the forehead and beneath the eyes?

Now it was fat and red, its cheeks too full and rounded, almost bloated looking. She felt its face, and was surprised at the warmth. The sunshine, she told herself.

Its eyes opened as she raised its head, and seemed to blink and catch sight of her and hold her image. So much the way a real baby would have. What a work of art, she thought. So real, in a grotesque way.

She carried it out into the hall. Gertrude would be delighted she had found it.

She stopped.

Then she crossed the hall to the room where Annie and Ted had died. The bed had been stripped, but the pillows were still on the mattress.

Jenny laid the doll on the pillows.

That was where it belonged, she told herself. Not upstairs in the display cabinet. Annie's grandmother had given it to her, the only thing Annie had ever received from her grandmother. It had not been an omen of death. It had been a quest for forgiveness. Jenny had to believe that.

So Jenny placed it as near Annie as she could, on the pillow where last she had lain.

Chapter 18

Jenny wrapped Gertrude's swollen ankle with long strips of white cloth she had torn from an old sheet. Night had fallen, and she hadn't closed the draperies yet, nor turned on any light except the one by Gertrude's bed.

"Did you lock the door, Jenny?"

Jenny looked over her shoulder. No, she hadn't, but she was looking to see that the door in the small hallway was closed, and it was.

"It's shut tight, Gertrude. I'll lock it when I finish here."

Jenny drew the white strip around the painful ankle and secured it with a safety pin. The ankle was now bandaged from halfway down the calf to the ball of her foot.

"That should help take the swelling down," Jenny said. "And in a couple of days you can probably walk."

"Where are you going?" Gertrude asked in a harsh whisper, reaching out as if to hold Jenny.

"Just to empty out your foot soaking pan. I'll be right back."

"Jenny, it's dark now. Please don't leave the rooms."

"I'll be all right, Gertrude. I'll be back. You're perfectly safe here."

"No! Can't you hear it? It's out there again on the balcony. It comes out of hiding at night. Can't you hear it?"

Jenny stared at Gertrude. All day she had seemed perfectly sane, worried that she couldn't get around on her own, concerned that Jenny was doing too much for her. And Jenny had hoped that Gertrude was going to be all right now. That in a few days, as soon as the ankle got well, Jenny could leave.

"It's only the mice, Gertrude," Jenny said, but she could see that she was not going to be able to leave the rooms. She put down the pan of cold water.

"It's not the mice, Jenny. It's the doll. It's going to kill us both, Jenny, if we're not careful. It's out there, coming for us."

Jenny said, "Gertrude, I found the doll today."

Gertrude stared at Jenny, the dim light from the lamp highlighting her cheek and making her nose look long, and her chin pointed and sharp. Jenny turned on the overhead light.

"It was in Annie's room, the one I was papering. Ted must have put it there. It was hidden beneath a sheet."

A slow frown gathered on Gertrude's face. "Why didn't you tell me?"

"I felt it was better if you didn't even think about it. It's only a doll, Gertrude. All these fears you've developed about it are irrational, can't you see that?"

She was handling it wrong, she saw immediately. She wasn't a psychiatrist. She didn't know how to handle people with screwed up heads.

"What did you do with it?" Gertrude cried in the low whisper she used when she spoke of the doll.

"I put it back in its cabinet, Gertrude," Jenny lied. Gertrude could not handle the truth in her present state of mind. It was better this way. "You don't have to be afraid anymore."

The image of it lying on Annie's pillow filled Jenny's eyes and she saw it smile, its pouted lips turning up at the edges. Two tiny white teeth gleamed in its mouth. Teeth? She had never noticed that it had teeth. She blinked the image away.

She watched Gertrude lie back on her pillows and close her eyes. She drew a long, deep breath. As Jenny drew quietly away she hoped Gertrude would sleep and rest, perhaps for the first time since Ted and Annie had died.

"Thank God," Gertrude said. "I just pray it hasn't gained enough strength to break out." Gertrude sighed again and added, "Thank you, Jenny. I don't know what I'd do without you."

Guilt entered Jenny in a sudden, dark rush. She was ashamed of herself. Why hadn't she put the old doll safely back into the cabinet?

Tomorrow she would do that. It really didn't matter where it was, but if Gertrude felt better with it behind glass, then that's where it should be. She would do it now, but she knew Gertrude would be petrified with fear. Jenny was afraid she might suffer a heart attack or a stroke. She was doubly sorry she had ignored Gertrude's wishes this afternoon.

"Good night, Gertrude. Do you think you can sleep now? Do you want a sleeping pill?"

"No!" She sounded terrified of the thought.

"Then if you need me, just yell, okay?"

"Yes. Good night, dear." Then, as Jenny was leaving the room, "But please lock the hall door."

Jenny took the key down from the hook. In the shadows of the square little adjoining hall, she tried to insert the long key in the keyhole. Metal rattled against metal as she pushed and jostled, but the key wouldn't go all the way into the hole. "These damned locks," she muttered to herself.

"What's wrong?" Gertrude asked.

"I don't know. I just can't get the damned thing in. It goes only about halfway, like something is poked in from the other side."

Immediately she wished she hadn't said that. It suggested that someone was on the other side of the door.

Jenny quickly said, "It's okay, I'll fix it." She put her hand on the knob and turned, but Gertrude cried out.

"No, please don't open the door, Jenny."

Jenny stopped, exasperated, and leaned against the door jamb.

"Don't worry, Gertrude. Remember, I told you—"

"Jenny, please, just don't open the door."

Had Gertrude seen through her lie? Since she had lied about the doll, she might as well lie about the door, too. She inserted the key again and pushed, but still it wouldn't penetrate far enough to turn the lock.

She removed the key.

"Got it," she said, as cheerfully as she could. She hung the key back on the hook by the door frame. "You go to sleep, Gertrude, and rest. Tomorrow will come sooner."

"It's locked now?"

"Sure is. I guess I just wasn't trying hard enough the first time. Good night."

"Good night, Jenny."

Gertrude watched Jenny until she went out of sight into the other room and closed the door. Jenny had forgotten to turn off the lights in Gertrude's room, but that was all right, she didn't want to be in the dark. She could also see the white porcelain doorknob of the single door that led out onto the balcony, and she had seen that Jenny had only pretended to finally make the lock work. The long key had not penetrated, the heavy inner bolt had not made that sound of falling into place. Gertrude knew the sound well, through years of locking the door.

She also knew that Jenny had not put the doll back into the cabinet.

If she had, what was making those soft sounds in the

305

hall? The sound of material against floor, against wall. It was very like hearing her mother come so quietly along the hall, her long robe sweeping, whispering.

There was a long time, after she had seen Mama bring the doll from Julie Sue's room, that she was afraid of her mother. Was it like Jenny had said, in her moments of talking about the gift of the doll to Annie, that Sybil had meant for the child to die? But never Ted. Gertrude knew that Sybil would not have harmed Ted in any way. Even though he had displeased her in his choice of wives. So that meant that even though Sybil wanted the deaths of some, others were probably not intended.

Rose's death was perhaps unintentional. She remembered how pale her mother had grown when she learned of Rose's death, and how near hysteria. *"Rose. My God, Rose!"* she had cried. And her suffering had been real.

It meant a frightening, terrible thing. It meant Sybil had possessed no real control over the doll. She had learned of its powers in some way, and had used it, but it would have turned on her as easily as it turned on others.

And now Gertrude wondered if that was the reason behind Sybil's fears when she became helpless and dependent, when she began to need sleeping pills to carry her through the night. When she would wake and cry out to know if Gertrude was near? Why hadn't Mama told her what caused her terrible nightmares?

What had been put into the doll to make it dangerous? What poison, perhaps, that only close contact activated? How could it be destroyed? If it weren't alive, how could it be killed?

She put her hands to her head and pressed hard. If only she could put the thoughts away. Dismiss them as easily as Jenny had seemed to dismiss her wonderings about the doll.

But tonight, persisting through her insomnia, Gertrude

306

was seeing more clearly than ever the connections. Sybil had approved of Jenny as a maid, never as a daughter-in-law. And at the last, when she was dying and when she wanted to see the granddaughter, Gertrude had thought she was softening. But now, lying in the uneven light in her room, staring at the white doorknob until it blurred and seemed to be moving about erratically, she saw it all clearly.

Sybil had called Annie to her, and had given her the doll. "She's yours now." In looking at Annie, the child of the woman who had taken her son away from her, Sybil was in effect giving her a death sentence.

Gertrude rolled her head in the sudden misery of that knowledge. The emotional pain seemed more than she could bear. Why hadn't she seen exactly what her mother was doing? The mother she had always been terrified of, the terror lying under the thin crust she had thought was love. The mother she was afraid to disobey. What life had she given up because she didn't have the strength to try to get away?

She had to send Jenny away. Tomorrow she had to get up and prove to Jenny that she could walk, could take care of herself. She had to tell Jenny to take her things and go.

Her eyes cleared and suddenly focused on the white doorknob. It was not her blurred vision that had made it look as if it were turning. She stared at it, widening her eyes to keep her vision sharp. The knob turned slowly far to the right, then swung back to its original position.

Gertrude held her breath and stared, her throat paralyzed with horror.

It couldn't enter, she told herself. In order to reach the knob it would have to crawl up the door. And it could not do that. Surely to God it could not crawl up the wall.

She stared, and saw the knob turn again, to the left,

and then slowly to the right. Far, far to the right.

The click of the latch was like a shot in Gertrude's heart.

Unable to move she watched the door swing slowly open.

Inch by inch the door moved inward, and then the yellowed white appeared.

The doll's head came through the opening. It was on its stomach, its head reared up like the head of a snake. Its open eyes had found her, and even in the shadows in the entry they appeared to glitter. Marble blue glass, catching the light and reflecting it. It came forward.

As it drew near she saw its upper lip lifted and protruded, and beneath it, the growth of teeth. Two . . . no, four. She stared at them, unable to pull her eyes away.

Gertrude's tongue grew heavy as lead in her mouth. She felt pinned to the bed, unable to move. She thought of Jenny, beyond the closed door of the bedroom. Safe, for the moment. But only for the moment.

It came across the floor, its hands reaching out, and pulling the body forward. The yellowed gown trailed behind it like a tail.

Gertrude could no longer breathe. Flashes of memory came and went like bits of lightning glimpsed from the corner of her eye. "Don't ever touch this doll." But at the last Sybil had changed her mind. "She's yours now."

And Gertrude knew. She had been talking to all of them. Even Jenny.

Jenny get out. Run. Break the window, jump, run.

It had reached her bed, and its fingers wrinkled the blanket as it climbed. She could hear the sound of crawling, of a long robe sweeping the floor as her mother came to her door to check on her, to see that she was still there. As long as Sybil could walk she had come to Gertrude's door to make sure she was still there . . . but now she had sent the doll for Gertrude.

It had reached her stomach and it crawled up onto her, the head closer and closer.

As if its glare paralyzed, its open mouth already drawing Gertrude's life away, she could not lift her hands against it.

Chapter 19

The world seemed deadly silent when Jenny woke, but welcome light came in at the windows. She got up and looked around. The room was cold. Very little warm air came through the vent that opened from the entry hall on the first floor.

Quickly she began to dress, pulling on jeans and sweater and long, heavy socks. She glanced at the clock. Almost nine.

"Gertrude?" she called.

The silence that followed the sound of her voice frightened her. It was so much like the morning she had awakened late to find the house cold and still, and Ted and Annie . . .

"Gertrude?" she called again, louder, stumbling as she tried to run and slide her feet into her loafers at the same time.

She flung open the bedroom door.

The first thing she noticed was the half-open door leading out onto the balcony. Thank God, she thought, sagging against the wall as she finished pulling on her shoes. Gertrude was better this morning and had gone to the bathroom.

Then she saw that Gertrude's room was still shadowed, the lights unable to reach the corners of the room. Gertrude hadn't opened her curtains, or turned off her lights.

"Gertrude," she whispered, suddenly afraid to go into Gertrude's room.

The house was deadly quiet. There was no movement from Gertrude's room, and no sound of movement down the outside hall toward the bathroom.

Slowly, her fingers turning to ice, Jenny put her hand out to the door frame as if it might help her to face the emptiness of Gertrude's room.

She crossed the threshold and stopped again and stared.

Gertrude lay on the bed in the same position in which Jenny had left her, but she was no longer Gertrude. She was a skeleton, her skin covering her bones, her eyes sunken and staring toward the ceiling.

On her chest, like a monstrous bloated worm, rested the doll. It twisted on Gertrude's wasted frame and looked at Jenny, its fat little fingers digging into the quilt as it pulled itself around. Rising onto its hands it crawled down the length of the body to the corner of the bed, its eyes fastened on Jenny.

It fell onto the floor, a soft, sickening plop. Then it reared up, its head lifted, and crawled rapidly toward her. Its cheeks bulged, almost enveloping the button nose. Its forehead protruded, and the ties of the bonnet cut into the fat bulges of the chin. The lips puffed red and obscenely insatiable. Beads of moisture slowly dripped from the jagged edges of the stained teeth as if the last of Gertrude's life oozed from within it.

Jenny turned. She felt herself mired in her nightmare, unable to move. Her voice lifted in a scream of terror, filling the house, frightening small rodents in distant walls.

She found herself able to run, even as she felt unable to move. She was out of the bedroom and on the balcony. The stairs were in front of her. She reached them and fell. She rolled, her head striking the banister, her arms flailing. At the bottom she gripped the banister and pulled herself up. Unable to appreciate that she wasn't injured, her consciousness filled only with the horror of what she had seen.

She fumbled with the lock on the front door, and as if she had burst from a nightmare, she found herself outside the door. She heard its solid slam as she desperately pulled it shut behind her. She ran, the cold winter air fire in her lungs.

Book Three
Inheritance

Chapter 1

"Kirsten!" Jane yelled for her older daughter, "Kirsten! I need your advice here please."

"What?" Kirsten responded, sounding distant. She was unpacking in her bedroom at the rear of the house. "In a minute."

Although she was only eleven she had a good eye for artistic balance. In that way she was just like her dad. Jane wished Don could have helped place things before going to work, but the job came first no matter where they lived, and this was no time to ask for a day off.

Jane took a breather while she waited, and went out onto the front lawn. It was newly landscaped, the plants still small.

She loved the house and the neighborhood. Before hers and the girls' arrival she had seen only pictures. Her husband, Don, had made a couple of extra trips back to Arkansas looking for a place to live that would be, they hoped, a safer and less crowded world in which to rear their two young daughters. He had found Wilfred, a small but growing town within a few miles of a large lake.

There were perhaps fifty new houses in the development, all roomy and well built, with shake roofs, individual floor plans, and one acre lots. At least fifty acres of forest had been dug into, leaving as many trees as possible, in order to build the houses. Jane's backyard butted into the privacy of a woods.

The two young men who had trucked their furniture from California were unloading the piano, and Jane turned her attention to checking her house plan. On it she had marked the spots she felt each major piece of furniture should go, but as she looked over the actual living room she decided the piano might look better angled in the bay window area.

"Yeah, Mom?" Kirsten came out of the hallway that led to the four bedrooms, with seven year old Lisa behind her.

"Where should we put the piano?"

Both girls were dressed in jeans. The June weather was comfortable for jeans, with cool mornings and evenings and warm afternoons. Lisa, as always, looked almost lost in hers. It was impossible to get a pair that fit Lisa's narrow little hips, and still have enough length for her legs.

Lisa stood behind Kirsten in the living room. She was carrying a Barbie doll in the crook of one arm, and had part of the doll's wardrobe in her other hand.

"Not the bay window," Kirsten said. "At the windows it would become, well, too important. I like it better against the wall, the way you have it on the plan."

"Put a chair and flowers in the windows," Lisa said, and slipped out of the way to sit in the corner and dress her doll.

"All right," Jane told the movers, who had paused in the hall to rest, the piano leaning on the dolly. "Put the piano against this wall."

The long yellow truck had been parked in the street in front of the house for hours, and it would be hours more

316

before it was empty and driven away. Don wouldn't be home for lunch, and they couldn't leave the house to go eat with him. In the kitchen Jane made lunch not only for her children and herself, but for the movers. Then she began the tedious job of unpacking boxes between giving directions for the placement of the rest of the furniture.

In the middle of the afternoon Kirsten, with Lisa behind her as usual, came and slumped against the kitchen table, looking sweaty and exhausted.

"Mama . . ." Kirsten began.

She never used the word "Mama" unless she wanted a special favor, and Jane sat down.

"What?" Jane asked with a grumpy note in her voice. Then watching Kirsten begin nibbling on a cookie, she said, "I never knew moving could be so time consuming. Or so utterly exhausting."

Her only experience in moving had been when she packed her clothes in a suitcase and headed west with Don when they were newly married. They had left their families in Iowa and gone to Southern California and had bought a small tract house in what was then a quiet neighborhood. Then as their children were born instead of moving to a larger house they had simply added what rooms they needed.

They'd been married twelve years when Kirsten was born. She had been afraid they were never going to have a baby. Now they had two miracles, two healthy daughters, both beautiful and bright. But sometimes Jane was overwhelmed with the wants. How could two such precious babies grow up and think of so many things to want?

"Can we go out and look around?" Kirsten finally asked as she ate the last crumbs of the cookie.

"What? No money for a trip to the store?"

317

"No. What store? Can we just go look around outside?"

Jane looked at her daughters with pride. Kirsten was growing tall. At least, she looked tall beside Lisa, who still carried the soft roundness, the lovely pale skin and hair of babyhood. Lisa was the three year old beauty who had won the Beautiful Baby prize, who had stretched up to seven years still looking very much as she had at three. Today her hair was braided, as it had been since they had started on the trip east. Jane liked to curl it into long ringlets that glistened like pure spun gold. Kirsten's hair was darker now, though it had been blond, too, when she was younger. But it had never been naturally curly, and she was less dainty and feminine than Lisa, and wanted her hair kept no longer than chin length, with bangs. Just a simple, easy cut. She had a pretty, heart shaped face with a faint dimple in her chin.

Jane looked out the windows beyond the dining area, and saw the large backyard, and the edge of the cool, shaded forest. There were no fences around the backyard yet, and the shrubs planted along the boundaries between their yard and the ones on each side were still small. Yet old habits and fears from city living linger.

"Look around where?"

"In the woods, maybe. Or up at the old cemetery."

"No, don't go into the cemetery. I'll walk with you up there someday." Being interested in the history of the land and in genealogy, Jane had a fondness for old cemeteries, and Kirsten enjoyed going with her. Lisa usually sat in the car playing with one of her dolls, while they checked out old stones and wondered about the lives of the people buried there.

"How about the woods?" Kirsten asked.

"Well . . . why not? If you come to a fence, though, don't cross it."

"Of course not, Mom. I know that."

Kirsten's exhaustion had miraculously disappeared, as it always did when she was tired of a job and wanted to do something fun.

Jane watched them go out the French doors onto the deck at the back, and then down the steps. Kirsten must have said something to Lisa, because the younger girl turned back to the deck and laid down her doll. Then they ran across the backyard and into the trees.

"What's back there?" Jane had asked Don the first time she saw the house. They had been walking around the yard, looking at the landscaping, which was great for the shape of the house. The grass was thick and green, and had been mowed. Sprinklers were hidden in stragetic places, though Jane understood that the annual rainfall was above forty inches, and the sprinklers wouldn't have to be used as they had been in the desert climate they had moved from.

"Woods," Don said.

"I can see that." She reached over and pinched his arm lightly. "But, how far?"

"I don't know. But don't worry," he added, knowing her through and through, "the kids are safe here."

She now had the old feeling of concern as her girls disappeared into the woods. But, she saw, they had slowed and were walking cautiously. They had been in mountain forests many times, on trips that lasted a day or a weekend, but those forests were different from this. Here the woods looked more dense, with ground growths of vines and smaller trees and bushes. She wished when they disappeared from view that she hadn't let them go. Yet she didn't call them back.

Kirsten led the way, trying to find the path of least

319

resistance, and finally came upon a thin little trail that looked as if it actually had been a path. At least once long ago. She saw something that looked like a red stone, and scratched the soft dirt with a stick and uncovered old brick. Scratching further, she found that it was a narrow path of old brick, just like the brick on the sidewalk in front of the parsonage. Except it was very narrow, only three or four bricks wide.

"Lisa!" she said. "There used to be a brick path here."

"In the woods?"

"Yes! There must have been a house here once," she said, but Lisa didn't answer.

The ferns lolled less heavily here, the brush was not quite so thick. She followed it, careful to push limbs out of their way and hold them so Lisa wouldn't get slapped in the face. The brick was gone, but there was thinner undergrowth, and Kirsten felt sure that once it had been a path that someone used.

"Look, Kirsten, an old house," Lisa said.

Kirsten hadn't had time to look up. The floor of the forest was too interesting, with the flowers and the fern and the tree roots that rose above ground like the spines of prehistoric burrowing animals. She had thought Lisa was still behind her, but her little sister was several feet away, standing beneath the low branches of a white barked sycamore tree.

"What? Really?" Kirsten saw nothing but trees.

"A real old, big house."

"Where?"

"Here!"

Kirsten went to stand beside her. Barely visible through the trees was the dark corner of a tall building made of the same dark red brick that had buried in the path.

"Gosh," Kirsten said, feeling as if she'd been tricked.

"This wasn't very much of a forest after all. A block of nice woods, and then somebody's house."

"Do you think anybody *really lives* there?" Lisa asked, her voice hushed. "In that old place?"

Kirsten's interest piqued. "Maybe you're right. It's not that it's such a shallow forest, it's that somebody deserted the old place, which was built right into the forest. Or the forest grew around it."

"Can we go see?"

Kirsten shrugged and looked back. She could still see the back of their own house, though with difficulty. You had to know just where to look to find it. If it hadn't been built of stone, with lots of glass windows, it would have blended too well with the trees to be seen.

"Okay, I suppose it's all right."

Kirsten led the way, pushing through vines that in places were almost knee deep. The house was suddenly closer, looming up through the trees and disappearing into the leaves at the top. All red brick, trimmed in wood, its windowsills were old and grey, as if they had never been painted. Some of them looked soft with decay, as did the long back porch. The screen was rusted, brown-edged holes large enough to crawl through in many places, and the back steps sagged.

The old brick walks didn't look as if a human foot had ever touched them. Weeds and vines grew between the bricks.

"Nobody lives here," Lisa said. "I can tell."

Kirsten shrugged, eyeing the second and third floor windows. The dusty glass looked blank and dark.

"Are we going in?" Lisa pleaded, excitement making her blue eyes big and round. She clutched Kirsten's sleeve. "Please, can we? You can see nobody ever lived here."

Kirsten hated having her sleeve pulled on. She jerked

321

it away. "Ever? Then why was a house built in the first place? Of course someone lived here. And maybe they still do."

Kirsten fought her away through the brush to the far side of the house. A brick driveway was barely visible beneath the growth which had rooted between the looser bricks. It led southward toward the road. Passing cars were hidden beyond the trees, their sounds muted.

"Nobody lives here now. Can't we just take a peek inside?"

"Well, I suppose it'd be okay."

Kirsten was more eager than she would admit to Lisa. She returned to the back of the house and climbed the steps to the porch gingerly, careful to step on the edge where the support wasn't so decayed. The backdoor of the house was closed, though a panel had fallen off.

"We should knock," she said, and raised her hand to the door. A shiver went down her spine when she listened to the sound of her knock. A glass in the door gave her a veiled view of a large kitchen that appeared to reach almost the entire width of the house.

"Boy," Kirsten murmured as she peered through the dingy old glass of the door. "Mama would love this. The furniture looks like it's still in there. An old table, still with a tablecloth, and bowls or something still on the table, covered by a cloth. Somebody must live here. They wouldn't just go off and leave their table with stuff on it." Yet as she peered through the glass she grew doubtful. The cloth was covered in dust. Webs created a spidery wall beneath the table, and stretched upward from the table to the light fixture above.

Lisa stood on her toes beside Kirsten, her hands cupped against her face and the glass to improve her view. "Gosh," she murmured in awe. She pulled away from the door. "Let's go get Mama."

"Okay, in a minute." Kirsten put her hand on the doorknob and turned. The door resisted. "It's locked."

"Let's go get Mama."

They went cautiously across the safer looking boards of the porch, and down again into the overgrown backyard. Nobody had lived there in a long, long time, Kirsten agreed. The weeds and brush hadn't been cut, and trees didn't grow up so large in just a few years.

"I wonder how long it's been since whoever was here died?" Kirsten said, as she pushed her way through the brush and around the corner of the house.

"Died?" Lisa wailed behind her.

"Of course. Why else would they leave all their stuff?"

"Do you think it's haunted?"

"I don't know. Maybe."

"Let's go get Mama, Kirsten!"

"Just a minute. Let's look around a little more."

Closer to the house the growth thinned, and walking was much easier. They passed windows too high off the ground to see through, even though they paused once and Kirsten lifted Lisa.

"I can't see anything. I think something's covering the window."

They went on, close to the house. When they came to a small porch and a door on the side of the house, with an overhanging roof, Kirsten saw the old bricks of the driveway. Brush, weeds and vines grew through the cracks.

"Mama would love this," Kirsten said. "Think of the history here!"

They reached another corner of the house and turned left, and came at last to the front entry. This porch was built of brick, and the steps were stone. Kirsten went up to the front door.

Lisa said, "Shouldn't we get Mama?"

323

It was a tall door, with no glass. In the center hung an old, rusted knocker. Just for the devil of it Kirsten lifted the knocker and let it fall, though she was convinced the house was unoccupied.

The sound was dull and empty.

"What are you doing?" Lisa asked.

Kirsten's hand was on the funny old door latch. It fit into the palm of her hand, and turned with difficulty.

"Are you going in?" Lisa asked, coming closer. "Without Mama?"

"It's probably locked, too."

But the door opened, surprisingly easily, and quietly. And the girls peered into the musty darkness of old Wilfred mansion.

Chapter 2

Jane went out onto the deck and looked toward the woods. The girls had been gone only thirty minutes, and she thought it was a safe neighborhood, but what did she really know? She crossed the backyard and stepped into the shaded woods.

Cool air moved gently from the world of trees and plants. Birds by the hundreds sang somewhere in the treetops. What kind of snakes lived in all that greenery, she wondered.

"Kirsten! Lisa!" Birds above her fluttered away, alarmed by her voice.

She walked to the left along the rear of her yard. Next door a woman suddenly spoke from behind a flower bed. Jane jumped.

"Sorry, didn't mean to startle you."

Jane saw her, on her knees at the side of the area where she was digging and weeding. She got up, pulled off her right glove and approached Jane with her hand out. She was middle-aged, and her yard looked as if the plantings were more mature than in Jane's new yard. A large, fluffy yellow cat moved out into the grass and stretched full-length in the sunshine.

"I'm Wanda Alden. Moving is quite a job, isn't it? My husband, Clyde, and I moved in last year. We were the first to buy."

Jane introduced herself and explained, "I let my daughters go into the woods about thirty minutes ago, and then wished I hadn't. I mean, it looks 'snakey' in there."

Wanda laughed. "There may be a few snakes, but don't worry, most are not poisonous."

"Most?"

"Well, a copperhead or timber rattler could possibly live there somewhere, but they'll make an effort to get out of the way. Snakes here don't attack. They run. I wouldn't worry. When our grandchildren come out they like to explore the woods, too. I think they have a playhouse in there somewhere. Maybe your daughters found it."

Jane looked with worried eyes at the forest of trees and undergrowth. "There's no danger of getting lost?"

"Oh my, no. I saw your daughters go into the woods. I wouldn't worry at all if I were you. My only orders to the grandkids are to stay away from the old house."

"There's a house in there?"

"Yes. But it's deserted. Somebody said for forty or more years. I'm sure they'll stay away from it. It's not an inviting place."

A house, deserted, brought to Jane's mind all sorts of horrors. Old bums, druggies, pot heads using the house as a temporary home. Spiders, bats, everything that would go into a deserted building, especially one that had been deserted for forty years. And, of course, snakes. Those poisonous rattlers and copperheads that aren't supposed to be aggressive. The more Jane's new neighbor talked, the more worried Jane became.

"Don't worry," Wanda said, as if she could see that she had made matters worse not better. "I'm sure they won't get hurt. They probably are following the paths in the woods."

"Paths? Where to?" Deserted houses. Snakes.

"Nowhere in particular. Just paths. Made by kids, or deer, perhaps. You get used to kids playing in the woods when you've lived here longer."

Wanda looked over Jane's shoulder just as a man's voice spoke her name.

"Mrs. Flanners."

The older of the two men from the moving van stood in the middle of Jane's backyard.

"Excuse me," Jane said to Wanda, and went toward the blond, husky man who had driven the long truck all the way from southern California.

"Mrs. Flanners, sorry to bother you, but we're bringing in a bunch of boxes now just marked bedroom, and we don't know which bedroom . . ."

"Yes, I'm coming."

She cast a last glance toward the woods as she told Wanda goodbye. She had to trust that Wanda was right. The kids were okay. They wouldn't get hurt. At least she didn't have to worry about gangs from the next neighborhood.

Jane hurried into the house to direct the placing of the bedroom boxes. What idiot had not written each person's name on the boxes? Herself? Well, she'd been in a hurry during that whirlwind week of packing and getting ready to move.

If the girls were here they would help, but . . .

Kirsten and Lisa stood in the large foyer. Very little light penetrated the window high in the wall over the door. It looked permanently fogged over with dust and cobwebs, but enough light came in at the open door behind them for Lisa to see that it was a big house. A long stairway curved up on the left. Overhead a balcony with railings stuck out over the foyer, and the ceiling was far above the second floor. A big chandelier hung down, but it was a mass of webs and dust.

"Excuse me," a voice called out loudly, and Lisa almost

screamed. Then she saw her sister stepping forward, and knew it was she who had shouted.

"Is anyone at home?" Kirsten yelled again, going a few steps deeper into the foyer. Her calls echoed back dimly, "at home, at home, at home . . ."

"Why are you doing that?" Lisa hissed, her arms stiffened at her sides, her jaws tensed. "You sound weird."

"Just trying to find out if anyone lives here," Kirsten said in a normal tone.

"Well, you scared me. Where are you going?" She had wanted to come in, but now that she was in, she wanted to leave. But she wasn't leaving alone.

"Look at that, isn't it fantastic?" Kirsten pointed at a huge old grandfather clock. A large pendulum hung still. Spider webs reached from it to the weights on each side. Beside the clock sat a funny old sofa with a curved wood top. Dust covered everything in a grey film. "Those are antiques, Lisa. I'll bet this house is full of antiques. Mom would love those. Why would anyone just go off and leave all this stuff and not even lock their front door?"

Kirsten's voice had grown very quiet, as if she were afraid someone might hear even though she had said no one lived here anymore.

Lisa looked at the stairway. She had always wanted to climb a real stairway in a big old house. In all the stores where there were long stairs Kirsten and Mama insisted in going up on the escalator. Lisa hated escalators. They were hard to get on, and hard to get off. She always felt like she was going to be tugged right along with the step that went out of sight beneath the floor.

"Can we climb the stairs, Kirsten?"

Kirsten glanced up. "They might fall."

Lisa went to the foot of the stairs and looked up. The steps rose and curved to the right, protected by the banister. Like the foyer floor, they were bare, but there weren't any holes that Lisa could see.

"They're okay, Kirsten, can we go up?"

"In a minute," Kirsten said, then she went slowly back along the hall that led into the darker depths of the house. Lisa heard her open a door.

Lisa started up the stairs. Her hand touched the banister and drew back. It was coated with a sticky, grey dust, almost like soft gum. On the steps were narrow, uneven trails in the dust, wavering to the side and back again. They didn't really look like footsteps, but more like someone had slid their feet along. Lisa stood looking at the trails a moment, then decided they weren't anything but just the way the shadows fell.

She stepped on a riser and heard the groan of wood as it gave beneath her weight. She jumped to the higher one, grabbing the sticky banister, and held on. She looked over into the foyer, but didn't see Kirsten.

"Kirsten!"

"What?"

The voice came back from somewhere below, slightly distant and muffled. Overhead Lisa heard her own voice echoing, drifting away eerily to silence.

Suddenly the silence was broken as somebody scrambled along the balcony above Lisa, as if her voice had shocked them awake.

Lisa put her hands over her mouth, staring up. She expected any moment to see a face peer over the banister toward her. What would she say? What excuse could they use, she and her sister, for entering a house without being invited? She looked down for Kirsten, but Kirsten was gone, snooping somewhere in this house that wasn't unoccupied after all.

"Hello." Lisa's voice squeaked higher than normal. "Sorry . . ." She had started to say she was sorry they had come into the house, but the sound on the balcony made her pause. She listened intently. Now it didn't sound like a person. There was no footstep, only a soft, sliding sound.

It was silent a moment, as if listening to her, too, as she listened to it. Then again it was moving. Like something soft rubbing against the wall, or the floor, a movement almost silent. Then it stopped again right above Lisa.

Lisa's heart pounded. She wished Kirsten were with her. Whatever it was in the upper floor must be a furry little creature because it had made such a soft sound. They are more afraid of you than you are of them, she'd been told so many times.

She took another step upward, looking as high as she could, trying to see onto the balcony. Whatever it was that had hurried along the balcony was lying still. Whatever it was on the balcony might have made the trails on the stairs that she had decided was nothing after all. She could almost see it sitting there, a bunny rabbit maybe, its little nose twitching and its eyes scared and watching.

"I won't hurt you," she murmured, and climbed slowly upward, her eyes blinking widely to adjust to the murky, shadowy world of the second floor.

The balcony went around three sides of the upstairs. She saw some steps at the back that went on up into a long, dim hallway that had a window at the far end, but she didn't want to go there. She only wanted to see what was on the balcony.

Her head was barely above the balcony floor. She held onto the banister and stretched to her tiptoes so she could see better. There was an open door into another hallway, but it was so dark she couldn't see into it. On the other side of the balcony two doors were closed. She wasn't interested in that side, only this.

Lisa edged closer to the balcony railing and peered through into the dim light.

Nothing. No bunny rabbit sitting up, his pink nose

twitching. Not even a mouse. Only spiders fat in their webs. Could that have been the noise she heard? A fat spider? Running along the balcony?

She would never hurt a spider, but she didn't want one on her. And she hated getting tangled in webs.

She started to draw back, to settle down from her toes and retreat to the hall below when she saw dark suitcases at the top of the stairs. There was a movement in the dark space between them, as something settled out of sight. The movement was so slight she could believe she had imagined it. Yet she had heard movement earlier, and now saw something like a small animal huddling lower.

Lisa stretched taller and peered through the shadows. She saw light cloth, like a scarf or handkerchief. Clothing spilled on the floor from a suitcase? She moved closer, slowly climbing the stairs. Not just clothing, after all. Something had been placed there, between the suitcases.

She moved her head to the right and saw a small face looking at her from between the old suitcases. Her heart almost stopped. She stared, breathless, then realized it was a doll.

A doll. Left here in this rotting old house by what little girl? Left here with packed suitcases. It was so sad, as if it had waited for a long time for its mama to come home.

"Ooooh," she breathed, and ran up the few remaining steps to the top of the stairs. That they creaked and groaned beneath her feet didn't matter. Someone had left a doll, and she loved dolls just like she loved all little things that could be carried and loved.

She reached around the newel post at the top of the stairs and pulled the doll toward her. Dust sifted from it like powder.

It was wearing clothes that were dingy grey, a very long gown that hung almost to Lisa's own feet, and a

331

bonnet edged in narrow lace. It was just like a fat baby, with cheeks round and red, and its mouth pushed out into a red, rosy pout. It had four little teeth that were as dusty and stained as its bonnet. Its eyes opened wider as she lifted it, and it was like looking into a living soul. She held her breath as she looked into the deep, blue glass that didn't look like glass at all.

"Oh, you beautiful doll."

She tried to knock a bit of the dust off the clothes. It fogged into the air, and she sneezed. With the doll cradled in her arms she hurried down the stairs, carefully avoiding the steps that had caved in.

"Kirsten!"

"What?"

Kirsten came along the hall toward the front of the house, her eyes gleaming.

"Look what I found, Kirsten." Lisa thrust the doll out at her. "It's a real . . . uh . . ." She had almost said a real live baby doll. But Kirsten would have snorted in contempt at the way Lisa was always acting as if her dolls were really alive. Of course, to Lisa, they were. They had their own names and personalities, and likes and dislikes.

"Where did you find that?" Kirsten demanded, frowning and drawing back as if the doll were something gross.

"Up . . . uh . . . up there."

"You climbed the stairs? You nitwit, you were supposed to stand right here by the door."

"You didn't say so!"

"Well, put it back and let's go. Mom will be wondering where we are. I can't wait to tell her about this place."

"Put it back!?" Lisa clutched it closer. It was larger than any of her dolls. The only baby doll she had, and she loved it. She'd never even seen a doll like it before. And she had already bonded to it.

"Yes, put it back. These things all belong to somebody."

"Well if the doll belongs to somebody, why don't they take it and clean it up? Look at it."

Lisa held it out. Dust fell from it and drifted in the breeze from the door. The tail of the gown swayed. In the light the crusts of dust on the face of the doll looked like dark lines and wrinkles, as if it were a very old, old person instead of a baby doll.

Kirsten snorted in contempt. "It is a mess. It's still not ours to take, Lisa."

"I only want to clean it up, Kirsten. Please?" Lisa bent over the doll, holding it against her stomach, doubling up as if she were in pain. She was trying so hard to convince her sister that she should have the doll that her stomach was really beginning to hurt. "Please? Whoever left didn't even take their suitcases. They're still there at the top of the stairs. Right where they left the doll. The dust is thick, Kirsten. If they were coming back they'd have been back a long time ago. *Please?*"

After a while Kirsten shrugged. She went out the front door onto the porch. Lisa followed her.

"You can take it home and keep it awhile, I guess. It does look like it's been deserted a hundred years, just like the house."

"A hundred years?" Lisa asked in awe, ready to agree with anything Kirsten said, now that she'd been allowed to carry the doll out of the house.

"Well, maybe not a whole hundred years," Kirsten said.

Lisa followed obediently behind Kirsten, objecting to nothing, the doll held tenderly in her arms.

Kirsten found a narrow brick path that led along the edge of the road and curved into the trees. "I'll bet this is part of the path we found in the woods."

"Gosh," Lisa murmured. "A hundred years. Did people have regular suitcases back then?" She held her doll carefully to avoid getting its clothes snagged on the limbs and twigs that swung against her in Kirsten's wake.

"Probably not. I wish I'd seen the suitcases. Maybe this afternoon we can go back, with Mom. None of that furniture in there is part of this century, except in that one room I looked in. In that room I saw a regular sofa and two chairs. But the rest was definitely antique."

They reached the narrow strip of trees between the road and the houses in Shadow Oaks. Kirsten led the way through the trees, between two houses, and out onto the sidewalk that curved along beside the street. Their house was the third one down, the one at the rear of the cul-de-sac.

The moving van was gone.

Kirsten began to run, and quickly outdistanced Lisa. They reached their yard and Lisa followed Kirsten around the end of the house to the deck at the back.

"Mom!" Kirsten yelled, pushing open the screen on the French doors. "Mom, you'll never believe!"

Their mother came into the kitchen and then stopped and looked Lisa up and down, while Kirsten was trying to tell her about the old house.

Lisa twisted uncomfortably under the scrutiny of her mother and looking down saw her jeans were coated with several layers of grey dust. She backed toward the door, slipped outside and with the doll safe in her left arm, tried with her right hand to knock the dust off her jeans. She could hear Kirsten's voice telling their mother about the house and the furniture. She told about the suitcases.

Then they both came out onto the porch and Jane asked, "Did you bring that doll from the old house, Lisa?"

Lisa knew the tone of the voice. Did you . . . *whatever?* Then undo it. Right now.

"Ah Mama," Lisa pleaded, turning to face her mother.

334

Jane was standing with her hands on her hips the way she always did when she wanted to make sure she was heard. "Mama, please, nobody wanted it. Why can't I keep it?"

"It does not belong to you, Lisa," Jane said, her voice not a bit cross. "I know it was left behind by whatever child it belonged to, but it belongs right there in the house where you found it."

"But Mama, I've already bonded to it."

Jane smiled faintly, then hurriedly got rid of the smile. "Then unbond, Lisa. The doll isn't yours."

"Well, I can't go back today," Lisa said, thinking of how many ways she could try to keep the doll. If she could just keep it until Daddy got home, he'd be on her side. He would know that any doll, left behind in a deserted old house might as well be loved and enjoyed by some little girl like herself.

"Why can't you go back today?" Kirsten said. "I'll take her back, Mom. It's only just over there in the trees."

Their mother hesitated, and looked at the clock she had hung on the kitchen wall. Lisa's hopes began to rise, then were quickly dashed.

"All right, Kirsten," Jane said. "I'd go with you but I don't have time right now. Kirsten, go ahead and take Lisa back and put the doll right where you got it. And then you girls will never go close to the house again, understand?"

"I know what," Lisa said brightly, glad she'd thought of it. "I'll wait until tomorrow when *you* have time to go with us."

"No, Lisa," Jane said. "You can't keep the doll. Not even overnight. I'm surprised you took it, or even went in the house. I'm surprised at you, too, Kirsten. I thought you knew better."

"The door wasn't locked, Mom."

"So why did you even try it?"

"But, it's just a deserted old house. I thought you'd like to see it."

Their mother said nothing. She wiped a dish and put it away in the cabinet with other dishes.

"Come on, Lisa," Kirsen muttered in disgust. "I don't know why you can't just be satisfied with what you've got. She's always wanting a new doll, like she didn't have forty million now."

"I only have a few!"

"A few! In all my life I never had as many dolls as you have. Come on. If you don't hurry, I won't go."

Lisa went down the steps behind Kirsten, her mouth feeling tight, as tight as her chest. She knew if she looked in a mirror it would be almost as pouty as the doll's. She had to put the doll back. And almost as bad as not getting to keep the doll, she also couldn't go close to the old house again, where so much adventure beckoned.

She held the doll against her chest, both arms wrapped around it. Its fat cheeks pushed against her neck, and felt warm and real.

She didn't want to give up her doll.

Chapter 3

Kirsten hesitated on the porch, looking up at the large front door.

"Kirsten, let's hurry, it's getting dark."

"Not me. You go on in. I'll wait here."

"Kirsten!"

"Hurry up, Lisa."

Lisa looked at the shadows beneath the trees. She felt layers of chilly air, like invisible ghosts brushing against her arms. The old mansion looked more scary now than interesting, and she knew Kirsten was getting mad, but she couldn't go in that shadowy old house alone.

"Kirsten, please?"

"You shouldn't have taken the doll in the first place. Hurry, Lisa. I'm leaving in two more minutes."

Lisa jigged in indecision. Kirsten meant what she said. "It's time for Oprah," she'd said three times on their way through the woods. "And I don't want to miss her show again. Hurry, Lisa! I haven't seen her in two weeks."

Lisa looked at the tall door. Its paint had peeled away, leaving dark wood beneath. "Come with me, Kirsten. Please?"

"No! Hurry up."

"Can I lay it just inside the door? Please?"

Kirsten began wandering around on the porch, humming, her hands in her pockets. "No. Take it back upstairs. Okay, I'll give you three minutes. Starting now. One, two, three."

Lisa stamped a foot. "You have to come with me. It was you who opened the door in the first place."

Kirsten stopped humming. "So, did that make you go up the stairs and get the dumb doll?"

Lisa tossed her braid and felt it flop like a rope on her shoulders. "All right!"

She even had to open the door by herself. With one hand she grasped the handle and tried to turn it. Kirsten finally came to help, sighing in exasperation.

"If you'd turn the doll loose for a minute so you could use both hands, Lisa! Here."

The door swung inward. The foyer was darker now, and looked like a huge cave. The sun was down behind the trees, and a cold rush of air came from somewhere along the dark hall.

Lisa looked back. Kirsten stood on the bottom step off the porch looking at the brick path.

Lisa took a step deeper into the foyer. She looked around with trepidation. It was haunted. She could feel the presence of something that was going to swoop down upon her in a minute.

I'm not afraid, she told herself. All she had to do was climb the stairs, lay the doll down, and run. Maybe later she could talk her dad into talking her mother into bringing her back to get the doll. "It doesn't belong to anybody," she mumbled aloud to keep from hearing the sound of her steps. "I just know it doesn't."

She climbed the stairs, avoiding the two broken steps. At the top she started to put the doll down right between the suitcases where she had found it, with a goodbye kiss on its fat cheek. She stopped. Her eyes swiftly covered the possibilities. If she had found the doll so easily what was going to stop other kids?

If she wanted to keep the doll for herself, she had to put it somewhere not so easy to find.

The silence of the second floor settled around her like

dust as she looked for a hiding place. Halfway along the wall was a door, partly open. It must lead into a bedroom.

She was afraid to make a sound, as if the ghosts that lived here would be drawn to her. Or what if a real person was still here? What would she say if she opened a door and a lady looked up from her dressing table?

Quietly she walked along the balcony to the half-open door.

She peered in. It was not a room. Just a small square place from which two more doors opened. It was another hallway, of sorts, that seemed to connect two rooms.

The door on the left was partly open. Lisa peered in. Dying light came from two narrow windows. Old, dark draperies hanging there looked shrouded in dust. There was a huge bed, so high it had a small stair step at the side. The headboard reached far up the high wall. The bed still had pillows and sheets and quilts.

Lisa stepped into the room and looked at the bed, puzzled, trying to figure it out.

People *must* live here. The bed was unmade, the top covers pushed back as if someone had just gotten up. She went closer, cautiously, and very quietly. The dim light at the window showed her the bed sheets were grey with dust.

No, no one lived here. Lisa walked slowly toward the door, feeling the hair on the back of her neck rising. She felt the presence of those she couldn't see. *Ghosts.*

Her breath caught, and the braid at the back of her head pulled, her scalp tightening. Out of the corner of her eye she saw the movement of something. She almost screamed. But it was only a door in the little hall, moving from a draft that came from the open door downstairs. But it might have been pushed, by a hand she couldn't see.

She didn't like this room. It was too shadowed, too

filled with things that belonged to someone now dead. She backed all the way into the connecting hall and stopped, remembering the doll clutched in her arms. She turned. The door to the other room was open now. Hadn't it been mostly closed before? She couldn't remember. It was the door that had moved.

Lisa stepped cautiously to the threshold. Another bedroom. Only this one wasn't so large, and the bed . . .

Lisa stared.

Someone was lying in the bed. A very old person. Her head lay on a thick pillow that lifted it. Black holes stared at Lisa. A black mouth gaped open with nothing but teeth, horrible dark teeth. The forehead was white and the eyes hollow and huge and deep. The bones of her chin were sharp and protruding. Lisa knew it was a woman because of the hair, long and limp, growing from the white skull.

Lisa stared, unable to move, or breathe, her body tight and frozen. No, it wasn't a person. Not a person, but the skeleton of . . .

Lisa screamed. The sound of her voice vibrated against old, hard walls, and echoed mockingly from distant halls and rooms. She ran mindlessly into the other bedroom and circled it before she dropped the doll and found the door to the balcony.

She fell on the top step of the stairs and rolled a few steps downward. When she tried to stand up her leg went through the broken step and something in the darkness below grabbed and held her.

At first Kirsten couldn't place the horrible sound. It could have come from the woods behind the house, and her first thought was owls. Owls scream horribly, in the darkest hour of the night, far away from cities. On camping trips they had heard those screams and Dad had said so calmly, "It's only an owl, go back to sleep."

Then it seemed as if it were part of the huge old house, as if something horrible within it vented its fury, and Kirsten had sent her little sister in alone.

She ran up the steps and into the foyer. The full force of the screaming reached her, and she recognized it as Lisa, filled with a fear that chilled Kirsten and made her movements feel as awkward as if she were made of glass.

"Lisa!"

The house had turned almost totally dark, and Kirsten could hear the continued gasping cries of her sister, but couldn't see her. She starting running back down the hall, then realized Lisa was overhead. Kirsten turned back and hesitated at the bottom of the long stairway, looking up.

Lisa was a pale blob against the darker stairway. She was lying on the stairs, not moving, screaming, gasping, crying.

Kirsten climbed toward her.

Lisa lay on a broken step, her hands clutching two railings, and one leg caught in the step.

"It's me!" Kirsten called in her ear. "Lisa! Lisa, it's okay."

Lisa turned to Kirsten and wrapped her arms around Kirsten's knees. She cried out something about being held and something about skeletons. Kirsten pulled her up. The broken boards of the stair riser had caught and torn her jeans, and Kirsten had to wrench her free. She couldn't leave her here while she ran for help. Poor Lisa was so scared she would have died alone.

"It's okay it's okay," Kirsten yelled in her sister's ear. Lisa's arms reached up and circled Kirsten's neck, and Kirsten lifted her free and carried her down the stairs.

In the light outdoors Kirsten put Lisa down. The little girl was shaking so hard her teeth clicked together and shattered her voice as she tried to talk. Kirsten under-

341

stood nothing Lisa was saying. She examined Lisa's leg, and saw it was scratched and red with beaded blood that was beginning to ooze down toward her ankle. But the scratches were shallow.

"Mom can fix you up, Lisa. You're okay. You just stepped through a hole in the stairs, that's all. Nothing was holding you."

Lisa held on to Kirsten with shaking hands, still jabbering and crying about something Kirsten wasn't able to understand.

"Ske-ske-skeleton, Kirsten. Th-th-there's a skeleton up there!"

She pointed toward the top of the house. Kirsten got her firmly by the hand and hurried her away. She kept hearing the same thing as they ran home. There's a skeleton up there, a skeleton up there. Until finally, by the time they had reached their own backyard and Lisa had calmed down some, Kirsten believed her.

Chapter 4

Detective Mary Swift, with her partner Mark Henley, sat in the living room of a family who had moved in so recently they weren't completely unpacked, and tried to make sense of the story.

"The two girls went into an old house in the woods and found a skeleton?" Mary asked. She had lived in Wilfred all her life, and had worked in the police department since she was twenty-three, eighteen years ago, and thought she knew the town and surrounding area. But she couldn't recall any old house in the woods. Woodlands around town were becoming scarce these days with the developments bulldozing them out. So an old house in the woods, with a skeleton, sounded like something out of Hansel and Gretel.

The man of the house, who looked to be in his late thirties and who was turning somewhat to the portly side, had introduced himself as Don Flanners, the girls' father. He said, "I didn't know they were going to enter a deserted house. And I'm sure they'll never do such a thing again."

He gave both girls a severe look. The younger of the two appeared to be trying to sink into the sofa behind her mother. The older girl sat on the floor at her mother's feet, her head bowed.

"We didn't mean to hurt anything," she murmured, her voice so low Mary hardly heard it.

"Where is this house?" Mark asked.

Kirsten lifted her head and her arm and pointed. "It's in the woods. It's not far from the road on the other side of Shadow Oaks. It has a long driveway, of brick. But it's all grown up."

A memory surfaced suddenly. Of course Mary had seen the edge of that old driveway, and even, in winter, the corners of the huge, old brick house. She said, "I know where it is. It's the old Wilfred mansion. I've heard my grandmother talk about it."

Sergeant Henley asked, "No one lives there?"

"I don't know," Mary said, at the same time both little girls shook their heads.

Kirsten said, "It's dusty and dirty. Nothing has been cleaned in a long time."

The mother, Jane Flanners, a plumpish woman in jeans and a loose shirt, spoke up, "It sounds as if the owner must have died in his or her bed, and no one ever checked. For some reason Lisa feels it's a woman. She must not have had any relatives."

"It seems to me," Mary said, "I've heard the owner lives in town. The house has been deserted for years."

"If that's so," Mark said, "Then there's no telling about who died there. Could be someone who decided to take advantage of a place to stay."

"Where was it you said you saw the skeleton?" Mary asked the older girl. She seemed more capable of communication. She reminded Mary of her own youngest child, a couple of years ago before Amber turned teenager. She couldn't help her feelings of sympathy. She wanted to reach out and touch both girls and tell them it was okay. Kids do go into deserted houses, barns, sheds, tunnels, old cars, whatever looks interesting.

"I didn't see it," Kirsten said. "My little sister found it when she—when she—"

The mother said, "The girls had gone into the house, and my younger daughter, who loves dolls, brought home an old doll from the house. I sent them back to return the doll. I should have done it myself, but I was very busy at the time and I just felt I couldn't . . ."

"It's all right," Mary said. "Kids would naturally explore an old place. You said it was open?"

Kirsten moistened her lips and looked away. "Well, not really. The back door was locked. I saw a side door I didn't try to open. The front door was closed too, only when I turned the latch it opened. We only walked in a little ways. I just went down the hall, and looked into some rooms, and I saw these really neat old furnishings, and I knew Mom would love it. She does family genealogy."

Mary Swift nodded.

"They know better than to go into someone's house," Don Flanners said, his face set with all the recriminations Mary didn't feel.

"We didn't know it belonged to anybody," Kirsten murmured.

"But," Sergeant Henley said, "Who found the skeleton and where was it?"

"I did," the little blond girl said in a very small voice. "I was taking the doll back to the top of the stairs, like Mama said I should, and I—and I went on into the two bedrooms that have a little hall of their own. And it was in the bed."

"And then what did you do?"

"I ran. And I fell."

"She broke through the stairs."

Don Flanners said, "It was probably already rotten."

Sergeant Henley got up, and Mary stood also. "Sure," he said. "Well, thanks for calling us. We'll check it out."

In the patrol car Mary said, "Haven't you ever heard of the old Wilfred mansion, Mark?"

He stared thoughtfully into the forest beyond the Flanner's house as Mary started the car and pulled it away

345

from the curb. She glanced at him. His round face made him look younger than his twenty-five years. She could see he knew nothing about it. But, it simply could be the younger generation, which she considered Mark to be part of, had grown so far away from the town's past that he wouldn't have heard of it.

"Not that I recall. Could there be any connection to the name of our town? Wilfred mansion in the town of Wilfred?"

"Yes, right. It's one of the oldest structures around. It wasn't exactly in town though. It had its own land, and probably still does. The lady who owned it moved into town, I think, and the house just sort of drifted into the past. Probably none of you younger people ever heard of it, especially if you don't have a grandmother like mine. She used to tell me stories about the people who lived there."

"What about 'em?"

"Oh, they were once very rich. But they had a lot of tragedies in the family. I don't remember much, except there were two or three young girls, in their teenage years, who died there. And their bodies were all put in the family mausoleum, except there was the rumor of a baby born to one of the girls. And no one ever knew where it was buried. Somewhere in the woods, it was said."

"Sounds like Halloween fare." Mark smiled.

"Maybe, a little. I remember Grandma and I once went to the funeral of one of her friends. She was buried in the old cemetery here by the church, and I asked her about the mausoleum. That's when she told me about the old mansion, and the young girls. But Gram wasn't trying to scare me."

"Just kidding. Do you think the Flanner kid really found something, or just got scared?"

"No idea. I guess we'll find out."

"What's the easiest way to get there?"

"It's on Highway 17, just around the corner from Shadow Oaks. Maybe we can still use the old driveway."

Mary drove past new houses, some of which were still under construction and some that were beginning to look occupied. Lights had been turned on, and glowed from windows with blinds not yet pulled. Probably many of the houses didn't even have their draperies and blinds yet. The yards were big, the sign at the entrance had guaranteed one acre plots. Plenty of room to garden and landscape.

"I wish I could afford to buy one of these," Mark dreamed aloud.

"Why Mark!" Mary grinned at him. She was sixteen years older than he, married for almost ten years, divorced for another ten. She didn't regret her divorce, but she regretted never having any kids. She had cats, dogs, and peace of mind. And Mark, sort of. He was her daily companion. She often teased Mark about his age and his girlfriends, just as he teased her about being an old lady who carried a gun. "You finally getting serious about your girl, honeychile?"

He sighed. He wasn't in a joking mood.

The street curved, as the streets in all these new places did, and small parks with trees came up in unexpected places. She could understand his desire to live here. She would have liked it herself. But still, her small house with its small yard looked very good to her when she went home tired.

"I'll be lucky if I can buy her a good ring. And luckier still if I can persuade her to accept it. I haven't even beat out my competition yet."

"She's pretty special, huh?" She looked at the thick forest on the right. How could an old driveway be found in this?

"Yes, she's special." Mark sounded lost in dreams.

"Mark," Mary said, and snapped her fingers in front of his nose. "To the right. Watch for the driveway."

Mary eased the car along Highway 17. They passed the west end of the stone wall of Shadow Oaks, and had solid forest on the right. Traffic had ceased. The sun was sinking, leaving the sky different shades of red and rose, cooling to deep blue overhead. Highway 17 wasn't very wide, but it was passable. The county hadn't even bothered to put a center dividing line in it.

On their right tall trees crowded against the road. Mark peered into them.

"Whoops," he said, twisting in the seat. "Back up."

Mary backed up.

"Okay, now turn. Maybe you'd better stop first and let me check it out. Very brushy."

She stopped the car on the shoulder, opened her door and got out. With Mark she walked toward the edge of the old brick driveway. It was almost hidden beneath weeds and brush and blackberry briars, but it looked passable.

Mary went back to the car, got a flashlight and returned to the brick covered culvert. Mark joined her.

The brick driveway, so narrow it must have originally been built for buggies, looked safe. The only problem was the culvert, and it was appeared solid. The driveway disappeared into the trees. Although it wasn't completely dark yet on the road, the woods looked dark. There certainly was no sign of a house.

"Back in there?" Mark asked.

"Yes, evidently."

"Do we walk or drive?"

"Why don't we drive."

"You don't think we'll knock something vital off the bottom?"

"We've driven over brush and briars before."

They got back into the car and Mary turned sharply

right and eased it onto the culvert and into the briars. They progressed slowly and came at last to a place where the brick had given way to young saplings. Even though she could have driven on, Mary stopped. The headlights picked up the corner of brick that went up, up into the trees.

"Hmm," Mark said in the moment before he got out of the car. "Lived here most of my life, and had no idea this was here."

With her flashlight shooting its beam in erratic directions, Mary cut through the brush toward the brick wall. Mark followed her, keeping the line of his light on the house.

With the flashlight beam probbing, Mary found the porch at the front of the house, the tall door, the windows above it, the roof. Mary went up to the door.

"Interesting knocker," Mark said, walking up to stand beside her.

Mary thought he was going to use it, and she cringed at the noise she expected. But he only grasped the rusted latch instead.

The door screeched as Mark pushed it inward. The sound was a highpitched, very faint wail that seemed to echo through the house, as a sound carries through a cave. Mary felt the hair stand up on the back of her neck. Mark looked at her with that quick surprise that followed finding something they hadn't quite expected.

"What the hell was that?" he asked softly.

"The door," she said.

He gave her another direct look that was almost a frown, a scowl of disbelief.

"Echoes," she said, trying to explain it.

Their flashlights found a floor with scattered rugs, the patterns hidden beneath dust. The lights passed over the frames of paintings, or portraits, quickly, and searched out the stairway the little girl had climbed.

"Why do you suppose the front door was unlocked," Mary speculated aloud, "With all this old furniture left in here?"

"More amazing is how did the vandals happen to bypass this place?"

"Maybe because it's isolated, and like you, the vandals didn't know it was here."

"Yeah," Mark grinned as her light washed briefly over his face. "What a place to bring your girl. One hour out in that old driveway, and she'd be all over a guy."

"Maybe so, but not with passion."

"Who cares?"

Mary started climbing the stairs, Mark right behind her. They stepped over the sagging steps and the one through which Lisa's leg had gotten caught. Mary paused and shined her light down into the hole. Nothing there but darkness.

At the top of the stairs were two old suitcases. They both bulged.

"Looks like somebody got this far," Mary said, aware that she tried to speak unnaturally softly.

They stepped past the suitcases and turned left and entered the door into the connecting hall of two bedrooms.

"Said she was on the bed," Mark muttered, going into the right bedroom. Both flashlights illuminated the mummified body on the bed.

Mary went closer, her light beam examining every surface detail of the dead face. She saw the open mouth, large teeth, dark and totally exposed from dried and receded lips. The eyes had sunk so far back into the head it made Mary shudder to look at them. Dust, heavy and grey, clung to everything. The hands still gripped the covering quilt. Dust had settled onto the long fingernails and obscured the pattern of the quilt.

Mary moved down the bed. One leg of the dead person lay on top of the quilt. It had been bandaged at the time of death.

"A woman," Mary said, her voice seeming to boom and echo in the house. Something in the wall, or outside on the balcony, scuttered away.

She felt an odd chill ice her cheeks. Mary looked at Mark, but he was shining his light about the room. Then, as if drawn by her stare, he turned. She could see he heard it, too. Something was moving on the balcony outside the room. Not human footsteps, not mice, rats, or raccoons, but something crawling.

Mary went toward the door.

She entered the connecting hall between the two rooms and stopped. Amazing, she thought, that a little girl would have the guts to come up here alone. She didn't even want to see what was out on the balcony. No wonder the child had been brought home in hysterics by her sister.

Mary stopped on the threshold of the outer door and shined her light along the balcony. Nothing.

Mary went back to the bedroom where Mark was still looking around, now from the other side of the bed.

"Woman, you say. It looks to me like it could be anything."

"Woman," Mary said, "I'll bet you a dollar. See the delicate face, and the hands. And the hair that looks as if it might have been worn in a pompadour." It was colorless, coated with dust and woven with webs.

She didn't pull back the cover. Or disturb the bed in any way.

"How long do you think she's been here?" Mark asked.

"Lord. I don't know. Twenty years? Forty? Fifty? More, maybe. That's not our department, thank God. I'd hate to touch the poor old thing."

"Speaking of department, we'd better go call."

Mary agreed. She was ready to get out of the house

351

and stay out. There was a smell in it that was getting to her, and a feeling she didn't like. She wasn't going to tell Mark, who was more sensible sometimes than she, but if ever she had believed in ghosts, now was the time to verify the truth of it.

"Let's go," said Mary. "And then let's pay my grandma a visit. She'll remember the names of the people who lived here."

Mary led the way out onto the balcony. She shined the light carefully along the side of the balcony on which they walked, but didn't go around to the other side. There was nothing. Dust had been disturbed though, in long trails, as if very recently there had been something.

Chapter 5

No one would ever have guessed Edra Logan to be eighty-three years old. She still walked two miles a day, had no grey in her light brown hair, and was into everything. She was busy with church, and with the senior activities. She played cards at the senior center a couple of times a week, and had turned down two marriage proposals since her third husband died eighteen months ago. Mary was proud as the dickens of her grandma, and hoped she could handle aging as well.

When Mary and Mark entered the tidy living room Edra was dressed in a blue robe, sitting in her recliner, her feet up. She had a paperback suspense novel in her hand and the television on. Mary had never been able to persuade Edra to lock her doors. So Mary had simply opened it, yelled in, "Gram?" and entered. That was the way Edra liked it. Locking one's door against one's neighbors just wasn't neighborly. Crimes were a distant happening. Even those that were moving closer and closer with the increasing population had no reality for Edra. "Who'd want to bother me?" she'd say when Mary worried. "I don't have any money or jewels, and my TV's ten years old, the VCR doesn't work half the time. Who'd want 'em?"

Edra brought them cups of tea, even though they didn't want it.

"In uniform?" Edra noted aloud as she sipped her own tea. "What have I done?"

Mary giggled. "There's no telling, Gram, but we're not here to make an arrest. What we want is information."

"Uhhuh. Now I'm an informant. Well, there's this one suspicious character that just joined the senior center, and brought his own deck of cards. I suspect he's going to try to scare up a poker game. Maybe even a nickle a pot."

Mark laughed, Mary smiled, and then turned all business.

"Listen Gram, you remember the old Wilfred mansion?"

"Of course."

"And the people who lived there?"

"Well . . . I was never acquainted with any of them. All I knew was whatever rumor was going around. The family died out, or moved away. The last I heard was forty years ago, I suppose. Back in the late forties or early fifties, the young man, Teddy Madison, and his daughter died, the same night. They were buried in the Wilfred mausoleum. And that just about ended the family as far as I know. Teddy's wife used to live in a small house over on Olrich Street. I haven't heard anything about any of them in years. They may all be dead now."

Mary leaned forward, her pen flying over her notebook. "What was her name, Gram?"

"Umm. Well, I'm not sure. I do know she once worked for the Madison's, and—"

"Madison?" Mark said. "I thought the family name was Wilfred."

"The Wilfred side died out. The only survivor was a woman named Sybil, and she married a Madison."

Edra turned and reached for the telephone book on the table beside her chair. She began leafing through it.

"There aren't a lot of Madisons. Most of these listed in the phone book came to Wilfred in the past few years with all the others who have moved in, and none of them are related to the old Madison family, that I know of. I asked a woman at the senior center whose name was Madison, and she'd never heard of them. Here, I'll bet this is it. J. Madison. Olrich Street."

She handed the book to Mary. Mary sat down on the floor on the other side of the table from her grandmother's chair and dialed.

"What's the sudden interest in the Madisons?"

Mark said, "There's a body in the old mansion. Someone was never buried."

Mary heard a silence in the room as she listened to the muted ringing of a telephone in the house on Olrich Street. Then a voice answered, and she lost out on the conversation between Mark and her grandmother.

"Mrs. Madison?"

"Yes."

"Are you related to the Madisons who own the old Wilfred place out southwest of town?"

There was a lengthy silence on the phone, and then the voice, more distant and muted, said, "Yes."

"I'm from the police department, and would like permission to come and talk to you."

There was another, even longer silence.

"All right."

She hung up.

"Okay," Mary said to Mark and Edra. "She said it was all right."

Mary was halfway to the door when she stopped. "She didn't ask why the police department wanted to talk to her. Which means she knows why."

Jenny's heart pounded, raced, shaking her body, causing pain in her chest, neck and arms. She wanted to get up and walk, and try to ease the pain away.

For over forty years she had been expecting the police

to show up at her door, and now she was too tired to get up and open it for them. For all this time she had closed herself in this tiny house and waited. And at night dreamed dreams of horror that made her a recluse and a coward.

The day she had run from the old mansion was almost a blank in her mind. She had run like a wounded animal trying to escape its pain.

With the falling of night she slowly came out of her insanity enough to return to the house. But she couldn't go back into it, not for her coat, not for her purse, or the key to her car. She realized she had to have help. There was nowhere she could go, except back to the house. Or to the police station.

Finally, shivering and cold, she had walked uptown, across the deserted square, and down the street to the police station. There was a light over the door of the one story brick building, but the door was locked. She remembered her feeling of relief. What would she tell them? She didn't believe what she had seen. How could she expect them to believe her?

Freezing, she retraced her steps to the church beside the cemetery where Annie and Ted were so recently buried, but that door was locked also. She thought of going to the parsonage, where she knew the minister would let her in, but she went instead to the mausoleum. Crouched in the freezing cold against it, she stared back through the woods toward the old mansion.

Go back in time, go back to the days when she, Ted, and Annie were homeless, back to the days when they went to visit her sister. Back to the day when the phone call came. When Gertrude told Ted his mother was dying and wanted to see him and her grandchild. Go back, and change it. Leave Carol's house before the phone call came. Leave and stay away, and let Miss Sybil die. Jenny felt in her heart that if they hadn't come home, if

Annie hadn't been standing there at Miss Sybil's bedside, the doll never would have been removed from the cabinet.

She couldn't go back. As she huddled against the mausoleum, hearing the brittle crack of leaves in the black, cold forest, she imagined the doll coming to find her.

With the coming of day she suddenly remembered that Ted had always kept a spare ignition key beneath the left fender. She could get it and drive away, and keep going.

She walked back through the forest to the house. In the car, the door closed, she turned the key. The starter ground slowly, too cold to start. She began to cry. Then she tried it again, and the car started. She hadn't made plans. With the heater warming her she drove to the square and parked in a sunny spot and turned off the engine. The gas gauge showed empty. She had no money. Her purse was back in the house, with her clothes, her coat, everything else.

She realized as the stores opened that she was parked in front of the bank. As if providence had brought her. She went inside. There were two clerks, and neither of them acted surprised or shocked at her behavior or that she wasn't wearing a coat. She was hiding her terror well, her disbelief at what had happened. She asked to speak to the president, or whoever might help her. She was mumbling, but the clerk smiled her into an office.

She was able to explain that she was Ted Madison's widow and Gertrude Madison's sister-in-law. She was the one who would be taking care of Gertrude, and she would be taking care of the money for Gertrude.

To her surprise the bank president simply brought out a paper for her to sign. As Ted's widow, she had that right.

She didn't leave town. Ted and Annie were in the mausoleum. She had to stay in Wilfred to be sure that nothing ever happened to the old mansion.

She found a small house and rented it, and years passed. She lived day to day. She didn't need much money to live. In the fenced backyard she grew a vegetable garden each year, and canned and preserved all she could. At the store she bought flour, cornmeal, milk, salt, sugar and food for the stray cat who came to live with her. Over the years a dozen cats and dogs came to her doorstep and spent the rest of their lives with her and finally came to their final resting place at the edge of the garden in her backyard.

She had passed the age of seventy, and she was tired of waiting for the day when someone would come and ask her about the body in the old mansion. She was tired of thinking and dreaming nightly of the horror of the doll. Over the years she had tried to tell herself she was crazy. She had gone crazy after the deaths of her husband and child, and somehow the doll had become part of the nightmare.

And perhaps that was the explanation. But it didn't excuse the truth of the body left on the bed, unburied.

No one had ever inquired about Gertrude. Gertrude had been such a shadow, living without friends, that no one missed her. If the minister from the church had gone knocking on the door, he had finally given up without saying anything to the police.

Very few people knew Jenny was connected in any way to the old mansion. Only a few of the old-timers.

The town had changed over the years. People and businesses had come in and settled out along the highway east of the old part of town. Housing developments spread. There was a new population that had never heard of the original founder of the town, or the land still undeveloped, or the old mansion around which bushes had grown into tall trees.

She had regularly driven out to the house to make sure no one had bothered it. She always parked just on the edge of the driveway and walked in, just far enough to see the front door was still closed. Gradually over the years the paint fell away from the wood, and bricks fell, leaving exposed the grey wood beneath, like a grey skeleton.

Then she had seen the bulldozers at work on the property next door, and for awhile she had been terrified they would damage the mausoleum. But although the developers built houses and yards where much of the forest had stood, the cemetery was left untouched. She still took flowers and laid them against the door.

The front door of the old mansion, she remembered daily, was not locked. She had never gone close enough to touch the door. At night she dreamed of that old latch in her hand, and she heard the door opening and saw the endless dark beyond the door. And into the dark would come a face, surrounded by the lace of a bonnet, and she would wake trying to scream.

She waited now for the police, each breath more difficult than the last. When the car lights turned into her driveway she got up and went to the door and unlocked it, but when she tried to return to her chair, she fell. She tried to rise and couldn't. Pain seared her chest, neck, and face. She let herself down on the floor.

Thank God it was almost over. But she had to live long enough to tell someone about the doll. Warn them. Don't go into the mansion. *Don't touch the doll.*

Mary knocked on the door. A dim light illuminated the drawn window shade. There was no answer. She knocked again, and at last called, "Mrs. Madison?"

Mary put her hand on the doorknob and turned. The door opened. She pushed the door wider and looked into the room. A grey-haired woman lay on the floor, facedown. Mary ran to her.

"Mark," she said as she knelt, "Call an ambulance."

Mark's footsteps pounded across the front porch as Mary bent over the woman. Her face was turned, her cheek flattened against the floor, her eyes staring. Mary's heart plummeted. Too late. Perhaps her phone call to Jenny Madison had caused her collapse.

Then Mary heard a groan. Jenny's eyes turned slowly and found Mary's face.

"You'll be fine," Mary assured her. "Help is on the way."

"Doll . . ." Her voice was weak and faltering. A cat came close, meowing, and rubbed against the top of Jenny's head, and Mary almost lost the few words Jenny was trying to speak. The meowing of the cat increased as it sniffed Jenny's face.

"Old . . . house . . . danger. The doll. Don't let . . . the doll . . . please . . . don't . . . let . . ."

"Jenny, what doll?"

Jenny sighed deeply and her eyes fixed on the wall beyond Mary. The woman lay still, the cat pushing against her head as if trying to bring her back. But Jenny Madison had died.

Mary stood up slowly and looked around the room. There was no doll that she saw. Later she could check through the house and see if there was a doll, but what had Jenny intended for her to do with it?

Mary stared down at the thin form, and felt a terrible sadness. She knew nothing about this woman except that she had lost her husband and child and evidently had lived here alone except for whatever animals might have lived with her. Jenny Madison was the only person who might have told them what had happened to the body left in the mansion. But her feelings of sadness were too crushing, as if something of Jenny still floated in the air, and Mary had absorbed a touch of the woman's feelings.

The next day Mary went through Jenny's house and found no doll. It was a simple little house, with only the necessary furnishings. The cat meowed at the backdoor, and she set out milk and food. It was eating slowly when she left.

She returned to the mansion. Trails had been made to the front door by the cars that had driven over the growth of vegetation. A couple of local police cars were parked near the house, as well as one unmarked car and two State Police, but still the aura was of an ominous silence. As she entered the front door the first of Jenny's dying words snapped into her mind. "Old . . . house . . . danger . . ."

Mary stopped inside the door struck suddenly by the messages she sensed. A woman had been left dead here a long time ago, and Jenny had kept silent about the death and moved to town. Her last breath mentioned the danger of the mansion and a doll. It created more confusion in Mary's mind than connections.

She found a member of the police department she knew and staked him out. Part of the State Police had come in and taken over, making tracks in the dust.

"What's happening?" she asked.

The officer, stationed here by the city police to keep an eye on the State Police, shrugged. He was slightly on the plump side, and his belly pushed out his neatly pressed shirt. He stood with his hands on his belt at each side of his waist.

"Nothing. They're just taking a look around. We'll be out of here in a few hours."

"Body gone?"

"Sure. Hours ago."

"How did she die?"

"I don't know. The state will let us know when the examiner gets through with it. The local coroner said he thought she must have been dead thirty or forty years, and probably of natural causes."

Mary shuddered.

"What's going to happen to the house now that its owner is dead?"

"Don't know that either."

"Did anybody say anything about finding a doll?"

He looked at her with a half-smile. "No. You lookin' for one?"

"I'll look around, okay?"

The ground floor had nothing left of police except a few tracks in the dust, going from door to door and along the halls. In the kitchen Mary found that food had been left on the table in bowls and on platters and covered by a cloth that once had probably been white.

She found a back stairs and climbed. Voices at the front of the house, like the murmurs of a radio turned low, indicated where the police were working. She looked into the bedrooms along the back hall. They were furnished, and some of them still had bedding. But there were no dolls, nor toys of any kind.

She finally found a doll on the third floor.

It was in a large display cabinet, a lady doll, thirteen inches tall, in Puerto Rican dancing costume. She opened the glass door and removed it. It had a tiny, well-sculpted face and delicate hands. Its feet wore black slippers. Dust clung to it as dust clung to everything in the house. Puzzled more than ever as she tried to exactly recall Jenny's words about the doll, she slowly replaced it. She closed the glass door. The cabinet was filled with old toys, most of them very small, and glass or wood figurines. What had Jenny said? "Doll . . . don't let . . ."

Mary stood looking through the glass at the black-haired smiling little doll. Was it valuable? Probably. It looked very old. But why hadn't Jenny taken it with her?

It was the only doll she had seen in her quick and

casual look through the house. There were rooms she hadn't seen, and hundreds of places where old toys and dolls were probably tucked out of sight. She would have to dismiss Jenny's words as being the confused words of a dying person.

Mary would have liked to go through the house more thoroughly, but she had a report to write. She left and went back to the station. By then more information was available.

"There's an heir," one of the girls told her. "He lives in Seattle, Washington."

Mary raised her eyebrows. "An heir, huh?" She pushed aside a stack of paper and sat on the corner of the desk. "Interesting."

The neighbors she had talked to about Jenny said the woman had never had visitors. No family was even known about. There was not one shred of evidence of communication with anyone, friends or family. In Jenny's house there had been no saved Christmas cards, no letters. Nothing except the barest essentials of furniture.

She had talked to the mail carrier. He had carried mail along Jenny's street for almost twenty years. He told her Jenny got the usual junk mail, and once or twice a year, for a long time, she had gotten a letter, or card, from somewhere in the state of Washington. But they had stopped several years ago, so he assumed that whoever Jenny communicated with had died.

Instead of living in the mansion, Jenny had chosen to rent a small house in town, and had rented it since 1950. Was the death of the woman in the old mansion, who now was known to be Gertrude Madison, a homicide? There had been no stab wounds, no gunshot wounds. But, if Jenny Madison had killed her sister-in-law, it might have been poison. They'd know about that in a few days.

"How did they learn about the heir?" Mary asked.

"Beats me. The state found it out. I think there were some old letters out in the mansion. She had a sister and a nephew. The sister was dead, the nephew is the survivor."

Mary looked out the window toward the building next door and wondered if the nephew would be here in time for Jenny's funeral.

"What's going to happen to Jenny's cat?" she asked.

"Did she have a cat?"

There was nothing to stop Mary from going back to Jenny's tiny little house and picking up the cat. There was room in her yard for another animal.

Curiosity about Jenny and why she had never reported her sister-in-law's death, why at the last she had called the mansion dangerous and was concerned about a doll, might remain forever with Mary. She felt as she knelt and opened her arms to the meowing, lonely cat, that she would never know much more than she now knew.

The cat, in her arms, began to purr.

She stroked him. "It'll be all right now," she said.

Chapter 6

Whenever Kirsten could sneak off from Lisa she checked on the old mansion. After Lisa made friends with the two little girls from the next street over, it was easier to get away. She watched the police cars in the first days after they had found the mummy in the upstairs bed, but then Lisa had been with her, begging her to come back. And their mother had demanded they stay away from the house also, so Kirsten had learned to slip around to do her peeking.

After the police left and nothing was happening again at the old house, Kirsten would slip through the woods and watch it, at times sitting on the limb of a tree she had climbed to get a better view. She felt both repelled and drawn by the house. There was something about it, something that seemed to be trying to speak to her, as if voices were trying to reach her.

A skinny little man in a business suit came out in his Buick and put up a No Trespassing sign at the road, and then he walked around the house, peeked in the front door, then fiddled with the latch. Kirsten wondered if he locked it. After he left she itched to go over and see. But she had strict orders to stay away from the house. Also, she was afraid now. In her dreams at night she wandered through a huge, endless house filled with twisting hallways and numberless small rooms, most without windows. She could never find her way out.

* * *

Two identical coffins were placed in the Wilfred mausoleum after a brief service conducted by the minister of the small church Jenny had occasionally attended. Jenny's nephew did not arrive in time for her funeral. Mary lingered after the graveside services were over and watched the final closing of the heavy wood door on the mausoleum. There had been so few people at the funeral it saddened Mary. Two people buried, and no one to remember them. Jenny's next door neighbors had come, a few of the police, Mary's grandmother, and a handful of strangers who were curious.

The minister's last words lingered with Mary. "And today we lay to rest two people who were not strangers to God. Gertrude Madison and Jenny Madison." Not strangers to God, but strangers to the town that should have known them.

Alone at the cemetery Mary laid a red rose against the door. She listened to the singing of the birds, Gertrude's and Jenny's only dirge. She opened her notebook and wrote down the names, dates of births and deaths of those listed on the brass commemorative plaque beside the door. But they did not open up the mystery of the last years of the old Wilfred mansion.

In the days following the brief funerals Mary talked to everyone in town who had any memories of the old Wilfred and Madison family, and learned little more than her grandmother had told her. She was ready to give up when it occurred to her the public library was another possible source of information.

In the library basement she checked through the microfilm of the old Wilfred newspapers. There were little items in the first newspaper printed in the municipality of Wilfred, in 1837. The paper was called the *Wilfred Daily,* and told of Martin Wilfred, president of the Wilfred Bank, being at a meeting in which Wilfred's first mayor was elected.

In the early days the town must have been only a crossroads, a trail between the river and the railroad. It was big news when Martin Wilfred built the new store. People of the town would be able to buy everything they needed in one store. The paper printed in its odd, uneven type, they could buy "groceries, yard goods, needles, thread, wool, harnesses, nails, hammers, wagons, seeds and all things pertaining to the livelihood of a household and a farm."

In 1840 a birth was announced. Born to Martin Wilfred and his good wife, it said, a son, named Charles Martin.

But, in a newpaper dated 1843 was Martin Wilfred's obituary. By that time the newspaper had grown to four pages, and ads filling two of them indicated more stores and business had been built in Wilfred. Martin's survivors included his son, Charles, his wife, unnamed. Two daughters were listed as survivors but they too were unnamed.

Women were so unimportant they weren't even named as a man's survivors? Only the son counted. She paused for a moment and considered that. It fit in very well with her growing idea that men weren't happy if they weren't number one. Of course she had to admit she still carried some bitterness from her failed marriage.

She had tried to get rid of her rage, her hatred, her disappointment. But at times it still rose into her throat and chest and made her feel ill.

She had dated a few men since then, but hadn't fallen in love again. She wondered if she ever would. She wondered if it mattered whether she did or not. She was content with her life now, far happier than she had been during the last seven years of her marriage.

She started reading again. This time she skipped to the Civil War. Now the newspaper, which had been a weekly, was published only once a month. Among the pages that told of various young men going off to fight, the paper at last named women who had taken over at home. But none was a Wilfred. Then she found again the Wilfred name. Charles Wilfred had returned home from the war.

She read of the ending of the war, and a month later the news of the marriage between Charles Martin Wilfred and Minerva Rose Addison.

Occasionally then, it was mentioned that businessman Charles Wilfred had returned from a trip to South America where he had business interests.

A year later, in 1867, a Wilfred daughter was born. Rose Marie.

Three years later another daughter was born. Sybil Rose.

The newspaper grew to six pages, and the print became as neat and legible as present day newspapers. Buggies and horses were drawn in black advertisements. Both were for sale at the Wilfred stables. Banking still occurred at the Wilfred Bank. There was occasional mention of Attorney's at Law, Wilfred and Mangrove.

Was Charles Wilfred an attorney, with business interests in South America? He still took an annual trip. Perhaps it was during one of those trips he had purchased the little dancing doll with the black hair and ruffled skirt.

Then in the winter of 1882 another obituary showed up, this one very elaborate, with angels and vines drawn around it. It announced that Rose Marie Wilfred, at the tender and innocent age of thirteen years, had passed to her heavenly rewards.

Mary felt something grab in her heart, and that strange prodding in the back of her mind increased, as if something about Rose Marie's death had shaken the curtain that hung between the world of reality and the world of the spirit.

Mary began to scan the old newspapers more carefully. Rose Marie's survivors were listed as her father, Charles, her mother, Minerva, and her sister Sybil.

Then, in the spring after Rose Marie's death, the mother died. She was listed, too, as having passed to her heavenly rewards. There was no reason given for either death. But the feeling grew stronger in Mary that someone was trying to tell her something about the deaths. In the silent basement of the library she looked over her shoulder, as if whatever it was lurked behind her. Yet she shouldn't be afraid, she told herself. It only wanted help. She could almost see it now as perhaps the spirit of one of those who had died. Rose Marie, maybe. Or maybe someone she hadn't read about yet.

In June, 1890, Sybil Wilfred married Walter Madison. The article described Sybil's gown, and showed a dark portrait of a tall young woman with her hair in a puff on top of her head, her waist very tiny and narrow, and the long white gown swirled around her legs and trailing behind her. It could have been the picture of any model. The features of Sybil's face were smudged, so that Mary saw only the shape of her face.

Mary found herself frowning at the picture. This young woman had lived in the old mansion?

She moved on, and found the birth of Rose Marie, 1892.

Rose Marie. The same name of the sister who had died. Mary suddenly had a very bad feeling for this baby, Rose Marie. She checked her notebook. Yes, Rose Marie had died at age eighteen. Why had the Wilfred-Madison family had so many deaths of teenagers?

Three years after the birth of Rose Marie another daughter was born. Julie Sue. She was going to be another of the teenage tragedies. Then five years after Julie Sue's birth Gertrude Minerva's birth was announced.

Gertrude.

It was her mummified body that little Lisa Flanners had found in the old mansion. She was born January 20, 1900.

Mary bent closer to the computer screen and turned the years by. She was watching now only for obituaries, for explanations, because whatever she was looking for had to do with the deaths.

She found the obituaries. Rose Marie, died, age eighteen. And two weeks later, Julie Sue, age fifteen. There were no reasons given. No explanations at all. Nowhere in the newspaper were the names of Rose Marie and Julie Sue mentioned, outside the obits.

She found another name, Beulah Stafford, age seventy-one. The obituary mentioned in one sentence that Beulah had been a maid at the Madison home for fifty-seven years.

She was almost a part of the family, then, it seemed to Mary. And the disturbing thing was, she had died just a few days before Julie Sue. The Wilfred-Madison family had suffered three deaths in a two week period back in 1910. If the rumors Mary's grandmother had heard about Rose having a baby were correct, then there were four deaths in a very short time.

Jenny had said . . . what were her exact words? Mary couldn't be sure now. Something about the old mansion being dangerous. And something about a doll. The two probably had no connection.

Mary pushed back the chair to which she felt permanently bonded. She was tired, drained.

There was something about all those deaths in 1910 that were important, even today. But Mary didn't know what it was, and there was no way to find out what she needed to know. Nothing spoke to her telling her to go on reading, yet after walking around and rubbing her rear with both hands, she sat down again.

She scanned marriages, divorces, deaths. She found the

death of Sybil Madison, January 14, 1950, leaving behind one daughter, one son, and one granddaughter.

Less than two weeks later Ted Madison and his eight year old daughter, Annie, died. Their obituaries were in the same column. Both of them had died the same day, January 28, 1950.

They were survived by Jenny.

Good Lord, no wonder Jenny felt the old mansion was dangerous.

Jenny Madison's obituary mentioned no survivors. It was the shortest obituary Mary had ever read. It was as if no one knew anything at all about Jenny Madison. Not even as much as Mary herself knew. She didn't know who had written the obit, but they obviously hadn't known about the nephew in Washington. There was no mention of Gertrude Madison in this newspaper, although there had been a short article on the second page at the time of discovery of the body.

Mary's search was stifled, but there was a lot more she could guess. She felt certain that Jenny knew about Gertrude's body being in the mansion, never removed from her deathbed. For some terrible reason Jenny had never told or had her buried. Then the shock of the police wanting to talk to her about Gertrude had killed her.

Of course that, too, was in the newspaper, but in a small article of police news. Jenny Madison, wanted for questioning about the death of Gertrude Madison, had died before police could talk to her. Most people in town reading that little item might be puzzled for half a minute, but then they'd forget it and go on with their lives.

The library lights blinked off and on, a not so subtle invitation to leave. Mary climbed the stairs and told the librarian good night. She went home feeling drained of energy and confused of mind. Tomorrow she was on duty again, and she had no really good excuse to go into the old mansion, although she would have liked to. The case of Gertrude Madison's death was closed in the police files. She had died of natural causes.

Mary had a strong feeling that was not true.

After the police stopped going into the old mansion the forest reclaimed it. Kirsten checked every day, from a spot near a large tree where she had a fair view of the front door of the house. She went down the road and to the driveway, where the weeds and brush were broken and mashed flat. She found the skinny little man had roped off the driveway, with a sign on the rope saying stay out.

A few weeks later Kirsten woke to the sound of large machinery. As soon as she could get dressed she ran down to the end of the street to see that bulldozers and tree cutters were working on clearing away another part of the forest. And, she thought in a rush of anxiety, perhaps the old house, too. With all its antique furniture.

She ran home to find her mother and Lisa in the kitchen. Mom was making French toast, and Lisa sat at the table with one of her Barbie dolls and a lapful of little clothes.

"Where have you been?" Jane asked.

"Mom," Kirsten cried. "They're cutting trees! I think they're going to tear down the old mansion!"

"What about the doll?" Lisa asked.

Jane said, "Forget the doll!" Then to Kirsten, "Of course they wouldn't just bulldoze it down, Kirsten. It belongs to somebody now."

Kirsten relaxed a bit. "How do you know?"

Jane looked at the wall. "Ummm. I heard it somewhere. Now go wash your hands and face and come and eat."

"I washed already."

"Wash again! You've been chasing through the woods."

"But I didn't touch anything."

"Kirsten!"

Kirsten went down the hall to the guest bathroom and washed her hands. Before going back to the kitchen she peeked out toward the sound of the machinery, but couldn't see anything.

She learned a couple of days later that the clearing was for a convenience store to be built soon. She hated seeing old oaks that were probably two hundred years old go down and become little chunks for somebody's fireplace. But there was an unexpected advantage, too. She found that from her back deck she could now see one portion of the old house. When she brought out the binoculars she had gotten for Christmas, she could see an upper floor window very clearly.

The bulldozing and tree cutting stopped, leaving a thin line of trees between the lot where the store was being built and the yard of the old mansion.

Her feelings surprised her. It seemed now that the old mansion was closer to her own house, and she realized she didn't want it closer. She looked through her binoculars at the one window that was so clear, and then moved the binoculars toward the back of the house and lost it. Trees were untouched there, and shielded it completely. She looked back and stopped again at the window and stared.

Someone was in the house.

She lowered her binoculars and blinked, but the window was too far away now, shadowed by trees leafed in summer foliage. Kirsten cut through the trees between her backyard and the mansion. She skirted the edge of the convenience store lot where work was still being done by several guys with chain saws and trucks.

She approached the old house slowly. The sound of the men working grew muffled and distant, as if they belonged to another world. The old mansion was like a dark monster hiding in the trees.

Kirsten saw the rope was still across the driveway, and there was no car near the house. She went closer than she had for several weeks. Still there was nothing to indicate that the owner of the mansion had arrived.

She returned home, balanced herself on the railing of the deck, and put her binoculars to her eyes again. She looked at the window. Lace hung in strips, rotted with the years. At the bottom of the glass she saw clearly, for just an instant, the face again.

It was small, the face of a child, or a very old person, perhaps. Kirsten wobbled on the railing, and grabbed for support. The binoculars slipped out of her hands. She almost fell off the railing of the deck, following the binoculars to the grass eight feet below.

The face had been looking at her. Directly at her. Watching her longer than she had watched it, seeing her and recognizing her.

She went down after the binoculars and focused them again. She found the face and then made herself look more closely.

Not a face after all, but a cobweb, or dirt on the window. The spots that looked like eyes were darker spots in the smudge. That was all.

Kirsten lowered the binoculars to her knees, and hooked her toes behind railing posts for balance. She stared at the dark wall of the house in the distant trees until it all blurred in a mass of green and brown. Her feeling of cold fear didn't go away. Curiosity was replaced by a new knowledge. There was something dangerous in the house, and it stared at her from every window, faceless and voiceless.

She began to wish the house were demolished and taken down brick by brick and cleared out of the woods.

* * *

Emily's handsome husband held out his hand to the lawyer and said, "I'm Mel Curtis, and this is my wife, Emily."

Mel was still flushed with excitement, or maybe embarrassment, and Emily felt sorry for him. From the moment they had received the staggering news that Mel had inherited property from an aunt he didn't even know, they had existed in a kind of dream. Mel had driven east in a high that reminded her of their pot smoking days when they were both teenagers experimenting with various dangers. Now he was as nervous as a kid.

"And our children."

Emily smiled at the lawyer as she extricated her left hand from holding the baby, switching her to the right. She added, for Mel, "Adam and Priscilla."

She looked down and found Adam, who stood slightly behind her as if he had reverted to a two year old peeking around at the stranger. She put her hand on the top of his head and pushed him forward. Then she felt that incredible pride as Adam put up his small hand to the lawyer's big paw and said his little piece.

"Pleased to meet you, sir."

She had instructed him only once. For a nine year old he was remarkably dependable.

Prissy was growing heavy in her arms and beginning to fuss. Now that she could walk she thought she had every right to get down and explore the office of the lawyer.

"Please sit down," Jesse Crafton said as he settled behind his desk and began sifting through a sheath of papers. "We'll need to go over a few things."

During the next hour Emily sat back, her attention divided between what the man was telling Mel, and trying to keep Prissy controlled. The plump little toddler waddled first in one direction, then the other, and Emily found herself wishing Prissy would just go to sleep. She dug the bottle, which usually was given to Prissy only at bedtime, from the diaper bag, and tried to entice the baby with it. But Prissy pushed it away.

"The house has not been lived in, so far as we know, since Jenny Madison rented a small house in town. She simply walked off and left it . . ."

Emily detected something in the air. The way the lawyer hesitated, the way he leaned back in his chair, brought her attention fully to him.

"I don't know how to tell you this easily," he said. "Just before your aunt died, a body was found in the house, still in her bed upstairs in a front bedroom. She was Jenny's sister-in-law, Gertrude Madison. She had been dead for many years. It's largely guesswork, but the death has been set at probably the same time that Jenny rented the little house, which was early February, 1950."

Emily sat frowning at the lawyer. She felt as if he had reached out, gripped the clothes at her neck and ripped them off, leaving her cold and uncovered.

Mel had said to her, how many times, there has to be a catch. Here we are with nothing, never had anything, and suddenly we're property owners? There has to be a catch.

"But," Emily said, wanting more than anything for Mel's dream of owning property to come true, "Mel is the heir?"

"Oh yes, without a doubt, Mel is the heir. There's very little money, but there's the house and eighty acres of land, most of it reverted to timber now."

She told herself it didn't matter that someone had died in the house and her body was not discovered for an incredible number of years. That had nothing to do with her and Mel. Yet, she was determined that if the house had enough bedrooms to accommodate her family comfortably, they would close off the bedroom where the woman had died, and leave it closed.

Prissy was about to pull a potted plant off a table, she noticed suddenly. But Adam was going after Prissy and pulling her away. Prissy opened her mouth in one of her screeching cries that lasted only a moment before her attention was drawn to something else.

Chapter 7

They left the office of the law firm that had handled the Madison estate, and followed in their dusty old sedan the shiny new cherry red Buick of the lawyer. Emily felt like a refugee from *The Grapes of Wrath*, with their car's luggage rack loaded with boxes and a couple of old cheap suitcases tied atop and looking ready to fall. The backseat of the car was so packed that Adam was crowded into one tiny spot and hiked up on a folded blanket. They had left barely enough room for the seat belt to reach him. In front, between Emily and Mel, the babyseat took up so much room that Emily had ridden cramped against the right door in order to give Mel elbow room. The only really happy one was Prissy, who had a lap full of toys to entertain herself with, and the lull of the car in motion to nap by.

Downtown Wilfred, or Old Town Wilfred, as the lawyer called it, delighted Emily. It reminded her of picture postcards she had seen. She loved its brick streets, surrounding a square that was green and shaded. In the center was an old-time bandstand. There was even a statue of a Civil War general standing stiff and straight with his long rifle at his side, and his face turned north. A bird rested on the top of his hat, lifting its beak toward the sky and pouring forth a lovely trill.

They left the square behind and continued on a narrow street, still made of brick, past small frame houses with wide front porches moulding beneath their cover of

378

trees. They passed a larger house next door to a cemetery. On the left the more modern houses began, rows of sunny rooftops replacing the cool, dark trees.

They passed a lot where a construction sign announced that Speedee Mart was being built by Bayer and Sons Construction. Just beyond the building site the trees began again, large, old, dense, with knotted limbs and rough bark, and among them the white, smooth bark of sycamore.

As Emily was admiring the trees she realized the Buick had slowed and was turning into the thick of the forest. Their car followed closely.

The house suddenly loomed at the side of the drive, another expanse of dark brick. Emily stared at it. The top disappeared beyond the treetops. It was huge. She saw beneath a long, narrow window a dark wound, where wood was exposed. Brick had fallen, and lay scattered on the ground.

"And I was wondering if there'd be enough room for my family so I could leave that poor woman's bedroom closed."

No one seemed to hear her. In the backseat Adam was struggling excitedly with his seat belt and the door at the same time. Emily got out of the car, and reached back for Prissy. Adam finally freed himself and left the car door standing open as he ran to his dad. Emily closed the car doors, adjusted Prissy on her hip, and followed.

They went around a narrow brick path. Brush growing along the path had been broken back, and the lawyer was explaining that the police had cleared their way to the front door. Emily said nothing. She brought up the rear, Prissy quiet for once in her arms.

They went around to the front of the house, climbed steps to a porch, and stood before a large door.

Mr. Crafton opened the door, and it swung back on silent hinges. "Somebody," he said, "squirted some oil on these hinges. It doesn't sound like it did the first time I went in."

They stopped in a foyer that was as large as their rented house had been. Doors opened off it on the right and left, and a long, curving stairway rose toward a balustraded balcony above. Straight ahead double doors stood half-open, revealing a hall, gloomy and nearly dark.

Even in the filtered and gloomy light Emily could see the dust and the webs. Spider webs had woven picture frames to the walls, and had taken over every nook and corner. The chairs seemed a uniform dark grey, with only a suggestion of pattern beneath the dust.

The floor was tracked with footprints through the center of the foyer and up the stairs. A few sets of footprints went toward each door, and through the hallway to the back. Emily also noticed, in deepening dismay, odd little trails, as if something had been dragged in all directions, crisscrossing, keeping close to walls

"I'm sure there are keys somewhere in the house," Mr. Crafton said. "Well, this is it." He stood uneasily, exhibiting a nervous attitude that seemed more pronounced here than it had in his small office. "I'm sorry it's so dirty, but, well, it's been empty a long time."

Looking up toward the dim upper story, Emily said, "Which bedroom was hers? I'd like to see it."

"It's up at the front, on the right side. There's a suite there, two bedrooms joined by a private hall, with one door opening out onto the balcony. It was the master suite, I guess. You can't miss it." He seemed reluctant to show her.

"Amazing," Mel said, his first remark since they had entered the house.

"What's that?" Mr. Crafton asked, looking about in alarm, as if Mel had spotted something unseen before.

"That this house has stood here for so long with the

front door unlocked, and wasn't vandalized."

There was a moment of silence, then the lawyer said, "I guess people just forgot it was here, hard to see from the road with all the new growth."

Emily asked, "How did it come to be discovered? The body."

The lawyer motioned back toward town. "You noticed the new houses next door? A couple of little girls were exploring. They found the door was open and just came on in."

Emily caught a glimpse of Adam in an old mirror on the wall. His dark eyes were enormous, filled with wonder and perhaps a bit in awe of the haunted house atmosphere. His dark, curly hair caught a streak of sunshine angling through the trees and the open door and became firey auburn for just a flash. His round, beautiful face looked more pointed at the chin, slightly distorted by the mirror.

"The police checked out most of the house, I'm sure," Mr. Crafton said. He looked over his shoulder at Emily. "Be careful when you climb the stairs. There are a couple of broken steps."

He looked pointedly at his watch.

"Well, I'm sorry I can't be of more help. We didn't bother to put new locks on or anything to keep out the curious. If thieves had wanted to get in, they would have anyway. But it doesn't look like anything's been bothered."

"I'm surprised," Mel said, "This furniture is probably pretty valuable, and there must have been publicity."

"Not as much as one would think. The discovery of the body got an article on the second page of the newspaper, and then one more, when there was a positive identification. Some old dental records."

Emily asked, "What was the cause of death?" She really wanted to forget there had ever been a body in the house, but she also felt a need to know why.

Why was it left? What caused the death?

"Natural causes, so far as they could tell. No poison, so I heard, or anything like that."

"Do you know if there was a falling out between Aunt Jenny and her sister-in-law?" Mel asked.

"Why do you say that?"

"Well, if Aunt Jenny moved out so long ago, perhaps she didn't know her sister-in-law had died. Maybe they just never communicated."

"That's possible, but there's evidence she did know. If you want to know more about what the police have on file, you could ask them. In the opinion of those of us who were interested, it looked like Jenny Madison left at about the time Gertrude Madison died. Very hurriedly. She didn't even lock the front door. There were some rumors that maybe Jenny killed Gertrude, but there was no sign of anything but a natural death. She'd had a sprained ankle. The bandage was still on her leg . . . on the bones of her leg." He made a sound in his throat, and looked at Adam as if remembering a child was present. Backing a few steps toward the door, he looked at his watch again.

"Anyway, it's all yours. You'll find keys somewhere, I'm sure. You might want to clean it up and stay here, or if you want to just unload it, you let me know and I'll recommend a real estate dealer."

Emily looked at Mel. He had been so excited about owning his own place, but there was a dark and somber quality about the house that depressed Emily. The lack of light made her feel as if her vision were impaired. The dust that was everywhere looked impossible to ever get control of.

Yes, it should be cleaned up before being put on the market, Mr. Crafton was saying, and yes it should have a cleaning crew. Mel nodded, and nodded, but Emily knew who the cleaning crew would be. Her and Mel.

They didn't have money to hire anyone.

"There are records that indicate the bills were paid regularly. The gas, lights, telephone. Jenny Madison paid them, all these years. All you need to do is have it put in your own name."

"You mean the lights work?" Emily looked for a switch, found an old-fashioned button arrangement at the side of the front door. But nothing happened when she pushed them.

"The bulbs are probably burned out, Emily," Mel said.

"Well," the little lawyer said again. He was ready to go out onto the porch. "If there's anything I can do, I'll be glad to do what I can." He hunched one shoulder nervously. "Anyway, it's all yours. You can stay here, or if you'd rather not, until you get it cleaned, there are some nice motels out on the highway east of Old Town. You'll find shopping centers out there too, and supermarkets."

Emily carried Prissy to keep her out of the dust. She heard Mel at the door saying a few parting words to the lawyer. She began to climb the stairs.

Halfway up she felt one of the steps sag beneath her and heard the threatening rip of a board. She stepped back and stood looking up. There was a source of light at the front of the house and turning her head, she saw tall windows. But like the others they were narrow and coated in grime, letting in just enough light to keep the house from total darkness. But she knew suddenly she didn't want either one of her children in this part of the house.

She turned and retraced her steps to the foyer. Adam backed down ahead of her. He had been following her up the stairs. She took hold of his arm and guided him toward the door.

"Adam, I want you never to climb those stairs, or go up there. Hear? It's *dangerous*." With the word spoken, her feelings sharpened. She sensed the danger of this part of

383

the house as if it were atmospheric, invisible in the gloom but floating in the air like a high pressure.

"But Mom . . ."

"No," she said. "I want you to take Prissy outdoors and watch her, while I go up."

"But, I'll be careful, Mom. I want to go too. I want to see where the body was."

"Don't be gruesome."

"I only wanted to see the room, Mom."

Mel said, "After the house is cleaned and the stairs mended, he can go up, can't he, Emily?"

Emily saw that Mel had not lost his former excitement. In the glow of his eyes she could almost see the house as it could be, as it would be to him, as perhaps it had been a hundred years ago. Gleaming clean, the woods polished until they shone. She saw that look in his eyes and felt weighted with her own depression.

"Maybe," she said. "Maybe then, if it ever happens. Meantime you keep Prissy right out here on the porch. Don't get away from her. And be very careful."

Mel went with her up the stairs. They stood briefly at the top of the stairs looking about. All the doors stood ajar, leading to dusty, silent rooms. At the rear of the balcony a hallway, with three steps leading up to it, led into a rear wing of the house.

"Must be bedrooms there," Mel said. "But these are much nicer, probably."

He went to the door that opened onto a square entry to separate bedrooms and looked in, then backed out and went around the balcony to bedrooms there. Emily went into the bedrooms where the lawyer had said the body was found.

Bedding was still on beds in both rooms. But Emily was drawn to the bedroom on the right. There was a residue on the sheet, a trace of a body having lain there while dust settled slowly over and around it. In that old,

384

high bed the dust had been disturbed just enough to indicate that here Gertrude Madison had died and been
left to mummify over the next forty-odd years.

Emily stood looking about without moving beyond the
threshold. She saw massive, dark furniture, so much like
the furniture in the other room, with the tall headboard
of the bed reaching toward the high ceiling. Webs covered the bedside lamp, reaching down and enclosing a
Bible.

Footprints of varying sizes, as pronounced as if they
had been cast in mud, made paths to and around the
bed. And tracing about the room, beyond the footprints,
those strange little trails.

Emily began looking more closely at the trails. They
were in the other bedroom, too, and out on the balcony.
And when she went around to the other side of the balcony where Mel was still looking at the two bedrooms,
she saw the trails even more clearly where the footprints
were fewer.

"How about this room, Em?" Mel called. "There's good
light, and Adam could have the room right beside it.
Prissy could sleep in a crib in our room for the time
being, and then—"

"No!" Emily said.

He came to the threshold, but she didn't look at him.
The little trails in the dust went on around the balcony
and toward the back hallway, and Emily followed. Over
her shoulder she tried to explain her feelings to Mel.

"It's too dangerous here at the front," she said. "What
if Prissy fell? Even Adam."

"Fell? I don't think they'd go close to the banister."

"Oh, Mel. Look, there are bedrooms back there."

She climbed the three steps into the rear hall. The
trails led through each door, as if something had explored
every room recently. The bedrooms in this section were
smaller, but every one Emily looked into was furnished

with a bed and dresser and sometimes a chest of drawers, a bedside table with lamp, a chair.

They stood together awhile, speculating on the abandonment of the entire house.

"And did you see those suitcases on the balcony?" Mel asked. "They were packed. One had a man's clothes, and one a little girl's. They were stacked against the wall."

"Mel," Emily said. "I don't want to live here."

Mel said nothing. They stood shoulder to shoulder looking into the room where old paper had been ripped from the walls, leaving it blackened now as if it had been burned. A few strips of newer paper still held its colors of blue and rose, but the background was yellowed. It had been a little girl's room, Emily thought suddenly. Perhaps the little girl whose clothes were packed in the suitcase. Emily didn't like it here. She didn't like the feelings of old tragedies, and perhaps, tragedies yet unlived.

"Let's leave, Mel. Let's sell it. I don't want to stay."

Behind her Mel sighed. "We have to, Emily. At least for awhile."

She said nothing. He was right, of course. They didn't have the money to rent a motel or a house. They needed what they had to live. They had driven over two thousand miles to get here. For the first time in their lives, they owned a house. They had no choice, at least for this summer, but to live in it.

"Well," Emily said, trying to make her voice more cheerful, turning to a room across the hall. "We'll take that bedroom, and Adam can have the one right next to it. As you said, Prissy's crib will be in our room.

"I need to go down and see the kitchen," she said, "And see if the water is also turned on."

"It has a well. Has its own system."

They walked down the hall to a door at the rear that stood, like all others, half-open.

"The lawyer tell you that?"

"Yes. Its own well and water system, its own septic tank, everything we need."

An enclosed stairway, almost as dark as a cave in a mountainside, dropped steeply. Near it, but rising toward more light, was a stairway to a third floor. Emily was glad to see the service stairs down. But she shut the door on the third floor stairway. At least, she told Mel, they wouldn't have to use the dangerous front stairs.

She felt on the wall for a light switch, and was surprised when it worked with a feeble, yellow illumination from above where a naked bulb dangled from a chain.

The peculiar, narrow trails wavered down the stairs, close to the wall. There were no footprints in the webby, dusty stairwell.

"Mel," she said, pointing. "What do you think made those odd little streaks in the dust? I've noticed they're everywhere on the floors."

"I don't know. The police, probably."

"How? With what?" she demanded. "Dragging a snuggy blanket for comfort?"

She followed him, down the stairs, into the big kitchen, which included a dining area with a round table that still held bowls, plates, and platters. Dust seemed even thicker here, spiders larger, their webs more intrusive.

Emily gingerly uncovered a bowl. It held dry, hard, brown things with a growth like old moss.

Adam lay listening. He felt as if he had been swallowed by a monster, and he was in its stomach. When he had gone to bed in this strange room he hadn't minded having a wall between him and his mom and dad and Prissy. But now, listening to the sounds in the hall, he wished the wall weren't there.

There was something moving in the hall. His heart pounded because he knew it wasn't his mother or his dad. It sounded more like Prissy, when she was smaller and crawled.

It passed his closed door, then came back and stopped. It was in the hall outside his door. He knew it was listening to him just as he was listening to it. He felt as if it could hear the hard beating of his heart. He wanted to scream out, but he was afraid of making a sound.

Go away. He eased farther down in bed and pulled the blanket to his chin and gripped it there. He listened. There was no sound now. It was quiet outside his door. But he could feel it there listening.

Mama didn't like this house. He hoped she could talk Dad into leaving. He had heard her saying they could sell, and buy a small house. One with three bedrooms, instead of this one with so many they'd never begin to use them all.

Something rattled suddenly, a soft, slow sound.

The doorknob.

It was coming in.

His breath stopped, and he felt smothered, the way he had when he fell off the swing.

When he could breathe again, he heard nothing. A mouse in the walls squeaked and rattled its paper bed, but in the hall there was no sound at all.

He wished he had a light in his room. He wanted to see the door better, so he could watch the doorknob. He stared toward it anyway, and thought he found it. A small, lighter spot in a wall of black.

The crawling in the hall started again. Sounded like Prissy had before she learned to walk.

Adam lay still, and his room slowly became visible. The dresser against the wall, and the door, and the knob. The knob was white. Like a large egg.

The egg began to waver as he stared at it. His eyes grew heavy, and he slept as daylight outlined the window.

Chapter 8

Kirsten tried to follow her mother's advice and turn her attention to other things. She hadn't found a friend yet, as Lisa had, but she didn't miss having a best friend. She helped her mom with the decorating of the house, hanging pictures, shopping for extras.

At night she looked out her window, and wished it weren't on the southwest side of the house facing the woods that held the old mansion. She let her new, rose, pleated blind down and felt more secure.

One night she saw a light through the trees, like a ghostlight floating over a swamp. She stared and stared, thinking at first it was a reflection, or the moon sinking behind the trees. Yet in her heart she knew. Someone had moved into the old mansion.

She took her binoculars and went out onto the deck and even without using them saw that the light was in the window where it had seemed a face was permanently implanted on the lower pane of the glass.

She put the binoculars to her eyes. The lace had been torn down from the window, and the pane glimmered as if it had been washed. As she watched, a figure moved past the window. A man? Then another figure came in sight, smaller, more feminine. They were hardly more than shadows, come to life in a room that had been dark for a long, long time.

Kirsten realized she was spying on real people, and she jerked the glasses down.

389

The next day, as soon as she had made her bed and cleaned up her room, she went out on a pretext of merely going for a bicycle ride. If she had told her mother she wanted to ride over and see who had moved into the mansion, Jane would have told her to mind her own business.

She took the long way around, staying on streets where she could ride the bike. She went along the curving street to the entrance to Shadow Oaks, and out onto the road past the lot where the convenience store was in the process of being built.

At the driveway up to the mansion she stopped. A car, barely visible from the road, was parked near the house. It looked like an old car. She rode closer on her bike. The rope with the No Trespassing sign lay like a coiled snake on the edge of the old, uneven bricks of the driveway.

She stopped. A baby cried out, muffled by walls and trees, and an older child's voice raised for a moment. Then the voices hushed, and Kirsten was left with the sounds of hammering at the convenience store, and the birdsong in the trees.

Finding the trail too uneven and rough for slow bike riding, she left her bike at the side of the driveway. Walking, she approached the house.

Kirsten felt like the trespasser that had been warned to stay away, but she had to know who they were and how long they were going to stay. She wanted to tell them they couldn't stay here. The house was *haunted*.

Yes, haunted. She hadn't really known before what was wrong with it, she had only felt in her soul the danger that lived there. But now she felt sure it was haunted.

A little boy, a couple of years older than Lisa, came running into view suddenly. He stopped at the sight of her and stared a second before his face lit up.

"Hi!" he said.

"Hi," Kirsten answered.

Footsteps on dead leaves announced the arrival a moment later of a tall man with a neatly trimmed beard. His dark eyes found Kirsten and stared a moment, just as the little boy's had.

"Hello there," he said.

Kirsten forced a smile. "I didn't mean to trespass." Intrude, she'd been going to say, and trespass, and the words had gotten mixed up on her tongue.

"Oh you're fine," the man said, going to the car and beginning to take down some of the stuff tied on the luggage rack. "What's your name?"

"Kirsten. I live in Shadow Oaks. Just over through the trees there."

"Well, Kirsten, I'm glad to see we've got neighbors."

"You're going to be living here then," Kirsten said. She looked at the eager face of the little boy, and almost asked, aren't you afraid?

"My name's Adam," he said. "I'm nine."

The man said, "He just had his birthday."

A pretty, dark-haired woman came into view from the back of the house. She was carrying a curly haired toddler dressed in denim coveralls. When she saw Kirsten she looked surprised, too, as her husband and son had, but she didn't smile. The baby struggled in her arms, and she stooped to put her down. The baby could walk, but only a few feet before she fell. Instead of crying, she pushed herself up and toddled on.

The woman said to Kirsten, "What a mess. Forty years of dust in that house. I hope you babysit."

Kirsten said, "I'm eleven." The information had slipped out, while in her mind a picture of herself alone with the baby in the dark old haunted house flashed.

"Oh," the woman laughed softly. "Well, maybe in a couple of years."

Kirsten understood then the woman had been joking, and she smiled.

Adam said, "Have you ever been in our house?"

"Well I was the one . . . my sister and I . ." She couldn't say it.

The eagerness on his face increased, "Come on, I'll show you!"

Kirsten backed away. "I can't. I have to go."

Disappointment darkened his face. He blinked and glanced away, and Kirsten felt pulled toward him in her heart, the way she did toward Lisa when Lisa was sad.

"Well," she said.

"Would you?"

The mother and father were talking together as they unloaded the car, but the father said over his shoulder, "We'll be going to the store, Adam, as soon as we get this stuff in the house."

Kirsten grabbed the excuse. "Maybe the next time, okay? I ought to go now."

Adam followed her as she backed farther away.

"Will you come back?"

"Sure." Kirsten waved. "And you come over, okay? I have a little sister, Lisa. She's seven. There are other kids over in my area too. It's just through the trees. The house at the end of the cul-de-sac is mine."

She turned and ran, dodging brush and tree limbs.

Adam followed her halfway down the driveway. She was half-hidden behind the trees but he could see she had a bicycle. He waved at her as she rode away, but she didn't see him.

He turned back toward the house. He didn't like the house very well. The first night he slept in his new room he'd been scared. But last night he had slept without waking, without even a scary dream. It had helped to tell his dad and mom yesterday, "Something crawled in the hall outside my room last night. It woke me up." His dad pulled him over against his knees and hugged and kissed him and said in a deep voice, "That was me. At night I turn into a big snake and crawl all along the halls and into every room that's open! Make sure you keep your door closed at night!"

"Oh Mel," Mom said exasperatedly. "You'll give him nightmares for sure."

But it hadn't given him nightmares at all. It had helped him sleep. He knew his daddy didn't turn into a big snake. Just thinking about it made him laugh.

"Time to eat," Mom said. "Then your daddy's going to town."

Adam ran ahead of her, careful as he picked his way across the old boards of the back porch and went into the kitchen door.

"Can I go, Daddy? Please? *Please?*"

His dad was already in the kitchen, making sandwiches at the table. A loaf of whole wheat bread had slices spilling out. A jar of mayonnaise had been opened, and lunch meat, cheese, and lettuce lay on one of the old platters Mama had gotten down from a cabinet.

"Here," Mel said and slapped a crooked sandwich in front of Adam. "Eat."

"Can I go with you?" Adam begged. It was so important that it felt like a big hand had reached in and was twisting his stomach. He wanted to get away from watching Prissy all the time, and he wanted to be with his dad. "Please?"

"Not today. I don't know how long I'll be gone."

"Daddy, I won't mind."

"No, your mother needs you."

Mama sat down at the table, Prissy on her lap. She said, "He's going to see about selling the place, Adam."

Adam saw the look that passed between his dad and

393

mom. The look said that dad was reluctant. He didn't want to sell. But he'd do it for Mom.

"That way," Mama said carefully, her eyes on Daddy, "We could take the money and buy a new house. Maybe one of those being built out on the lake. Or we could go back home."

Dad said, surprising Adam, "Our roots are here. My grandparents lived here. Aunt Jenny's parents. And yours are back here somewhere, Emily."

"Sure. Three generations ago. Oklahoma, actually, and Missouri. Your other grandparents didn't come from here."

"Well, no, but their grandparents came from Ohio. Everyone out west had roots farther east."

"I don't have anything against the country. I just don't want to live in this house, Mel. Good Lord, look at the work that would have to be done to get it in shape. And you don't even have a job yet."

Adam suddenly lost what little appetite he'd developed. Talking about jobs again. He didn't like hearing about his dad being out of work.

Adam looked at his dad, and saw that he wasn't as happy as when he first found out what he had inherited. "Eighty acres," he had told Mom. "Eighty acres, with a big house. Furnished." Both of them had looked happy and laughed a lot on their trip cross country. They hadn't known Aunt Jenny, so it wasn't like a real family member, Mom told Adam when he asked about her.

Then, when Mom saw the house that look of happiness changed. Adam thought it was all the work. Dust was everywhere except where tracks had been made by the people walking around.

She had worked the whole first day cleaning up the funny old bathroom, and two of the bedrooms between the bathroom and the back stairs, so they'd have places to sleep that weren't filled with spider webs and dust.

Mel got up from the table, leaving a half-eaten sandwich, and Adam began to feel sick. Every time Mom mentioned that Dad didn't have a job, he left them. Not for long, but he left. He'd walk out of the room and be gone for awhile.

This time in the silence left behind him there came the sound of the car starting. Adam ran toward the door, frantic to catch him before he drove away.

"Adam!" Emily called. "You come right back here!"

Adam stopped on the porch.

"I need you to watch Prissy, Adam."

Adam returned to the kitchen. Prissy had cookie crumbs on her face, mixed with the mayonnaise. But Mom didn't seem to notice when she put her down. Prissy went running toward the door to the hall, and Adam took after her with a damp rag in his hand. He caught her at the bottom of the back stairs, where the door had been left open. Tracks in the dust on the stairway reminded Adam of the paths of animals in the woods.

Prissy squealed when he caught her, as always. She wanted to climb the stairs. He dragged her back, and she wiggled in his arms and slipped away.

"Prissy!"

"Climb!" she said clearly, pointing to the stairs, "Up!" And then she did something that always melted Adam's resolve and made him glad he had Prissy for his baby sister. She reached up and patted him lovingly and said, "Pease, D'am."

He smiled. "Okay." Then he yelled back toward the kitchen, "Mom, can I take Prissy upstairs?"

"If you'll be very careful."

Prissy not only allowed Adam to take her hand, she reached for both of his and held onto them. He wriggled one hand out of her grasp so he could hold onto her wrist, too.

"Okay," he said. "We climb. Stairs. Up. We climb up the stairs."

"We climb stairs," she repeated. "Up."

Her face glowed, her shining eyes looking upward as she trusted him to help her stretch her short little legs from step to step.

Chapter 9

"Jenny's last words were that the old mansion is dangerous," Mary said to Mark as she drove the country road out past Shadow Oaks. The convenience store was almost finished now. Pavers were working on the entrance and parking area. Mark seemed more interested in the work being done there than in what Mary was saying.

"Another convenience store," he said. "They're popping up all around."

"You haven't heard a word I said."

Mark looked down the road ahead as the convenience store slipped past. The car moved slowly as Mary watched for the driveway.

"I heard," he said. "And I've thought about it. We didn't know Jenny. Nobody seemed to. But here's what I came up with. She was there when her sister-in-law died. And it scared her and she left and never said anything. In the week or so before, her husband and daughter had died. Don't you think Jenny's mind just couldn't take all that? And she subscribed something supernatural to explain it, and lived all these years afraid of the old mansion."

"Why were there so many deaths so suddenly?"

"Did you check the death certificates?"

"I did. On Jenny's husband and child. The child was listed as dying of acute pulmonary edema, and the husband, Ted, of heart failure."

"Well."

"But Mark, those aren't causes of death, they're only conditions found afterwards. His heart stopped, they didn't really know why. A lung condition such as little Annie had could have been caused from being smothered."

He threw her a sharp look. "You mean you think she was murdered?"

"By someone in the family? No. Otherwise, why would Jenny have seemed to be warning us about the house? Her very words were that the old mansion is dangerous."

They came to the driveway and Mary turned the car sharply right. Bricks loose over the culvert rattled beneath the tires.

"It's old," he said, "Maybe she felt it would be rotting down by now."

Mary sighed. "Oh I suppose you're right. But now a young family has moved in, and I'd like to see if they're okay. Find out if they intend to keep it or what."

"Check up on them. Snoop a little."

Mary grinned. "I guess."

But she just couldn't dismiss it as Mark had. All these nights since she had bent over Jenny and heard her last words, the look on her face had haunted Mary's dreams. She remembered more and more the desperation in Jenny's eyes, the need to deliver a message of importance. Yet, Mary had asked herself a hundred times, if it had been really important, wouldn't Jenny have done something about it while her health was still good?

Maybe Mark was right, and the deaths of the three people who were closest to her had left her mentally ill.

There was no car parked near the house. The house looked as deserted as the last time Mary had seen it. She stopped the car and turned off the engine, and then sat a moment before getting out.

"Do you suppose they left?"

At that moment a face peered through the window not

far from where the car was parked. Mary saw vague outlines of a youthful person, with dark hair pulled back.
She got out of the car.

"Coming?" she asked Mark.

"Naw. I'll just sit and look at the scenery."

"I won't be long."

By the time Mary reached the back walk a young
woman was coming down the steps. She was on the small
side, very pretty, and didn't look a day over twenty-two.
She was probably closer to thirty, because her information was that there was a family of four, including a girl
less than two years old, and a boy nine. Mary had noticed that the older she got, the younger people looked.
Her grandmother had told her, "Just wait until you're
eighty, Mary, even the sixty year olds will look like kids."

The young woman looked with dark eyes at the police
car, then gave Mary a quick up and down. Mary understood. She was wearing a cool skirt and blouse, no uniform.

"Is something wrong?"

"No," Mary said, smiling, holding out her hand. "We
were just in the neighborhood and thought we'd stop in
and see if you need anything. I'm Mary Swift of the
Wilfred police, and that's my partner, Sergeant Mark
Henley."

His voice at her shoulder startled Mary. She hadn't
heard him approach. His long arm went past her to
shake hands with the young woman. Youth and beauty
had drawn him out of the car.

"Welcome to Wilfred," he said.

"Thank you. We're the Curtises. Mel and Emily. I'm
Emily." Emily smiled, but it was shy and hesitant. "My
husband isn't here at the moment. There were a lot of
things he had to do in town. The kids are in the house
playing."

She didn't invite them in.

Mary looked up at the house. The slope of the roof above the long back porch and the limbs of overhanging trees shielded the upper floors from view. The house didn't look so imposing from this perspective. Now that she was here, she didn't know what to say. She couldn't tell her what Jenny had said. There was no real purpose. She had actually considered coming to Jenny's nephew and giving him Jenny's message. But when she tried to put it into words for anyone but Mark, it just didn't work.

Emily didn't invite them in. She still had a wary, concerned look in her eyes.

Mary explained, "We've been driving by regularly to see that the house wasn't vandalized, since there was some publicity that might have brought it into the public awareness. Your attorney let us know when you arrived. So this is just routine, to see if all is well."

Emily nodded. "Just fine. Thank you." She looked down at her jeans and brushed her hands against her thighs. "Just a lot of dust, that's all. I'm a mess. I've been cleaning."

"Are your children enjoying the house?"

"Oh yes. Children manage to enjoy themselves, no matter where they are."

"They've probably found a lot of things to entertain themselves with."

"Yes."

Mary took a step backwards. She felt like an intruder. "We interrupted your work," she apologized. She heard Mark's footsteps as he returned to the car and saw Emily smile and nod, probably in response to his motion of goodbye.

"Thanks for keeping an eye on the place," Emily said.

"Call us if you need anything."

"Thank you."

Mary retreated to the car, and turned it around, following the trail made through the brush by the turning of many other automobiles in the past month. When she looked back at the house Emily was gone, and the old mansion was deserted again, as if Emily had been an apparition. Mary felt even worse than she had before she met Emily. A deep sadness sucked her into its gloomy marsh. She had a feeling of doom that she'd never had before.

Emily watched the police car from the privacy of the screened porch until it disappeared from view. There was something about police driving into the driveway that scared rather than comforted her. When she was a child, a police car had driven in and brought the news that her father had been killed in a car accident. And ever since, the sight of a police car made her want to cringe.

She sighed deeply and went back into the house, poured herself a cup of coffee, and sat down. Just for a moment, she told herself. She wondered how Mel was getting along. She wished they would get a real change of luck, a real break, for once.

It seemed to Emily that one set of problems had been replaced by a million. Back home it had been money. After Mel lost his job as a lumberjack, because of cutbacks in the timber industry, they had to depend on her small wages. Waitresses in small towns didn't make much. Tips were hardly anything, and minimum wage hardly paid the utilities and the groceries. She worried, too, about something happening to her and Mel, and the children having no one. Mel was the only living child in his family, his parents were dead. On her side it was almost as desperate, with no one to turn to. Her mother and stepfather had a family and problems of their own.

She had never expected to be rewarded by someone's death. She had never even heard of Aunt Jenny Madison, and it was a while before Mel could remember her. But then he recalled that his mother and his aunt Jenny used to exchange Christmas cards until his mother died when he was fifteen.

At first the inheritance had seemed almost like winning a lottery. They had sold their whole houseful of furniture for enough to make the trip, and had money left to buy groceries for awhile.

Then, she had seen the house.

It was enormous. There were rooms in it she hadn't even looked at yet. It was heavily furnished and she suspected the furniture was worth quite a lot of money. A lot of it was ruined by the dampness, but much of it was still in good condition, too.

They couldn't afford to hire someone to clean, so the job fell to her, mostly. Mel had a way of avoiding things like brooms and dustmops.

She sat at the kitchen table looking at the long kitchen. She had scrubbed part of the old, dark cabinets, and had torn down rotting curtains. But the faucet dripped constantly, and Mel said he'd get a washer and fix it. But she didn't have a lot of faith in Mel. He was a logman, a timberman. He was used to working with trees and logs and saws, not faucets.

He might try, though. He wanted to keep the place, house and all. To him it was a mansion filled with valuable antiques. He didn't see the rot, or smell the decay. He didn't see the "woman's work" that would have to be done to make it liveable, or the carpenter's work that must be done to make it safe.

Emily got up. She was tired. But she was always tired. Another cup of coffee would only make her heart pound in a caffeine fit. It wouldn't give her energy.

She opened a cabinet she hadn't looked in before, and saw it was stacked with plates, saucers, cups, bowls, glasses.

"Good Lord," she said aloud, "Why on earth would one family want so many dishes?"

She reached for a stack and placed it carefully on the counter. Each plate was encrusted with the sticky dust that had seeped into every inch of the house.

She ran hot water into the sink. At least she had hot water, she thought. She began to wash the dishes.

A stray and unexpected feeling of happiness coursed through her like a thrill. She hadn't thought of it before, but this was the first time in her life she had security. The house might be too big, and hard to clean, but at least they had a roof. And it was a roof that they *owned*.

"Up," Prissy demanded, after they had reached the top of the stairs. She pointed toward the ceiling.

"What are you, nuts? This is as far as it goes."

"What are you, nuts?" she repeated, and broke free and ran down the hall.

He dashed after her and caught her just as she started to enter a bedroom. He pulled her back, but he allowed himself a peek in.

There were two tall stepladders in the room, and some old wallpaper hanging in strips over the top of one. With his hand gingerly against the door, he pushed the door wider open. Prissy crossed the threshold, and he followed.

Someone had been papering the room with new wallpaper, a long time ago, and then quit. The part of the wall that hadn't been papered looked dark and moldy where old paper had been partly stripped off.

He got Prissy's hand just before she reached into a bucket of something that had hardened and cracked. There was a brush in the bucket, held by the hardened stuff. Prissy wanted the brush.

"No, let's go look for something else, Prissy, okay?"

"No. No. No."

"Come on, stop saying no. Okay, Prissy?"

"No. Okay."

He let her walk, keeping his steps short and slow so she could keep up. She was getting too heavy to carry. After her first birthday, six months ago, she suddenly got big, it seemed to him.

He led her out into the hall. The room two doors down was the room his mom had fixed for him. It had eastern light, so he would know when the sun rose. Right next door to his room was his mom's and dad's, and in one corner they had put Prissy's crib, which they had brought all the way from home on top of the car.

"Wanta go to beddy bye?" he asked hopefully when they passed the other bedroom. If he could get rid of her, he could . . . but what could he do? He didn't dare go off and leave her alone up here in the crib. "Never mind," he said.

She led him past the door and past other doors. They came to the three steps that led down to the balcony.

"Up," she said, pointing down.

"Sure, sure, sure."

He let her go down by herself. She turned around and crawled down backwards, slowly. It would take her awhile, and meantime he could look around. He had only glimpsed this big front part of the house. His mom wouldn't let him go past the steps because it might be dangerous. He wasn't really going down to the balcony, he just wanted to look.

It was neat, he decided, as Prissy climbed the three steps again and turned around and climbed down, then back up again, then down, saying, "Up. Up."

Adam slipped farther toward exploring the front of the house, that forbidden place where the dead body had been found. Something cold and icy gripped the back of his neck and his stomach, at the same time, but he crept on, doggedly, filled with curiosity.

A board made a mouselike sound beneath his feet. He stopped. Adam thought for a moment he might fall through the floor, but the squeak ended and he stepped cautiously on.

The windows at the front didn't let in much light, and the spooky feeling of this forbidden front gathered around him like black ghosts. Still, he slipped on, one step, then another. Ahead he saw a closed door, and he knew. That was the room where the body had been.

He stood listening to the house, aware of little sounds. It was like the house talked to itself, whispering, moaning.

Something pushed against him, as dark as night, filled with all the scary things he had ever imagined, and he turned and ran back toward the three steps that separated the front from the back.

He stopped, forgetting the invisible dangers that had turned him back. Prissy!

Prissy was not on the steps, climbing up and down, where he had left her.

"Prissy," he hissed, "Where are you? Prissy!"

For a terrible moment he imagined her swallowed by the house. The whispering he had heard, the moaning, had been the house eating Prissy. Tears choked him. Fear froze him so that his legs felt like sticks.

He ran, clumping, down the hall, calling in a hoarse whisper, "Prissy?"

He whirled back and stared.

Prissy sat in the middle of a room that looked like a skeleton of a bedroom, with a bed that had been stripped and a dresser with nothing on it.

She held something, and when she saw him she lifted it.

At first he thought it was real. It wore a bonnet and a long, white dress, and it was almost too big for Prissy to lift.

"Dolly," she said. "Baby dolly."

Chapter 10

"Oh Lord," Adam said with such vast relief he felt emptied of everything inside his skin.

He sank to the floor, and then almost instantly rose again and pulled the doll from Prissy's hands.

She began screaming. He held the doll just beyond her reach and looked at it. His lips curled. "Yuck!"

Its dress and bonnet were a mess, old and yellowed and dirty. Dust fogged as he held it away and dropped it on the bed. It stared at him, its eyes stuck open. It had funny, bulging apple-like cheeks, and its eyes had puffy lids. There were no eyebrows and its lashes were thin and ragged. Paint had come off the ringlets on its forehead, and were part white and part golden. Paint had flaked off the left side of the chin, and the white, pebbly stuff underneath looked like a disease. The mouth pooched out, as if it were trying to blow bubbles, and its hideous, long teeth were stained with dust.

"Stop yelling, Prissy! You can't have the ugly old doll. Why did you run off like that?"

He tried to pick her up, but she was getting so big he couldn't carry her if she didn't cooperate. She squirmed and twisted in his arms and reached out for the doll, her scream dropping to a whine.

"Baby dolly, baby dolly."

"No! Come on, Mom'll be mad."

He covered Prissy's mouth briefly with his hand, and in the moment of silence listened for a voice yelling at him. But Mama hadn't heard.

"Listen, Prissy, let's go down the stairs, okay?"

She made sounds of complaint, still reaching out for the doll. "Baby dolly. Mine."

"No, not yours. We have to ask Mom first."

Prissy screamed when he tried to pull her away. One arm reached back toward the doll, and the other shoved at him, her elbow beneath his chin, right where it choked.

"Stop it, Pris—" He gagged and wrapped his arms so tightly around her she couldn't move.

He carried her, screaming and crying, toward the back stairs.

A voice floated up from below. "Adam! What's wrong?"

He shouted an answer. "It's okay, Mom." Then, "See, Prissy? Now you're going to catch it!"

Only it wouldn't be Prissy catching it, it would be him. He set her down at the top of the stairs. "Up, down, see, Prissy? Stairs."

Their mother appeared suddenly in the doorway at the foot of the stairs. She looked up. Prissy was still trying to get away and go back after the doll, her cries mingling with tears that ran down her cheeks and a blubbering, "Dolly, dolly. Baby dolly."

Emily started up the stairs. "What on earth does she want, Adam?"

Mom's blouse was streaked with dirt, and in her right hand she carried a blackened dishrag. She wasn't pleased at being interrupted from a job she didn't want. Adam dodged away from her hand when she

408

reached for Prissy, even though she had never hit him in all his life that he could remember. If she ever felt like hitting him, it was probably now.

"Baby dolly," Prissy was whining over and over, "Baby dolly."

"An old doll, Mom. A dusty old doll."

"What about it?"

She picked up Prissy, and Adam felt the load lift from him.

"She found it in one of the bedrooms and she wants it."

Prissy stopped screaming and fighting and leaned into their mother's arms sobbing, "Dolly. Dolly. Baby dolly."

"Well why didn't you let her have it, Adam?" She went walking down the hall toward the bedrooms, and Adam hurried after her.

"I told her we had to ask you first, Mama, that was all. It's somebody else's doll." He didn't want Mom to give the doll to Prissy. He couldn't think of a word that described his feelings about it. It was *creepy*.

"Everything in this house is ours, now, Adam. Where is the doll?"

Adam sighed. "But it's so dirty, Mom!"

"So what else is new? Everything in the house is dirty. So we'll clean it up, just like we did your bedroom. Where is it?"

"In there."

He followed his mother and baby sister into the bedroom where Prissy had found the doll, where he had dropped it on the bed.

His mother stopped, a few steps into the room. "Where?" Her voice sounded tired and irritated.

Adam stared at the bed. It was the skeleton bedroom with a bare mattress, no quilt or pillows or spread.

409

But the doll was not where he had left it.

He rushed forward and got down on his knees in the dust and looked under the bed. Dark webs wove through the bottom of rusty springs.

"Adam," Emily sighed. "Look how dirty you're getting. Get up."

"But I left it here." He got to his feet and brushed his knees.

"Under the bed?"

"On the bed. But it might have fallen."

He heard his mother expel another long breath. She turned away and went back into the hall. Prissy had grown quiet.

"You must have been in a different room. There are so many of them, all so much alike. Look for it, will you?"

He stood watching as his mother carried Prissy away. He listened to her footsteps on the stairs going down, and heard the creak of the wood.

He didn't want to find the doll. Let Prissy play with her own doll. She had a plastic one whose toes she had chewed until they all had little holes at the ends where the nails were supposed to be. He didn't want to find the fat-faced dusty doll with the bonnet and the long dress. But he went down the hall, peeking into each bedroom, because his mother had told him to.

Then, having taken a brief look into all the rooms, he drew a long breath as his mother had done, and went running toward the back stairs.

When he reached the kitchen he found his mother sitting in the rocking chair by the windows, Prissy sleeping in her lap.

"Shhh," she said, and nodded when he asked if he could go outside.

He ran out, careful to close the door quietly. For an

hour or so, he didn't have to watch Prissy. He could go play, climb trees, look into old barns and sheds. He could do what he wanted to for a change. He might even see Kirsten again.

Chapter 11

What angels babies are, Emily thought, feeling that marvelous sense of contentment that motherhood brought her. What lovely creatures God has wrought in a baby. In many ways she had enjoyed Prissy more than she had Adam. With him she'd been a little scared. They were so young when Adam was born, and she'd had to hurry and take care of him and then run out to her job. She had taken off only three weeks, and it hadn't been enough time for her to rest.

When Prissy was born times were easier. Not only had she reached the age of twenty-seven and far more maturity than she'd had at nineteen, but Mel had been working steadily for several years. He wanted her to quit work and stay at home with the kids, and she was all too willing.

It was cookie baking time in her life, and she loved it.

But Mel's job had ended, and nothing came to replace it.

The rocking chair creaked faintly as she rocked. She made herself look at the old, long kitchen. It wasn't so bad now that she'd scrubbed and scrubbed. There was still a lot of cleaning to do, but it wasn't such a bad kitchen. At the moment she had a languid feeling of content. A feeling even of optimism. Maybe Mel would find a buyer today.

They had reached a compromise, she and Mel. She had agreed to keep the land, if he would sell the house.

In bed this morning at daybreak they held hands and made plans. Mel could keep his land, and she could have a new house. It was going to work out great after all.

She got up and laid Prissy in the cradle they'd found in a room upstairs. She had ripped off the old ragged lace and washed the dust out of the white wicker, and it now looked pretty good.

She took her mop bucket and mop and went into the back hall and paused at the foot of the enclosed stairs, listening. Adam had gone out and the house seemed unholy quiet. The front was shut off, the wide double doors between the rear of the house and the front closed. Someday she'd have to tackle that job and clean it, but she was still working on the back.

Prissy would sleep for an hour, maybe two. Emily climbed the stairs and started mopping a bedroom. It was small, thank goodness, and had bare floors that once had been varnished. She rolled the one throw rug, which looked as if it might be very pretty once it was cleaned, and laid it on the floor of the hall. Working quickly, she got up most of the dust on the floor and uncovered wide, smooth boards like those of the rest of the floors, which Mel said were maple rather than oak.

Emily bent and looked under the head of the bed. There was a mouse hole, a little larger than her thumb, in the wide baseboard behind a bed leg. She took a handful of the cotton from the mattress and stuffed the hole full. They could live in the walls, but not in the bedroom. Later she'd bring up a piece of metal and nail it over the hole. God made many kinds of life, and they were all wonderful in their own way.

She closed the bedroom door and moved on to the next bedroom.

The room was much like the other, small, furnished very simply. She didn't feel like tackling it. She closed the door and went back into the hall. Later, she told herself.

413

She looked into the narrow stairway that rose to the third floor. She hadn't even thought about cleaning up there yet, and the thought of it now exhausted her. She hadn't even climbed the stairs. Mel had gone up and told her there were six rooms there, some of them used for storage, one a sitting room or music room. It held an old organ.

It was the organ that drew her to climb the stairs, wielding her mop ahead of her to wipe dust and webs from walls.

When she reached the top and stepped onto the wood floor she paused. Windows at the other end of the single, straight hall let in enough light she could see the dust that coated the hall floor. There were footprints through the dust, going into each room. Only two people had walked here, both with the large feet of a man. Mel had been one of them, and a policeman the other, probably. There was also in the dust those disturbing little paths, angling close to the walls on each side, and into each room, criss-crossing, wavering. It looked exactly as if something had been dragged. But there were no footprints, only the uneven trails, each about six inches wide.

Emily dampened her mop and went to work on the dusty floor, wiping up footprints and the puzzling trails. Then, ten feet down the hall, she stopped. Make Mel look at them, she told herself. Insist he look. She was beginning to feel uneasy. There was something in the house that crawled along the halls, into each room, through the years of dust.

She looked into the first room, and saw a bedroom, with an iron bedstead, springs but no mattress. There once had been a featherbed, and now there was nothing left but scattered feathers and rotted cloth. She closed the door.

The more she looked, the more hopeless it seemed.

How long would it take them to save enough money from the small monthly income to hire a cleaning crew? Who would buy the house if it weren't cleaned and repaired? Who would buy it anyway?

She found the room with the organ, and brushed just enough dust from a couple of keys to try them. Nothing. Dust and weather changes had long ago ruined it. But it was a nice old organ, even though the varnish had peeled and it looked as if it would fall apart if moved.

She heard a sound that brought her to a halt. She listened. Prissy? Or Adam, perhaps, coming back into the house? She wasn't even sure what she had heard. Maybe just the house. It was filled with doodads, as Mel called stuff like that. She loved doodads. She used to go to garage sales and flea markets, looking for something she could afford to buy. Now she had a houseful of doodads.

She looked into the cabinet and marveled at the variety of things. There were little glass animals and birds, music boxes with jeweled tops, a black-haired lady doll on the top shelf in dancing costume. She looked very old and fragile. There were fancy thimbles and pincushions and another tiny doll made entirely of lace and tatting. Like a child she wanted to touch, feel, examine.

The door of the cabinet was closed, and just as she was trying to figure out how the latch worked, she noticed the large doll.

It was leaning against the outside of the china cabinet, as if a child had carefully placed it there. The moment she picked it up she knew it was the baby dolly Prissy had been crying for.

"Hmmm," she murmured. How did it get up here? Adam, of course. Why would he do such a thing? She had told him to look for it, she remembered, to quiet Prissy. She had told him to give it to Prissy. He had hidden it instead. That didn't sound like Adam.

For having been left in this old house, it was remarkably dust free, except for the creases in its face, and the whole front of the dress, which looked as if it had been dragged through dirt. Adam was right, it was one messy doll. But it could be cleaned up.

Other than its ungainly head, it was soft and cuddly, the sort of doll Prissy would like. She must have truly wanted it, to yell so long and loud when Adam took it away from her.

She went downstairs, the mop and bucket in one hand, the doll in the other. After leaving her cleaning equipment in the laundry room, she went to see about Prissy.

The baby was beginning to stir. A thin line of perspiration had dampened her dark curls and held them to her forehead. At first glance her hair looked like the painted curls on the forehead of the doll, except Prissy's hair was darker.

The doll clothes were filthy. She removed the bonnet and found the back of the doll's head oddly flattened. The doll maker hadn't bothered with molding or painting hair anywhere except the forehead. Evidently he had not intended for the bonnet ever to be removed. But, like the long gown, it had to be washed. The yellowed material would never whiten, but at least the accumulation of dirt would be removed. Undressed the doll was like some ugly little skinned animal. It wore no undergarments.

Well, Prissy wouldn't care whether it had eyelashes or clothes.

Prissy sat up in the cradle and blinked her eyes several times.

"Hi, sweetheart. How's Mama beautiful baby?" Emily bent and held the naked doll down to Prissy. "See what Mama found for Prissy."

Prissy drew back against the side of the cradle, her face puckering. Emily thought she was going to cry, but she only sat with the odd scowl on her face staring at the doll.

416

"Oh, the clothes," Emily said. "See, here are the dolly's clothes. Mama's going to wash them."

Prissy leaned harder against the cradle, her eyes on the doll. Emily thought oh what the heck, and started dressing the doll again. She could sneak the clothes off tonight and wash them, after Prissy was in bed. A little more dust wouldn't kill her, after all the dust she'd been crawling around in these past few days.

"Now," she said, holding out the doll with its bonnet and its long gown. She watched as Prissy's face smoothed and a slow smile broke through.

Prissy reached up, pleased laughter bringing out her dimples.

"Baby dolly," she said. "Mine."

Chapter 12

"Let's make a path between your house and mine," Kirsten said to Adam. Even though he was two years younger than she, and half a head shorter, she liked him better than anyone else she had met since her move to Shadow Oaks. "Then, if you had to come for help, or anything, you could run straight through the trees."

"Okay," he said with enthusiasm. "There's a bunch of tools and things in one of our old sheds. Come and see."

They ran back toward his house to the door of a shed. Kirsten backed away from the dark interior. Shapes loomed, dark and rusty. The dirt floor looked littered with strange tools.

"We need a light," she said.

"I'll get something," Adam assured her, going in without hesitation. "I can see. I've been in here before."

Kirsten followed him gingerly and peered in as Adam extricated something. A metal item fell, clanking against another metal item.

"Maybe we ought to get ours," Kirsten suggested, but they only had a hoe and a riding mower. And she wasn't allowed to use the riding mower unless her dad was present.

"No, that's okay. Here's a thing you use to prune. I know because we had a neighbor back home who was always pruning his hedge."

He came forward from the gloomy shed and handed Kirsten the pruning shears. Then he sank back into the shadow as if he were part of it.

Kirsten drew a long breath and looked toward the house.

"Do you like living here, Adam?"

He came out of the shed with an old, rusty ax. "Sure," he said. "I guess so."

"You're not afraid?"

Adam began to hack at limbs and bushes and for a moment didn't answer.

"Sometimes at night I hear things," he said.

"What?"

"I don't know." He brightened suddenly, his face turned toward her. "Let's hurry up and make our path, okay? If we work real fast, couldn't we get through before I have to go home?"

"When do you have to go home?" She had seen him in the woods today, swinging on a tree limb, and had met him halfway. But she'd been thinking about a path since meeting him and his family. A path, to her, meant an escape for them, if they ever needed one.

"I don't know. I just can't stay out too long. Mama needs me to watch Prissy."

"Well, I have already marked a short cut through the trees. I went through and broke limbs, so I could find my way again. This is going to be your escape route."

"Sure, and yours, too."

He didn't understand what she meant. But that was okay.

She began pruning, snipping away thin twigs of trees that would slap a person in the face when he was running. He followed, hacking at the roots and vines. Sweat trickled down into Kirsten's eyes, and she lifted her wrist and wiped it away. She looked back at Adam and saw his hair was damp on his forehead, coiled like pin curls.

Kirsten pruned faster. Ahead was her own backyard. She could see the deck. And on the deck steps Lisa sat with one of her dolls. She was changing its clothes. Kirsten paused to wipe sweat from her eyes and saw Lisa look up and stare toward them.

Lisa ran down the steps and crossed the yard, the doll held carefully against her chest. She ducked under a tree limb that Kirsten planned to prune back, and came to stand directly in the proposed path.

"Adam," Kirsten said, drawing the project to a halt. "This is Lisa, my sister."

Adam looked up. For about ten heartbeats he and Lisa stared at each other, then Adam flushed, his tanned skin turning rosy across his cheeks. He pivoted, kicked at a root.

Lisa said, "Hi."

"Hi."

"Are you the boy who lives in the old mansion?"

"Yes."

"Gosh," Lisa breathed in awe, her blue eyes widening even more. "Aren't you *afraid?*"

"That's what Kirsten said." Adam seemed suddenly more at ease. He squared his shoulders and swung the ax at the trunk of a sapling. "Naw. I'm not afraid."

"I would be. I wouldn't go back in there for all the money in the world."

Kirsten said, "Nobody asked you to. It's his house."

Adam swung at the tree, slicing it through with the third hit. It fell, and he pushed it out of the way. He kicked leaves after it, clearing the path.

"I'm not afraid," he said. "I even go into the front of the house sometimes."

Kirsten explained, "Lisa found the . . . you know."

"Yeah, I figured that. They said two girls found it. The body."

"And it doesn't bother you?" Lisa asked. "That the body was there?"

Adam shrugged. "I don't live in the front of the house,

420

I live in the back."

"But—"

"Why don't you shut up, Lisa?" Kirsten demanded. "Go dress your doll, or something."

"What are you doing?" Lisa asked.

"We're making a path between our house and Adam's."

"I want to help."

Kirsten and Adam exchanged looks. Adam shrugged slightly, and Kirsten said, "Well, okay. You go start at the other end and come to meet us. But you'll have to put your doll away."

Lisa ran. Adam watched her go, and Kirsten thought she saw a shadow of doubt on his face. Now that Lisa wasn't here to watch, his macho image had drained away.

"Don't listen to her," Kirsten said. "She's weird." She felt guilty for having put her sister down. Lisa wasn't that bad. She'd had some nightmares since she found the body, and Kirsten understood. Still, it wasn't polite to talk about Adam's house the way she had.

"It's okay," Adam said.

"Anyway, now we've got a little path, and if we keep working on it we'll have a nice path, so nice you could find it in the dark. If you need to."

"Sure."

They worked toward Lisa, and then the three worked together. Lisa surprised Kirsten with her eagerness. Before long Lisa was talking to Adam as if she had known him all her life. She picked up the twigs and saplings he cut down, and threw them out of the path. Kirsten went ahead of them pruning away the twigs most likely to fly back and slap a face. They were coming closer and closer to the yard.

"Listen," Lisa said, her head tilted. "Somebody called." Her pretty, oval face was streaked with dirt and sweat, for the first time in her life. Kirsten almost laughed.

Adam flung down his ax and ran back down the

421

barely visible little path toward the old mansion. And thinly now, Kirsten heard the call. It was like a spirit, a ghost, its voice wavering. But it must have been Adam's mother. The call died away, and Adam disappeared through the trees. Even the sound of Adam running was gone, as if he had ceased to exist. Kirsten stared at the still green of the woods.

"I wouldn't go there for anything," Lisa said, and shuddered.

Kirsten turned. "Oh shut up."

"Where on earth have you girls been?" Jane asked. They both looked as if they had crawled through a jungle. Lisa had never looked so disreputable in her life, and Kirsten's face was red blotched and damp with sweat.

"Making a path," Lisa said.

"A path to where?"

"To Adam's."

Kirsten sank to the floor. "Adam is the little boy who lives in the old mansion, Mom."

"Oh. So you got together to make a path, eh?"

"Yes."

They explained, talking at the same time now and then, and Jane struggled to separate the two. Facts were that a young couple with a nine year old son and a baby girl had moved into the old mansion, and her two girls and Adam, the new boy, were making a path through the woods. The part about the family was not news. Kirsten had talked about them before, but Jane acted as if everything they said was not only new but very interesting.

"I see," Jane said, and finally, "Now go wash."

Kirsten got to her feet. "Mom, I was thinking. Couldn't you bake your fabulous vegetable lasagna and take it over to them? Wouldn't that be nice? They only moved here a few days ago, and they probably don't have much food. Adam says his mom is cleaning house all the time, and he has to watch Prissy."

Jane said, "Well, just wash your face and hands and help yourself. You know where my recipe file is."

"I'll help," Lisa offered.

They went to the utility room and Jane heard water splashing. Taking food to a newcomer to the neighborhood was a custom she had nearly forgotten.

"Are they actually living in the house?" Jane asked as the girls came back into the kitchen. She stooped to the cabinet drawer where her Pyrex baking dishes were kept, and extricated the largest one.

"Yes, they are," Kirsten said. She disappeared into the pantry and came back with pasta and several cans.

"And he's not even afraid," Lisa said. "I wouldn't go back in that house for a million dollars."

"I hope you didn't tell him that," Jane said, and began helping Kirsten. She got a pan and filled it half full of hot water, put in a dash of salt and put it on the stove. Kirsten turned on the heat and tore open a package of pasta.

"She told him," Kirsten said with disgust. "But she likes him. A lot!"

"I do not!"

Kirsten giggled. "Sure, sure. I could tell. And he likes her, too."

Lisa flushed. "That's not true!"

"There's nothing wrong with liking someone, Lisa," Jane said.

"But she meant . . ."

Kirsten snickered again. "In love, Lisa's in love. She even threw down her doll just to help Adam work on the path."

"Don't tease," Jane said, with a sideways glance at Lisa's red-cheeked little face. She wore a pout on her

423

mouth that to her mother did not detract from her natural beauty. "Lisa, you can start opening the cans, please. We'll all bake the lasagna and we'll all take it to Adam's mother. I hope she won't mind us busting in all gung-ho, uninvited."

Kirsten said, trying to keep a grin off her face, "Lisa won't be going with us."

"I will, too!" Then, "Why not?"

"You said you wouldn't go back in that house for a million dollars."

Lisa looked down in silence. After a thoughtful moment she said, "Well, I can go along, anyway."

Jane smiled. Ah, what changes are wrought within me by the force of my love.

Chapter 13

Jane started the drive to the old mansion, the hot lasagna casserole on a cookie sheet in the back, covered by waxed paper and a heavy dish towel. Lisa and Kirsten were arguing, as always, about whose turn it was to sit up front. Kirsten had won the first round, but the argument continued.

"You rode up front just this morning, when you went with Mama to the grocery store, Lisa."

"You weren't even along! That doesn't count."

Jane had enough. "Cool it!"

A blessed calm fell. All she could hear was the hum of the engine and the sound of the tires on the pavement as she slowly followed the curving street out to the gates to Shadow Oaks. She stopped, looked both ways and pulled right. Kirsten sat forward to watch for the driveway.

"It's hard to see, Mom. Slow down."

They passed the convenience store. Overnight, it seemed, the building was up and a roof was on. A dozen or so men worked, as industrious as ants.

Lisa yelled, "There it is."

Jane saw the edge of old bricks and crushed vegetation joining the blacktop of the road. Tracks made a curving trail off through the tall trees. Set far back, visible only if one looked for it, stood the house.

Jane cautiously drove the narrow trail, hearing the scratch of weeds and twigs on the side of her five year old station wagon. It had eighty thousand miles on it, but it was still a good car, and had survived city parking lots with only a couple of dings. And here she was scratching it up. Kirsten and Lisa had both wanted to walk the new path they'd cleared, but Jane hadn't thought much of the idea of carrying a hot Pyrex baking dish down a brushy trail. Lisa was repeating for the fortieth time that she wasn't going into the house, she was only going as far as the porch. The whole project was beginning to look like a bomb. Also, it was almost time to start dinner for her own family. Fortunately, while they were cooking lasagna, they had made two. Also, she felt a little nervous about going to a stranger's door without having called first. But if they had a telephone, she hadn't been able to get information to divulge the number. She doubted they had a phone.

Kirsten carried the casserole. They went to the back of the house and up creaky steps to a long screened porch.

"They don't live in the front," Kirsten hissed back at Jane in a low voice.

"I'm not going in," Lisa said from about six feet behind Jane.

They crossed the porch. Jane knocked on the door.

They waited. It was darker here than Jane had expected. The trees shaded every inch. Cool air wafted from around the house, up from the hole in the porch, from the forest itself.

The door opened and a tall young woman with stunning good looks peered out at her. She had dark, glossy, wavy hair, hanging shoulder length. She had pushed it back with barrettes, but it had fallen again on one side.

Her children were beautiful, too, Jane saw. On one side a little girl, perhaps eighteen months old, grabbed a handful of her mother's jeans. And on the other a boy, in size halfway between Lisa and Kirsten, looked out, then with a big smile on his face pushed past his mother and Jane.

426

"I hope we're not disturbing you," Jane said, feeling dowdier than she'd ever felt in her life. She'd been getting lazy about the extra fifteen pounds that had crept on lately, and now was acutely conscious of it.

The young woman's eyes quickly found Kirsten, and the offering she carried.

"Oh," she said. "No, of course not. Hello again, Kirsten."

Jane put out her hand. "I'm Kirsten's mother, Jane, and back there . . ." She glanced back and saw that Lisa had climbed the steps after all, "that's Lisa, my younger daughter. This was Kirsten's idea, and I thought it was a good one. We aren't here to take up your time, I know you're very busy—"

"Oh, come in." The young woman reached out and took Jane's arm and pulled. "I'm so glad to see you. My name is Emily. My husband, Mel, had to go back to town. He had an interview. Not that we don't have a ton of things to do around here."

Jane went into the long kitchen. The right end of the room was furnished like a sitting room, with a cradle, a rocking chair and a braided rug. Another overstuffed chair occupied the corner, where there was an end table with a lamp that had a fringed shade.

"Oh my goodness," Jane said, "Look at the marvelous condition of that lampshade. It must be a hundred years old."

Emily followed her, and gently brushed her fingers down the side of the old silk shade. "I found it in one of the front parlors. It was on an old gas lamp."

"Marvelous."

Jane saw a mop bucket and mop, the handle propped against the table. Emily looked as if she'd been cleaning. Her old shirt had bits of dust and webs stuck like glue.

She took the casserole from Kirsten and thanked her.

Jane declined the offer to sit down and stood talking a

427

few minutes longer than she had intended to. She learned more than she had ever expected to know. They had come from the state of Washington, and had never known Aunt Jenny, or any of the people who had lived in this house. Emily had never even heard of them before. Her husband Mel had been delighted about his inheritance. He had no close relatives. She had a sister who lived in Washington, also several aunts, uncles and cousins. Mel's family had dwindled down to him, and now was picking up again with Prissy and Adam. Mel wanted to keep the place and fix it up, it would be a real showplace, but she wanted to sell and build a small house and keep the land. They would probably have to keep the place, though, even the house, at least for awhile. They were going to clean it up. As soon as Mel got a job they would hire someone to help clean.

Jane tried to leave without being abrupt, but it was almost impossible to get a word in, even to say good night. The poor girl acted as if she hadn't had a friend in years.

"Did you know," Jane said, "our kids have been clearing a path between our houses?"

"Really?"

Emily came out onto the porch with Jane. "It's very hard to see, but they tell me they'll have it easy to use in a few days. So come on over, and see me."

"I'd love to," Emily said wistfully. "I'm so glad you came."

Jane said goodbye to Adam and Prissy. She waved at the three of them, standing on the old stone walk at the back of the house. There was something very depressing about leaving that young family there in an old house that seemed filled with invisible beings left over from a different age.

Kirsten said suddenly, "That house is haunted."

A tremor moved over Jane involuntarily. "Kirsten!

428

Places aren't haunted. Haunted by what?" Yet she felt guilty for criticizing Kirsten. Hadn't she been feeling something of the kind herself? She would never admit it to Kirsten, though.

Lisa said, "I wish Adam didn't have to live there."

"It's a fine old place," Jane said. "A bit overgrown, maybe, but still a very nice old house. It probably doesn't need as much work as one would think, to put it back in shape again."

Kirsten said, "I think they should sell it."

"Who would buy?"

"Maybe it could be a museum."

Lisa said, "Prissy had the doll."

"The doll?" At first Jane didn't know what she was talking about, then she remembered the old doll Lisa had brought home and which had been the cause of Lisa finding the body. If she hadn't been made to take it back, the body might have stayed hidden for many more years.

As if Kirsten had been thinking along the same lines, she said, "Mom, that makes us kind of responsible for them, doesn't it?"

"What?"

"Well, for years and years the old mansion was empty. Of people, I mean. Then we moved here, and Lisa and I were exploring, and we found the mansion. We went in. Lisa climbed the stairs. I went in the parlor and another room. Lisa found the doll. She took it home and you made her bring it back. Then she found the body." "But if she hadn't, the mansion would have been left alone and Adam and his folks wouldn't be here now. Right? The police came. And they checked up to see who the owner of the mansion was, and found Jenny. And she died. So then her nephew inherited the house. And here they are. And it's all our fault."

Jane muttered, "Thanks a lot, Kirsten."

Jane found herself examining the chain of events that had led to this summer, to the meeting of Emily and her children. She felt uncomfortably that Kirsten was right.

At what point in the chain of events could they have changed the outcome? Well, maybe the outcome would be good. A young family, an old place that needed love and attention. The sound of laughter again, as surely there was long ago.

Jane drove into her garage and turned off the engine. Lord, she thought. Of all things, she hadn't expected to feel responsible for the family in the old mansion. But she did, just because it was her child who had taken something that didn't belong to her.

"Well," Jane said as she got out of the car, "We'll have to see what we can do to help. We can take our own mops and go over and clean."

"I'm not going in that house," Lisa said.

Chapter 14

"Here, Prissy, let brother have it."

Prissy hung on to the doll and let out a squall.

Adam threw a hasty glance over his shoulder, but both his mom and dad had gone upstairs. His dad had come home with that look on his face that meant still no job, no luck. Adam had learned what it looked like, because all last winter and spring his dad had carried that distant, sad face. It made Adam feel bad. But what could he do except try to keep Prissy happy?

Only not with that ugly doll. He didn't like it. There was a mean look on its face that he didn't like.

"Baby dolly," she whined, clinging to it.

"No, mean old doll. Bad doll. Ugly doll. Let Adam get Prissy something pretty."

"No, no." She cried louder, holding to the doll with both hands as Adam tried to tug it away from her. Its old, yellowed gown tore a little, and Adam released the doll. Prissy turned onto her hands and knees and crawled away, dragging the doll along on its back. Its face looked up at Adam with a satisfied smirk that made it seem, for a minute, as if it knew.

Adam looked around, and saw a shiny glass figurine in a china cabinet in the dining area of the kitchen. He rushed over and took it out of the cabinet. It looked like a deer or a horse.

"Look, Prissy, here's Bambi, all in blue glass. Want to see it?"

Prissy sat on the braided rug at the end of the kitchen, near the chairs and her cradle. He teased her with the blue glass animal, holding it inches away from her hand when she reached for it. As he had planned, she let the doll fall aside, got on her hands and knees and crawled toward Adam, one hand stretching out.

"Awww," she wailed. "Horsey."

"Yeah, okay, horse. Here, you can look at it. And here, I'll get you some more, lots more. But you mustn't break."

He put down the blue figurine and went back to the cabinet. He found a dish that was red and wavy at the edges, and two thimbles made of glass. He looked at the thimbles, then he put them back. She'd probably put those in her mouth. He grabbed a couple more figurines and hurried back to her before she changed her mind and returned to the doll.

With Prissy occupied for the moment, he snatched up the doll and ran out of the kitchen. Then he looked about. He could see the open door of the back stairs, but if he went that way he might run into his mom and dad. So he went down the hall toward the front of the house.

He opened the double doors. Mom hadn't cleaned the big front foyer, nor any of the rooms beyond the double doors. Adam looked for a safe place to put the doll, a place where even Mom wouldn't find it for a long time. He gave up when he heard Prissy's voice and shoved the doll under the settee in the foyer.

He ran back into the kitchen to find her crying and crawling toward him.

"Baby dolly," she cried.

432

"Sleepy town," Adam said. "Baby dolly went to take a nap."

That seemed to satisfy her and she stopped fussing when Adam made a special arrangement of the little glass horse, the red dish, her small doll and blocks. He looked longingly toward the backdoor. The path was waiting, and so were Kirsten and Lisa. They had a lot more work to do to make the path really smooth and clear of limbs, and it was so much more fun than trying to keep Prissy happy while his mom and dad worked upstairs.

But the sun was going down, and his folks wouldn't let him go outside now even if he could figure out something to do with Prissy. He drew a long sigh. Maybe tomorrow he could play with Kirsten and Lisa, and work on the path.

Wind stirred the curtains gently at the open window, and sounds of a night bird drifted in from far away in the timber. Mel's voice was hushed, so that he wouldn't disturb the sleeping kids.

"I was thinking about starting our own business, Emily." His hands nervously kneaded the fingers of her left hand, a habit he had started when he lost his job.

"We have a big houseful of antiques. I thought if we turned the front of the house into a store, and kept this back part for our family. What do you think, Em?"

She found herself caught up by his idea. The house was perfectly divided. Double doors at the end of the wide hallway downstairs totally separated front from back. They could even put a lock on the doors.

She whispered eagerly, "We could build a door across the end of the upstairs hall, too, just like the downstairs!"

433

"Yes!" His hands clasped her hand, a painful pressure. She said nothing about it. She didn't want him to release her.

"And we could build a family room where the old screened porch is!"

"Oh yes, Em. Sure we could." He put his arms around her and hugged her as painfully tight as he had clasped her hand.

"It would make a great family room. It'd be bigger than our rented house was!" She laughed, and he laughed with her. They hugged and kissed.

For an hour or more they dreamed aloud, making plans. Mel went to sleep, but Emily's mind kept racing. She felt the excitment, she realized, that Mel had felt from the beginning. And she was glad. Glad that at last they had come to a decision they could live with, and be very happy with, and make a future with.

Her attention was diverted by a soft sound in the hall. Adam going to the bathroom? But Adam usually slept through the night without waking, just as Prissy did. She was lucky to have kids who were healthy and basically happy. They were all lucky to have this great old place, with the acres and acres of trees. What a fantastic place for Prissy and Adam to grow up!

How quickly her feelings about it had changed. What a great idea Mel had. But hadn't she always known he would make a good life for them?

She slipped out of bed and, guided by the dim glow of the nightlight plugged into an outlet near the crib, went over to check on Prissy. Her plump little arms felt cool, and Emily gently pulled up the blanket to cover her.

Emily went out into the hall. She felt her way along the wall to the door of Adam's room next to theirs. She went in, felt in the dark for the lamp on the table and turned it on.

He didn't look as if he had been out of bed since she kissed him goodnight. He was lying on his side, his blanket clutched tightly in his arms and half wrapped around his body. His legs were drawn up tightly against his arms. Maybe eventually he would relax, Emily thought, as the whole family became more relaxed. She could hardly wait to tell him about their plans to have their own antique business right here at home. *Home*.

Then she turned out the lamp and in the dark felt her way to the door. She closed it behind her.

The closing of the door woke Adam and he lay listening. He heard his mother's footsteps as she went back into her room with Dad and Prissy. She had left him in the dark, and he was afraid. He wished he could call her back. He wished he could go sleep with them. He had never felt so far away.

He lay still, listening, his whole self drawn toward the hallway, it seemed, where even now he could hear that movement again.

The soft movements in the hall passed on by, the crawling, the sliding of something soft against the floor or the wall. He heard it pause outside his door, and then it went on again toward the front of the house, toward his mom and dad's room. He listened, and felt himself drifting on the sounds. He wanted to stay awake and listen for the crawling along the hall, but he knew he was going to sleep.

He would open his eyes as always to find day had come, and the crawling in the hall silenced.

Whatever it was crawled only in the dark. It was as if the ghosts of the people who had died here came back nightly to drag their feet in the hall.

435

Afraid of the noise he would make if he turned over, he eased the sheet up to cover his face. He ached to move, but he only doubled up tighter, his legs drawing closer to his face and arms.

And somewhere in the house a door opened.

Emily looked toward the door, expecting to see Adam. Light outlined the edge of the door in a faint, failing glow, and she watched it open slowly, one inch, two, three.

"Adam?" she whispered. Behind her Mel slept, turned on his left side away from her. His breathing was slow and deep. Prissy, asleep in her crib in the corner beyond Mel, made no sound at all.

"Adam?" she spoke in an open voice, softly. She raised to her elbow, leaning, watching the slowly opening door.

Adam didn't answer, nor appear in the narrow opening of the door. It had opened several inches, and now stopped moving. A tingle of uneasiness kept her still, as she wonderingly watched the dark strip of hallway. Could the door have swung open on its own? The sound of the knob turning had disturbed her dozing rest and startled her awake. Adam had not slept well in this house, probably because of the change. She remembered he had said something crawled in the hall outside his room. Mel had dismissed it with teasing about a snake, and Adam had said nothing since. But as Emily stared at the door she remembered also hearing a sound that could have been described as crawling. To her it had sounded like a swishing of clothing, and not even to herself had she admitted her vaguely unsettled feelings.

Long gowns swishing. Something crawling.

Narrow pathways, trails made in the dust.

It was not Adam who had opened her door, unless he had opened it and slipped back to his room before she whispered to him.

A deep disquiet, like the memory of a bad dream, slowed Emily's movement as she rose. She put back her light cover and slid her feet to the floor. The wood felt icy beneath her bare feet, and she walked through a darkness that swam around her ankles like thick mud.

She was halfway between the bed and door when it moved again, a fraction more, then another, slowly. A faint squeak of the hinges made her know she wasn't imagining the slow opening of the door.

She felt her mouth turn dry, her lips stiff, her tongue clublike. She stood still, too far from the door to see what it was that was pressing against it. She heard the swish of the movement again, of long, ghostly skirts in the hall, or perhaps coming through the narrow opening of the door. Her skin was like brittle glass, holding her in a sudden senseless terror. She wanted to call Mel, and at the same time wanted to protect him from whatever it was invading their room.

Something dimly lit appeared on the floor of the doorway. No more than a strip of clothing, a rag. The door moved again, pushed by it—whatever it was. Suddenly it reared up a few inches. Emily stared down at a small grey object against the black dungeon of hallway.

It moved forward on the floor, crawling, like a baby who had just learned to use its hands to pull itself along.

As it narrowed the space between them, it crossed a dim trail of light that passed beneath the bed. In horror Emily saw clearly the face of the old doll. Its eyes gleamed oddly, reflecting the light, and they were looking up at her as if somehow they could see.

Emily couldn't move. She could feel the drooping of

437

her facial muscles and bones, the drop of her chin, the gaping of her own mouth. As the doll's mouth pursed, as if readying itself for nursing, she felt her own disbelief changing her from a thinking human to an animal under the power of something beyond, a supernatural energy she could not understand.

She hadn't realized she was moving until she backed up against the bed. Without taking her eyes from the doll as it moved from the streak of light to darkness again, she gripped the bed and pulled herself up. She drew her legs up. A sound began escaping like steam from her throat. A gargle of horror, expressed only in sounds of animal choking.

Behind her Mel stirred, lifted himself to an elbow.

"Emily? Em? What's wrong?"

She moved back on the bed, drawing her legs away from the edge. Her mouth moved, but all sounds had dissipated and her breath came in gusts. She stared at the edge of the bed.

"Em?" His voice was low, to keep from waking Prissy, but puzzled and with growing concern. "Emily? What's . . ."

Its head appeared at the side of the bed like a distant, dark moon rising over a toxic planet. It came up above the bed and into the light. Its eyes picked up the light again and reflected distant evil gleams.

Emily had pushed back against Mel, unable to point toward it or audibly alert him. Then she knew that he saw it, too. She heard a curse of disbelief, felt the hard grip of his hands on her shoulders.

Then it appeared to leap, coming suddenly full into her face and bearing her back. She tore at it with her hands, tried to dislodge it from her face. She heard Mel's voice, and glimpsed his hands near her face, his fingers dug into the thing attached to her. She grew

438

faint.

She was unable to breathe, too weak with horror and disbelief to move. She was dreaming, she told herself. She had to wake up and tell Mel to put a lock on all the doors because there really were ghosts and they walked the halls at night and opened doors. There was no doll crawling. That was too crazy. Not even in her dreams could she have created that horror.

Where was Mel? She couldn't hear him, or see him. Where had he gone? A spark of life in Emily heard Prissy moving about in her crib. "Mama?" she whimpered. Emily tried to answer, but could not.

There was a sound in the bed, a sound of suckling. She willed herself to turn, open her eyes.

Mel was lying down, and it was on his face. Its hands held his cheeks as its mouth suckled at his. He was no longer fighting.

Emily tried to move. It lifted its head and turned toward her. The nightlight fell on its full, red face. As if it had sucked blood its bloated face hung in the air before her, edging slowly nearer. She had no will to escape it. She was sinking into the world of her nightmare, this thing that couldn't be real, and not even the cry of her baby could help her.

Prissy was crying. On and on, her voice like a dream.

Adam sat up in bed.

As if a bubble had burst in his head, he was suddenly awake. He blinked and widened his eyes, and thought in a burst of helplessness he had gone blind. He couldn't see. But he had to go to Prissy. She was alone. He had never heard her cry that way before.

And Mama and Daddy were not answering her.

439

Adam rolled, trying to extricate himself from the blanket. He felt for the edge of the bed, and fell. The floor struck him, jolted him to a stop, and the blanket unrolled behind him. He pushed himself to his feet and with his arms out felt for the door. The distance seemed miles. He could touch nothing of substance, as if he were going around and around in circles. And still Prissy cried, on and on.

His hands touched the wall, and he felt for the door, and found it. He opened it and made his way along the dark hall, his hands on the wall for guidance.

Prissy seemed even farther away until he came at last to the doorway. The door was partly open, and a dim light began to reach him.

Fear pulled at his skin and entered his body through every pore. It turned his brain cold and his stomach tight and sick. He wanted to speak Prissy's name and tell her it was okay now, he was here. He wanted to cry with her and call for his mom and dad. *Where are you? Mommy, Daddy. Where are you that you haven't heard Prissy crying?*

His hand, cold and numb, felt clumsily and slowly along the wall for the light switch. His fingers found and pressed the button.

Light suddenly illuminated the room. Although the bulb was dim and high in the ceiling, its light at first hurt Adam's eyes with its contrast to the dark it had displaced. Prissy's sobs sounded breathless, as if she wept without hope. She kept crying.

Adam stared at the bed where his mom and dad should have been, and stared and stared, unable to accept what he saw.

Two skeletons lay in the bed. Two skeletons with skin like wrinkled paper, hair growing from bony skulls, eyes bulging at the ceiling. Their hands were jointed claws

440

on the sheet that only half covered them. His mama's dark, pretty hair, spread on the pillow above one skeleton's head, and his daddy's beard grew like long moss on the other. Large, gumless teeth in shrunken mouths gaped at nothing. This was not Daddy, not Mama. No. NO!

A scream filled his total being, but didn't find release. Prissy's cries surrounded him, and at last he looked toward her.

She pushed and clawed at the inner corner of her crib as if trying to climb the wall, trying to get away from something.

There was a white thing crawling up the side of the crib. Adam saw the back of a small head wearing . . . *a bonnet*. It suddenly turned its face. He saw the ruined skin, the bursting cheeks of the old doll, the open mouth like a red wound, and the stained, growing teeth like protruding fangs. Dust motes like moths drifted in the light away from the doll with each movement. It looked twice as large as when he pushed it under the settee downstairs.

It was crawling toward Prissy, up the side of the crib. Even as it turned its glassy eyes on Adam, it kept crawling.

He was paralyzed with his terror, and his stomach felt as weak as mush as it sank around the sick knot in the middle. His flesh burned with intense cold. His mom and dad were dead, like the woman in the front bedroom had been. The doll was going after Prissy now, and then it would come after him.

He hardly knew he was moving. He had to get Prissy, get Prissy, get Prissy . . .

He was suddenly at the foot of the crib, and the doll's hard, glassy eyes watched him. Its mouth opened upon a red, gorged interior and its large face seemed within

441

inches of his own. At that moment he garnered strength enough in his arms and shoved the crib out from the wall.

Prissy leaned and reached toward him, her cries of terror as forlorn as the terror in his brain. They were alone, with a *thing* that had killed their mom and dad. They couldn't get away. They would never get away.

He grabbed her and pulled her over the back railing of the crib. Her weight bore him down and he fell with her. He grabbed her up, lifting her feet from the floor.

A plan for protection flashed through his mind as if from somewhere beyond.

He would run to the door and get back to his own room. Then he would shove all the furniture against the door.

He heard a thump on the other side of the crib as the doll dropped. Carrying Prissy, he started toward the door. It looked so far away. Twelve feet away the door was open on the dark hall, but it was like miles.

The doll was no longer behind them at the crib. He threw a terrified glance toward the shadows beneath the big bed, but didn't see it.

With Prissy a dead weight in his arms he struggled toward the door and escape. He had to take care of Prissy. Mama would want him to save Prissy, get her out of the house, away from the horror that had tried to make itself look like a doll.

In the face of his terrible death, he knew the history of the thing that lived only to kill. He saw the doll as once it might have been. Little and soft, like a baby, dressed in a bonnet and long dress, with a little round mouth and eyes that opened and shut. One night it started, and it used up people. It tried to keep itself cuddly and pretty, like a little baby, but killing changed it. Now it made a sound that drove through him like threads of fine wire, piercing his lungs, his stomach, his heart, his brain.

He had to save Prissy. Then he had to go back and get his mom and dad.

The door moved, and a long icy strip of weakness replaced his spine. He stared at the moving door, and heard the latch as it snapped shut.

His gaze dropped to the old yellowed gown on the floor against the door. The bloated, red face of the old doll turned toward them again.

As Adam drew back, it rose to its hands and began crawling toward him and Prissy. It had trapped them in the room, where it had killed Mama and Daddy.

Chapter 15

Kirsten ran down long dark halls. It ran behind her, closer and closer. She could hear it running on its skeletal feet, through the long, winding, strange halls of the old mansion. She tried to scream, and couldn't. She could see it behind her, its eyes sunken, its teeth exposed beyond lips dried to thin, tissue skin. It had long, sparse grey hair, flowing back over its bony shoulders. Even though Kirsten ran, she hardly moved. It was reaching for her now, its long, fleshless hands touching her shoulders.

She woke, upright in bed, cold with fear, choking on the aborted screams in her nightmare. The sounds came out as if she were gagging, and dwindled away in the pounding of her heart.

Then, trembling, she sat with her hands over her face, so relieved that it had been a dream. But she felt as if she were still in the old mansion.

She turned on the lamp at the head of her bed and looked at the clock. 2:50 A.M. The deepest part of the night, the time when even the night owls slept.

She got up and went to her window and looked out. A full moon made the backyard seem like a dim, silent day. She had always loved moonlight, but tonight it made her shiver. She pushed the curtain aside and stared through the moon touched trees toward the mansion. Adam was there, and his baby sister, and his parents. And Kirsten had a really bad feeling about it tonight, as if something were terribly wrong, and her dream had tried to tell her. She squinted, and thought she saw a light, a distant beam, through the trees.

She took her binoculars and went quietly out onto the back deck. She lifted the binoculars, and saw a few inches of a window frame, the gauzy fall of curtains, and the bedroom light. It was in that window she had seen a face, before Adam and his family moved in. Tonight the light was like a beacon. At 3:00 A.M. in the morning, it seemed out of place, and her feeling that something was wrong grew stronger.

She returned to the house and went down the hall to the master bedroom. The door was closed. She opened it without knocking.

"Mom?" she whispered loudly from the doorway.

The room was lighted only by moonlight falling like old silk through the wide, deep windows on the west.

She didn't want to wake her dad. He'd tell her to go back to bed and mind her own business. He didn't understand that Adam, and his family, was her business. If it weren't for her, and Lisa, Adam wouldn't be there, in that haunted old house.

"Mom," she whispered, crossing the thick carpet silently, peering down at the person on the near side of the bed. Yes, luckily, it was her mother.

"Hmmm?" Jane said, and her arm moved, a pale object in the dark. She mumbled sleepily, "What is it, Kirsten?"

"Mom," Kirsten whispered, "There's a light over in the old mansion."

"Ummm. So?"

"It's almost three o'clock!"

Her dad said suddenly, "Go back to bed, Kirsten. Maybe they like light."

"But . . . it's three o'clock!"

Her dad turned over, groaned, and pulled his pillow over his head. "And I have to get up in three hours. Go to bed, Kirsten."

Her mother turned over also, onto her side, her face settled into her pillow.

Kirsten stood a moment longer looking at them. It was nothing, their attitudes told her. You're a silly, hysterical girl who thinks the old mansion is haunted. Grow up.

She left the room and went back to hers. She sat on the side of the bed, stared at the floor, and tried to convince herself she should go back to bed.

Instead, she went again to the deck and peered through the binoculars. The light was still on. She lowered the binoculars.

Every night she came out to the deck and looked toward the old mansion. There would be a light in that room for only a short time, and then darkness. Everyone went to bed early. They didn't have a television to stay up and watch, as did most people in the neighborhood. Every night at ten the lights were out. Was it Adam's room? Or his baby sister's? Or maybe his parents'?

She returned to her bedroom and began to dress. Without knowing exactly what she was going to do she began to hurry. She jerked on jeans, a sweatshirt, and tennis shoes with soft, rubber soles. From her nightstand drawer she took her flashlight.

She was careful to make no sound. The new wood floor in the house was solid and didn't squeak beneath her steps. The French patio door slid open silently, and closed as silently behind her. She was on the deck, and across to the steps and down. She began to run. In the edge of the woods, where the path began, she turned on the flashlight.

The path seemed far longer, far less defined than it had when they were working on it. She stumbled over a fallen limb that hadn't been moved, and thought she had lost her way. Her light, shining ahead, revealed nothing of the boundaries of the area that once had been the yard of the old mansion.

Then suddenly her light touched the corner of the house, and she had a full view of the lighted window on the rear of the second floor.

She stood still, looking up. She became aware of sounds. The shifting of the house, settling of wood, a steady nibbling of a rodent, and another sound that unnerved her.

Sobs, cries, reaching her at one moment and fading the next, as if on shifting air currents. It sounded muffled by walls and far away. But it was in the house, and it was upstairs where the light was. She *knew*. Prissy, crying, gasping as if she had been crying a long time.

Kirsten hurried around the corner of the house and up onto the screened porch. From here, where the only light came from her small flashlight, the crying seemed to have stopped. She stood still a moment listening. Had Prissy awakened, and was that why there was a light in the window?

Her parents would be taking care of her.

Kirsten felt like a fool. Her own parents would be furious with her. If she knocked on the door, who would hear her? They were upstairs, a long way from the kitchen door.

Tomorrow she could ask Adam if Prissy had gotten sick in the night.

She left the porch and went along the wall to the corner of the house again. Her flashlight pointed toward home, she searched for the path.

On this side of the house she could hear the baby crying again, on and on. But it was none of her business. She could see the light from the window

447

shining out into the trees.

She started forward.

A choked, hoarse scream stopped her. The baby's cries intensified. The scream didn't repeat, but the cries sounded breathless and gasping, sob after sob, cutting off the baby's breath.

Something was terribly wrong there.

Kirsten thought of calling Adam, but instead she ran around to the screened porch again and across the old boards to the kitchen door.

She pounded, then tried the knob.

It seemed she could hear them, both Adam and Prissy. Yet, when she paused briefly to listen, she heard the whisper of leaves, the creak and moan of the old house as if it were changing positions in its sleep.

She vascillated between breaking into the house and going upstairs to see what was wrong, or assuming that nothing unusual was wrong and going back home. She thought of going again to her parents. She thought, too, of running home and dialing 911 for the police.

Kirsten stood on the porch and listened to the moan of the house, and distant thumping sounds like irregular footsteps, and Prissy crying, crying.

Adam clutched Prissy to him. The doll crawled toward them wherever they turned, pulling itself with its hands, its arms stiffened and its shoulders and head lifted, while behind it the feet and long gown dragged. He heard the sound of the crawling, he saw the narrow trail it made across the pattern of the old rug at the foot of the bed. With Prissy in his arms he pushed back as far as he could go, huddling between the dresser and the wall. They sat in the dim light thrown by the nightlight, and Prissy trembled against him, her small body feeling im-

448

possibly heavy and cold, yet slick with sweat. Her face turned toward the doll and her cries sharpened, numbing Adam's senses, beating into his brain. Yet above her gasping sobs and screams he heard the sound of the crawling as the thing that looked like a doll drew nearer to them.

His stare tore from the bloated and horrible face to the door. Beyond it was a hallway of lightless dark. They had to run.

With his arms around Prissy, he picked her up. She slid as he stood, his hold on her loosened. Her feet dragged the floor as he ran, putting all his strength into getting to that door, out of this room. If they could just get to the hall, some remote part of his mind planned to slam the door shut. Shut the *thing* in the room. Then they would run again, and keep running.

He had to pass within inches of the horrible old doll. Blindly, he struggled to run. Then he felt himself drawn to a halt, the burden of Prissy holding him back. He felt Prissy dragging away from him. He turned, losing hold of her. Her screams intensified and didn't sound like Prissy. He felt as if he were in a strange, prehistoric world, and all he could hear was the scream of a small, frightened animal.

The room focused in his vision again. Adam saw the doll had grabbed Prissy's leg and was crawling upwards, its hands pulling at her. Its red, round, bulging face within inches of Prissy's.

Chapter 16

Jane gave up and opened her eyes. Moonlight cast a dim glow into the bedroom and she could see the ceiling fan in the recess above. As her eyes wandered about its outlines, her mind sought Kirsten. Where was she? Had she gone back to bed? What kind of nosiness was her daughter up to? Back home, Kirsten behaved just like any normal kid. Here, she helped hack a path through a wild woodland to an old mansion she thought was haunted. She hadn't settled down to watching her favorite TV shows. She hadn't even been riding her bike much.

Jane turned onto her right side, leaned up on her elbow and peered toward Don. But he was sound asleep again. He'd been working so hard since they moved, getting into his new job, learning where everything was and getting acquainted with the people. Waking him would be cruel and unusual punishment, especially since he had to get up so early.

She slipped quietly out of bed, pulled her robe on, and went into the hall where the girls' bedrooms were. At Kirsten's door she called softly, and when she got no answer, she turned on the overhead light.

Kirsten was not there. The covers were thrown back. But even more revealing were the pajamas tossed on the floor.

Kirsten had dressed and gone out.

"Oh Lord," Jane said under her breath.

She went out onto the back deck. Moonlight fell unfettered onto the deck and backyard. Kirsten was not in sight. But lying on the railing was something small and black, and when Jane went closer she saw it was Kirsten's binoculars.

Puzzled, Jane picked them up and held them to her eyes.

The window of the old mansion came into startling focus, with only a couple of limbs and a few dozen leaves to obscure the view. It was a second floor bedroom window, so far as Jane could tell.

Just because the bedroom light was on, Kirsten had gone over there?

"Oh Kirsten!" What kind of nosey kid had she raised? What would Emily and her husband think . . .

A chill covered Jane's back as if something very cold had splashed against her. She raised the glasses again and looked at the window. She could see the thin curtains, a gauzy veil between her and the room. But she could also see movement there. Not a man or woman, but someone much shorter. A child. The head moved erratically, as if dodging. She glimpsed just for a moment the head of a second child, lower but very close to the first. And then, a third. Smaller yet, and close to the second. Although the three heads were very close together it seemed they were moving too erratically, dodging about in a frantic way that puzzled and disturbed Jane. And then suddenly they disappeared, and the window was like a frame in which the picture had been removed.

Jane found her breath had grown short and inadequate. She dropped the glasses back onto the railing and stared at the dark wall of the forest in which one single window light shone.

She whirled, and ran back into the house.

Kirsten heard the screams. She didn't have time to stop and wonder why. She knew only that it was Prissy and Adam, the voices of children. Where were the parents? She had to get in and see what was wrong with Adam.

The flashlight beam revealed two kitchen windows were raised. The windows were low, near the area where the table would be. Only the screen stood between Kirsten and entry.

With the flashlight tucked tightly under one arm, Kirsten tried to remove the screen. It held, fastened at the bottom by a hook.

Kirsten looked around for something to poke through. The screen looked dark with rust, and she hoped it was weak. She shined the light along the porch, while upstairs the cries of the baby drifted to a softness that sounded more and more like the wail of the wind.

Adam saw the doll's pouched lips skimming Prissy's cheek, reaching round for Prissy's tear-dampened mouth, cutting off Prissy's cries.

With a scream hoarse in his throat, Adam ran to the table by the bed and came back with the metal lamp. He swung it at the doll's head, and heard it smash. But he had aimed too low and it glanced across Prissy's forehead, leaving a bloody streak. The doll fell away.

Adam threw the lamp aside and lunged for Prissy. Oh God, she was dead. Her body was limp, her eyes closed. Her cries had stopped. But the doll was rising again on its hand, dragging its long gown, its eyes fastened on Adam.

He had to reach within inches of its face, but he snatched Prissy away and lifted her. Lifted her easier than he ever had in all her life. He ran with her to the door.

Behind him it came, so fast that when he turned to look back, to pull the door shut, it was within inches of reaching him again.

He kicked, and struck its head, and it reared backward. Then it regained its balance and started forward again, the cheeks bulged, the mouth in a red, moist, glistening pout, the eyes glassy and steady.

Adam grabbed the edge of the door and slammed it shut between them. The darkness in the hallway seemed now like a comforting blanket. He couldn't see, but he knew the doll was on the other side of the bedroom door. They were going to get away. He'd find the stairway and go down, and then find the doors that led to the outside and the path to Kirsten's house. Mama would be so glad he had saved Prissy.

Light suddenly pierced the darkness of the hall as the bedroom door opened. He threw a glance back and saw they were only a few feet away. It had seemed to Adam, running in the total dark, they had gone a long way and were maybe going to escape. But the doll was coming, ten feet away, nine, eight . . . dragging its hindquarters and its long gown.

He whirled, looking for a way out. But he had cornered himself. The doll came rapidly toward them, closing the gap.

Kirsten jabbed the flashlight into the rusted wire, jabbed and jabbed again. She saw the screen bulge inward, and then it split. With the end of the flashlight she enlarged the hole, then reached her fingers through and pushed on the hook.

She felt like crying. There was silence in the house now, but it was a silence that terrified her. She couldn't back away and go home. She had to see Adam.

She pushed on the hook, and it cut through her finger and brought a drop of blood. She drew in her breath and pushed harder.

The hook gave suddenly, flopping loose. The screen was free.

She crawled into the kitchen, then following the beam of her light ran into the hall and found herself blocked by closed, double doors.

She pushed on the double doors, and they opened. She ran into the big front foyer, and to the curving stairway that led up to the balcony and the room where Lisa had found the body.

She shined her light up the stairs and called, "Adam! Emily!"

She thought someone answered, but she wasn't sure. She climbed the stair, carefully. There was a broken step somewhere. She found it, stepped over, and hurried on up. Their bedrooms were in the back wing, Adam had told her. Three steps led up from the balcony to the hall of the back bedrooms.

Kirsten found the three steps and ran. The hall was dimly lighted from the partly open door of the bedroom.

With her flashlight still burning, she ran to the door and stopped just over the threshold.

She stood unable to move as her light beam fastened to the bed. Dazed, she stared, as time stopped. The bed held two dead people who looked as if everything had been taken from them but the bones and skin.

Kirsten's awareness took in the entire room, though she looked at nothing but the bodies on the bed, the horror of their deaths holding her rock still. Yet she saw the crib was empty. She saw that neither Adam nor Prissy were in the room.

"Kirsten . . ."

It was a feeble, pleading cry, somewhere behind her.

She didn't have time to wonder what had caused such awful deaths, but in the depths of her mind she connected it to the horror of her nightmare, to the cruel soul that had never escaped the mansion, to whatever ghosts lived here and lived upon any human who walked into its dark halls.

Kirsten's light guided her. She heard the cry again and turned her flashlight down the hall, and to her left.

An empty room, she first thought. Then her light fell upon Adam.

He had pushed back as far as he could go between the chest and the wall. Prissy lay limp in his arms, her forehead bruised by a narrow, red streak.

But they weren't alone. A very small person seemed to be trying to get close to them, but Adam kicked out, a low cry coming from his throat.

Kirsten's light outlined his face, white and trembling. Prissy's, unconscious, with a raw, red streak across one side of her forehead. Then the light beam fell upon the face of the small person. In stark horror she saw it resembled a human face only in its contours. *The doll!* The doll Lisa had found and brought home with her.

It did not look at her, but its eyes reflected the light in glittering shards of blue and red. They were almost buried in the red bloat of its enlarged face. It was trying not only to get close to Adam and Prissy, it seemed to be attacking them in a grasping, clinging way, pushing its engorged face against Prissy's, grasping Adam's shirt with its tiny, mechanical fists.

She couldn't believe this. *The doll.* A thing that drew life from living humans.

Kirsten gagged on vomit that rose to her throat. Her stomach felt as if it were being pulled out of her. Her fingers grew numb, and the flashlight fell and rolled.

And the sound brought the doll around to fasten its glassy eyes on Kirsten.

Chapter 17

Kirsten screamed, "Adam! Run! The path, Adam!"

He didn't move. He huddled over the limp body of Prissy, his arms beneath her. Between Kirsten and the two quiet children in the corner, the doll-creature came, lifted by its hands, crawling rapidly toward Kirsten.

Kirsten's instinctive urge to run and save herself gave way to her inability to desert Adam and his baby sister. It held her stationary for a moment too long. She couldn't leave Adam and the baby. She had to run to get away from the *thing*. She couldn't leave . . .

It reached her. She felt it against her, its hands tugging at the legs of her jeans. Its face shadowed while the beam of her light danced like a fireball gone mad on the opposite wall, on Adam, across the room and ceiling.

With one hand clawing to pull it away from her, she raised the flashlight and brought it down on the doll's head. It clung, as if it had been glued to her. She struck again and again, missing, the doll's head too close to her own for her to strike it. A weird, high-pitched sound hurt her ears and burrowed into her brain. It came from the doll, close to her ears, burrowing into her brain like maggots, sending her over the edge of terror.

The flashlight hit the floor and rolled crazily out of reach, its beam spinning.

Kirsten turned and stumbled toward the door. She had to find the path . . .

The doll was at her face, its sharp little hands digging into her cheeks.

Kirsten fell, and rolled, trying to dislodge it. With her bare hands she began digging at it, tearing off its bonnet, ripping the back of the long, dusty gown it wore. She felt pain rip up her arms as her nails tore away, but the sensation was only marginal. She was filled with the sound of the high mewling, the almost soundless vibrations that came from the doll, like a psychic wire that had been plucked.

The flashlight had stopped rolling, and its light angled across Kirsten and the doll. Kirsten lay still, no longer fighting. The doll perched above her, but turned its face toward Adam.

Adam's mouth worked silently. His thoughts stumbled in split pathways, unable to form. His eyes saw only Kirsten, who had come to help, and who was dead now too, like Prissy. He could not let the doll make them empty and hollow as it had done Mama and Daddy.

He got to his feet, his legs wobbly and weak. He adjusted the heavy weight of his little sister in his arms, looked toward the door as if fixing his goal in his mind. Then he turned and walked backwards, his eyes on the doll. When he saw it was following, leaving Kirsten, coming for him, he whirled and ran.

The flashlight showed him the hall, and the back stairs, and then faded away, leaving him in darkness.

He stumbled down the dark stairs, Prissy dragging him down. At the foot of the stairs he bumped into the closed door, and Prissy fell from his arms.

In silence he stooped to pick her up, and heard the

bump of it coming down the stairs above them.

He heard the mewling, so high it was at times inaudible. His skin tingled and tightened, terror dried his throat and made his tongue thick. With a clubby hand he felt for the doorknob, and found it. He opened the door and ran out into the hall.

Utter blackness surrounded him. He was lost in the dark world of the old mansion. Where was the door? The door that would let him out in moonlight so that he could find the path?

He had to find the door.

It was closer now, coming after him and Prissy. It wanted Prissy. It wanted him. Everything that lived in the house was its to be eaten. Someone a long time ago had given it that right.

The mewling was closer, and the stink of death. He heard the crawling, the dragging of itself along the hall. It was following him, and coming closer because it didn't have to have light to see.

He stumbled on, trying to keep Prissy from sliding away from him as he used one hand to feel for a doorknob.

The cold porcelain was at first a shock, as if he had touched ice. Then with a sob in his throat he realized what it was.

A doorknob!

He grasped it and turned and stepped through, and was falling, down, down. With Prissy's body heavy against his, his left arm scraping a rough board that didn't feel like a wall, he grabbed and held on.

He was on steps again. This time the wood was rough and splintery beneath his bare feet, and the support he held to was rough and had sharp edges.

He could have screamed with hopelessness at what he had done. The basement. The steep steps down, the watery floor, the mud, the webs and darkness. Behind him, cutting off his only escape, the thump, thump on the steps . . .

"Where are you going?" Don asked.

Jane hurriedly pulled on her running shoes.

"I didn't want to wake you," she said. "Sorry. Go back to sleep."

"What's up?" he asked, sounding wide awake.

"Well, Kirsten has this thing about the old mansion, and—"

"The haunted thing?"

"Yes, you knew?"

"How could I miss." He stretched and yawned, his arms passing through a dim ray of moonlight. He rolled, reached for the lamp and turned it on. "But that doesn't answer my question. You don't usually go for a run at this time of night."

"Kirsten's gone. She thought something was going on over at the old mansion. I told her to go back to bed. Then I found out she'd dressed instead. I'm going out to look for her."

"She's not in the house?"

"Nor on the deck. Her flashlight's gone."

"I'll go with you."

"No, you go back to sleep. She's safe enough, I'm sure. She's probably out in the yard somewhere."

Jane went to the utility room where she took down the electric flashlight. Without turning it on she went out, leaving the deck light on.

She didn't dare call very loudly, if at all. There were neighbors on both sides.

She paused to look through Kirsten's binoculars again. Frowning thoughtfully she lowered them and

460

stared at the dim little speck of light through the trees. What was so unusual about a light being left on all night?

She wanted to be angry at Kirsten, but a growing uneasiness allowed no room for anger.

Putting the binoculars down, she crossed the deck to the steps.

Jane turned on the electric flashlight. It had a strong, white beam, and with no trouble at all picked up the path the kids had been making.

Adam felt cold water on his feet. He went forward, blinded by dark and fear. He had been in the basement once before, with his dad. They had come down the steps, their way lighted by a bulb hanging from one of the floor joists. Dad explained to Adam what everything was.

Adam had squatted that day in a dry place near the furnace and watched as his dad struck a match on the side of the matchbox. He watched his dad light the water heater, and saw his dad place the box of matches on the floor beside the furnace.

"What's that?" Adam asked, pointing at a can with a spout, and something dry and brown stuck on the end of the spout.

His dad pulled on the dry brown thing and smelled the spout.

"It's a can of kerosene. And this thing was once a potato. People used to use a raw potato to cover the end of the spout so the kerosene wouldn't evaporate. Smells like it worked."

"What's kerosene?"

"It's a derivative of petroleum. It burns. People used it for lamps and cleaning and stuff like that. Don't ever touch it. It's dangerous. Don't bother these matches, either."

He had left the match box on the floor.

If Adam could find the box now . . . he'd have light . . . if he could find the furnace . . .

Prissy dragged him down, sliding from his arms. He felt the floor, and found it dry. The furnace was in a dry place. The furnace was near.

Back in the unrelieved darkness to his left there was a sound on the steps, the thump of something falling from one step down to the next. It was following, it was off the steps now. He could hear the sliding crawl.

He had to find the matches.

He didn't know why he wanted the matches. He only felt the desperation of having to find them before it reached them again.

Leaving Prissy on the dry dirt floor, he scrambled about on his hands and feet, feeling, reaching. The basement filled with the sudden whine of that sound, rising as if in a call of triumph. Adam knew it had located Prissy again.

He jerked up, and his head struck something sharp and hard. Pain radiated through his neck and shoulders. He put up his hands and felt the corner of the furnace.

With a cry, he fell to his knees and began feeling the floor. It was dry and powdery, and he heard a soft sigh as the water heater lighted.

Light.

Beautiful light as thin and pale as the light from a firefly, coming through the cracks of the little door of the water heater. Just enough light to reveal the box of matches on the floor.

He grabbed them up and fumbled the box open. The first match he tried to strike flamed and then died. But in the instant glow he saw the doll, its bonnet gone, the gown hanging only on one arm. It hadn't reached Prissy yet, but it was crawling on its hands, through the thin, shallow lake of water between the steps and where Prissy lay on dry ground.

Adam grabbed a handful of matches from the box and raked them down the rough side. They lit, exploding into a torch. He held on, feeling the heat of their fire, but looking over them at Prissy and the doll. It had reached her.

Adam screamed and ran toward it, and kicked it before it could clutch Prissy. It rolled onto the dry ground near the furnace and immediately lifted itself.

Adam dodged around it toward the can of kerosene.

"Don't touch it, ever, Adam, its very flammable."

He grabbed the can and threw it at the face of the doll, then he threw the handful of matches.

He heard a low explosion. Flames leaped. The clothes of the doll became a torch, its body burning. Its face, now with a bonnet of fire, grew moist and livid. Still, it lifted itself to its hands and reared toward him.

Adam fell backwards. Flame leaped upward toward the dry joists of the underfloor of the house and spread, eating into the wood. The doll, with clothes flaming, rushed toward him. Adam rolled, reached Prissy and grabbed her up into his arms. Holding her close he rolled over into the shallow pool of water.

Heat singed his face. When he turned, he saw the doll, coming through the water, its head reared. Its bonnet flamed a halo of fire but the water through which it crawled had extinguished the fire on its gown. It came straight toward him and Prissy. They couldn't get away, after all. There was no way out of the basement now. Fire was spreading across the ceiling of the basement and onto the steps. The door to the basement was beginning to burn. He could hear the fire, a whisper of movement like something alive, and the thin, high wail of the doll.

He stood up, Prissy heavy in his arms, and turned his back to the doll. Lifting his face toward the burning door, he began at last to weep, tears rolling in silence down his face.

Chapter 18

Adam fastened his stare on the burning basement door and began to climb. He was walking into a world of fire that moved like oceans before his tear-filled eyes. He hardly felt the lick of heat against his cheek: Prissy's clothes hung heavy and wet against his arm. He didn't look back to see how close the doll-creature was. He faced forward, one goal in mind.

The door hung half-open. With his head ducked against the blaze he passed through and into the back hall. He could see better now. Light danced and played with shadows in the hall and revealed to him the side door. The fire in the basement seemed like a burning hole in the earth, which threatened to drag him back by the force of its deadly light.

He heard the sound of crawling, and saw the licking reflection of fire on the floor at his feet. Through the whisper of the eating flames, he heard it, as he had heard it those nights when he had thought he was safe.

He almost dropped Prissy when he freed a hand to open the outside door. Flames had followed him along the hall. Bursts of light like rockets on a dark night. He was not going to look to see if it was there. It had stopped making its sound, as if putting all its effort into climbing the steps and coming through the fire and into the hall. He knew it was there, following, but he wasn't going to look back.

The door opened, and he slipped through.

He had wanted to take Prissy to the path, but he had to go back and get Kirsten.

Prissy seemed to stir in his arms as the night air bathed her. He could almost see her opening her mouth and gasping, taking in the air as he had. But he wasn't going to look at her face because he knew she was dead.

He found a soft growth of grass beside the brick driveway, and laid her down. Then he straightened and looked at the door through which they had exited the old mansion. He could see the faint glow of light from the basement fire. He had to shut the door so the doll-creature wouldn't find Prissy.

He went up the steps to the door and paused on the threshold. It was the only way in. He had seen his dad lock the backdoor. And the doors in front, the big entrance door, and the door from the sitting room out onto a brick patio had been closed and locked the first day they came into the house.

He had to go back into the hall, where fire licked upwards from the basement, where the doll had followed.

He crossed the threshold, and pulled the door shut behind him.

He ran past the burning basement door and on to the door of the back stairs. The stairwell to the second floor was dark, but he could feel heat, as if the fire were burning just inside the wall. There was a strange sound in the house, a whispering, a murmuring soft and secret but growing louder like a group of insane elves laughing. He felt a trembling in the floor beneath his feet, and warmth he'd never felt before.

He climbed through the darkness as fast as he could. Maybe the doll hadn't escaped the basement. Maybe he had only thought he heard it crawling behind him. Or maybe it had slipped through the door when he had and even now had found Prissy, or maybe it had turned and gone back upstairs to Kirsten.

He tried to hurry faster, his breath burning in his lungs and throat, his heart close to bursting. He came out into the upper hall, and was surprised to see the faint touch of light from the open door of his parents' room. The ceiling light still burned.

He hurried into the room where Kirsten lay twisted on the floor, her arms drawn up over her face.

He pulled at her. "Kirsten." He hadn't known he could still cry, but he felt tears run down his cheeks. "Kirsten, don't be dead."

He willed her to rise, but she didn't. He tried to lift her and couldn't. So with his arms beneath hers, he pulled. She moved, and it seemed she was trying to help him, but it was only the straightening of her body as he pulled.

He strained, and put more effort into moving her. The house was burning. The whole house would fall, with them in it. He could hear more clearly the maniacal laughter of the elves, the delight of the fire as it ate the wood. He had to get Kirsten out. He had to get her away from the doll-creature.

He reached the hall with Kirsten, and going backwards, began pulling her to the stairwell. He came to the door and the top step.

The sound at first seemed only somewhere in the back of his head. He felt it, too high for him to hear. It drew closer. *The doll-creature.* Somewhere near. Its sound angry and high with warning, like the hiss of a snake. Adam tried to look for it, and missed his step.

He fell backwards down the stairs, his elbow striking the wall, his knee cracking against the steps as he rolled. Kirsten fell with him. At the foot of the stairs he tried to stand and couldn't. A pain shot through his leg and into his hip.

Down the hall a few feet away the fire licked at the ceiling, rushing with greater force out of the basement. Adam tried again to stand, and the pain receded. His legs and arms weren't broken. He was going to get Kirsten out of the burning house. He was going to get her out.

With his hands gripping her arms he pulled, down the hall, past the flame, beneath it, and to the closed door. He reached past her to the door and pulled it just wide enough to get her through.

More steps, but this time he held her from falling. And once again it seemed she was trying to help him. It seemed he could feel a stiffening of her arms and legs, and she lifted her head.

"Kirsten," he gasped, trying to hold back the sobs that rushed into his chest. "You're not dead. Kirsten, don't be dead."

He got her down the steps. Moonlight touched Prissy where she lay in the grass, and Adam pulled Kirsten over to lie beside her.

Light, bright and full, outlined him suddenly.

Adam straightened and turned.

A car was coming up the driveway to the house.

Yards away it slowed, and the passenger door opened and Kirsten's mother called, "Adam!"

She came running toward him, her body dark in the headlights of the car. The car had stopped, its engine still purring, a sound soft beneath the cry of the fire in the basement. He saw a man get out of the car, and pause just a moment at the door.

"The house is on fire!" Kirsten's mom yelled. "Call for help, Don!"

Adam saw the man reach back into the car and bring out a phone.

Kirsten's mother ran to Prissy and Kirsten on the grass and went down on her knees.

"Oh my God. What happened, Adam?"

Adam whirled and ran back up the steps and into the hallway. He ran past the burning basement, one arm up to shield his head. He felt the heat, the awful, searing heat, but he ran through it and kept going.

When he came to the back stairway, he began to climb. It was like going into hell now, the heat had increased so much. But he had to keep going.

Sounds filled his head. The fire had a louder voice, rising to a shrill cry. The elves were no longer laughing, they were screaming. The fire was alive and growing. Adam heard all the sounds. He heard the voices of people, calling, screaming, *"Adam, where are you?"* He heard the wavering scream of sirens.

But above it all he heard the rise of the high-pitched scream of the doll, like a wire in hell plucked by a playful hand.

Mary drove through the brush out of the driveway beside the old mansion, her heart beating dangerously fast. She had not been able to sleep well, and had been awake to hear the first call for help over the radio. She had dressed hastily, and by the time the fire sirens were activated she was on the road. She drove into the dark tunnel of the old mansion's driveway ahead of the fire trucks, but at the end of the tunnel was an ominous red glow.

She paused for a couple of deep breaths beside her car and forced her heart to slow. Why hadn't she done something for this small family that had moved into the old mansion? She'd been warned. By Jenny. By the facts of the strange and untimely deaths of some of the people who had lived here, of death reports that had no real basis. And by her own vague and formless worry. But that was the problem. She had only considered her inability to get her mind off the Curtis family and the old mansion as baseless worry. Now she prayed they were all safely out of the house, but her feelings of doom were more pronounced than ever.

In the first sweep of lights from the fire engines she ran to meet a man who came running toward her. The soft leaping glow of the fire in the rear of the house turned his face darkly red, but she recognized Don Flanners. A quick glance to the left where a woman squatted with a child in her arms and someone else prone on the grass brought Mary's worst fears to the surface. Where were the others? Don and his wife Jane were the only two adults.

"We have the baby, but the others are still in there! The boy was out but he ran back in!" Don called to her breathlessly, motioning toward a side door that was filled with flames. "He ran back in! I couldn't stop him!"

Mary was already running toward the front of the house as she screamed back at Don. "Stay with them!" She didn't want him trying to stop her from going into the house. She had never met the little boy, but somewhere within herself she knew him, and she knew he would go back because his parents were still in there.

She knew the house. She knew it better than anyone who would be coming to fight the fire, or any of those who waited outside. Night after night she had gone through it again in her mind, searching out the meaning of Jenny's last words. She had tried to find the danger without actually returning to it. More than searching out a danger, she had tried to convince herself that Jenny's nephew and his family were going to be fine there.

The front door was locked. Darkness surrounded her. As she stood there briefly she mumbled a curse at herself for not bringing her weapon. She could have shot the lock open.

Mary dropped to her knees against the wall at the front of the house and began feeling along the ground. The old brick had fallen in places, she remembered clearly. She cried out with satisfaction when her hands touched the rough surfaces of a small pile of brick. She grabbed up one in each hand.

The first fire engine was pulling into the trees at the front of the house when she finished breaking out the glass of the window beside the door.

There were warning shouts from all around her, it seemed, as she climbed into the house.

Heat struck her, as if she had opened an oven door. Above, behind the railings on the banister, the wall of fire danced in the bedroom hallway. Standing silhouetted against it, as if he intended never to move, was the little boy.

"Adam!" she screamed, her call competing with the roar of the fire. "Come here, Adam!"

He stared down toward her. She started running up the stairs, pulling off her jacket as she drew nearer. She saw his face, drawn tight with horror. Yet he stood still, as if he couldn't move.

She climbed into heat that was a searing pain on her skin. There was no way out through the back of the house, only the front. Adam's parents were still here, somewhere.

She reached the little boy and threw the jacket over his head and picked him up, whirling, running again, all in one motion without pause.

The child in her arms whimpered something that sounded like "Mama . . . Daddy . . . Prissy's baby . . . dolly. . ." but she had no answer for him.

Below her the firemen had chopped their way through the front door. Shouts reached her. Curses, too, that meant nothing.

Adam was safe in her arms.

Chapter 19

Mary Swift stood safely beyond the smoldering ruins of the old mansion, alone. She was off duty, tired and dusty, still dressed in her jeans.

The children were safe, thank God, but the parents had died in the fire.

She had carried Adam from the house just as the rear of the second floor sank into the inferno of the basement below. She would remember the sound as long as she lived. There came at first a loud whoosh, like a great sigh, and then above that was a shrill whine. She had no idea what it was, but Adam had stiffened in her arms. It was his only movement, and seemed instinctive, and filled with fear.

The parents of the children for some reason had not made an effort to leave the house, perhaps even to leave their bedroom. She had not wanted to question Adam. He had seemed almost catatonic, staring in fright at nothing in particular. Later, after he had slept, she would try to talk to him again.

All three children were safe and resting in the hospital now, and all three would recover physically.

But there was something strange that wasn't being told. Mary felt it, saw it in the eyes of the children. They were silent. The older girl, Kirsten, acted much as Adam did, as if she were stunned by it all, staring off at the window when Mary talked to her this morning.

"I thought something was wrong," Kirsten finally said

softly. "So I went through the path over to the old mansion."

She paused, staring steadily through the window. Her eyes unblinking, a faint scowl between her eyebrows.

"And why did you think something was wrong?" Mary asked.

"Well, I don't know. Just the old mansion, you know. A dead person had been there, and it seemed like a bad place." She squirmed slightly, reluctant to talk. Her stare relented and came back to fix itself on her fingers as they pleated the hospital sheet.

"A bad place?"

Kirsten shrugged. "I just don't remember."

Adam hadn't talked at all. He lay in his bed, speaking only a few words. "Is Prissy okay? And Kirsten?"

"Yes. Can you tell us what happened, Adam, why . . ." She hated doing this. The child's face had second degree burns on one cheek, and the hair on one side of his head had been singed. One shoulder and arm had third degree burns.

But in his eyes was the same distant look as in Kirsten's. Mary hated to ask him questions that would undoubtedly be painful. He had gone back to save his parents, and she could only imagine his sense of failure and loss.

"Adam, why weren't your parents able to leave their room?"

Their bodies had been found, still in the ruins of the bed, partially incinerated. It looked as if they had never risen, or attempted to rise.

His dark eyes met hers, but there was an invisible wall between them.

"I don't know," he said.

She left the hospital feeling in her heart he did know.

Relatives from Washington were coming to get Adam and Prissy. An aunt and an uncle. As soon as the two children were able to travel they would be gone.

The case would be closed. And perhaps it was just as well.

Mary stood with her thumbs hooked in the front of her belt and stared at the ruins of the old mansion. A couple of brick walls still stood, smoldering, with small puffs of black smoke dissipating into the air as if a troll were hiding there smoking a pipe.

Trees all around the mansion had been blackened. Brush had been broken down and crushed beneath the wheels of fire engines. Nothing had been saved from the house. And two lives were gone there, with only fragments of their bones removed from the ruins.

Mary turned away and went back to her car. She would always wonder what had really happened, but it was time to try to put it aside.

The police department had donated money for the children, part of which Mary had used to buy them a couple of nice presents. She had chosen a Nintendo GameBoy for Adam, and a beautiful doll for Prissy. It wore a lovely pink, frilly dress and bonnet, trimmed in white lace.

She drove back to the hospital and went up to the third floor, the gifts in a large plastic bag.

The baby was in a room two doors away from Adam. He hadn't been able to rest until they had taken him to her room, and let him see for himself that she was alive. Then, he had slept.

Mary looked in on Adam, and saw he was still sleeping. She placed the Nintendo game on the bedside table.

Prissy was awake, sitting up in her crib. She looked at Mary with large, dark eyes. She couldn't know that her mama and daddy were gone forever, yet there was a sad, forlorn look on her face.

"Hi Prissy," Mary said, reaching out slowly with her hand. Prissy stared at her, then extended her own dimpled hand. Mary took it, felt the softness, the vulnerability. Tears came to her eyes. She wished she could adopt these children. She would talk to the relatives, she thought. Maybe it could be done.

"Hi, Prissy, how are you today?"

She didn't expect an answer. The baby stared at her, yet held tightly to her hand.

"I have something for you, Prissy."

She eased her hand away from the baby, and pulled the doll out of the bag. It was such a beautiful doll, Mary had fallen in love with it instantly. Its lovely dress flared from beneath plump arms. The bonnet framed a face almost as perfect as Prissy's. Mary offered it to her.

Prissy stared at the doll, and then like a small creature wild with terror flung herself away. Trapped in the corner of her crib she screamed, her eyes fastened on the doll.

A nurse and doctor ran in. Mary stood in stunned paralysis with the doll in her hands. There was something about the doll that terrified the child, but Mary's hands were numb and slow to move. The baby sobbed and screamed, trying to get away from the doll, her voice filled with horror.

The baby grew quiet only after medication. When Mary last looked in, she saw the baby being rocked by a volunteer grandmother. The old rocking chair creaked lazily, and the baby lay with her head against the soft breast of the elderly woman, her eyes closed, her plump little hands clasping a bottle of warm milk.

The doll had been taken away to the children's ward.

The volunteer grandmother smiled and nodded at Mary, her actions saying, "She's all right now."

But Mary wondered. Was the baby all right? What horrors did the sight of a doll bring to her, and why?

As she left the hospital she remembered something that had slipped her mind.

There had been a doll in the old mansion. It was the

finding of that doll by Lisa and Kirsten that had led to the finding of the body, and then to Jenny, and at last to the young family that had been destroyed by the fire.

There had been a doll . . .

Jenny had mentioned a doll. It was the last word she had spoken.

Adam had mentioned a doll also, as she picked him up in the burning house. It had hardly registered at the time. She was intent only in getting him safely out of the fire.

Mary drove back out to the gently dying fire in the ruins of the old mansion and walked around it. The large house was merely a hole in the ground now, the wall having fallen, the basement still a bed of red coals and hot ashes. Pieces of bed railings, metal from tables or chairs, were like thin, black bones in the rubble. Someday it would cool, and when it did, Mary was coming back.

Perhaps she would find the remains of a doll.

THRILLERS BY WILLIAM W. JOHNSTONE

THE DEVIL'S CAT   (2091, $3.95)

The town was alive with all kinds of cats. Black, white, fat, scrawny. They lived in the streets, in backyards, in the swamps of Becancour. Sam, Nydia, and Little Sam had never seen so many cats. The cats' eyes were glowing slits as they watched the newcomers. The town was ripe with evil. It seemed to waft in from the swamps with the hot, fetid breeze and breed in the minds of Becancour's citizens. Soon Sam, Nydia, and Little Sam would battle the forces of darkness. Standing alone against the ultimate predator—The Devil's Cat.

THE DEVIL'S HEART   (2110, $3.95)

Now it was summer again in Whitfield. The town was peaceful, quiet, and unprepared for the atrocities to come. Eternal life, everlasting youth, an orgy that would span time—that was what the Lord of Darkness was promising the coven members in return for their pledge of love. The few who had fought against his hideous powers before, believed it could never happen again. Then the hot wind began to blow—as black as evil as The Devil's Heart.

THE DEVIL'S TOUCH   (2111, $3.95)

Once the carnage begins, there's no time for anything but terror. Hollow-eyed, hungry corpses rise from unearthly tombs to gorge themselves on living flesh and spawn a new generation of restless Undead. The demons of Hell cavort with Satan's unholy disciples in blood-soaked rituals and fevered orgies. The Balons have faced the red, glowing eyes of the Master before, and they know what must be done. But there can be no salvation for those marked by The Devil's Touch.

HAUTALA'S HORROR—HOLD ON
TO YOUR HEAD!

MOONDEATH   (1844-4, $3.95/$4.95)
Cooper Falls is a small, quiet New Hampshire town, the
kind you'd miss if you blinked an eye. But when darkness
falls and the full moon rises, an uneasy feeling filters
through the air; an unnerving foreboding that causes the
skin to prickle and the body to tense.

NIGHT STONE   (3030-4, $4.50/$5.50)
Their new house was a place of darkness and shadows, but
with her secret doll, Beth was no longer afraid. For as she
stared into the eyes of the wooden doll, she heard it call to
her and felt the force of its evil power. And she knew it
would tell her what she had to do.

MOON WALKER   (2598-X, $4.50/$5.50)
No one in Dyer, Maine ever questioned the strange disap-
pearances that plagued their town. And they never dis-
cussed the eerie figures seen harvesting the potato fields by
day . . . the slow, lumbering hulks with expressionless features and a blood-chilling deadness behind their eyes.

LITTLE BROTHERS   (2276-X, $3.95/$4.95)
It has been five years since Kip saw his mother horribly
murdered by a blur of "little brown things." But the "little
brothers" are about to emerge once again from their under-
ground lair. Only this time there will be no escape for the
young boy who witnessed their last feast!